TOSS A BRIGHT GUINEA

Toss A Bright Guinea

A Novel By

Harry Child

Harry Child (signature)

Bloomington, IN

authorHOUSE®

Milton Keynes, UK

AuthorHouse™
1663 Liberty Drive, Suite 200
Bloomington, IN 47403
www.authorhouse.com
Phone: 1-800-839-8640

AuthorHouse™ UK Ltd.
500 Avebury Boulevard
Central Milton Keynes, MK9 2BE
www.authorhouse.co.uk
Phone: 08001974150

First published by AuthorHouse 6/19/2007

ISBN: 978-1-4259-9301-6 (sc)

Printed in the United States of America
Bloomington, Indiana

This book is printed on acid-free paper.

Acknowledgments

The author would like to thank the Local Studies Section of Newcastle-upon-Tyne Libraries and Information Service for help in his research; in particular for giving permission to use the map of Newcastle inside his book and to use the illustration of 'The Side' on the cover.

London Published for the Antiquarian by Dean & Munday Bradley Public School

Chapter One
The London Road

"Give them back, Sir; give them here, at once!" The major ground the muzzle of his pistol hard into the socket of my left eye. White stars danced bright edged in the darkness before me. But already I knew well enough that no man in my situation could spare any time for simple anger. Just as I knew that given even the half of another chance I would try again…later. Damn him, I had to! I allowed the ring of little keys to fall into Farquahar's fat hand. Then I did curse. For, I heard the tinkle as he stowed the keys to both my sets of irons into the breast of his scarlet coatee. Now it was going to take a damned sight more than any sudden lurch into a pothole along the London road for me to get my hands on those keys again.

But then and to my astonishment Farquahar began to chuckle. It sounded like a handful of musket balls being shaken about inside a trooper's mess kettle. "That was a damned handsome try, Doctor. I grant you that! Altogether a most commendable effort! Though, I should tell you now, Sir… that a traitor can hang just as easily with his knee bones smashed by a pistol ball…just as easily!" I sucked breath hard as he brought down the barrel of his horse pistol sharply to hit me on the kneecap.

To take my mind off the sharp surge of pain I forced myself to concentrate on Farquahar's voice. Again the bastard

1

had slipped into his counterfeit of a Guards Officer's languid drawl. By now I knew that when he took the trouble to do it the fellow's affectation could sound very like that of a Guard's cavalry officer – though never quite exactly so. In Paris I had heard one of the Bourbon officials who had delivered me to him at the prison of *Sainte Pelagie* confide to his colleagues that the major had been a commissary officer in Spain. This was one rogue, it seemed, who had made himself useful enough to be advanced higher than any mere carrier of beef and biscuit to Wellington's army.

I had heard old soldiers swear often enough that slack guts will serve to put a sharp edge on even the dullest recruit's wits. So by that time my own faculties should have been scalpel keen. For in the four days since our little carriage had rolled out of Paris I had eaten almost nothing. At Dover that very morning the shabby Lieutenant, Cable, who was now snoring away across in the corner from me had slipped me a heel of ration bread and a piece of cheese. But before I had swallowed one full mouthful of that food, Briggs, our other passenger, had protested noisily to Farquhar about his lieutenant's act of simple charity. Farquahar himself had stepped forward at once and knocked the bread flying from my hand. By Christ! If ever I could get free… that snivelling little snot of a man… I choked off the curse. For by then I had reminded myself that I was as certain as I could be that this same Mr. Nathanial Briggs was already as near to his own coffin as made little difference! Soon enough, I fancied, that same spiteful bastard would be far beyond any vengeance that I might inflict! Already the dog had a stink about him that foretold of his own death. Again in the dark I could hear his fat lips sucking little sips at the silver flask. Briggs was fighting his pain with some sort of opiate. Though that did nothing to hide the awful stench of the fellow's breath. And more than occasionally we had all been made aware of the disorder in his bowels.

I suppose that – and in spite of my own best efforts to resist it - I had at last fallen asleep. The drumming of hooves and the rumble of wheels will have that effect on a weary fellow. Even a man already well on his way to facing an English jury, indeed to stand before a London jury, twelve respectable tradesmen, and every one of the same bastards overstuffed with good food and safe patriotic zeal, will need to sleep at some time. I woke with a start. Farquahar was shouting. The major's bouts of raving fury were something I had become used to. Mostly it had been Lieutenant Cable who had drawn all the fire; this time it was Butterworth, our soldier coach driver, who was taking the full volley of aimed musketry. I eased myself forward. Already, Farquahar had his window down. His body was turned edgewise to me. He had thrown back his military cloak. By then I could sense rather than see the pistol hooked into his belt.

"Damn your fool's eyes, man! I know we're slowing down but just you tell me... *why* are we doing it?" I took a breath and drew back my shoulders. Butterworth's clipped military responses came down clearly.

"Three lanterns is burnin' in a triangle ahead, Sir. That means we got t' stop. Plain as day that is, Sir! Clear signal o' danger..." Corporal Butterworth, I knew, had been alone at the reins all the way from Dover. In the winter's weather the poor bastard must have been near to frozen.

But, by God, I was ready enough! Almost I could already feel my grip closing around the butt of that horse-pistol hooked into Farquahar's waistband. Now for certain sure that same torturing bastard was going to die. I had decided. And this, I had assured myself, could be nothing other than my own desperate necessity; there could no longer be even a trace of simple dislike in my decision. All the foul abuse I had stood from the same hound had been put well aside. Now I was simply going to put a ball into Farquahar's navel. In my mind's eye I had already planned the entire movement. It would all be precise. I would shoot George Ninnian Farquahar. Then, with one sweep, I would bring the pistol's barrel across and smash it down on Lieutenant Cable's skull. Kind enough that fellow

3

had been to me, but I had already decided. Poor Cable had simply drawn the wrong duty! After all the man was a serving officer. Like a hundred thousand other men in the last years he could as easily have died on any battlefield in Europe.

Then, and within the next half second, my own desperate plan had been thwarted. I winced as I took Farquahar's hard kick on my ankle. As his leg jerked up I caught a whiff of the varnish on the major's Hessian boots and the horse dung caked into his instep. Then suddenly it looked as though George Farquahar had gone quite mad. Like a lunatic in a fit the fellow was trying to squirm his way out of the carriage window. And the sound he was making now was like that of some gin soaked toper, a man trying to spew out his innards. Then I caught the white flash of the silken scarf. And at once I realised what was happening. My chief gaoler's head was being drawn, dragged upward out of the lowered carriage window. Yet even then I saw that Farquahar's fleshy shoulders could never have squeezed their way through the carriage window. But that did not seem at all to bother the man outside. He was busy at his work - garrotting the major!

"Have a care, Niccolo…I don't want the fellow dead!" The urgent warning was in a young woman's voice. And she had spoken in French – in good French. A waft of freezing air blew through the carriage as both doors were swung open. Though by then I had already had the wit to reach out and grab at the major's pistol. That was the instant when Lieutenant Cable chose to awake. The poor fellow had just time to enjoy the briefest instant of consciousness. I heard his skull bones ring out as a club hit hard home.

"Here y'are, m' Laddie! Gi'izz that barker here!" I felt Farquahar's horse pistol plucked out of my hand. There was a sharp click as the hammer was pulled back to full cock. The flare of the priming powder lit up the inside of the carriage. My ears rang from the confined bang. Then from within the swirl of white powder smoke I heard the soft chink of the iron staple that had secured my leg irons to the coach's bodywork. It was hanging loose.

"Now, Kidda! Y' can help yer' sell... an' move ya' damned arse!" It was not what the fellow's words were saying to me that had drawn my sharp start. More surely it was the accent itself. And the one use of that special form of address: 'Kidda'! God Almighty! One at least of the men rescuing me had to be a Geordie born!

No more than five paces stood between the coach and the light racing curricle that was drawn up alongside it. Though, twice my chains made me stagger so that I almost fell headlong into to the piled slush in trying to get across to it. Then I realised that what I had stumbled over was the prone body of Nathaniel Briggs. He was lying face down in the snow. The urge for me to kick the bastard in the head rose us within me. But all at once I was gripped. I felt strong hands under my elbows as I was lifted aboard. One of the men thrust something at me. My hand closed on the rough teeth of a new file.

"Try to get those irons off yourself, Doctor." It was the woman again. Now though she was standing to spread a heavy sheepskin rug over me. It was only then that I realised that she herself had taken the driver's seat.

The rest of that night lay between a dream and a nightmare. Yes; I was free. Working with that file I was able to cut through my patent Birmingham manacles, piece by piece; and as I had them off I flung them into the bushes along the London roadside. But several times, and that was for sure, I was convinced that this young woman was about to kill us both. That girl drove her matched pair of dappled greys like a crazed bitch or, perhaps more aptly, like some sporting English buck with a hundred pounds wager in minted sovereigns riding on the outcome! I just hung on as best I could. Nonetheless, the grey break of dawn saw us rattling across Southwark Bridge.

Only then did the woman slow her pair of greys. For even at that early hour the traffic on the capital's streets required care. For a long time it seemed that we moved through narrow streets. I had lost track of where we were long before we at last drew up behind an inn.

"Inside, Doctor, and do that at once... if you please. A gentleman will greet you there. This bag will identify you to him. "She reached down and laid a leather valise across my knees. "And he will make himself known to you as Mr Squires Taylor. Take my best advice, Sir, and accept that man at once as your master in all things – at least until he has seen you well on your way to the North."

I suppose it was then that I turned about in the low glimmer of the yard's lantern lights trying to get a better look at the girl. And to be sure I was able to steal little enough to bear in memory. At least the face well matched the voice. Yes; the mademoiselle was close to being beautiful. Framed around by the pale satin lining of her bonnet that face had looked oval, but it was not elongated; this lassie was certainly not one of your horsy looking Englishwomen. Those lips of hers too were full enough for any man. But it was her eyes that had at once caught fast my attention. It may well have been the poor light. Or it could, as I knew well enough, have been no more than the zany haverings of my own mind. A man who has been as good as been standing in the hangman's tumbril for the last four days is surely allowed to have some strange fancies! By then, though, I could feel my exhaustion closing about me. Nonetheless that morning I also knew I had seen those eyes, looked into them; seen the long dark eyelashes. And although I found I was unable to even guess at their true colour, I knew for certain that if ever I got as close a look again at that lass I would know her!

Nor was there any doubt that I was expected at the *Bull and Mouth*; anymore than that my arrival there was to be kept other than a matter of discretion. I was watching – nay I was admiring - the way the girl turned her racing curricle around in the yard. And I honestly had heard nothing behind me. But all at once he was there, standing at my side. I felt the valise taken from my hand.

"Doctor Robert Fenwick Shafto…" It was a gentle almost a kindly sound. But my arm had stiffened and I knew that he had felt it. "I have a fancy, Sir…" The voice was cheerful, "that a bite of breakfast would not be unwelcome to you…"

Bull and Mouth! The name came back to me. Somewhere in the depths of memory I fancied that I had heard that name before. And truly if ever a traveller's hostelry served a breakfast to restore the measured beat to a man's heart that place was it! Before a roaring coal fire in one of the inn's private rooms I sat down to a heated china plate loaded, indeed piled high, with sausages, mutton chops, curls of fried bacon, slices of black pudding, and topped with no less than three quite huge fried eggs. And to cap it all Squires Taylor had ordered a pot of coffee. It came from the hands of someone downstairs who truly did know how to make good coffee!

I drew on the cigar, turning it in the spill's flame that Squires Taylor was holding out to me. The rich smell of the Cuban tobacco wafted across the room. Outside it was snowing again. I heard myself sigh softly. So too did Taylor. I watched him tap the ash from his churchwarden's pipe bowl.

"Charles… Eggerton…Dacres." It came from the man's mouth like a pronouncement from a judge's bench. And at once I knew that the real business of the day had begun.

"A good egg…is he? This Dacres fellow…" I drew on my cigar and looked at Taylor through the twisting blue smoke. There was about the same measure of wickedness in both our smiles. For we both knew what the answer had to be.

"Truth to tell, he is neither a very good nor indeed a greatly wicked man. As we speak he is conveniently out of the way in Portugal, and is likely to remain so during the next few years. These are his papers… and this is his pocket watch." He allowed the gold chain to coil itself down into my hand.

"But, Mr. Dacres…" He did not catch me out. As Squires Taylor had spoken I had raised my chin and looked him directly in the face. He smiled. "We are both a little ahead of ourselves. So, and without wishing to give you the slightest

7

offence, my dear Charles, I have to tell you that there is a great deal about you that will need to be changed before you can go many more steps to the fore." Taylor lifted a little silver bell from the table and made it tinkle.

"Our Timothy Gann may look a little odd to you, Mr. Dacres. But be assured that his labours would cost you a half crown piece in the Bond Street shop where he normally plies his trade. And that on any day o' the week!"

Nor was there any doubt about the truth of what Taylor had said. Indeed it had been a warning. Odd was not in it! The fellow looked what the Germans would have called a *kobold*. He came into the room noisily scraping a badly clubbed foot. And that face of his was surely a phantasm from some absinthe drinker's nightmare. But the white towel that was wrapped turban fashion around the pale blue of a close shaved skull was his barber's badge of office. Mercifully the rest of his Maker's handiwork was hidden under his wide apron.

"Timmy Gann…this is the gentleman of whom we spoke. 'English' him for me at once, if you please. Apply to your Mr. Goite for your usual payment! And while you do that I'll leave you both. I have other business to be about…elsewhere!"

Gann, it seemed, had scant use for scissors. The wretched man did most of his work with the same little ivory handled razor. He set me before a cracked mirror between two candlesticks and began his cutting. Nor at any time did the fellow solicit the slightest co-operation from me. His huge hands moved my head as he needed. Nonetheless, I had to declare myself well satisfied with barber Gann's work. As I looked into the mirror my own face had seemed almost to emerge from a six months growth of hair and beard. My matted locks were falling freely about my shoulders when I became aware that the fellow was humming a tune to himself. It took me a few long minutes to recognise it; and a few more yet to recall the ballad's words. Suddenly I had it. It was called 'The Night before Larry was Stretched.' Our glances met; and Taylor's Mr. Gann grinned wickedly as he showed his rotten teeth.

8

"By George, Sir, but our own Timmy Gann has done you proud this day! He really has…" Taylor was obviously delighted. He stood in the doorway beaming at me. Then I saw that he carried a good armful of clothing. "Here we are, Mr. Dacres… get your body into these."

Damn me, but I looked a sight better than I had done for many a long month. For to be sure six months in a French prison will usually take much of the gloss off any fellow. That the woollen under drawers and vest I had just put on tickled like Hell I did not mind one bit. The linen shirt was itself a joy to look upon. I pulled on the pale whipcord breeches and buttoned the broadfall.

"What the Devil are these things?" Taylor picked up the grey slippers I had arrived wearing. The coarse felt was still dripping wet. Suddenly I too found that I could smile.

"Major Farquahar took his gaoler's duties very seriously, Sir. So he put much thought into securing his prisoner. Those same slippers he had exchanged for my own best Paris-made boots when he had them rivet the chains on me at the Prefecture in the *Rue de Jerusalem*. Yes; indeed, Sir, Louis Bourbon's commissioners all thought Farquahar a very droll fellow!" I listened to the hiss when Taylor tossed the wet slippers on to the fire's coals. But whatever other pleasures I enjoyed that day there was little to touch the joy of wrinkling my toes inside a clean pair of knitted Worcester stockings. He handed me the top boots. These were not quite new; but for certain sure they would do. And – quite miraculously - they fitted me like gloves. The confidence that a well-fitting pair of boots gives a man is beyond belief.

Now, Mr. Dacres…" Taylor gave me a wan little smile. I want you to tell me tell me how your escape was affected along the road from Dover." I told him what had happened. The events were still very fresh in my mind.

"So you could say that Mrs Rachel Brydon conducted herself…well? "

"The lady has my entire… approbation, Sir. I doubt that the whole business took five minutes…" Even as those words were in my mouth I was trying again to see the face I had sought for in the lamplight. Though now I had a name to put to it…Rachel Brydon!

"That news will please certain people…for sure it will." Already Taylor was thinking about something else. "Some of us were a mite worried about the widow's…" He shrugged. "Competence! Though we must both know how useful the ladies can be for certain types of work! Though mark you well! Without doubt the same old fellow who commissioned her services is truly quite as mean as any tom cat's shit…but that aside I can say no other than that I've always found his given promise always holds - for good, or ill." Squires Taylor thumbed open his watch case. His eyebrow went up. "The stage to Newcastle will be leaving in twenty minutes, Mr. Dacres. My instruction to you now is that you should make certain sure that you do arrive in that city…I believe that you are being offered an… opportunity, and surely this is one chance that only a damned fool would decline!"

Chapter Two

I had been thinking of Dante Aligheri, the Italian poet. That had been the lad who had written that traitors would suffer forever in a freezing Hell. Damn my eyes but the fellow had been right. The last stage of our long stage ride up from London, the journey from Durham to Newcastle, had taken us all of four hours. And like every other soul aboard that mail coach my bladder felt near to bursting. For certain sure every one of my fellow passengers bore on their face that same distant look of a misery hard borne. It was the cold's harsh bite that was doing all the mischief! Through rugs, sheepskins and the gross animal heat of six tight packed bodies that night's killing frost had groped its way to us all. Long since, the bricks in the pea straw at our feet had yielded up the last of their heat. And the cause of it all was that twice the stagecoach, *Union*, had suffered accidents: a trace had broken; then one of our wheelers had cast a shoe. And now as we were running the last three miles of our journey down from the heights of Gateshead Fell we were fleeing headlong before a swirling blizzard. Altogether the London stage was coming in close to five hours late. Half past nine had been the due time for the London coach; now it was near enough to two in the morning. This had been one night when the weather had defeated even the company's tight timing of its stages. It was four badly tired coach horses that clattered their way up Newcastle's Pilgrim Street that morning. We, the inside passengers, sat like so many marionettes. We lurched together and slumped in our seats as the driver leaned on to the brake to bring his coach to a screeching halt. We were at *The Queen's Head*. There was an instant of silence before folk let out their breaths. The old lady clutching at my elbow sobbed out her heartfelt thanks to her Kindly Saviour. Then the tumble began.

The staging inn has a long yard. Convenient to the nearer end are the privy-stalls provided for men; at the other - the distant end - is the noisome little shed that affords some shadow of immediate decency for the lady travelers. Though at that moment every last shred of the ladies' decorum was blown to the winds - all notions of rank and precedence were forgotten. Like so many startled rabbits, *les dames* scampered off towards their appointed place of relief.

It took the ostlers in the yard of the *Queen's Head*, two men and a lad, almost less time than it takes to tell of it to free the near exhausted team from its harness. Steaming like so many wraiths the poor beasts were trotted away smartly to the stables. Fresh animals were lead out and harnessed up. Within twenty minutes, set by the driver's pocket watch, that coach would be off again, along the road to Edinburgh.

I screwed my face into a raw smile when I saw that while the redbrick inn did offer even its late guests a fair welcome; though to be sure, once that welcome had been delivered, it was not something to be held out overlong. Two great torches had been lit to glare at either side of the inn's door. But now that the Royal Mail and its passengers had fairly arrived a lad hurried out to lift them down and douse the flames with a bucket of sand. Acrid black smoke hung heavy on the freezing air. Geordie's welcome was being tempered by a decent prudence. Yes, and now I knew it, too damned truly I knew it, Bob Shafto was home.

When a stagecoach's boot is opened for the baggage to be distributed a coach's passengers will always squabble. It is the same across all Europe. Already the men, their bladders blessedly eased, were returning. But I was far ahead of them. At York I had given the guard two shillings to keep my baggage by him and to take it straightway into the coach office the moment we arrived in Newcastle.

For my own instructions had been that I was to find the man who had been trusted to greet me. John Nesbitt was the name I had been given. So while the other passengers were shouting out for their cinnamon brandy and mulled wine I stepped quickly across to the lamp lit window of the coach-company's offices. I stepped in and looked around me. An elderly porter was lying by the iron stove.

"Jackie Nesbitt?" I was brisk. The porter looked up. He squinted at me – no more than a little to one side. Few men on Tyneside who were baptised John were ever called anything but Jack, or Jackie. Like some Lazarus miraculously quickened this fellow sat bolt upright from the wooden bench where he was lying. Almost I laughed. Plainly he was an old soldier; for certain sure he had a cavalryman's bowed legs. One eyebrow was raised: I was being scanned like a doubtful cut of meat pie.

"Name of Minto, Jackie Nesbitt... George Minto!" That was the password that had been whispered in my ear when I had left London. Jackie Nesbitt would know me by no other. "You have a letter for me, I believe?"

"Oh, aye, that'll be the big 'un from Bristol..." His fingers hovered over a set of pigeon-holes mounted on the wall.

In London I had been given no specific commands. I had not received any written orders at all. What orders I had been given were whispered to me – and were no more than: "Your instructions are but one post ahead o' you. For what you don't know, my friend … you can't tell…"

From the docket he took an envelope bound with hemp; leaden seals were clamped over the knots. "There's six-shillun t' pay..."

"The post was paid at t'other end, my friend! As it always is! That much I do know." Then I passed across the counter to him the envelope that I'd been given. It was addressed to the British Linen Bank at Edinburgh. It would go on to let my employers know that their agent had at least arrived safely in Newcastle. "To be put aboard the next Edinburgh mail coach... understood?" He nodded.

Now however my mind was racing. These people were uncommonly efficient. With my orders sent off a single post ahead of me there was little enough chance of their being read by anyone else - not even by me!

An' aahm to tell y', Sir, that a lodgin' has been found for you. It's... er...a well recommended house."

"And paid for?" This was getting to be an important consideration. Though there was no way I was going to be tempted to lodge beyond one night at anywhere but a place I had chosen for myself... and that damned carefully! Protection of my anonymity and hence of my skin, would always be my own affair - nobody else's. That was the way things had been done when I had served the Emperor.

"Aye, Sir, a month 's been paid up in advance from last night... the place is only a few steps from here... down near the bottom of the Butcher Bank. You'll be lodgin' wi' a respectable widow woman... everythin' there'll be nippin' clean and she's said to be a good cook. Tommie, here, will take your bags and show you the way." I nodded.

Even after all these years I could almost swear that it was my own boot soles, unaided, that were finding their own sure way down the bank to towards the riverside. But I walked behind the porter and to try to ensure that we were not followed. We were. Though whoever this fellow was he was keeping his distance; but with the night' frost so hard underfoot we might both as well have been treading on broken gin bottles.

The house was old. It was one of the big merchants' houses that clustered close together down both sides of the Butcher Bank. And it was well matched to its owner. The widow Dilkes herself was a hatchet faced, old biddy. Wisps of white hair poked out from under her linen cap. I fancied my porter's knock had caught her snoozing. But she had opened her door and then stood aside with every semblance of good grace.

"Will you be good enough to come in, Sir..." It was a greeting not a question. "Your room is made ready and there'll be a hot meal on the table as soon as I can serve it..."

It always showed. Clearly this Mrs. Dilkes had once been in service. Everything about her, the woman's white apron and cap, and her neat, plain gray dress, told me that. Also I knew that whoever had chosen my lodgings probably knew the old woman well, and she him. Perhaps, even, the widow Dilkes had been a servant to some noble household. *Noblesse oblige*, indeed; though for someone in the agent's trade it had been a stupid thing to do! At best, I could afford use my room at Mrs. Dilke's as a store for my gear. But before another day had passed I knew that I would need to lodge myself elsewhere.

The house was large and Mrs. Dilkes, I quickly divined as much from her manner, was mistress of it all. She lived alone, and that in the kitchen. The rest of the place was empty, near gutted of its furniture. Her likely tale was an easy one to guess. Her husband had died and left her only the house and its furnishings. Piece by piece she was selling off her property.

But, thank God, coals were still cheap in Newcastle town; so the kitchen was blessedly warm from the blaze of a good fire. I sat myself down at the table by the hearth and allowed the widow Dilkes to serve me from a big willow pattern tureen. She piled my plate up with a thick beef stew. So famished was I that I went at my food like a hound at broth.

"You've had instructions about me... well in advance, Mrs. Dilkes?" I could but try.

"Yes, Sir; I have that." The old woman was standing with her hands folded across her apron. She had obviously enjoyed serving a man again. "My instructions are that I am to answer any questions you may ask me as best I can... but to ask none of you." Just the faintest twitch of a smile flicked at the corner of the old woman's mouth.

"Well then, Mrs Dilkes, we both understand one another well enough." I matched her wan smile and looked up at the face in the firelight. "However m' dear, and much as I regret

15

it, I am unable to risk spending even this one night under your roof. As I came down from the *Queen's Head* I know I was followed..."

"*That* you were, Sir! I've always obeyed my instructions to the letter. There's a man in the street and another in the lane at the back. They've both been well paid for seein' you here safe. One of them is m' own nephew. Wor Cuthbert 's a canny lad and as big as an ox; moreover some folk will say that when he's been sore vexed he's handier than most lads wi' his fists."

That night I slept in a great four-poster bed. And by then, by God, I needed it. The linen was still hot from the warming pan and a huge patchwork eiderdown sealed me in against the draughty chill of the bedroom. My preparations for bed however had to be a little more involved than those made by most peaceable men. Under the door I kicked into place the three oak wedges that lay in readiness. Those little pieces of oak alone would give me perhaps half a minute's warning against a rush. Clearly Mrs. Dilkes's house had been used for some secret purpose before.

For all their so careful sealing, my orders did not tell me that much. But at least there were three banker's orders for ten pounds; each was drawn on a Mr. Backhouse's Bank on Theatre Square. The first would come due in two days. I lit a cigar at my candle and lay back smoking in the freezing bedroom.

And as I drew in the smoke I began to retrace in my head all that had happened during the past week. Almost by then I was too weary for sleep. Rachel Brydon's sweet but husky voice began echoing about again inside my head. But then the twisting blue smoke of Cuba tobacco served to carry my thoughts backward a deal further than the last few days.

In the November of 1801 I had finished my medical apprenticeship under old Doctor Bowren. For over a year I had scraped a pittance working between the town's charities and the folk who lived down in city's the poorer wards. Daily I had shoved clystres up paupers' fundaments and lanced the boils swelling on madmen's backsides. For to be sure in my apprenticeship years with Doctor Bowren I had learned much of malingering lunatics; and yet more again of the sheer barefaced robbery practiced by physicians and apothecaries than ever I had about either medicine or surgery. Then in early March of 1803 I was summoned at short notice to assist a Dr. Martin in cutting a patient for stone. The patient was Sir Jowett Munck... and, without a doubt, he was quite the slimiest bastard ever born to woman!

We got a pint of good brandy and a close to two hundred drops of best Calcutta laudanum into the man. Nonetheless it took four big porters from the meat market to hold the rogue down. And under old Doctor Martin's knife our bold Sir Jowett squealed like a contralto pig. But, nonetheless, the operation was a success. We took a very fair cluster of stones out of him; the biggest was quite the size of a walnut.

And that was where Bob Shafto's young life took its sharpest turn. Dr. Martin, doubtless with one of his own protégés in mind, had advised Sir Jowett that he would need to keep a physician at his side for at least a month. At once and at the direct insistence of Lady Munck I was offered that post. Bob Shafto was to accompany Sir Jowett and his family to France as his personal physician. The emoluments I was promised were damned generous and I was, of course, to eat at the family's table. Within the week we sailed for France aboard the _Zenobia_. And I must own that for six weeks I enjoyed myself, at first in Rheims and then later, and much more, in Paris. Sir Jowett was one of your fellows who enjoy being treated as an invalid. So I served both him and - after resisting as long as mortal flesh might - his young wife.

Then both First Consul Napoleon and my own lusts brought me to ruin. On May 19th of 1803 war with England was declared. On the morning of May 20th I staggered back from a minor debauch with friends. Almost politely I was arrested as I stood swaying at the hotel's door. Sir Jowett and his lady, I was told, had left for Calais in a hired phaeton the night before. For a modest consideration the two grinning gendarmes allowed me to pack my few things and then they marched me to the carts to join the other English *detenues* on the road to Verdun.

I was woken by the clang of a pieman's bell. While I had slept it had snowed again. Within half an hour I was up and out of the house. My bodyguard was still there across the street, huddled into a doorway and stamping his boots against the chill. As I stepped out into the street he shuffled quickly by me and into the house. He was welcome to eat what was left of my breakfast of smoked gammon and eggs. After his long watch in the snow the poor beggar surely deserved it.

'Always walk your ground carefully, my young friend. Discover precisely where you are and carefully note its bounds.' That had been one of what Papa Dimnet, the man who had trained me, had called his 'precepts'. But, I fancied to myself, I already knew the full extent of Newcastle both within and outside of its walls. Not so very much could have changed even in twelve years. Though, of course, that little could be important to me. So I walked down on to the Quayside. There I sat myself down in a shaver's booth. As I expected the barber was a young lass. Without ceremony she lathered me up smartly and swept her razor close. Damned handy with her blade she was; even in that morning's freezing cold my cheeks scarcely smarted at all. Then I turned about and walked up the bank again into the town. Already my ideas were forming.

At Charnley's bookshop on the Bigg Market I found what I was looking for. The middling sorts of folk, the English as much as the French, greatly relish seeing their names, their trades and professions printed plain in 'directories'. With them it is a sort of *Almanach Imperial*. Almost of itself any entry between its covers bestows both rank and respectability. It was worth two of my half-crowns to get my hands on a copy of *The Newcastle Directory* for the year 1814.

A pleasant young fellow served me. He was able to offer me the latest editions of *both* the *Newcastle Chronicle* and the

Tyne Mercury. I guessed that if these worthy newspapers did not exactly give me any direct clues then at least they would feed my local knowledge. Perhaps too they would tell me those areas of the town's life where I would be wasting my time in examining. Then when I hesitated, looking around for what else I might need, the young fellow invited my attention to a pile of little books bound in buff coloured paper.

"A new book of poems, sir … they are fresh from the printers this morning!" The lad was pathetically eager. "New come from the hand of a local poet, Sir... and at just three pence the copy."

A man who buys your poems, and there was no doubt in my mind that this lad who had penned them, was entitled to ask a few questions about the city's literary life. Within a few minutes I knew a great deal - though from that deal I knew I probably had little enough profit in the knowing. Nonetheless on another occasion I might be able to ask other questions; as might indeed any man who expresses himself as being quite enchanted with your new printed soul's work!

It was as I stepped out again into the street again that my elbow was gripped and I was swung about. My fist was already in full swing when an expertly blocking hand reached forward and caught my punch.

"Don't do it!" That order came at me with a harp hiss. "You'll surely want to save yourself a cracked head, Doctor..." I felt my head give a short nod. There was no help for it! A sardonic smile spread across each of the three faces. "Obliged, t' ye, Sir... Now if you would now care to step up into the carriage…"

In more ways than one I was being lifted. Already both my feet were off the ground. "There's a gentleman just along the street a little ways… He begs the favour of a few words with you!"

Chapter Three

But the men who had lifted me were not Law Officers. That was plain enough – and I was thankful for it! Their ways of doing their business had not been in the style of those cheap hooligans. The first time I had met the gallant major he had smashed his fist into my mouth. That whoremonger might well hold King George's commission, but beyond that and for certain sure, George Ninnian Farquahar was no gentleman! Apart from a restraining hand against the swaying of the carriage these lads did me no violence at all. Though, from the instant my backside touched the cushions that carriage was off at a fair cavalry gallop.

It had been my fond fancy that I knew the back streets of Newcastle as well as I knew the back of my own hand Now all I could see was that we were speeding through narrow unlit lanes. It would have been a good man who was able to follow us. Then we turned again into a close. Our tyre iron grated on the cobbles as the carriage took a corner rather too sharply. That manoeuvre threw me hard first to one side and then the other. At once there was a hollow-ness in the clatter of the horses' hooves. We had passed through a stone archway and there was the boom of a gate being closed behind us.

Then I felt my mouth drop open. I had stepped down out of that hackney carriage to find the bell-mouth of a blunderbuss being shoved hard against my chest. I saw a blue bonnet. The rest of him was wrapped tight in a grey plaid. For the life of me I couldn't help myself: my gob fell open! I heard that spiteful snicker-snack as the fellow's gnarled fingers cocked back the gun's hammer. A bloodshot gaze wavered over me.

"That'll be alright, Alexander!" Where the order was coming from I could not tell.

"But just you mind you don't blow that gentleman's bowels across the yard... He's needed. At once the thought passed through my head that Bob Shafto was being made to serve as the butt of some joke! Not least because the look of a crazed drunkard disappeared from the watchman's face. Though, truth to tell, the smile that replaced it was near enough as bad.

"If you would be good enough to step in through yonder door, Sir... There's a gentleman waiting to meet you..." To my surprise the watchman spoke now in the seemly accents of Aberdeen.

"Doctor Shafto... or are you transmogrified already into Keir..." The stranger stepped into the lamplight. His hand was extended. His grasp gripped hard. There was a look on his face that might have been amusement. Or it might have been a natural wryness.

For these last three days at least, Sir... I am become, Keir." I had found myself trying to match his grand manner, and at once I cursed myself for it.

My name is Richard Grainger...how do you do?"

"Without doubt this man was an aristocrat. Grainger had surely been born into that class which in reality rules both England and Scotland. In France many such men as Grainger had gone down with the Revolution of '93. In these islands they continue. They usually have wealth and have had it for centuries; often they are handsome and can be charming; some of them even have brains. But I knew that, try as you may, it will take all of three generations of careful copying to become one of them, or even like them. Ape them all you please and all you will succeed in doing is to make yourself look ridiculous. This Richard Grainger had that same lean-shanked look about him as the British dragoon guard officers I'd seen since the

21

Peace, lording it about along the streets of Paris. He was tall – all of three inches taller than I. And when he had shaken my hand I had looked into a face that was genuinely humorous. Though I also saw that in the eyes - and behind them - there was the spark of a very keen intelligence. It was at that same moment that remembered Squires Taylor's words of warning: "Don't forget, Lad…these same people will hang you without a thought!"

"If you would be good enough to follow me…" Grainger smiled at me. As we walked he made conversation: "Until November last we used to have a fine old house of our own down close to the Quayside. From there we did all manner of odd bits of work for the Bank. But then last summer some madman flung a bombard shell through our window. Damn-me but I can still hear that fuse spittin'!" He was half joking - but I think only half.

Grainger's long legs took the upward spiralling stairs three at a stride. The building we were in appeared to serve as chambers for several partnerships of lawyers. The signs, in gilt copperplate lettering on polished boards, were neat, and yet discrete; though the actual names had more than just a touch of whimsicality about them. On one landing I saw a 'Dunberry, Dinsbury & Dunberry'. Possible, I supposed. But a Felapton & Ferio looked to be just too unlikely! As we climbed I had the chance to catch only a glimpse or two along the side corridors. What I quickly saw however was that every floor could be sealed off from the next by an ornate wrought-iron gate. Every barrier looked to be strong enough to hold back any rioting mob.

At the stair's head however there was a plain black board with white copperplate lettering. It read 'Talaeus Dekker – Dealer in Antiquities'. For a few heartbeats we stood before the last gate. I could sense that we were being watched but, again, I was damned if I could see where from. Then I heard the snick of sprung levers. Without visible human agency the wrought iron grill swung open for us.

At first sight I had to suppose the room had once been a library, a place where a leisured gentleman might withdraw to his studies. This hypothetical scholar of mine had clearly been a man of classical tastes. As a room itself the place belonged to the last century rather than this. The bookshelves themselves were of polished Honduras mahogany. Though of books, save a few of what looked like ledgers, there were scarce two dozen altogether - and the bindings of those were well worn. The rest of the furniture too had seen better times.

From the very outset, indeed almost from first glance what I sensed in that room was contradiction. Nothing fitted or matched. It was a room that was worked-in, and worked in every day. Its whole atmosphere was redolent of brisk business; the very scent of the place suggested that just few minutes before we had entered the room half a dozen clerks had been busy there. There was the sharpness of fresh ink on the air. There was the smell of the damp wool of drying coats, tobacco, and men's sweat. A chipped china plate with knife, fork, and the yellowed fat from a beefsteak had been left balanced on the edge of one of the writing desks. While at its side there stood a tankard of porter. It was still three parts full. Someone *had* just left.

And as I walked forward the very floor under my feet began to tell me something more. What once had been a splendid expanse of Brussels parquet was now badly scarred. And *that* too I knew had been deliberate. Without even having to test it I knew at once that anyone taking two steps across that floor would set up a warning clatter. I stopped, stood where I was, and looked over towards the narrow window. Set up there on a tripod was what surely had to be from the fervid dreams of any Peeping Tom: a man o' war's brass spyglass. Through the grimy windowpanes beyond it I could look out back across the rooftops and chimney pots of Newcastle.

As I stood with Richard Grainger at my shoulder I was still trying hard to gather in anything that might tell me more. Clerks, I saw, were allowed to smoke here. That certainly would not have been permitted in many of the counting houses of either Paris or London. Cigar ash and pipe dottle dusted the floor. It was then that I became aware of the warmth. Heating too was not a luxury that was often provided for the comfort of mere clerks. In an alcove a huge Hamburg stove of yellow glazed brick shimmered. But then that was the end of my unhindered reconnaissance. A clerk, or at least a skinny young fellow in a plain suit of decent grey swept up silently behind us to help us out of our greatcoats. Without a word he moved to a side table and took up a tray with a bottle and some glasses. From behind his hand he whispered to Grainger. He was good at it. I caught scare a word of what was said. Then he handed his master a fat bundle of letters.

Richard Grainger poured sherry for us. He smiled as he raised his glass to me. But then hurriedly he excused himself and begged leave to sort through the letters. I smiled at him and graciously waved him on, sipping appreciatively at my wine. Though, that was not feigned. Whatever it was it was damned good. However, as I sipped, I turned slowly and began again to scan that room. With me it was a natural habit. I was still an intelligencer - an agent! This was what I had been trained to do. Now too I was busy reminding myself that a well-honed sharpness would be as much a necessity here as it had been on in France. Indeed for a moment I so far forgot myself as to slip into thinking that I had somehow conjured my way into one of the *cabinet noir* of the Emperor's enemies! Though, that might not have been such a deep folly. The war might be over but nonetheless it would be stupid for me not to try to peck up every last grain of information I could about this place. For nothing was surer to me now than that for all this Richard Grainger's pleasantness he was one of the men who held my life in their hands. Even as watched his eyes scan along the lines of writing I had to remind myself that this young fellow had the power to put a hangman's noose about my neck. Any magistrate in Newcastle town would be likely to believe anything this man swore! I sensed it. Like my old master, Fouche, this tall cheerful Englishman in the blue tailcoat and buff waistcoat was possessed of double handfuls of simple, raw Power. I was not free; I had simply exchanged one master for another. These people had simply reached out and deftly plucked me out of Major Farquahar's fat fingers?

Grainger went on slitting open sealed letters and reading the close written sheets. I stole a few more seconds to blink and look about me again. Now I tried to see the room in a new light, with a different eye. Definitely this was no merchant's counting house. It had none of the neatness and order for which British business was becoming famous. Yet without doubt work similar to that of a counting house was done here. That was sure. Here and there I picked up the small evidences for it. There were no candles in the wall sconces. But each of three separate desks carried a pair of the new Carcel lamps. With its reflectors polished and its lamp glass clean the invention threw out five times the light of any ordinary lamp. I'd seen such lamps in France. The ruinous quantities of cabbage seed oil they guzzled was so viscous, so thick, that it had to be raised up from the lamp's base by an ingenious little clockwork pump. The very smell from such lamps brought to mind a green marble office in an annexe of the *Palais d'Angloueme*. There on most nights the Carcel lamps had ticked away as merrily as any watchmaker's shop. They lit the work of the clerks who laboured to make copies of the Emperor's official despatches. So this too then might be an office from where messages were received and sent. With a single step forward I had satisfied myself that the lamps were indeed Paris-made. Now how could such luxuries have been spirited to Newcastle time o' war? Why, Sir, best put your question to a banker!

Then my attention settled on the abacus. Ebony beads were strung on brass rods. It was a device polished with much use. And in spite of my caution I found myself whistling softly in sheer astonishment. If those rows of beads told true, then surely that abacus had recorded on it a sum that ran to over a million pounds Sterling. Behind it I saw the slate slab fixed to the wall. A £'s symbol topped each of the columns chalked on to the slate. It showed vast sums of money.

"So, Mr. Egerton Keir, I have here in my hand the full dossier on an interestin' sort o' fella, a lad called <u>Dr</u> <u>Robert</u> <u>Shafto</u>..." Grainger tapped at his chin with a dark green folder. He waved it. There was no mistaking the laurel wreathed 'N' on the cover. And at sight of it I found myself cursing Joseph Fouche and all his works.

Naturally all we agents knew that Napoleon's Minister-of-Police kept a detailed file on almost every notable citizen in Europe. Like many other people I too had already wondered *how* and indeed if, Fouche, the *regicide*, could even hope to survive for long under the restored Bourbons. Probably he would. Scum ever rises! Now, however, I found myself elated, thrilled almost, to know that this same Monsieur Le duc d'Otrante no longer had his talons on the dossier of Dr. Robert Shafto. And of that I was sure – quite uncannily so! The file that Grainger waved was no copy: it bore the embossed stamp and the cipher of the secret archive in Paris. Without warning Grainger laughed and flung the dossier riffling through the air towards me. For just an instant I was a man reaching out to catch his own soul. For if there were no file...why then I could have no official existence! I caught it.

"Faith and Trust, my friend, is what we all need most of all in these troubled times." Richard Grainger looked at me keenly. "Read your biography, if you so wish. Take your time over it. It'll serve to tell you, better than any words of mine, exactly where you now stand." Grainger's statement was pure fact: fact edged sharply with threat. He turned away.

"While you have a look at that I shall go and take delivery of the rest of the morning's messages."

Hated, bitterly despised, Joseph Fouche might be, nonetheless his system of records had to be the envy of every government in Europe. Moreover very few men have ever been given the privilege of scanning their own *dossier*.

The file on the *detenue*, Robert Fenwick Shafto had been opened on the 7 Brumaire 1803. At that time, as I recalled, the Minister of Police had himself been out of favour with his master, Napoleon. But like a snake beheaded his system had writhed on. Government clerks had continued to receive and assiduously to record every trivial piece of political gossip that came to them. I smiled grimly when I saw that my dossier's number was preceded with the inked-in designation: *'Anglais'*. How clearly I could remember it.

Their first approach had been when I was at Verdun. For two days I had scarcely eaten. Nor it seemed was I any longer welcome in any of the clubs where I had been making a little money at cards. That too I later learned had been their doing. Quietly the name of Shafto had been sorely fouled among the British *detenues* in the town. All that morning I had been light headed, dizzy with hunger. The day too had been bitterly cold. Then the so-amiable Monsieur Royer, a Strasbourg merchant he claimed, had approached me in the street. Very civilly he had asked me to translate a short letter from New York for him. He had paid me not in cash but with an invitation to dine with him at *La Cockatrice* on the Market Square. We had eaten, I remembered the taste of it distinctly, a ragout of stewed mutton with parsnips and baked potatoes. That was not in the dossier; though on that same day one Carcaud, a clerk, had recorded in my *dossier* the fact that I had 'appeared receptive'. As well I might! Sourly I recalled that what had finally seduced me into the Emperor's service had been a single Louisiana cigar. And of course my first assignment had been both ridiculously well paid and simplicity itself – the first one always is!

Page after page it ran. It was all there. Italy: Rome, Milan, Venice, Savorna, Genoa, and of course Naples. There was also a guardedly complementary note about my work at both Ulm and Cracow; there was some more fulsome praise for my part in *L'Affaire Sussenbrotius* in Bruges in '08. I should bloody well think so too! There were also the names, many, to which now I could put faces, some of them long dead faces. Here too there were certain entries I read with very distinct surprise! Had it really been twelve years?

"Well then...?" Grainger whispered quietly. He was standing by the window in wan sunlight and looking back across the room at me.

"Well then indeed, Sir..." There was little else I could say. I spread my hands and shrugged. For a Mr. Egerton Keir whose documents showed him beyond doubt to be a loyal North Briton it was an oddly Gallic mannerism.

"It may surprise you, Shafto, but when first I read your dossier I entertained a certain sympathy for your plight." His smile was distant as he confided. "In the winter of '04 I myself had to steal my way across France all the way from Lausanne." The smile broadened. "That however is quite another story. The real crux of my present tale is that this county's finances have been plunged into a case of 'Needs musts when the Devil drives'. Which is why we have been able to procure from the Attorney General *stays* of arrest for half a dozen or so men. Men who, in the ordinary course of events..." There was no need for him to proceed to his conclusion.

Then Richard Grainger began to tell me a tale that I had already suspected, indeed had already more than half known:

"Gold... that is what this is all about. Also you might reflect that it also the reason why Major Farquahar has been denied the pleasure of having you thrown into the Tower." He went on:

"One way and another since 1793 the Boubon dynasty of France has cost the tax payers of these islands more than twenty millions in gold." Grainger was looking at me directly. "Now however this country's trade is swift approaching a crisis. Essentially, and as of three weeks ago, the British Government has scarce eight million pounds in gold left within the Bank's vaults. Sir, this country is in crisis!"

Of course I knew that the British were short of gold. That had long been clear. They had to be. What I had not guessed was exactly how near to bare their cupboard really was. Grainger continued:

"While at this moment there are men, men we must suppose to be agents of the exiled Napoleon, out and about and busy in all the clubs and coffee houses of all this county's major cities. These damned peddlers are offering as much as thirty shillings worth of French silver *ecu's* for every English guinea they can get their hands on. Such an offer must be very hard to resist. And they are also so damnably clever at it. Here on the Tyne last month a ship was seized for attempting to take out of the port a sum close to ten thousand guineas in gold. The shipmaster had dropped the coins into a barrel with a few pints of red-lead paint poured over them.

It was obvious that Grainger expected me to comment on the ruse.

"But you smoked the whole business, eh?"

"It was the smell from a keg of raw turpentine. It would have been needed to flush away the paint once they were clear away to sea. But one of the excise men caught the reek and put two and perhaps three together."

Richard Grainger was pretty close to a blush! Most men are a little susceptible to vanity - gentlemen born more perhaps than most.

"We have the beggar, safe in the town's gaol!" I sensed Grainger's satisfaction. "And soon enough we'll have the names of his ... employers!"

Grainger's laughed sounded bitter. "What we are dealing with here is a group of men, perhaps just one or two men who are - in their own right - wealthy." He began to tick off his points on his fingers. "Probably they also have political power. *That* is a commodity that the late war seems to have spread about far and wide. For, not only do they seem to have the guineas to hazard but they must also have the means to bring in the silver. They are able melt it down. Then of course they have to put their new won wealth to work! The Devil of it all is of course that the law can require no man in England to answer any enquiries about his simple *possession* of either silver or gold."

The turn of the doorknob was discrete. The Tom-o-Bedlam who walked in was like a sun burned prune. I had the distinct feeling that had the fellow have been put to steep overnight he would have doubled in size. He wore a dirty flannel nightgown and an old periwig. But whoever he was Grainger stood up for him when he entered the room. And I of course was a bare blink o' the eye behind Grainger.

"Good morning, Colonel Dekker! And what news has Mistress Jane brought for us this morning?" Grainger was eager. He took the tiny roll of paper that Dekker slipped out of a little piece of goose quill and handed to him, unrolled it and focussed with a magnifying glass. There was a long silence.

"So it is as you suspected, Colonel Dekker, and that I now own freely, and I'm damned glad to have to do so..." The two men exchanged bows. Again Grainger focussed the lens. Slowly he drew it along lines of tiny handwriting done on finest rice paper. "Though this can't be allowed to slow the enterprise at this end of the business..." He smiled. "We must look after our Mistress Jane well. She's earned her grain today!"

For a moment I was puzzled. Grainger saw the expression on my face. Suddenly he sniffed at the air, long hard, slow. I did the same. Then I too knew. When we had climbed he stairs there had been what I had supposed had been a distant reek of bad drains. Now I knew it had not been that. It was fowl droppings; to be precise it was pigeon dung.

"Yes, Mistress Jane is a four year old Liegeoise pigeon. In the summer months she's good for nigh on to two hundred miles; and that at a timed thirty-seven miles to the hour! We fly her between Edinburgh and here. Today she'll rest; tomorrow she'll be back on the mail coach north. Her sister will take the same message down to York. Hopefully! Sometimes, though rarely, their Lordships of Admiralty allow us to use their telegraph at Deal to speed on our messages up to London...

when it suits them. But for carrying detailed news we find pigeons are more effective."

"Ah!" Talaeus Dekker was clearly interested. "I myself would like to have sight of whatever the decoding tells us. Meanwhile, Richard, I will need to have some talk with our friend here…" The words were soft and came as a civil request. But I had already sniffed out who the senior man was. Here it was Dekker who gave the orders. Grainger left us.

"So… Dr. Shafto…" Dekker's voice was now coming from under the dirty nightgown. As he freed himself from its billowing folds the grey periwig dropped to the floor. His bright eyes followed my gaze down to the thing. "Ah," He said. "Pigeon shit, my dear Sir; it plays the very devil with a fellow's hair and will damned soon burn a hole in your coat… "Under the night gown Dekker was wearing kerseymere breeks and a shooting coat of coarse tweed.

D'y know if we had a garden hereabouts I could grow gooseberries the size of turkey's eggs. We've the rich manure for it!" For just a few seconds I was deceived by the stray fancy that Dekker was one of the so-called Eccentrics I had heard about. But this Talaeus Dekker was no bumbling fool. He turned about suddenly.

"Tell me now… What will be the prime danger that will face a man who wishes to transport, say, one hundred thousand guineas from the port of Newcastle to anywhere on the Continent of Europe?" I recognised his opening gambit. I was to be 'wrung out'!

"As always, Sir, his own accomplices…" It was a good answer. That much I could see. Dekker went on. Now though he was a professor lecturing to a class.

"His first problem must of course be the assembling of such great pile of coined gold. Gold is scarce everywhere, and getting scarcer. Someone among the hundreds of small banks must surely know the names of the men or indeed of the companies which might keep such sums. But in this country they are, of course, in no way obliged to confide that information to their government."

For what seemed an age Dekker talked on. He asked questions but did not wait for my answers. Then for a few moments he appeared to go to sleep. As he nodded he closed his eyes. Of a sudden he had a haggard look to him. It was only then that I saw that he was not near so old a man as I had first thought. What his prematurely whitened hair had not contributed to the effect was made up for by the sun wrinkles on his hide. In his time this Taleus Dekker had obviously spent much time overseas.

"A man who seeks to smuggle golden guineas out of these islands gives himself a number of problems not experienced by other merchants. For as soon as he assembles his coin he is liable to attack from all quarters. By the very act alone of putting his treasure aboard a ship he becomes a felon. So thus there is no one to whom he may appeal if he is then robbed."

It seemed for a moment that the last word he used had begun a new train of thought for Dekker. He smiled wickedly and rubbed his hands vigorously. Then as quickly he was back. Again he had his wits focussed sharply upon me.

"Then he has to ship his guineas over the seas... but to do that he has to entrust his treasure to a shipmaster and a crew. And surely nobody but a fool would watch his precious gold drop out of sight below a distant horizon with anything like an easy heart!"

I think the man would have gone on for hours. Though of course I knew that had been his intention from the start. I was being both interrogated and at the same time prepared for my task. Though, all the whiles the old bastard had offered me neither a seat nor a glass of wine. It was deliberate. Yet it was all so damned pleasantly done. This Colonel Dekker was indeed an expert. Quite the best I had met. He was so very gentle in the way he led me in and out among the pathways of Money. His voice was even becoming soothing:

"Gold exchanges for perhaps sixteen times its weight in silver. Though with the inflated rate of exchange now offered there could be as much as twenty four times the weight, the bulk...."

It was then that I realised that I hearing the voice as though it was coming at me from a distance. It was like an echo calling for me down a great hall. Then I felt myself sway on my feet. I gave a little start.

"Anton Mesmer!" Loud and clear the name came leaping up from the store of my memory. It almost snapped from my lips like a command. Dekker had made no mystical passes across my face with his hands but nonetheless the outcome had been the same. And at the sound of that name I found that I was smiling directly into the old man's face.

"Older than that it is, my friend...much older." He spoke very quietly.

But whatever might have followed was aborted in the instant before its birth. The curtains across the door were flung aside. The young clerk hesitated for a second before he ran into the room. Tight lipped and keeping his eyes upon me he sidled by me to hand a slip of paper to Talaeus Dekker. I learned more from the working of the old man's mouth than from anything he might have said. His teeth clacked noisily.

"Mr. Grainger!" The power that was suddenly in Dekker's voice took me unawares. The shortness of Richard Grainger's footsteps told me that he had not been far away. Probably he had remained within earshot.

"Arrest the bastards! Take Big Dougie wi' ye - now - down to this town's Tollbooth and clap those idle whore-masters in their own double shackles! Before half an hour has passed I want them separated and in cells. Stay there, Grainger... And before I talk to them I want every man jack of them terrified near out of his life!"

I stood waiting. For a long moment I was like a post in a courtyard. All the excitement went on around me but nothing concerned me.

Then as just as quickly Dekker had switched his attention back to the business in hand. He stepped forward and clapped his hands to my shoulders. I felt the warmth as he took hold of my hand and shook it. "A Hindoo priest taught me that dodge in India more than thirty years ago..." Then his eyebrows went up and he was looking at me directly. "You'll do, laddie. Indeed, I shouldn't wonder if you did very well... " There was a pause, a long silence during which I could hear the hushed murmur of voices in the other rooms. Then Dekker made up his mind: he was going to confide in me. "You come very well recommended, Doctor Shafto. When I gave the Brydon girl leave to go to France to find you it was on the advice of the man you knew as Hypolyte L'Amph..."

The sharp breath I drew sounded across the silence of that room. It was, as they say, as though someone had stepped on my grave. And the elegantly booted foot that did the stepping had belonged to Colonel des Ingeniers, Henri Hypolyte L'Amph, the officer we had called 'Le Duc'.

"But Colonel L'Amph was burned alive in 1810, at Savorna...I was there!" Vividly I could still see the body lying prone, spread-eagled on baled wheat straw at the bottom of the broken ladder. I remembered how the smoky flames from the burning casks of olive oil had licked around his boots. Dekker smiled. He was obviously more than a little pleased at what I had said.

"Oh, yes, of course you could not know! The man you knew as L'Amph, Dr. Shafto, is very much alive." The smile became amused. "Indeed in a way you could almost say that now you are almost comrades-in-arms again. He is at work in the City of London. Indeed it is largely because that fellow speaks so highly of you, Sir, that you are here!"

My laugh came out as a short bark. I was amazed. So that was it! I had often wondered. Afterwards we had found nothing of L'Amph's charred corpse among the ashes of Salvatini's warehouse. So *Le Duc* had been an English agent. And I owned to myself fairly that at no time had I suspected a thing. I had not even thought it strange that a British sloop had been close inshore on the Ligurian coast that night.

"Without hesitation he chose you from a list we had drawn up ... all of them known as competent agents: Grice? Oliver? Miss Haydon-Uys?"

"Yes, Sir... It was all I could say. Dekker too had done with me. He waved he towards the door.

"You shall start this day... The weather is foul. But nevertheless, Doctor Shafto, I want you to take yourself off down into these damned Black Indies of yours. Aye, we've evidence enough to make us certain that the trade in smuggled gold out of the Tyne is as brisk as it is up in Edinburgh. I've just learned that before Christmas a hundred and fifty thousand pounds worth o' British guineas was put ashore in Antwerp. Newcastle is nearer to the Continent than Edinburgh; the more so in this weather. Leave the difference between the laws of Scotland and England to me. Just you catch me the bastards. We've a judge hereabouts who'll work out a way to hang them high! Dekker waved a hand in the air. Already the man's mind was turning to other problems.

"Grainger will be settling the details at this moment. You won't be long detained here."

For a moment Talaeus Dekker seemed to have forgotten something. He hunted about patting at his waistcoat before dipping his head to search through a drawer. He lifted a walnut box on to the table. "Here we are... this is a brace of Hunter's best." I saw at once that I was being offered the work of one of the finest Scottish gunsmiths. The octagonal barrels had been cleverly browned to show a pattern; the neat locks were of blued steel. "These days the rage is all for Forsyth's new percussion firing." His face was suddenly grim. "Poor George Tooke had a brace o' the new style of barkers with him when we sent him North from London. They didn't do much to save him! Take it, Doctor Shafto. You'll find flints and powder in the box. Just you be assured that where you're going they're like to be damned necessary! The beggars who did for George

35

dealt with him expertly enough …very, *very* expertly. White arsenic powdered on to hot apple pie! See that it doesn't happen to you!" It looked for a few seconds as though Dekker had finished with me.

"I will, Sir… be assured of…" I stopped. Dekker's lifted eyebrow signalled that another stray thought had occurred to him.

"Bye-the by, Shafto…how did you find our young Miss Grant… that is to say the widow Brydon?"

"She's a charming lady, sir…" That had not been the response Dekker wanted.

"T'cha! Spare me your blather, man! How did she manage the business of getting you here?"

"Fine, Sir… very well indeed…" Dekker looked weary again.

"You're a handsome young fellow, and as like as the next man to be smitten by a bonny face. For that reason I feel obliged to tell you this much for nothing…" His eyes narrowed. "Keep your beastie in y'r breeks, Doctor Shafto. An' see y' keep it tight muzzled at all times. You may feel at liberty to enjoy whatever lascivious fancies you will about her, Sir. For I know that all my young men do that. There was never a charge for dreams. But always remember this: that lassie is not for the likes of you! Perhaps when this business is over she'll wed Dickie Grainger - if his daft mother is ever fully won round to the notion. But be that as it may, all you'll need to know for the present is that the lass is the widow…of a truly decent man, a friend of mine… "

Chapter Four

The note I had been given at Dekker's office needed a response. That would be my starting point. Though I guessed, of course, that this could easily be a test piece for me to demonstrate my skills upon. The scrap of yellow paper with an address written in it was all I had been given. Also I saw whoever had received the letter had torn off the body of the work. I was being sent to question this Eneas Knox. Here, as elsewhere, there would be a need for especial caution. Nowhere would I dare to blunder!

The Hillgate I remembered was just across the river in Gateshead. I walked down to the Side and joined the increasing flow of folk whose business took them down towards the Tyne Bridge.

Even on a single passage of Gateshead's main street it was plain enough to me that as a town she still stood sore blighted by her next neighbour. As ever, Gateshead stood in the shadow of Newcastle - and likely always would. For the most part the shops there were smaller, meaner even. Here there were few of the luxury goods that adorned the wide windows of Newcastle's grand emporia. The note had said Hillgate. Whoever this Eneas Knox was he had clearly stretched his longbow here – and that more than a little. Better had he written 'behind' or 'within' Hillgate. The tenement yard was entered by way of a narrow alley. There was a single wooden stairway and three landings. And before I had gone even five paces I knew that my presence had been noted on all three. It was that sort of warren. A rag of filthy curtain shifted, a door latch clicked shut. A couple shrieking the foulest abuse at one another stopped dead. This however was the kind of curiosity I knew well enough how to discourage. I drew myself up like one of the Emperor's *Chefs de Brigade* on a tour of inspection. As I glowered at each empty window in turn I narrowed my eyes. For a short moment I stood there; knowing that I would be seen as the living embodiment of harsh Authority. The oldest tricks work best.

Fourteen was second from the end of the topmost landing. I stood before it's door and lifted my hand to the knocker. And then I paused. Smells differ. Smells of cooking, smells of brown soap and washed clothes, even the smell of human sweat will change a little between countries and even between provinces. The sharp stench of burning wool told me that close-by some thrifty housewife was tossing a sheep's head on to the coals of her fire. Patiently she would scrape the grinning head until it was white and clean. Those who have not tasted sheep's head broth cannot know how good it is; that especially when there's naught else in the house! But there is however another smell and that is surely the same for all of Humanity. I slipped the brass key into the lock and turned it gently.

I was hit by the heavy stench of a dissecting room. Before I had gone three paces across that room, that living stink had gripped me by the throat. Like fingers forced down my gullet the reek I had not known for years had me. Gagging like some lily-arsed student I snatched up the poker from the fireside. My stomach heaved; I tasted the hot acid of bile rising up into my mouth. With a hand clenched to my nose I stumbled across the room. The paint of years had sealed the window sash tight. I fumbled as I thrust the poker's point between the frames. Savagely I levered at it. The wood splintered. Two glass panes fell inward and smashed around my feet. I stumbled back to the doorway. For long moments I stood there, gasping, trying to get enough air into my lungs to blow away the smell of death.

But viewed as a plain job o' work, the murder appeared to have been simple enough. Death had been guillotine swift. The man's life's blood had gouted up high above the fireplace. There it had dried across the clean lime-washed plaster in a hideous fan shaped splash of red-brown.

However, and with of a sudden rush of professional interest, I knew that I had at least to satisfy myself. I had to look more closely to see just exactly how, and if I could, to guess by what blade Eneas Knox's throat had been slashed.

Once I'd heard an army surgeon describe such a wound as 'exuberant'; and indeed that single slash that had let the life out of Knox was truly … operatic! Only the white bone of the fellow's spine had saved the scrawny neck from parting with the head altogether. A razor of some sort had been used. And there was no doubt in my mind that such an uncommonly deep slash could only had been delivered by someone with a very strong left arm. Yet when the killer had struck the murdered man looked to have been taking his ease in his armchair by the fire. The other curiosity too was that the broad-fall of Eneas Knox's breeches was unbuttoned; the poor old bastard's kegs had been left pulled down around his knees! Odd it was, but also, perhaps, telling!

What was I looking for? How had the murderer gained entrance? Had he been admitted freely, welcomed even? From the clotted splash of the bloodstain down the corpse's front and into his drawers what did look certain was that Knox had been persuaded to get his breeks down first – *before* the killer had slaughtered him like a sheep! Another idea began to insinuate itself. Had the murderer been a woman, a strong woman? Or perhaps it had even been the Revenue officer's catamite. That was a fair guess, I supposed, and it might yet be well worth bearing in mind!

It was strange but my immediate feeling at that moment was that - against all common sense – I had all the time in the world. Indeed already my experience was whispering to me that this was not the time for hurrying. So far as I knew Knox had been Dekker's only informant in Newcastle; perhaps he had been the only man who had known *anything* at all about guinea smuggling. And now before I could ask him a single question the fellow's mouth had been separated from his lungs! But great as that loss was there was still a deal that his corpse, this small room and the few possessions in it, could tell me. That is if only I could hold my spew until I had worked over the whole place with a louse comb. But in early March the daylight still goes fast. On the mantle-shelf above my head there was a tinderbox. Now, for me, the simple knack the striking a light has always been a damned awkward business. From the box I pulled out a boll of fine combed flax and a few strips of charred linen. Some folk will swear by a good piece of black flint; others by the quality of the steel. Seldom had either made much difference to my efforts. Yet this time I was lucky. At the second strike a shower of sparks flew among the fine strands of flax. The suddenness of the flare up almost caught me out. Just in time I had the charred linen ablaze and the stump of a wax candle burning with a clear flame.

For once the freezing weather was working to my advantage. Had it been the month of August then Knox's cadaver would already have been black with flies; or later all a' crawl and lifting with maggots. The stench alone would have had the body discovered in no time. I reckoned the man had been dead for less than two days: *rigor mortis* was just beginning to slacken. Now it was simply a cadaver.

"Well, Bob Shafto… " I realised that I had spoken aloud and clapped my mouth shut. "… as old Doctor Bowren used to say: 'A man's body is but the vessel of the Holy Spirit…'" I sighed. First of all I would examine this cadaver – professionally, though of course this could be no full *post mortem*.

Eneas Knox had been, I judged, near enough to sixty. The first thing I saw was that his open mouth held a set of very well made false teeth. He wore his gray hair in the fashion of a sea-officer, clubbed and tied with an eel skin. At some time long time past a sword slash had opened the flesh across his chest.

When he had died he had already drunk, or had spilled, a fair quantity of Scotch whisky: that I knew only because I could still smell it on his shirtfront. Perhaps he had been already too drunk to know what was happening. Then suddenly I knew. The attack had come at the instant the old man had thrown back his head to sup from the tilted the whisky bottle. Only then had his neck been so fully exposed. That was it. I had been slow in my wits. But then it really had been a long time since I had done such work.

Yet I went on, and at the end of an hour I think I could flatter myself that I knew about as much about the late Eneas Knox as any physician … or as well as any physician working by the light of two candle stumps might expect to.

It was indeed a gross piece of slash-work. Knox must have been dead from shock before his scream had time to bubble out of his slashed windpipe. So much given for the poor fellow's body.

For my purposes however the man's clothing yielded more. My liaison had indeed been an officer in the king's Revenue Service. The crown and fouled-anchor on the gilt buttons of his dark blue coat told me that much. I searched his garments to the very seams. Oddly enough it looked as though the killer had not stayed to rifle his victim's effects. Revulsion often comes close on the heels of intense passion. On the floor at his chair's side I found a turnip repeating watch with a nine-carat gold chain and a Ceylon cat's eye set in the fob. There was also a little whale ivory scrimshaw box half full of a pungent snuff. The name Eneas Knox was engraved on both the watch and the snuffbox. And finally, stuffed into his side pocket there was a handkerchief. The silk was caked stiff with the dried phlegm of the snuff taker. But that, save for a handful of small change, was all. Nor was there anything else to be found at all in the pockets of his blood-stiffened waistcoat. Finally I pulled off his boots. In such situations the comic often contrives to present itself: Poor Eneas Knox must have suffered greatly from the huge bunion on his left foot.

It was a nuisance but when I had finished with the cadaver I put everything back – more or less – the way I had found it. I restored both the watch and the snuffbox, and, as an afterthought, much of the small change. For I knew that before long the keen eyes of the town's Justices would be scanning the corpse. A King's servant with a slashed weasand will always give rise to searching questions. And I did not want to have to answer any of them! That soon enough they would find some poor bastard to swing for the killing was… unfortunate.

How very much of a man's life and habits we can tell from a careful search of his possessions. Under the bed there was a big chamber pot. The edges the drying stale was rimmed with yellow crystals. At another time I suppose I might have tasted it. It would have been my diagnosis that the dead man had the sugar. No matter now, poor Eneas! By that time I was well beyond disgust. Knox's bed and straw palliasse yielded nothing except a few fleas. There were two pictures, both cheap Dutch oil paintings of bright flowers. I knew their sort, just as I knew the Amsterdam workshops where cheery young lasses sang as they daubed such canvases by the thousand for sale abroad. However inside the frame of one there was a sixteenth share in a lottery ticket. It had been drawn months before.

At the center of the table on an embroidered cloth lay a big black King James Bible. Between its pages, the place marked with a thin brown plait of braided hemp, I found Knox's Revenue Officer's commission. There was also a single page letter of special commendation from the Excise. It was for his part in the capture of a gang of tobacco smugglers at Blyth. Perhaps after all the dead man and I had had something in common.

By the hearth I found a tinned iron caddy. Carefully I poured the black tea out on to a sheet of newspaper. It was nearly empty when a single Spanish gold *onza* rolled out across the table. Prize o' war! And so I went on with meticulous care.

But it was only when I had kicked back the corner of a rag mat and seen that edge of one of the floorboards was polished with the rub of fingers that I began to hope that I had uncovered Revenue Officer Knox's own *cache de secret*. And almost at first glance I knew that I probably had everything that had ever been of importance. There was a starched cloth packet of letters and two leather-bound notebooks. These were too important to read kneeling on the floor in a freezing room. I stuffed them into my pockets. I was about to replace the board when I caught sight of the edge of the greasy chamois bag. It hefted heavy. That too went unopened into my greatcoat pocket.

Instinct warns. Another half minute and I should have trapped. I had turned the brass key and pulled the door shut behind me when I heard the scrunch of boots on snow.

I suppose I might have bluffed my way out and simply walked past them. My dress was that of a gentleman. It would have been considered a distinct impertinence for such fellows to challenge me at all. But looking down at the fallen snow I saw at once how easily I would have betrayed myself. My footprints came across the yard and up the stairs to Knox's door and to nowhere else. I patted at my pistols. It was at that instant that I knew for a certainty that this time - if I had to – I would use them. If I were challenged there were going to be two dead men lying on the snow in a Gateshead close. And that was something, I told myself, that I had decided without trace o' malice. For I had reminded myself once again that Robert Shafto was still standing under the gallows' shadow.

But then of a sudden a kindly salvation winked at me from across the landing. I saw that the ragged scrap of rag that curtained a window had twitched. Someone was watching me. Two steps and I had my shoulder against the tarred timber. The sneck that held the door shut offered almost no resistance. I fell inside.

She was a young lass. Or say rather that she had been that - once. Once, and that only a couple of seasons before, the girl

43

had been bonny; now like any plucked flower she was fading fast. Her mouth opened. I reached a hand out at her, grabbed her jaw between my thumb and forefinger, and clamped it shut. There was that look on her gaunt face that told me that the lass had long since been broken to a man's abuse. She had resisted me hardly at all.

"Ten minutes o' your best hush, m' Love…" I whispered. " And there's a half crown piece in it for you." Brown eyes widened their agreement. There was a sound behind us. Somewhere in the room a hungry bairn began to grizzle. I loosed my prisoner. She hurried across to the little creature. As she went she began to haul a shrunken breast from her shift.

To see anything outside I had to pull out some of the rags stuffed into a crack in the door. Below me two pairs of heavy boots had started to thud on the stairway. A fist banged hard at Knox's door.

"Mr. Knox, Sir… are y' in?" The gruff respect in the man's tone led me to suppose that he was himself some low rank of revenue officer, a gauger or a tide-waiter, or somesuch.

"Either he's been a' bed these last two days… or the bastard 's dead." He had turned to his mate. But this fellow was short on both patience and respect.

"Smash that fuckin' door down, Joe… or I'll do it myself."

He had to do it himself. With two savage kicks from his heavy sea boots he had broken the door timbers to splinters. The two men tumbled inside like dragoons into a wine shop.

Within seconds they were both out. The revenue man was spewing up his beer and black pudding. The big fellow, I saw now that he was a seaman, a master or mate, swore obscenely as he hawked and gobbed fulsomely over the rail and down into the close beneath.

Only the seaman went in again. He did not stay long. Though while he was inside he plainly had made Liberty Hall of the place. When he came out his pockets were swollen tight and he was carrying the two Dutch pictures, and, oddly enough I thought, Knox's big Bible. They went off together.

"Now, Mistress…" I wondered how often the lass had been addressed in such a fashion! "There's a dead man in that room over there. So here's the half-crown I promised you… See if you can't manage to forget that you've seen me altogether." I lifted her chin and smiled at her. Yes; this one would know how to keep her mouth shut. "And I dare say that there'll be a reward o' some sort from the town's magistrates if you run and report that you've just found poor Mr. Knox's body. Take your bairn wi' y' and it'll be best you go down first to the curate at St. Mary's. He'll know best how to manage this business." I smiled and winked at her. "Though, I'd ask that you give me a few minutes head start before you begin."

I caught up with the two men just as they parted company at the Gateshead side of the Tyne Bridge. The revenue man in his tricorn hat and with his naval cutlass hung from a black leather baldric with brass anchor on it would not be difficult to find again. I followed the seaman. It was no hard task. Keeping myself to the off-side of a loaded cart I kept him in sight as far as New Greenwich. There I watched him get into a jolly boat. He rowed himself out to a collier anchored in the river. Her name was the *Countess of Raby* and her number, painted white on black at her bows, was 179. I'd done a good first day's work.

By then the afternoon was drawing in. From across the river the soft glow from behind the curtains of a thousand windows was showing. Now it was getting on for the time for respectable folk to blaze up their fires and shut out the night. That reminded me. I too had to find somewhere to lodge. I did not want to risk spending another night under Mrs. Dilkes' roof. Though that was a pity because I had enjoyed the old woman's cooking. No; for whatever else now, this lad was his own hound; though I needed to afford the risk of looking up an acquaintance of mine, *someone* from my time in Italy.

Before Jonathan Stokoe came into the *Seven Stars* taproom I had sat alone in a corner seat. While he argued in loud Danish with two men who had the look of shipmasters I stood up and shifted my place. Now I was sitting on the settle by the fireside and I knew that my profile was shown up plain in the flicker of the firelight. I sat there quietly drinking my glass of hot rum and lemon juice. It had to be all of another ten minutes before Jotty turned his head in my direction. I knew then that the rogue had seen me. I saw his eyes narrow. Most men will look twice at something they find hard to believe. Jotty Stokoe looked across at me all of three times before I smiled back at him through the drifts of blue tobacco smoke. Only then did I catch his gaze and saw him fork two fingers up at his nostrils. Then deliberately he raised a quizzical eyebrow at me. At last and only then when he had struck hands with the two Danish shipmasters did he stand up. Without even glancing in my direction he walked out through a curtained doorway. Within a bare minute's space of time the taproom's lame potman was leaning over me. With a waft of breath from him that was like an opened tomb he gritted softly:

"Mr. Ochsteiner begs that you take glass of wine with him…Sir." I nodded and stood to follow him.

"Jonathan!" The big hands were a lot softer than the last time I had clasped them. "Why, man, Doctor Shafto…by God, many 's the time aaah've wondered what became o' you!"

"And I of you my friend! And I of you…." Though, to speak the truth that was not the strict case. For a year before and that by the sheerest chance I had had sight of a considerable correspondence from one of the Emperor's agents in Copenhagen.

"The man Stokoe is a resourceful agent – but exactly of *whom* we have been unable to discover…" At sight of those words I had roared with laugher. As always my friend Jotty was his *own* agent!

In the May of 1809 Jotty had been an able seaman aboard H.M.S.*Mnemone*. I looked at him. Suddenly it seemed that Jotty Stokoe had been reading my thoughts:

"Aaah'm as safe as any man could wish, Doctor...These days I've a genuine Danish passport in my pocket. And that, I may tell you, works a damned sight better than any arse-wipe of an Admiralty protection!" His smile soured. "Just so long as the bastards don't strip off my shirt..." That too I recalled – of course I did. When I had been at Legorno Jotty Stokoe had been brought ashore by the crew of a fishing boat. From his shoulders to his waist the man's back had been like raw steak. The poor bastard had taken a hundred lashes with a navy cat-o'-nine-tails. Yet in spite of his terrible injuries the man had slipped over the man o' wars' side and begun swimming. By the time I got to him the poor lad had been close to dead. For want of anything else I had tried an old remedy and bound his hideous lacerations with the flesh side of a new flayed goatskin. It had worked.

"I need a safe room, Jotty...somewhere I can be private and without fear of disturbance." He nodded slowly. He was thinking. Though in truth there was nothing for him to think about. For Jonathan Stokoe and I were chained to one another by the certain knowledge that one word from either of us would have the other hanged. If ever there had been a safe alliance it was ours. But more than that, I had an honest call upon the man. I had nursed him for six weeks. And then when he had recovered I had got him a berth on Yankee merchant ship and given him the money to buy seaman's gear.

"So you've turned merchant, Jotty?" I smiled approvingly. He was dressed very much in the *haute ton*. Though perhaps with more *haute* than ton! His waistcoat was of heavy Chinese brocade and there were diamonds on his fingers worth enough to buy a collier-brig, all standing. Stokoe smiled back. We had always understood one another, perfectly.

"I'll tell you the whole tale when we dine together. But in a few minutes I'm to meet with a man who tells me of the sale of twenty thousand stand o' new French Government muskets – all straight from the Rochfort arsenal. With all his troubles behind him his Blessed Majesty, Louis Bourbon, it seems wants shot of them! It's too good a chance for me to miss!" Stokoe tapped his nose with his forefinger. "Those two Danes you saw me with…they want to buy some decent muskets. They're minded to do a bit of trading somewhere down on the West African coast." He cocked an eye at me. " These days, wi' the war over an' all that, there's soon like to be plenty o' men without work…but by Christ, Doctor, an' I may tell this you now, it won't be me!"

For just an instant the ghost of a fear crossed my mind. Might I not be sitting here with one of the very men I had been sent to find. It was certain sure that Jonathan Stokoe was a man who had no reason to love England. A deal less, truth to tell, than had I. But no; no matter what, that wasn't friend Jonathan's way. His vengeance had been, and probably still was aimed at a certain Nathaniel Siskin, sometime First Lieutenant of the frigate H.M.S. Mnemone. It was a personal thing. Besides, as I judged him now, Jotty Stokoe might have become comfortable. Though I guessed he was not yet a truly rich man. For a few years yet my friend Jotty was likely to be one deal ahead of ruin. He wasn't big enough – yet – to trade in English gold to the tune of a hundred thousand guineas. Though, he might well know someone in the town who could.

I took Jotty's note of hand with me and walked up to the address on Westgate. That scrap of paper worked like a charm. Without question I was welcomed into the house. Nor could I have wished for a better room. It was at the head of the stairs above 'Mr. Ochsteiner's' own lodgings. The room smelled fresh and it was clean. Its furnishings were very decent and the floor was covered with a huge Ottoman carpet. At once Jotty's manservant ran up from below with a shovel of burning coals and soon had a fire roaring away in the grate.

"Dickie's the name…Sir. Dick Triphook. He stood before be like a man who knew his own worth. "Like t' Master you'll want to be left private?"

"Thankee, Dick…that's about the way of it…" I treated him to wink.

Now that I was settled comfortably it was time for a survey of any progress made. And it would ease matters a lot if I were to draft a report of some sort and have it put on the mail coach for Edinburgh. This of course was mere form. It has been my experience that those who employ agents become very ill-at-ease when they are without a posting of news for even a few days.

Of course I would not have been a mortal man had I not first of all turned out Eneas Knox's heavy chamois bag. Damn me but it was a score to swell out a fellow's heart. A veritable shower of gold it was. On to the table before me lay twenty years gleanings of all the scraps of the Tyne's trade. There were ten French Louis d'Or, five Russian half-imperials, there was even a couple of Yankee twenty-dollar pieces; the gold coins of half the world were there. Then at the bottom of the poke there was a butterfly shaped lump of silver: it was two Louis XIV ecus fused together by heat. Excellent! This was the stuff I needed. Around this scrap of silver lone I could easily embroider a report that would satisfy Talaeus Dekker. It would go by the first Edinburgh stage. I poured myself a good glass of my friend Jonathan's port.

However, as I tried to read the rest of the papers I had taken from under the floorboards of Eneas Knox's room I found myself sadly disappointed. They might mean much, or little. For myself, however, I could make neither head nor tale of any of them. And to me that was a considerable source of annoyance. None the less though, it would all go as grist to the same mill. It would fatten up my report very handsomely.

Suddenly and like an idiot I realised that just the ghost of a smile was beginning to play around my mouth. Again an odd feeling of well-being had begun to spread through me. I held up my wineglass to the candlelight

"Admit it Bob Shafto…" Quietly I was growling the words to myself. "This is the sort of work you were born to do… You damn well love it, you stupid bastard!"

And it was true. Since the year 1803 this was the work I had done, and been good at, damned good if the truth were acknowledged. Moreover this could hardly be the hardest case that had ever been laid upon me. Why, it had at best to be no more than a gill of small beer! There were less than thirty thousand souls in the city of Newcastle-upon-Tyne. Of all these people no more than half a dozen at most were ever going to catch the faintest whiff or sniff of anything to go with gold smuggling. Perhaps another twenty, twenty all told, would ever be even half-privy to the entire business. Some men would know a little and have guessed at a great deal. But, and looked at under the right sort of lens, the fellows who stood at the centre of the trafficking would stand out as proudly as the pustules on a pauper's bum!

Chapter Five

Again I had slept deep and, thanks to Jotti's manservant, breakfasted very handsomely on a great slice of gammon and fried eggs. Even so, the after effects of my long coach journey from London were still telling upon me. I had to go first to the stage office to see if there were any orders from Dekker for me. There were none. But I knew at once that the bowlegged Jackie Minto had had me well described to him. The fellow's eyes lit almost as soon as I had stepped into the office. But with my business soon done I walked out to steal a little time to wander about among the morning crowds in the upper town. Up at this end of Newcastle the streets were better paved than I remembered. Altogether indeed the place looked to have done well out of the French wars. On this side of the river too the shops were still bursting with good things. And their quality too was a fair match for anything from London or even Paris. Nor was it difficult here to see why British manufactures were being so eagerly sought after all across Europe.

Half on a whimsy I stepped into the select room of the old *Black House* on the Pilgrim Street. The alehouse was where I had taken a last drink with friends on the night I sailed for France. Between sips of brandy and hot water I sat working out a plan. For I knew that on everything I did during the next few days my performance would be weighed. Just as I knew also that Talaeus Dekker would be a damned harsh judge. My first reports to him would be carefully scrutinized. Masters, of whatever nation, will always bear a fierce hunger for checkable results. Just as in the same fashion those bastards' allowances for petty disbursements tend always to be tight. Though, of course I saw the reason for Dekker's caution in my case: with little money in his pockets Bob Shafto was not going to be able to flee the country. But, as I reflected, with Eneas Knox's hoard of coin in my pocket I was now in much better case than I had been only the day before. I remembered too exactly how damned close I had been hunted by Major Farquhar in Paris. How, on the night that same Farquhar had clapped his manacles on me, I'd had scarce enough loose copper in my pockets to buy a glass of the cheapest red wine.

I lingered a little over my drink in the *Black House*, using the time to see how my appearance struck the local tradesmen. Soon enough I was satisfied that I fitted my surroundings well enough. Not a man who entered that taproom spared me so much as a second glance.

I don't know what made me turn my head when I did. Nonetheless I did. I looked out of the bow window to see if it still snowed. Just in time I saw the flick of a fashionable bonnet passing before my eyes. I saw her. Or say rather that I saw *them*. It was Rachel Brydon walking with a companion. My immediate reaction was to call out to her. Only just in time did my jaw snap shut. I stifled my greeting - hard. Fool! That would have been a stupid thing to do. For a few seconds I sat, clutching at my glass. Damn me but I was blushing like a maiden caught in her shift, and I knew it. That after nearly thirteen years of service as one of the Emperor's best agents I should consider such piece of stupidity was unthinkable! Already this damned Albion had seemed to breed a carelessness that could finish me! Along the London road the widow Brydon had done her work well. She had got me free of my three gaolers. She had directed me on the next step of my journey. But that was all! I tried to tell myself that we owed one another nothing, nothing at all, save discretion! Nonetheless, and then almost without my realising it I got to my feet and set out to follow the two women.

I waited across the street while they went into a smart millinery shop. Already the latest Paris 'modes' were displayed. The elderly companion came out first. She had thrown back her hood. I saw her face clearly. This old woman had never been a great beauty but even now she was certainly still striking enough. Nonetheless I soon gathered that the elderly woman was Rachel Brydon's trusted companion. Companion! The English have such a genius for euphemisms. It was one of the few occupations open to a gentlewoman, for a lady in what genteel folk with their usual hypocrisy call 'reduced circumstances'… church-mouse poor!

Slowly I stalked the pair. They turned the corner into Mosely Street. There were carts and driven cattle on the street enough to mask my presence. The companion walked with her head lowered to watch for her footing on the frost rimed pavement slabs. Rachel Brydon, herself, moved along like a queen in mourning.

It was only when they got to the crossing at the end of the street that Rachel looked in my direction. But I didn't move for cover. For by then my gaze had been attracted elsewhere. That was when I saw for certain that I was not the only one who was following the ladies.

When the two women went into a watchmaker's shop the pair behind them stopped dead in their tracks. At once they turned away to look intently into the window of a grocer's shop. They were a man and a woman. Both were more or less respectably dressed. At dusk and by a lantern's light they might both just have passed for respectable! But one glance was all I had needed to mark their docket! This pair's trade was writ plain on their faces. If nothing else the sharp dart of their rat-eyed glances betrayed them both. These two were footpads, common knock 'em down an' rob 'em gutter thieves. Paris had swarmed with vermin such as these two. I quickened my pace to shorten the distance between us. For, I knew by then that it could not be long before this pair played their cards. There is an art in everything. Footpads working in daylight have to find some place where they can hustle their victim quickly in off the open street. And up ahead of us I soon saw where they had chosen. It was an alleyway, narrow and dark, between two houses.

The rush began when the two ladies were only three paces from the alley's entrance. The bitch of the pair got there first. She reached out and I saw the companion's frail body stiffen as a hand was clamped hard across her mouth. The little creature was lifted. Her feet left the ground kicking. But Rachel Brydon tried to make a real fight of it. At once for her pains the girl was felled with a 'pimp's clip', a short jabbing punch. I heard the click of the man's knuckles against her pretty chin. She crumpled and was neatly caught. These footpads were very good. Indeed a year before I might gladly have employed them both! That snatch-up had been done in an eye's blink. The last I saw was the black swirl of the man's coat skirts as they disappeared into the alley... *Presto*!

As I moved forwards I found myself reaching for my pistol. But before I got to the dark entrance the alleyway I heard the sharp click of another hammer being cocked. It brought me up short. Fool that I am I still stepped in between those narrow walls. But that shot when it came was not at me. In the little flash of the priming I saw the pale ivory oval of Rachel Brydon's face. She had been thrown to the ground and lay there in the filth. But in her gloved hand she was holding a little muff pistol. The bang was not loud. Whoever had loaded the little gun had used no more than a pinch of gunpowder. Yet soon enough I saw that that same little pinch had thrown a heavy ball.

Her shot had hit the fellow just below his sternum. When she had loosed off at him Mrs. Brydon's hand had been very close to the man's chest. The footpad staggered backwards. I saw the white flash mark on his waistcoat. Already he was leaning back against the wall and looking down in disbelief at the dark red flower beginning to bloom above the horn buttons closing his greasy moleskins. Nothing would save him now. That much I could see as a medical fact. Already this rogue was fast bleeding to death, internally. My professional opinion was that the fellow might last another few seconds - hardly longer. Even as I watched my prognosis was verified. He went down with a wavering groan.

The companion lay prone, moaning softly. Then from the darkness of a corner there was the sound of a breath being drawn sharply in horror at the sight she saw. It was the footpad's doxy. The woman had gone into the alleyway as a fine brazen creature, gypsy-looking, with dark eyes and black hair in tight ringlets. Now her backside was on the ground and her legs were splayed wide. She was well stricken. Her sheer terror at what had happened had wiped away whatever youth the lass still owned. Now her swarthy skin was the colour of a dirty shroud. Eyes like black bullets stared at us – stark and wide. The narrow face was like a bleached skull.

"Kill the bitch!" Rachel Brydon's order rasped out like a bayonet from its scabbard. Still though, to me, it sounded like a schoolgirl's theatricals. But she had spoken in French. And on hearing her words the gypsy woman's mouth fell open. The scream had been there but it had refused to come.

"She understands... so she can tell us more." Then she mewed at the girl: "Bitch... you know where he kept everything ... get them out." And with a whimper the footpad's woman scrambled, crab crawled almost, across to do as she had been bidden. She turned up the top of her partner's left boot and took a wad of paper. At once Rachel Brydon reached out to snatch it from the woman's hand. The dark girl did indeed know where everything was hidden. She undid a brass watch and chain from the waistcoat. Her hands came away bloody. She tore her dead lover's shirt front open and hauled out a cloth bag. From his pocket she took out a *jackie-legs*, a clasp knife with a blade close to a foot long. Deftly I plucked the weapon from her fingers. That was everything.

Feathers of snow flurried across the light at the street-end of the alley to blot out the street beyond. Once a drunken man staggered past, mumbling vague obscenities to himself; then there was a couple of serving maids who giggled as they hurried by under a shared shawl.

"I'll help Lady Donkin... You go first... and you see to it, Mr, that you guard that Spanish besom! She won't make trouble. And since the minx has been watching my house since this morning she'll know very well where to go."

So Rachel Brydon's companion was a lady. Well, we live and learn!

I was glad of the cover the driving snow gave us. We moved easily across the town. There were folk about but they shuffled along with their heads well down against the cold wind. We moved as two separate pairs. Rachel and Lady Donkin went as a young woman who looked to be helping an old lady taken suddenly faint in the street. For myself I kept my prisoner well within arms reach. But for the time being at least I knew that this lass wasn't going to give me any trouble.

"If you dare try to run, my pretty one..."I whispered pleasantly to her in French as I shook my hand in my greatcoat pocket. "I will certainly blow out your spine." She had seen what had happened to her man. My threat made her walk with her shoulders thrown well back.

Rachel Brydon's townhouse was on Charlotte Square. Somehow I had rather expected something rather grander than it was. Before it there was a little park with a few trees and what in summer would be a rose garden. Inside however the place was truly the house of a dream. Elegance was the key word. The whole place murmured softly of family wealth, of money safely secured. Rare woods cleverly carved were waxed and polished; the velvets were rich, their colours dyed deep. Everything spoke of care and many servants. The smell of *pot-pourie* hung on the air. Yet at that moment it was the odd silence of the place that of itself struck a false chord.

The cough came from behind us. It was Nicolo, Mrs. Brydon's Neapolitan footman, that same Nicolo who had applied his garotte so neatly to Major Farquahar's neck on the London road. Now here he stood quite splendid in the full fig of footman's livery, right down to a scarlet shoulder knot. He had moved across the carpeted floor with no more noise than a viper on wet grass. As I turned to face him I raised an eyebrow and punted my prisoner towards him.

"Keep this partridge in a secure cage - she is the property of your mistress... so you will know better than I with what care that lady is to be obeyed." It had been half a joke. Italian is not a language with which to put a real cutting edge on a command. But the handsome young fellow I had last seen so expertly tightening a white silken cord around a man's neck, stiffened. He struck. Grabbing at a handful of the woman's hair he hustled her away. She swore at him in Catalan. But footman Nicolo knew his business. I heard her yelp with sudden pain.

Alone, I stood in the hall and listened. Above stairs at least, the rest of the house was probably empty. That much I sensed by the many absences. There was no smell of people about the place. The house was well heated; it was well tended. But it had not been lived in for a long time. Then I heard Rachel Brydon sharp rap on the front door's knocker. Her Neapolitan servant ran to let her in. As he went forward I saw Nicolo's calf muscles ripple like a dancer's under his white silk stockings. With a burst of loud Italian he threw up his arms and then lifted Lady Donkin. Tenderly he carried the old woman into a side room. Yet he was out again almost at once. I heard Mrs Brydon call after him for cognac and that he should hurry and bring her the bottle of spirits-of-hartshorn.

But Rachel did not spend long with her companion either. Soon I heard soft laughter. And when she returned the girl fluttered like any young lady of fashion, unlacing her bonnet as she stamped the snow from her neat buskins and allowing her cape to fall away into Nicolo's hands. For anyone at that moment to accuse her of just having let the life out of a common footpad was a notion scarce to be believed!

"Well…that settles it… we must leave here!" She looked across at me. Perhaps I showed that I had been surprised.

"How is Mrs. Donkin?"

"*Lady* Donkin will soon recover." Her response to my question had been as sharp as any sudden box along the ears. "I have insisted that she should go to bed for the rest of the day. However we have still some business which may not now allow that…"

"Madam, I am a physician… "The bold wryness in Mrs. Bryon's little smile told me that I had failed from the outset.

"No, *Sir*! You are not! You are a quite awful fellow, by the name of *Mr. Dacres* as I recall. And in any case… I think *not*. I do however thank you for your kind consideration!" She was looking after her darling and I, strangely, was content enough about that. "Now, I must go and have a few firm words with that brazen faced bitch who attacked us…. No, *Mr*! You go down to the kitchen. My ways will not be yours. There's a good fire down there. You may keep Nicolo company. Speak Italian to the fellow. He's been moping for want of his beloved Naples these last weeks. Practice your quackery on him if you will… see if the lad needs a dose of black draught!

And I did sit with Nicolo. He made excellent coffee in the Neapolitan manner and served us both in fine porcelain bowls. Any man who had saved *La Signora* from street brigands was the friend of Nicolo Mario Cipocci… for life. That he swore by the Virgin.

After half an hour Rachel Brydon returned. She placed a silver locket open on the table before me.

"She's a Catalan… She took up with her light o' love when Sergeant Bates deserted Wellington's Army in the winter of 1813. They've wandered loose in Europe ever since. Last Thursday-week they were hired, in Calais… to do a murder." Rachel Brydon thumbed open the locket's catch. The miniature within was quite exquisite. The artist had caught precisely that almost mischievous smile. It was more than just a perfect likeness. It had an inner spirit that radiated from it like sunshine. It was herself.

"Hired by whom?" Easily I slipped into the role of interrogator. I had questions; I wanted answers.

"They were never told. The work was given them by a *maitre* in Calais."

Of course, I knew the way such things were arranged. The assassins themselves would never have clapped eyes on whoever it was had hired them. Both their instruction and their final payment would be done through a *maitre*, a middleman. It cost more - but it was usually safest for whoever wanted the killing done. I waited. Mrs. Brydon had something else to tell me.

"The last time I saw this locket was a year ago, almost to the day. It was in this house... on the night that my husband was murdered."

Rachel Brydon led me into the salon at front of the house. There she opened a door and stood aside.

"That gentleman was my husband, Sir... The late Mr. Roland Brydon..." Rachel held up a candelabrum to play its flickering lights on to the oil painting over the fireplace. Without doubt the man had been almost elderly. Blue eyes, merry eyes even, seemed to twinkle at us out from the canvas. The mouth was strong. As a younger man Roland Brydon might even have been called handsome. When that portrait had been painted the man had clearly already been well into his fifties.

"What I am about to tell you is nowadays common enough knowledge hereabouts, Dr. Shafto. Once I tried to pretend that it was not so. But now I no longer waste time in attempting to deceive either myself or indeed others. The County people hereabouts all knew about it at the time, of course, and I believe that at the time the match was generally approved of... save by a malicious few." Whatever Rachel Brydon had been about to say then, she suppressed with a sharp up-tilt of her chin.

"I was just turned sixteen; Mr. Brydon, my Roland, was fifty two." She paused and I watched her bosom rise and fall. It was still costing this young woman dear to talk of her late husband. And I sensed that in a way I was being confided in. It had been a very long time since anyone had knowingly done that. Strangely enough I felt myself flattered.

"Such matches are nowadays perhaps less common than once they were. Also as you will appreciate such a marriage could hardly be based upon love. "She looked up suddenly and stared me full in the face. "But truly from the first there was a liking between us. We were two people, a young girl, barely out of the schoolroom, and a man who was almost," Again her look was distinctly defiant. "... old. Both of us were simply doing our duties." She gave the merest ghost of a shrug. "Roland stood to inherit a large fortune quite unexpectedly from a great-uncle. Our families were close and depended upon one another in various matters of business. My mother and our lawyer explained everything to me very carefully." She breathed in up her nose slowly before she went on. "The plain fact was that without our alliance both our families faced simple bankruptcy. And..." Rachel Brydon's nostrils flared. It was as though she had expected me to laugh. "... dutiful child that I was, I agreed."

But without effort I neither laughed nor even smiled. She went on. "According to the terms of his inheritance, were Roland to have died without marrying *and* without having an heir... that fortune and a great deal of land both on here on Tyneside and in Scotland would have gone to his cousin, an extremely nasty and profligate fellow." Again she was looking at me directly, intently." Doctor Shafto, what I am saying is that the well-being of far too many people depended upon our union for either of us to have refused to marry; indeed many of my _own_ family stood in danger of simple ruin. It was a case of saving the modest incomes paid to maiden aunts and of ensuring a decent future for several young nieces and nephews. I suppose that at bottom of all it was a marriage... not so much of convenience but say rather one of desperation..." She was looking now directly into my eyes. "Truly I did quickly come to like Roland Brydon... greatly. And I did love him dearly... for all his kindness..."

A feint little smile wisped its way across Rachel Brydon's face. She was past the difficult part of her story. "Then when we had been married four years, the wicked cousin died - of drink – on the steps of his London club. As they say, Dr. Shafto: 'The best laid plans...' And I will confess honestly that I was glad when news came of that wicked man's passing." She lowered the candles and the painting was in the shadows again.

"However... and all this is really a little beside the real tale. My husband had not always been a rich man, not in his own right. For many years he earned his living as a minor official in the Royal Mint. Roland loved his work. So it struck me as being especially cruel that it was his knowledge of the assaying of precious metals that caused him to be murdered. For whoever it was had my Roland killed had also sent his agent to this house to steal just one thing. Though thankfully whoever that man was he did not recover <u>all</u> of the proof he came for!"

There was a sandalwood box inlaid with mother-of-pearl on a side table. Rachel Brydon opened it and lifted something out. She bore it forward, held high up between her breasts like some pagan priestess bearing a chalice. It was a dark grey lump. Indeed until I saw the slight glint on its surface At first sight I thought it might be an *aerolite*, a shooting star. Then Mrs. Brydon allowed it to fall into my hands and I knew then that it was no fragment of any falling star. It was some pure metal, very heavy. The edges were jagged; indeed for a few seconds it reminded me of a jagged iron fragment from an exploded siege mortar shell.

"Bring it over here, she said softly. "Let me light more candles then you can look at it through the magnifying glass."

Without thinking I took out the clasp knife that I had taken from the footpad's corpse. I scraped at the substance. A glance of brightness appeared and a tiny spiral of metal curled up under the blade's sharp steel. This was another piece of the same fused silver; indeed it was identical with what I had found in Eneas Knox's room.

"Tin? Silver?" I asked raising my eyes to her's. She said nothing but handed me a strong magnifying glass.

In the glass's focus I saw what Rachel Brydon had wanted me to see.

"Coins! These are silver coins all clotted together; fused by heat but not quite melted."

"Good, that is exactly what Colonel Dekker, my husband's good friend, had supposed they were. It was he who sent them here post-haste for Roland's opinion. But that piece was only one of two lumps that were brought to my husband on the night he was murdered."

'How murdered?' The question froze almost before it reached my tongue - but sooner or later I should have to know. Just _how_ a man, or indeed a woman, killed another might tell me much. When I got the chance I would have to ask Dekker for exact detail.

"I remember..." Mrs. Brydon's eyes clouded. "I sat over there by the fire with my embroidery. Roland came in, he was so excited." Her face lit a little and then the light faded. " It was his custom in his workshop to wear a quite dreadful green canvas apron over his clothes and a silly embroidered velvet cap." The young Mrs. Brydon was seeing the scene again. "He had used a fine clock-maker's saw to cut open one of the two silver lumps. He showed me the clearest outlines where some parts of the coins had escaped melting." Tiny jewels of teardrop were gathering at the corners of her dark eyes. Rachel lifted her chin and breathed in for the final effort. "He kissed me, and went down again to his work. I retired to bed. The next morning the servants found Roland lying stiff and cold in his own blood..."

I waited until Rachel Brydon had recovered herself. Her fine hands were spread on the table before her; the gold of her wedding ring gleamed in the candlelight. She patted gently at the polished mahogany wood and raised her face to me. She was ready.

"Mrs. Brydon, do you know *what* coins they were?

"Oh, yes! They are old silver *ecus* of King Louis XIV... We knew that. What Colonel Dekker had wanted to know was whether Roland could tell him anything about the *way* in which the silver had been melted."

My ignorance was of course almost entirely feigned. I had known at first sight what the coins were; just as I knew *why* they had been melted and *why* they were in England. It was a trade we had known all about in Paris. We should have done - we had initiated it! From the outset this was, had been, the Emperor's business. Always Napoleon had sought to gather gold; that metal he had always hoarded jealously for his war-chest. Moreover and like every other ruler in Europe it had always been English gold that Napoleon had needed so desperately to sustain his armies. That was a paradox! Where he could neither sequester, nor steal, where he could not coerce 'loyal gifts' or credit of indefinite extension, the Emperor had to pay. And those merchants who lay safely beyond the grasp of his armies *could* - and did - demand to be paid with his new minted gold Napoleons. So to get the gold he needed our Emperor had traded the huge quantities of the old silver ecu's he had inherited from both the Republic and the Bourbons.

Suddenly this was a bigger game than I had supposed. Like the echoes down the corridors of a State bank it came. I could hear again the crash as the heavy bags of gold coin were thrown on to brass scale pans, the scratch of banker's quills as drafts were signed; I could smell again the spice of seal-wax being heated and the calf-leather bindings of account ledgers. Once again I was in a world I understood.

Before I could ask another question however there was a light knock at the door. Mrs. Brydon walked over to open it.

It was Nicolo. This was strange. A lady did not usually rise to open the door to her own footman. In the flicker of a glass shielded candle he held up I could see that the Neapolitan had changed. Now he wore a suit of respectable dark green. The whiteness of his fresh neck linen showed up his olive complexion. Without his footman's wig our Nicolo was a very handsome fellow. For a moment they talked softly. So she knew Italian too. I had not expected that. Rachel Brydon thanked him and wished her servant a goodnight. She answered his bow with a gracious inclination of her head, a cameo caught in silhouette by the candlelight.

"News. Nicolo has been down to the *George*. He cultivates ... acquaintances there. The body of..." She hesitated and I saw that she trying to draw herself erect. "... of the man who was shot this afternoon has been discovered." The tremble in her voice as she chose her words was faint. "Though Nicolo says that already some of the town's physicians have begun to make offers to the... resurrectionists."

Usually, whenever I had let the life out of a man it had taken most of a bottle of brandy to calm my nerves. Rachel went on:

"But there is more to tell. A messenger has brought a letter from London. Our Mr. Taylor was attacked and wounded - that was in London three days ago, shortly after he left us."

"Is he?" On short acquaintance I had liked Squires Taylor. It had been he who had chosen the suit of clothes I was wearing. I was grateful to the man.

"No; it seems that he took a cutlass slash across the forearm. He will need some days in his bed."

Yes. I knew that it would require that long at the least. Mr. Squires Taylor would be weak from loss of blood. A man chopped at with a naval cutlass usually bleeds like a slaughtered pig. I would have prescribed that he ate large quantities of near raw lamb's liver.

"Farquahar?" Of the three men in my escort from Paris only the major, I thought, could have swung a blade against

Taylor. But then I also realized just what excellent time my pursuers must have made in picking up my trail.

"Not Farquahar... another man."

"Cable? Phelps? Surely neither man would have dared to draw steel on Squires Taylor."

Rachel Brydon bit a little at her lower lip, then realised that she was doing it, and stopped.

"So of course this changes everything." She stood with her hands steepled before her. Slowly she began to tap her fingertips together.

"I was given a list... all of them recommended as good men: Grice? Oliver? Haydon-Uys?"

"Yes, ma'am... so Mr. Dekker said." It was all I could say. The woman had dropped her gaze. Now she was looking at me from under her long dark eyelashes. Rachel Brydon was letting me know just exactly how much she - a woman - had been able to find out about my past. Though, I suspect too that she was a little ashamed that she should have been rummaging so freely in the basket that held so much of my personal dirty linen.

"But it was *you* I chose, Dr. Shafto... for my own ends. I chose you because I sensed that it would be you, if anyone, who in the course of his other inquiries could find whoever it was had paid the assassin to murder my husband! That killing was to do with gold and with silver; and _we_, Roland and I, were as nothing to them. They killed the poor man because of their greed. All they wanted to do was to go on making money..." Rachel Brydon gave her head a little shake: "Forgive me... a woman's sorrow must remain a thing of small consequence. In this business I am not perhaps the proper person to explain these affairs to you. Though today matters have reached such a head - so much more has happened than I could ever have anticipated. And I will own to you, Dr. Shafto, that sometimes I can still sometimes be more than just a little naive about the intentions of these wicked people. And I - personally - have much underestimated the power they possess."

The glowing crust of coals banked up on the grate fell in; for a moment the flames flickered bright.

"Colonel Dekker does not believe me but I have recently felt that someone near me, it seems, has a very long reach and a grasp that is steel hard! It is very likely that these same agents are already here in Newcastle at this moment. Even now they could be watching us." She turned to the curtained window. "For whoever hired those two murderers must know far more about me than I had ever supposed, and about my... friends. There was a silence in the room. I waited.

"Tonight, Dr. Shafto, I propose to put on a little masquerade, a ruse. If it is thought that I am not in Newcastle then there will be no point in our enemies trying to keep any watch on me!"

It was in my mind to suggest that she take the next morning's mail-coach to Edinburgh. No such thing! For I soon discovered that all the while I had been talking to Mrs. Brydon, her own arrangements were already well in hand. I had seen few servants about the house but it seemed that the lady had a call on much help from within the city itself.

The house emptied. As I stood by the curtain's edge in the bow window I watched. A closed carriage was standing out on the road outside. Then I saw a stable boy run out from the stables holding up lantern. The small figure of Lady Donkin could hardly be mistaken for anyone else. Then I heard myself give a low whistle – it was one of simple admiration. The shaped shadow in a black cloak and bonnet walked slowly towards the coach. What I was looking down at was Mrs Brydon. It was a ruse that would have fooled me! I saw Nicolo jump forward and bow to his mistress as he opened the carriage door. Both figures showed clearly against the lamplight. But as the woman lifted her skirts to get into the carriage her head went down and her bonnet shielded her face from the light. Noisily the coachman whipped up his horses and they set off at a brisk gallop.

"That was my new maid, Martha Dolan. Little Daisy Phelps who has been with me longer is of course madly jealous that I could not choose her. But I'm afraid that young Martha owns the height... and I think has more of the actress in her... don't you agree?"

I did. Plainly Rachel Brydon was much amused with her own cleverness.

Chapter Six

At the eating house on Percy Street I had ordered up bread and cheese, with a peeled Spanish onion for a relish. And as I tore open the hot crust of the stottie cake I saw my chosen victim's head turn. But he was not looking at me. No; his was the gaze of a man famished – and it was sighted fixedly on the slab of yellow cheese I was slicing carefully on to the new baked bread. I knew at that moment that here I was busily doing the Devil's own work – and to be sure I had the good grace to feel just a little guilty about the business!

"Oh, Dear God... aah can'nit dee it... I'll spew my guts at the first mouthful, aah know aah will... *that* for certain sure! The very smell o' it sets ma' belly nigh on t' tippin itself oot..."

I put my handful of bread and cheese back on to the plate and breathed my gin fumes over him as I confided: "We started off at seven o'clock last evenin' in the kitchen at Sir John Mather's house at Chester-le-Street..."

It was a tale I wove as I went. I was a valet newly out of a position. For the last five years I had been in service with a Swedish gentleman, a Count no less, who with the ending of the wars was returning to Stockholm. He had just paid me off. "Wi' a handsome present o' money, the better part of his own wardrobe..." I drew my thumbs down my lapels. "... Aye, *and* a set of real lawyer's scribed testimonials that makes me out to be a better man than the Apostle Paul himself!"

God forgive me, but how I did strive to excel myself over that poor wretched man. It surely was a story designed a' purpose to arouse all the jealousy that ever stirs in the hearts of servants. I was the fortunate one. I'd money in my pocket and letters of recommendation that would soon enough get me another position. Almost as an afterthought I motioned to the pewter plate.

"Dee us a favour, Geordie, and eat that…as a good turn to me." I watched his jaw fall. "I'm reminded that my dear mother always swore that the deadliest sin a body could ever commit was to waste good bread… Here, if you'll allow, let me stand you a pint of porter to wash it down. For I know now that my guts won't keep a bite of it down this side o' supper time."

His name was Jacob Storey. And, while he didn't know it yet, this poor beggar was already mine. An hour and three pints of strong beer later and I was being conducted about the snow covered lanes that threaded their ways behind the city's better houses.

Of course like most men-servants Storey was inclined to purvey pure filth. Though, in that he was no worse than I might have expected. What else would a fellow manservant be interested in? So I gave him his head and let him talk. Later when he felt the need for a drop of spirits I could ask him the questions to which I really needed answers. Though for now I could well imagine what would have happened if all those worthy folk at whose backyard doors he was pointing at could have half guessed just what I was being told of their private doings. We would surely have heard their shrieks of outrage from where we stood! For truly this fellow knew how to serve a steaming ragout of stinking black gossip; though there were perhaps a few thin shavings of information enfolded within it. At least however it did serve to eliminate many people from further enquiry. And of course while what I was being told had only a slight intrinsic interest to me! I tried to look aghast as I learned which gentlemen were in what he quaintly called 'carnal congress' with which supposedly respectable ladies.

Perhaps more usefully, I learned also the names of two of the town's leading citizens who laid out hard money to have little lassies brought to them, 'If you'd credit it, sometimes by the bairns' own mothers'. And I noted particularly the names of those sporting fellows who preferred little lads. Fewer but still with more obvious glee Storey also pointed out to me the houses of those gentlemen, "Both bachelors "and *married* men alike!" who hired '*directrices*' to visit their private rooms.

"And they're well paid to welt those fellows bare arses bloody'. The garrulous old scoundrel even asked me if I had ever heard of such a thing before! Oddly enough Jacob Storey knew of only *one* lady in the whole town who was said to join her own maid in acts of unholy passion. Stupid English! Did the fellow think that perversion had been invented in Newcastle town?

But soon it was growing dark and I was tired. The day had been slow. It had been at my own suggestion that we stepped into a chophouse. I had meant to fill Storey's guts, give him a shilling or two and, for now, to be shot of the rogue. Tomorrow I would find another man who might know something. But then suddenly there was a jolly laugh. We were being hailed from across the street.

She was young, pretty and with the joy of life still bubbling up from within her; but nonetheless, for all of that, I saw at once that this young lass was still a whore. I knew that much from the first appraising glance of those big bright blue eyes of hers.

Her given name was Miss Henrietta Bellis. Or that at least was the name by which Jacob Storey made bold show of introducing her to me. And as he did so I was already impressed by the delicate poise in the little courtesy she made me; by that and by the courtesan's coyness in the smile that she fired off broadside at me with from under her bonnet. But for sure and from my first glance I'd had Ettie Bellis fairly weighed up. Aye, and she me! I knew young Ettie as I had known dozens like her all over Europe. She was just another lassie struggling to fight her way out of the festering filth into which she had been born.

Whores, by the very nature of their trade, must always find a cold winter a sore trial. If they show too much of their wares they freeze – and yet they must perforce entice with some small display of their charms. Around her shoulders young Ettie wore a heavy plaid shawl; a pair of cut down man's boots protected her feet from the trodden slush. But I could also see that underneath the plaid she was wearing a high-breasted dress of fine muslin; and in a net bag she carried a pair of beaded dancing pumps. Strange, and doubtless because of it, I told myself that I must be getting soft in the head. For I had found myself wondering how many times she had had to endure the sweating grunts of some man's lust to earn the cost of that dress! Yes; from the first I liked Miss Henrietta Bellis.

And Jacob Storey, it seemed, was indeed a close relative of the girl. But it was also soon plain enough that the pimping old bastard was all for setting me up with her for the night.

"The gentleman is between positions, Henrietta. He's just been discharged, though very *handsomely* after serving a Swedish nobleman for some years."

It's always reassuring indeed to hear another man retail your own lies to someone else as the plain Gospel truth! But our Miss Bellis it seemed was not to be drawn by any mere passing trade. Her pretty lips made a very pretty little *moue* before – with apparent regret - she shook her head.

"I fear, Sir… that I have a previous appointment. One of my friends is a French gentleman newly up from London and set to stay for a month…" Her eyes danced merrily under the flutter of lashes darkened with Turkish kohl. "Another time, perhaps…"

But Jacob Storey was intent still upon screwing his half crown out of an already dead transaction: "A nice drop of gin then, Pet?"

Now young Ettie was truly magnificent. She may have been what was, but by God the lass flounced like a lady-born, tossed her head like a Spanish mare and allowed her pretty mouth to fall open as though in genuine astonishment. I saw then too that Ettie Bellis had uncommonly good teeth.

"Now you know very well, Uncle Joseph, that I have *never* allowed ardent spirits to pass my lips!" At that moment she might indeed have been a young lady from the upper end of the town itself. This was a girl who had schooled herself well. Those lively blue eyes fluttered at me just a little before she spoke again.

"But it is extremely cold…" She conceded this with all the grace of a duchess. "So perhaps a small glass of sherry wine would be… warming."

We sat in a booth in the corner of the taproom at Charleton's in Farringdon's Court, further down the Bigg Market. I ordered hot rum for Storey and myself, and a glass of the house's best sherry for our Miss Bellis. And we talked. We discussed where a fellow might secure a valet's place. Though it was soon agreed that I might well spoil my chances if I made too much of my having worked for a Swedish nobleman. In the North the folk like their servants as they like their breeches – cut plain and serviceable.

For the most part though our chatter was the usual skim-bawdy banter and all our laughter was a counterfeit entire. Nor had I chosen Charleton's wine cellars at random. From the old days I knew it for an honest place. There at least I knew that nothing would be slipped into my drink. But for now what I was interested in learning from Ettie Bellis was something of this Frenchman.

I had to wait until Storey excused himself to ease his water. Then off-handedly I broached the question of the Frenchman. It was a shot loosed off at extreme range. Surely these days there could be few Frenchmen in Newcastle? What had entered my mind of course was that some French agent had been sent across to oversee the safe shipment of the gold. However I had realised too that he might also be no more than some old roué left over from the Revolution. Many royalist émigrés, I knew, had stayed on in England. However this Miss Bellis was well versed in the etiquette of her trade. She was not inclined to discuss her 'friends'.

Quickly I made up my mind.

"But now however I fear that I have pressing business elsewhere..." As I stood up I took out my pocket watch and thumbed open the case. "Indeed I should say that I *had* business elsewhere all of half an hour since." I put a shilling on to the table before her. "Would you be so kind as to give that to your... er... uncle? It is a trifle I had to borrow from him this morning for want of small change. And if you would be so kind as to tell him that I would be delighted to take a dram with him... tomorrow, at noon, in the bowling alley of the *Rose* down on the Pudding Chare. I looked down into her bonny face and bent my neck in a bow. "Ma'am!"

Within another five minutes she was out of Charleton's. I had waited for her in the shadow of a doorway across the street. I watched as she tossed her head and retied her bonnet strings. Then she was off! And damn my eyes but the lass led me a fair gallop. She flitted away up towards the Newgate. Once or twice I thought I'd lost her as she skipped her way between the big wheels of the carts and drays. But then I saw her again and followed her, closer now, keeping mostly to the opposite side of the street, and away from the smoky yellow glow of the naptha lamps that burned outside the shops. Damn me, but soon enough that lass had me panting away like a blown cuddy. At last however she slipped away into a side lane off Lisle Street. I got to the corner just in time to see her form outlined against the opened backdoor of one of the houses. From inside I heard another girl's peal of laughter. The door slammed shut. There was little else I could do then but walk around and take note of the front of the house. The curtains were drawn. But from within I could hear tune being played on a pianoforte. Then I heard the scrape of a chair and a man's voice raised in welcome. Even slurred with the drink as it was there was no doubting that the Frenchman's accent was that of Toulouse.

As I made my way back to my lodging my mind was busy. In all fairness I'd had to own to myself that most of that day's work was like to have been a false trail. In my eagerness to find some small thing I might latch on to, I could perhaps have been persuaded that here was a lead I could scarce afford not to follow up. And without doubt Ettie Bellis was bonny. Though, I warned myself that to me she could be just that and nothing more. For sure this was no time to let myself be led astray.

But no! This was to be no leisurely evening for Bob Shafto. Call it if you will the intuitive sense. Damn me call even it the pricking of my thumbs! All I knew at that moment was that something had made me look up. And there before me on the bricks of a wall a poster was plastered. The paste was still glistening wet. '*Mr Harvey's Renowed Players*' it read,' *will offer their new rendition of William Shakespeare's Macbeth in Loftus's Long Room at the Turk's Head.*' I snapped my fingers. Of course! In weather like this, entertainment of any sort would be scarce. And where better to get sight of Newcastle's folks? Tonight at Loftus's a very fair sample of the town's citizens would likely gather to see the play.

First however I had need to wash and change my shirt. A day tramping about under the greasy smut of Newcastle's chimneys will always leave a man's neck linen as black as any coal-hewer's snot rag. Besides which there were a few questions for which Jotty Stokoe's manservant might well be able to get me the answers.

"Dick!" I yelled down the stairs. Triphook appeared in an instant; though to be sure he held a gnawed-at mutton chop in his hand. "You'll know the town and its people well enough, Dick?"

"Aye..." The man volunteered but did not elaborate.

"Well then, Dick, you take the night off..." I laid silver coins out on the table before me. "... but mind that you're to stay more or less sober. I want you to find out all you can about a chap called Jacob Storey. I pronounced it 'Storrie' so that there would be no mistake.

"Him what hoyed the hot cock-o-leekie ower 'is master?" Dickie Triphook's face cracked and then split altogether. "Why, sir, there's hardly a man nor woman along the Tyneside who doesn't know about that!"

I listened while the old sailor recounted the tale. Though, of course, I didn't doubt for a moment that it would be a legend much embroidered by many tellings. And at once too I could see too just how it was that Jacob Storey had plunged himself into such a sorry case. That was one fellow who would certainly never work in any respectable house in the city - ever again. Many upper servants go through their lives in a state of barely disguised drunkenness. But what Jacob Storey had done was a deed scarce to be imagined, even in a bad nightmare!

It was a damned good yarn, the tale of a spiteful master who gets soused with a gallon of hot soup. Hearing it must have cheered the hearts of many a servant who worked below the stairs. In their eyes - if nowhere else- Jacob Storey might even have become a hero, or, more like, a martyr. But still it told me little.

Then y'd know something of a young lassie called Ettie Bellis?"

Dick had heard the name but knew little else. I would send him out to find out. "But, *Mr...*" My warning caught him in mid-stride. "Ga'an ye canny, ma bonny lad! Tomorrow mornin' I don't want the *Town* to know more o' *me* than I know about it..."

"Oh, there's no fear o' that, Sir... The lassie aah'll be askin' knows well enough that when Mr. Stokoe's man wants the word on some matter she's better off for keepin' her gob well battened down - all secure!"

Loftus's Long Room at the *Turk's Head* was a place distantly familiar to me. During the Christmas of 1791 my father had taken me there to see Katafelto, the famous clown. And as I had expected many of the town's leading gentry had gathered there that night to watch *Macbeth*.

However for these good folk it was to be, from the very start, an evening of petty accidents. For they couldn't have it both ways: the hall's doors had to be either open or shut; and that night because of the biting cold outside most folk wanted them kept shut. That was until the lack of ventilation caused the whale oil in the flare pots along the stage's edge to give off a foul smoke. The Three Witches appeared as mere parti-coloured shapes moving within drifts of stinking black vapours. Incidentally it looked most effective. Soon enough however the ladies were complaining bitterly again. Their eyes were bleared and smarting from the smoke. This caused their gentlemen to demand gallantly that something be done. Within minutes the ladies were protesting shrilly about the icy draught.

I stood by a pillar to watch the merry by-play of what was not performed up on the stage. I heard men's names mentioned and I set them securely to faces. There were coal owners, and at least three bankers. Both the Navy and the Army both were well represented. Though there were more scarlet coats than dark blue with white facings. Nor could I help noticing that most of the soldiers were very young officers: lads who, like as not, had had their commissions bought for them so that they could strut about in the King's coat.

Between acts I moved among them. Yet as I knew well enough all the patchouli and Eau de Cologne in the world will not serve to stifle the smell of massed humanity.

The trick of passing barely noticed in such situations however is simple enough. All you need do is to walk about with a bright almost-smile upon your face. But then if someone does seem about to speak, and just as your gaze is about to meet theirs, you lift your chin, look beyond him or her. You can squeeze past them with a slight bow and a murmured apology. That way too I was able to look closely at damned near every soul in the hall. And of course you will hear snatches of all sorts of gossip. There was much talk that night of introducing the new gas-lighting on to Newcastle's streets. With practice a good agent learns to sieve out such chatter. Most of the talk was a reflection of men's current fears. Among the redcoats it was all talk of 'selling up'; while with the naval officers the discussion was all of 'half-pay' and unpaid prize money long overdue. With the merchants it was the growing slackness of trade.

Had I heard the name only the once I might have missed it; but three times I heard mention of Mr. George Humble. And it seemed that not one of those people had a good word to say for the fellow.

"Tell me, ma'am, I hear much of a fellow called … er, Humble?" It was a bland venture. The old lady was already a little the worse for her gin. Her husband had his stout back to us and was talking in a loud voice to a group of his friends. At mention of the name her chins wobbled like calf's foot jelly. But the hand that gripped at my forearm was like a hawk's claw. At last she had someone who would listen and she was not going to let me get away.

"George Humble, sir, is a scoundrel! That wretched fellow is taking the very bread from the mouths of the poor, and squeezing honest merchants!" In her anger the woman's flushed and her eyes seemed close to popping from her head. Her husband turned, glanced, and turned away again. His look had been one of sympathy. I bent towards her, gazing into her face like a man staring down into a deep well.

"D' ye know, ma'am, a fellow really don't know what to believe at all these days…" I drawled. "There are some people who speak so well of the fellow…" I feigned a sudden doubt, a weakening of opinion. The vapours of the sloe gin she breathed at me caused me to wince but nonetheless I stayed by her, if only to listen to her furious response.

"George Humble, sir, has set himself fair to ruin this city with that damned *Grand Lottery* of his… He squeezes, he sucks the very coppers from the pockets of our servants. And where does it all go? Why, Sir, it goes away out of the town altogether… they say direct to Edinburgh! Then she revealed the true wellspring of her anger:

"My own scullery maid spent an entire month's wages on a twentieth part of a ticket. Then without the grace of so much as one word of notice the besom just disappeared! I have learned since that she won one-hundred and twenty pounds as her share of last Thursday's draw…"

My heart went out to the young servant lass. But at last I had gained something to bite at. I took up the lady's puffy fat hand and drew it to my lips. In passing I noted that the pink pearl in one of her rings was badly pitted.

"Ma'am, you are a very wise lady… and you have convinced me quite entirely…" I gave her my best dancing master's bow and left her simpering behind her fan just as the bell announcing the next act began to clang.

But the next act of *Macbeth* was to be delayed. More exciting drama was in promise at this side of the footlights. There was a scuffle. A woman shrieked as she was jostled and thrust aside. She went down. This was now an entertainment for us all. For that same lady it seemed did not favour the new fashion for drawers. I, we all, saw the smooth ivory of thighs thrashing above pink stockings. Then there was a loud bellow from a man whose dignity had been sorely affronted. All the murderous perfidy of Lady Macbeth was forgotten. A sudden gleeful interest rumbled from the back of the Long Room. The audience pressed forward.

As I might almost have known it was an officer of the militia and he was very much the worse for drink. I have often wondered why it is that it your county militiaman is always the most eager to get him self into 'a meeting'. Perhaps his touchy temper comes from the distance that his duty keeps his from the smell of real powder smoke. I heard the drunken slur in both the challenge and its roared acceptance. I heard the words 'pistols' and 'acting for'.

That seemed to have settled the matter. Half a row of seats stood empty for the performance of the next act. Duels, I supposed, had to be another of the consequences of the Peace. But then and almost next to me I heard a man clear his throat before he answered a lady's giggling question.

I felt my neck hairs lift. I stiffened at the passage of a single galvanic pulse down my spine. And I knew. Without having to turn to look I knew precisely who it was.

Chapter Seven

I saw the man's big brown eyes glisten, they had seemed to swell, almost fit to pop out they were, and that under the heavy pressure of their owner's lechery. George Ninnian Farquahar was gazing down intently into the chubby face of the lady with big breasts. Nor was it difficult to see, as much from the smile on her own face, that this bitch was already as well on in her heat as the dog himself. I watched as a little runnel of sweat trickled its way down through the fine rice powder that had been dusted over her handsome cleavage.

"Oh, indeed, Major…You must think we're all fools here in the North!" She rapped smartly at his shoulder with her closed fan. The last time I had seen Farquahar lap at his fat lips in that fashion had been in the Prefecture of Police on the *Rue de Jerusalem*. That had been the night when the swine had produced his warrant of extradition. I tore my mind away from that memory. Tonight it was obvious that our bold major was intent upon his whoring.

I suppose at that moment my own instinct for safety should have had me fleeing away from the Loftus Rooms. But I didn't. Standing or rather, I should own, hiding behind one of the room's cast iron pillars, I went on watching the evening's jolly pantomime.

For his theatre wear the Major had laid aside the scarlet coatee of a king's officer. This evening Geordie Farquahar was wearing a suit of civilian clothes. Though, to be sure everything was of the best. His new rig had come – no error in the matter - directly from a London tailor. The double lapels on his evening coat were edged with a shiny satin braid. And he was also wearing the new fashion in gentlemen's trowsers, tightly under-strapped and cut tight at the knee. It was perhaps unfortunate that the same skilful cutting had not quite allowed Farquahar to hide the distinct swell of his belly.

But then my attention was snatched away from the major's amours. As the man standing next to Farquahar turned, my eyes at once fell upon this other profile. In spite of my own caution I heard myself draw a sharp breath. There had been no help for it. This was none other than the same mean-minded little snot who had been felled to drop headlong into the snow by our coach along the London road. Indeed my surprise was all the greater that this particular <u>mouton</u> was still alive at all. All along it had been my confident diagnosis that the man I had known as Mr. Nathaniel Briggs had been sent home to die. The harshness of his body-wracking cough, along with his steady sip-sipping at a silver flask of opiate cordial, had told me that the fellow could only be going home to England to die. Obviously I had been deceived. For here the spiteful bastard was, standing straight and dressed like a prince in a dark chocolate coat that was handsomely set off by a full cravat of peacock silk. That coat alone, I could guess, must have cost him all of twenty pounds. Nonetheless there could be no mistaking that face. The dark hair was newly barbered; his moustache and sideburns too had been expertly trimmed. When he had climbed into the carriage at Paris I had taken him for some sort of underpaid confidential clerk. That had been confirmed when I had heard him suggest to Farquahar that the Government's maintenance provision scale for military prisoners could not be held to apply to civilians. On that wretched fellow's nod alone my belly had flapped free for close to forty hours!

I watched and listened for a few minutes; though to be sure I heard little to inform me; and less that was of any value at all. What I did notice however was that when the man

I had known as Briggs spoke the entire company standing there paid heed to him, even George Farquahar and I saw this distinctly. A tall waiter barged through the crowd to take a tray loaded with wine to the little company. I waited until he was returning to the bar and followed him.

Pay first then ask your questions: I allowed my shilling to stop spinning on the waiter's tray before I laid a hand to his arm.

"Yonder gentleman …the lad wi' the dark brown coat…I believe that I have been introduced to…" I got no further, without even turning his head he had earned his shilling. And his answer was certain. "That would be our Mr. Hetherington, sir, Mr. Arthur Hetherington. He owns two separate lead works down by the river and, I do hear tell, three coal pits elsewhere." I was on my way out of Loftus's Long Room before the fellow's fingernails had scraped up my shilling from the tray.

It was only as picked my way between the day's rubbish piled across the cobbles of the Bigg Market that I realised fully just how badly I had been shaken. My sudden fear was that, after all, the man I knew now as Hetherington had seen me; had perhaps even been watching me well before ever I had caught sight of him. Now, and for certain sure, I knew that no disguise of mine was going to

deceive this lad – just as it also dawned in upon me that this bastard had already mocked me. While I had listened to all his feigned groans aboard the coach on the Calais road, this same chap had sat there crouched in the darkness – watching me. And all the whiles I'd been convinced that the wretch himself was heading - post haste - for his grave!

Three times on the way back to my lodging I stopped and listened hard. By then the falling snow was swirling into a near blizzard. Though that at least reassured me. I was glad when I saw how quickly my footsteps were filling up behind me.

I left the smoky glare of the torches that lit the market stalls and turned down into the shadows of St. John's Lane. On any ordinary nightfall that should not have disturbed me at all.

Now all was ghostly silent. All I could hear over the thump of my own heart was the soft hiss of falling snow.

Yet, as such, I was not afraid. Nervous I was, yes; but not fearful. Out there in all that cloaking whiteness it would have been no common duel; instead it would have been a duel fought blind – two men equally matched in the near darkness. Almost without thinking about it I cocked back the hammer of the pistol in my pocket. Yes! If I kept myself alert I might yet shoot Farquahar out there in the street. And then stupidly – and against all common caution - I heard the ferocious snarl of my own voice.

"So come tae me, ma' Bonny Lad… an' aa'l undertake t' blast yr' knackers off!" With a shock I heard myself mouthing those last words, "…yr' knackers off!" That had surely been in the Geordie accents of my boyhood. And why not! For this night wasn't Bob Shafto on his own ground? Yet still I tore my mouth away from my gritted words as though I had had bitten into a rotten apple. This would not do. Of a sudden I was embarrassed, ashamed of my own folly.

Nonetheless I had still to admit to myself that my coming unawares to within a short arm's reach of the man who held a king's warrant for my arrest had gripped cold and hard at my bowels. And after such a severe rattling I was uncommon glad to reach my lodging on the Westgate without mishap. Nor did I take any persuading that this after all was a night for staying within doors; though to be sure these were not hours I could afford to squander in idleness. Too much had happened for that. Indeed hadn't I been the one who had wanted my mission to open up? By God now it had. That much I could feel creeping up the very core of my spine.

Though for an hour I did sit by a blazing coal fire, filling my belly handsomely with a great slice of Dickie Triphook's steak and onion pie. It was late when I began to write my two reports: one for Richard Grainger and another – more detailed - for Talaeus Dekker:

"*...Thus I have reason to believe that a great quantity of gold coin is collected daily by the many agents who sell the tickets for this Grand Lottery...*" My quill scratched dry against the paper halfway through the final sentence. I paused to take a mouthful from a pot of ale. I gulped it down and then I smiled into the firelight. Once again the wisdom in the teachings of Papa Dimnet seemed suddenly to sound out inside my head:

"*These so-called Topics of Invention offer us a narrowing wicket through which we may shepherd and guide the headlong tumble of our ideas.*"

Indeed they did. For by using this classic method of composition I was able to expand my meagre handful of half facts into a neat web of plausible seeming events. I also appended a request for '£2. to pay small bribes to certain menservants who play cards at the *Three Kings.*'

By its very nature a fellow is usually well able to invent a great deal of what goes into an intelligence report – though one should always remember to colour one's text with the faintest tincture of real and verifiable detail. A request for funds will often add such veracity. It had always been worth a try before. Why, even my own old *maitre* had once or twice approved the payment of a *douceur* of a few francs.

It was only when my report had been signed and sealed that I realised that - all unthinkingly - I had penned it out in French. No matter, it would be seen as a wise precaution... both Dekker and Grainger would be able to read it with ease.

Yet, and tired though I had gone to bed, next morning I did not sleep late. Though to be sure I found it uncommon hard to quit the warmth of my eiderdown. At first light I had looked out. This was surely no day for walking Newcastle's streets. That morning the bank of Westgate Hill might have been the road back from Moscow. Below me down in the street the snow had been blown to drift up under the windows' sills. Nobody, save those poor devils who had their crusts to seek, was like to be much about that day! But I sat up at last when Dick brought me a handsome breakfast of pork sausages and fried duck eggs. And I could see at once that the old sailor was uncommon pleased with himself. Though he waited until I had eaten before he began to tell me what he had been able to find out about Miss Henrietta Bellis.

"She's a rare one that..." Dick licked his lips. I saw at once that the man stood in sore need of a livening-up tot. I nodded towards the brandy bottle. He half filled a tumbler and slew it in two gulps. "Until that lass was all o' fourteen she was a virgin pure... and that 's a rare thing hereabouts for a poor man's bairn, one orphaned at ten."

I waited until Dick had drained his glass. He had a story to tell and would likely make the most of it. And of course I knew well enough what he was talking about. Plain want of something to fill her belly with will force even a decently raised child to submit to the world's depravities.

"When she was just turned twelve she was taken into service by a decent woman, a Mrs. Mary Inglis in Albion Street. And for nigh on three years things went well. Then, the story I'm told is, the poor lass was laid hands on and raped one night by a young lieutenant o' Marines, name o' Crozier. He was home on wound leave and stayin' at the Inglis house..."

Dick shrugged. His tale was being held on a firm bridle. "Now hereabouts the forcin' o' a young servant lass an' puttin' her into the pudd'n club has never been a great matter... specially when the poor slut 's got no family to take her part. So this bold Marine offs his'self back to the wars leavin' our young Ettie a' backin' and fillin' very nicely." I nodded to the brandy bottle again.

"Well, Ettie Bellis had the bairn, an' a fine laddie it is by all accounts. But by then news comes that the father 'd been cut in half by a chain-shot from a French frigate off Ushant. That o' course left the Crozier family without their son and heir. So then, as you might expect, those pious buggers tried to get their graspin' hands on wor young Ettie's bairn. Though of course it was only *him* they wanted, not her! And the tricks they tried get him from her would take a month t' tell." Dick raised his eyebrows and paused for a breath while he made sure that I was following his tale. I nodded him on.

"But the young lass wasn't havin' any o' that, thank ye. She ups an' takes herself off somewhere out of the way and pays to have the bairn raised by decent folk. Then within a month of havin' the bairn she was back in Newcastle. Though mind this now, she wasn't on the streets by any manner o' means! For her Uncle Jacob was quietly doin' his bit pimpin' among certain elderly gentlemen o' the town. And soon enough the lass had enough regulars not to need him. In the end it was Storey's own drunkeness and the disgrace that came from flingin' the tureen o' hot cock-a-leekie ower his master that finally got him dismissed-the-ship wi' young Ettie."

"The Frenchman, Dick? What were you able to learn of him?" The life story of Miss Henrietta Bellis had been interesting enough; but was hardly likely to tell me anything about smuggled guineas.

"All I could learn was that the servants have been told that they are to address him as D'Oeuys... Mr. Charles D'Oeuys. He's been there for a fortnight"

"D'Oeuys! Jesus!" My oath stopped Dick Triphook dead. The old fellow goggled at me; his mouth clapped shut. For me this was troubling news. The name had come echoing up from the depths of my memory.

Of course the Frenchman's real name wasn't D'Oeuys. If this fellow was the same turd truffler I had known in Italy then his family name was Mc.Hinge. He was the grandson of a Scot who had fled to the Continent after the '45. D'Oeuys and I had worked together at Verona. Our mission together, however, had not been a notable success. Coincidence too was damned unlikely. It was almost certain that Mc Hinge's business in Newcastle had to have something to do with the shipping out of guineas. Both Dekker and Grainger would have to know about this at once. Though of course I had already considered the possibility that the Frenchman and I might already be comrades – we might both be working for Talaeus Dekker.

Besides, and if nothing else, it all meant that my report would have to be re-drafted. This would swell it by a page or two. I would also take the opportunity to increase my request for expenses to four pounds.

Before I charged my quill again I paused and looked into the fire. Of a sudden the chessboard I was playing on had become very crowded.

I began to write, starting with an account of my own first meeting with monsieur *D'Oeuys* in Italy. It is usually best to keep nothing at all significant back when you are writing of an old accomplice. I expanded the record. Stirring my pot to begin with by revealing that at eighteen Charles D'Oeuys had been a *forcat*, a convict in the state's galleys at Marseilles… and how Joseph Fouche himself had ordered his release.

With my report written and a careful copy for my own record I knew that I had not quite wasted the morning. As the garrison's signal gun boomed out to mark noon I found myself sighing. Then I remembered that I had promised that I would meet Jacob Storey at the *Rose* down on the Pudding Chare.

It was an effort but I managed to get myself there. And to my surprise I did find the rogue sitting apart at a bench by the *Rose*'s bowling alley. He'd been waiting for a long time – the gill of small beer at his elbow was as flat as a witch's tit. I stood over him for a moment before he looked up. Only then did I see the mess the old fellow's face was in.

Somebody had given Jacob what most Newcastle folks would have called 'a canny howkin'. The flesh around both eye sockets was split, cut deep; one eye was swollen, almost closed altogether. He'd been stitched but it was surely no surgeon's work. I examined his hurts closely. The damage had not come from some tavern brawler's fists and boots. Then I saw a peculiar mark, the shape of a bruise, and recognised it. Someone had been laying hard into the old rogue with the antler horn handle of a riding crop.

I called for a half bottle of Barbados rum, a kettle of boiling water, brown sugar, and a lemon. Considered purely as a drink I know that rum may do little or naught to heal a wound. But for certain the supping of it hot will surely make a man feel that it does. With his hands clamped around the hot tankard Jacob Storey gulped at his toddy as though it was the Elixir of Life itself; and he did that for all that both his lips were swollen fat and deep split. At that moment too I saw that now Storey really did look the old man he was. His skinny shoulders began to judder and shake.

"Tell me everything, Jacob. Leave nothing out." I put the edge of surgeon's bonesaw on to my voice. Perhaps Storey had good right to feel sorry for himself; but, for now, any kind soft words from me would only give him someone to lean on. That was not what I wanted. For a long time he made no answer. I filled his pewter tankard from my jug of hot rum and pushed it towards him. He drank.

"Aa'h divin't knaa... What aa' saw was that French bastard a' layin' in tae wor Ettie wi that heavy ridin' stick 'e carries ... that was in the lane. The poor lass was scratchin' at him like a wildcat... That bloody miserable Crapaud was tryin' tae get his damned guinea piece back off her." Storey's hands waved in the air before him. " Aah got this f' putting me bloody neb in an' trying to save the lass..." He reached again for the hot rum. "She's down at my lodgin's now... Aaah tell y' Sir...that bloody French whoremonger has nigh on killed the poor bairn!"

Chapter Eight

"That mangy bastard!" My anger rang out across the *Rose*'s bowling alley. Though to my small surprise the outburst caused little enough stir among the men watching the bowls game. Likely enough they'd seen it all before. Though at once, too, I began to ask myself why I should be so angered. Why? Surely I myself had seen all this before. Whores are misused often enough. It is the common hazard of their trade. When a lass sells her body she must not complain overly much about what is done to it! Moreover, in me, this had to be so much simple folly. I tried to tell myself that there was still the real possibility that this business would have nothing whatever to do with what I was seeking. Though I suppose that at that moment I was telling myself too that I might yet learn something about Charles D'Oeuys. I recalled well how he had behaved – in Marseilles – and yet when the drink had its claws into him - this same rat could become something close to a madman. Such a red-eyed rage about the simple matter of a coin he had given by mistake to a young whore might yet be no more than his drink-crazed fancy. Then I felt that old twitch. No! This was not a bone I could leave without - at the least - taking a little trial gnaw at.

Though I certainly could not afford to be seen helping Jacob Storey to get back to his lodgings. On those snow covered streets we two together would have stood out like a couple o' toads in a chinaware poe. I sent the old fellow hobbling ahead of me while I followed him at a distance. Our path was downhill all the way. Which was as well , for from the way Storey held himself I judged that at least two of his ribs were cracked. At his age, I reckoned, the old man stood a fair risk of pneumonia.

The very poorest folk in Newcastle are crowded mostly into the two wards of Pandon and the Sandgate. It is where the houses are old and lean close together like drunken men. We came to a ramshackle old place near to the ruin of the Wall Knoll Tower. Only then did I catch up with Jacob. He had stopped and stood panting at the foot of a crazy stone-built stairway. I helped him up to the first landing. There a little lad was waiting, cheeks mottled blue with the cold and with two snot streams like church candles dangling from a freckled nose. He stood gazing at us with wide eyes. Then he was gone. A few seconds later a stout old biddy wearing a man's tricorn hat and a butcher's apron had come down to scoop up the old man. She bore him upward like a bairn in arms.

"You scabby-arsed little bastard…" As they went she railed on at him. "Where the Hell ha' you been? From the stink on you, ye little shitbag, ye've had money through your hands an' already drunk it aa'l!" Her abuse welted at him. But I noticed that the woman set him down by the fire tenderly enough.

Perhaps the very smell of the place should have forewarned me. But it was only when I saw what was hanging in translucent drapes from clothes lines stung across the room that I realised. Damn my own fine innocence! At first sight I had thought they were sausage skins! Then I saw the three little lasses huddled close to the window. They needed the light to stitch the things. It was only then that I realised that I was in the little workshop of a cundum maker. Without a word more the woman went back to squeezing the filth out of lambs' guts into a wooden bucket. When she had a pile of guts voided and turned outside in she soused them around briskly in a cauldron of hot soapy water. Damn my eyes but every soul there was working with such intense industry. It was marvellous to watch the deft way the children cut off the lengths of intestine, closed the tube at one end and sewed in a silken drawstring. And it was all so very neatly done! Hundreds of the devices were being given their last careful drying on a frame strung above the fireplace. From the pile on the table I picked up a pasteboard box. *Britannia Cundums*, the stamped label read over the garish red and blue of the union flag, then, *Geo. Bell (Widow of) &. Son, Love Lane, Newcastle-upon-Tyne.*

"Four pence the skin… Only eighteen pence for the box. An' that's half the price you'll pay up at Reid's by the Newgate."

Somewhat to my own surprise I bought a box. A fellow never knows when he may be in need of such things. And for sure, after the event, what man would not willingly pay twice the price to save his flesh from the searing scald o' the clap?

Ettie 's in there…" Mrs. Bell pointed to a little door. "But that poor bairn's been badly used, she has…" Her eyes narrowed until they were like chips of coal in the steamed suet of her face. "So don't you go…"

"Madame, I am a physician!" My voice boomed in the little workshop. Again the same old ploy had been a mistake. The woman looked me full in the face. The intensity of her contempt for me was something to see. "Oh, aye, m' Love…" She sneered at me. "An' aa'm the Empress Josephine's chief lady o' the royal arse wipe!"

Nonetheless, by any man's reckoning Ettie Bellis had obviously been badly beaten. Of course the poor lass had done her best to defend herself. Like all whores she had tried hard to protect her face. It was her fortune. And as with all women she would know well enough the evils that can come of any sharp blow to the breast. It was only when I peeled down her blood drenched dress that I saw the extent of her hurts.

The lass had been punched in the face. Most of the blood that now caked her dress had gushed from her nose. She had also been slashed at with the same riding crop that had marked Storey so badly. But then I saw from the long scrapes to the flesh of her flanks that she had dragged over the ground for some distance. I replaced the coarse blanket and looked up at Mrs. Bell. She had chaperoned my examination, watching me like a carrion crow eyeing a dead drummer boy.

"It's bad…" She was telling me, not asking. Then she said: "The poor lass crawled here through last night's snow… A gentleman was he…Or is that just another name for a Godless, heathen bastard!"

"It can be m' Dear… it surely can be." I nodded but said nothing more.

Since 1803 I had practised little enough of my medicine. Indeed so little that I could remember most of the occasions. Once, along the road to Orly, I had delivered a bairn to a blacksmith's wife. The mother had called her Ernestine for me, or at least for the name I worked under then. Beyond that I had purged a few drunkards, stitched up a few sword slashes, and taken pistol balls out of men. Twice I had taken them out of my own meat.

"Sit with her…" I gave Mrs. Bell a look that would ensure that she would. "I must go to an apothecary. At least I can spare the lass some of the pain… and she'll be the better for having her wounds cleaned.

From my time as a Newcastle medical student I remembered the apothecary's shop known up in the town as Gilby's. Who would not? Though the old fellow who had owned it was like to be long dead. But what I did remember was that in spite of its name the business sold honest drugs and did a good trade in ready-made remedies and nostrums. The shop itself was at the far end of a short entry lane off the Denton Chare. And I found it more or less by the stink of tallow smoke from an iron crusie lamp burning outside the door. A drunken sailor staggered out clutching a brown bottle to his chest. I gave myself good odds that he would not get a hundred yards before he smashed it. As I pushed my way into the shop the sprung bell above the door clanged like a devil among fire irons.

Of all the trades and mysteries I have always held that your common apothecary is best equipped to dazzle and deceive his customers. Folk enter his shop and step straightway into a place of magic. Gilby's had ten foot of stuffed Nile crocodile suspended high over the counter. That the monster had hung on its iron hooks since Queen Anne's reign mattered not at all. Up on the highest shelves there stood also the great wonder of the leech flasks. They of course were filled with mere coloured waters. Leeches do not thrive in light and are best kept in buckets out in the back shop. But the greatest pride of Gilby's shop had to be the great cabinet of one hundred polished mahogany drug drawers. Each and every ivory knobbed drawer was labelled in gold leaf with Roman lettering. Just conceivably too some of the ciphers in doctor's Latin might once have meant something. But what I did see from my first glance was that the new apothecary himself was an opium eater.

At once I had noted the red tinge to the veins in his eyeballs. Of course it might have been an inflammation of his conjunctiva. But before I had taken three steps into the shop I had smelled the stuff on him. I suppose that a decent, unworldly sort of chap might have dealt with such a fellow for a dozen years and seen nothing to make him suspect it. Many addicts are extremely discrete. But I had been trained at great expense to look at a world that so often is all double crooked. To me at that moment, the man standing with his fingers splayed out on the counter before him might as well have been wearing a dunce's cap and a painted board.

However his shirt linen was immaculate; his silk cravat was tied to perfection. And the plum coloured coat with crystal buttons was new. Of course very many men take precious care with their dress. That does not make them all 'drinkers of darkness'! But with this creature it certainly did. The reek of the raw drug lay around him like a haze.

And, close-to, what an ugly little sod he was! He was lantern jawed, thin lipped, Saturnine even. The flesh of a wrist that showed below one of his lace shirt cuffs was uncommonly hairy. His fingernails were yellow and had wanted a trimming a month before. Stripped of his finery this chap would easily have passed for a Barabary ape!

Yet still all the signs of the poppy addict were there. He had looked at me too long before he spoke. The man was still struggling to haul himself out of his last draught. I smiled and gave him time. For this was exactly what I had been schooled to do by that sinister old bastard, Monsieur Monge in the chill salons of the *Hotel D'Arcol* at Rheims. Yet with this face before me it was an effort for me not to laugh out loud. I heard the stumble and recovery to his words of greeting. But then his actual words struck at me like a sword slash.

"And how may I serve you, Doctor Shafto?"

When you're recognised there are very few things you can do. I grinned. Even as the corners of my mouth curled upwards I knew that my expression was as greasy as shoulder o' mutton. But I showed my teeth and thrust forward the sweaty hand of deception. In such a situation it's about the only action that will serve. Then at the last instant my own inner *daemon* bestowed its gift. I knew what was needed. And it was like to be the only safe way to deal with this rat's-arse. I would just have try to overwhelm this fellow with my own sheer brass faced *bonhomie*

He took my hand and shook it. And as he did that I heard the slight whine in the back of his throat. Then the bastard breathed over me. Whatever it was he had taken it had never come from the East India Company's factory.

Nonetheless, this particular piece of bad luck was plainly mine to deal with. Of all the men in Newcastle whom I could most have done without meeting I had blundered into the one fellow who actually remembered young Dr. Shafto from the old days.

"Why, it is…" The name came. "… Everard, isn't it?" His face lit. And just in time too I was able to dredge up the Christian name. He'd been a mere pill pounding 'prentice lad the last time I had spoken to him. He smiled and I saw him again as he had been when he was younger. Hollow cheeked he'd been even then. More than once I had heard other doctors remark loudly that the lad had the sort of face that would yet get him hanged. Even then his teeth had been blackened. There's more than one man who'd become addicted to opium pills taken first to soothe the pain of rotten teeth. Twelve years before this same Wilkieman had leaped about the shop, as we say, like a linty at old man Gilby's bidding; and yet as even then, I recalled, he'd been something of an eavesdropping little sly boots!

"Or *Mr...* Wilkieman, as perhaps I should now address you..." I corrected myself hastily. Damn me, but the fellow was still a calculating little get! Though fair dealings! I had to allow that even a poor wretch like this would have a need to announce to all he met that he had – young – come to own this thriving apothecary's business.

"This is uncanny!" There was a drama in the way he smote at his brow. "D' you know, Sir, just today your name came up in conversation With Doctor Mudie it was. He's still physician to the Keelman's Hospital and the Workhouse... he mentioned to me that a gentleman had been enquiring after you."

"And did Mudie...er *Doctor* Mudie say who this gentleman was?"

Deliberately I put an angry edge on the question; and as I spoke I tightened my mouth and lowered my head like a bulldog beginning a growl. Now I would have to frighten this fellow; but first of all I had to know exactly *who* it was had been asking after me.

"Was it a man wearing a King's coat, a damned Irish bone-setter called Surgeon-Major Peabody?" To snatch up that name from memory I'd had to malign the memory of a damned good fellow. It was a fiction created upon the instant and delivered stone cold. Though to emphasise my feigned anger I punched my fist into my palm. "Damn me..."Now I simulated an angry man raving at himself. "It's always ready money as will do it... and *that* every cursed time!" Then I looked directly into Everard Wilkiman's eyes. At close glance the whites of the iris were indeed close veined with a spider's web of crimson. But still there was no mistaking that there was still a deal of cunning there. I lowered my voice. It was then that I played a physician's own ace of spades.

"I would suppose, Mr. Wilkieman, that Dr. Severus Mudie *did* indicate to you that not one but *two* of quite the city's finest medical practises are shortly to come on to the market?"

Nothing ever quite throws a stick among the geese as talk of a change in the fine balance that holds in the *status quo* among a town's medical men. For certain this tale burst upon the apothecary like a bombshell from a mortar. And damn me but I found myself at once warming to my own creation! This false news of mine had for the moment chased away even the fellow's curiosity about me. For this surely touched upon his own business.

Any changes among the town's doctors would have implications for the apothecary's trade. Many long standing contracts for the supply of drugs, and many cosy understandings about precisely *what* pills of coloured chalk and peppermint were actually supplied might soon have to be negotiated anew. Already I could see the flux of greed and unease beginning to meld together in Everard Wilkiman's narrow face.

"Though of course I may expect your absolute silence in this matter..."

Suddenly I was a worried man, someone remembering himself in the midst of an indiscretion. As a trick this had always seemed to me to add veracity to a tale. And then as though to seem in a hurry to change the subject I began to list what I needed from his stock. The apothecary hurried to get what I wanted; but it was plain to me that my fairytale was still disturbing Wilkieman - greatly.

"I shall also require a few ounces of *aqua fortis* ... and a box of twenty grain Calcutta opium pills" It was little a prod from me. And that particular request brought another knowing look from the apothecary. Then suddenly he gave what might have been taken for a little skip.

"Aah!" His cry mewed down the length of his counter. "The 'affair' at Loftus's last night! I heard that one of the officer's was sorely wounded!"

Already I had forgotten about the business at the theatre. So the quarrel had after all led to two drunken men standing to aim loaded pistols at one another. It came as a distinct surprise to me. It also presented an opportunity for me to weave another story. But I decided at once that this business was too damned risky. When the true story came out it was like enough to prove me a liar.

"No... last night I was physician in attendance when two other gentlemen - entirely - 'met' in a wood up away towards Fenham." I smiled grimly. "*These* two spirited fellows must needs have gone at one another with their hundred guinea sabres. And in this case, since they are both experienced swordsmen, both gentlemen were able to open wide one another's aristocratic faces very handsomely before honour was finally and quite *fully*... satisfied!"

Everard Wilkiman clapped a hand up to his cheek. Then I watched as his shock turned to an unholy glee at prospect at another's discomfort. So there'll surely be a full court-martial this time. For I've heard Colonel Westwood has sworn that the next time any officer under his command dares lift his blade to another."

I found myself tempted to smile. Not even the Emperor himself had beenhad been able to stop his officers from duelling!

Quickly however I held up a hand. Again my tale was beginning to take on a life of its own. "These officers were not at the Barracks, Mr.Wilkiman...This was a *very* private meeting." I tapped at my nose with my forefinger. "Yet I will go so far as to confide to you now that I am presently in the North as the guest of an old and noble family in the County..."

Now I had made so bold as to take the lords' names in vain. Almost, I was persuaded that I could use the tale to apply a very effective gag on the mouth of Mr. Everard Wilkiman.

Here in the North the old nod was still as good as the ancient wink. There was no need for me to say more. I knew. Our sharp man-o'-business might trade gossip about the sale of medical practises until his tongue turned black; he could even retail about the town all he heard about duels between officers of the militia. But if he had learned nothing else in his trade, young Wilkiman would surely know better than to tittle-tattle abroad anything he might hear of the goings-on among a certain few still powerful families. He would have heard the tales. The soft whisper would come down from above: 'Who trades with my enemy cannot remain my friend! Overnight, and to no man's astonishment, Gilby's, the busy apothecary's shop, would be lucky to sell a tub of blue unction to salve a sailor with crab lice. This was no more than the simple power o' money.

The apothecary was busy bundling my purchases into a paper sack when the banging at the yard door began. Of course he tried to ignore it and continue to serve me. But whoever it was wanted, as we say, ready money.

"Pray see to it, Mr. Wilkiman..." I fancied that I had now successfully tagged my name to matters of themselves important enough make the rogue think twice before he spoke aloud of them.

Behind the curtain which hid from view the back shop, I heard a man grunt with heavy exertion. "By gobs, these buggers is heavy!" At first I thought it was just the carter angling for his ale money. Then I heard Wilkiman draw a sharp breath. He snarled with alarm.

"And they are also very, very costly! What is in one of those jars would cost two year's of your wages to buy."

"Aye, Master, but then most things do that - on the little pittance aa'h earn!"

"These demijohns had to be ordered up special from London, Joe Sallis. So just you make yourself damned sure you handle them as you would a babbie!" There was the chink of small coin.

"Do I smell *Oil of Lebanon* ... cedarwood, Mr Wilkiman?" I had. And truly my comment had been no more than a mere pass-time observation. Its effect however was to bring him up like a reined back horse. For just an instant Everard Wilkiman was taken aback. Then he seemed to recover himself and gave a little shrug.

"This is a special order, Dr. Shafto." He had decided. Quite suddenly the apothecary was almost eager to share his secret with me. His voice became hoarse as he confided:

"The family of a foreign gentleman wishes to have his mortal remains borne back to his mother soil. The cadaver is to be embalmed. Doctor Mudie has undertaken the task. Because of that he has honoured me with an order for two firkins of Marjolin's *Patent Preservative*. Mind you though, I've had to have it brought up from London. So to be sure it is a transaction from which I shall make very little... very little indeed."

"Didn't they bring Nelson home in a barrel of full-proof rum? That should be good enough for any man." I mused aloud. Then again, at a tangent: "I believe a large syringe is used." I had had enough of the fellow's company. Miss Ettie Bellis needed my attention. But now Wilkiman's mouth was working slowly. My talk of syringes had clearly disturbed him. Out of sheer wickedness I made a slow plunger pushing motion with my hands. "That is of course after a full evisceration... the brain too must be removed."

I rambled on: "Doctor Mudie will likely need to have his fluid gently heated beforehand. I contributed another idea. "I would also advise the use of artists' carmine... two ounces will be sufficient! Though mind you use only the best, the real Mexican cochineal. You'll find it adds an attractive pink tinge to the corpse. It has been my experience that a corpse's family will usually admire that greatly! That's the thing , Mr Wilkieman, that 's what's needed. And there's the chance of an extra fee for you!" Wilkiman began hurriedly to put my purchases into the sack.

"Will you wish to reopen an account with me, Dr. Shafto…" His expression became suddenly sharp. "Or shall I write you out a receipt so that you can claim back your disbursements from…?"

There was no need for him to say more. At least this new proprietor of Gilby's shop had learned one of the main tricks of his particular trade. He was leaving open the way for us both to indulge in a piece of time-hallowed roguery.

"Thankee…" I smiled full at him. I had spent eighteen shillings on apothecary's stuff. But the bill he wrote was itemised for close to five pounds. *'Balsam of Ephesus…my arse!'*

I spread two sovereigns on the counter. Without a word he scooped them up. Expensive it was - but also a sound investment. Already in Wilkiman's mind I had limned in the outline of a noble family whom I served as physician.

"Bye the by…" I turned at the door with the bell above me poised to clang. "The gentleman who was asking for me at Doctor Mudie's, d'ye happen to recall the name?"

Wilkiman did: "It was, if I recollect it aright, a Mr. Cable, Doctor Shafto… Though a damned shabby sort of a gentleman he was, by all appearances!"

Chapter Nine

I turned my head and forced a wink. "Indeed you rightly say so! I know the same gentleman well… and I dare say that I shall find him, more easily than he is like to find me…" I feigned my laughter. " I think a deal more easily!"

So Mr. Lieutenant Cable was in Newcastle; and probably the fellow had been in the city for some days. Farquahar was here too; so why not Cable? Well, I supposed that where the master walked, his dog could not be far behind. I knew it, I would bear it in mind, but it was not something to get my bowels in an uproar about.

As I made my way back down the bank towards the Pandon ward, and just in time, I remembered my manners so far as to realise that I could hardly go back to Mrs. Bell's home without taking back for her a present of some kind. I went into a drysalter's shop and bought a gallon demijohn of 'broon sirrup'. That was what local folk called West- India molasses. It would put a taste to her bairns' porridge for many a morning. Moreover it's something I've often seen little ones thrive upon. But for the woman, for herself, I had no doubt about what was needed to sweeten her temper. In England, China tea, 'scandal broth' is the drug that women delight in - that and snuff. At Cross's Emporium I went by price alone and bought Mrs.Bell a pound of the coarsest chopped leaf at two shillings. Many a woman on Tyneside might take her pinch of snuff, but not even among the poorest classes would she ever be slut enough show so much as a stray grain of it on her person. Nonetheless

I'd smelled rather than seen the snuff on Mrs. Bell. I called in at Elstob's, took the shopman's advice, and bought her two ounces of 'Sampson's Wig'.

"She's asleep now, though not before she sobbed her little heart out… " Mrs. Bell had heard my feet on stairs. She stood in the doorway blocking the lamplight. For the beat of a heart she barred my way. Then with a swish of her skirts she stood aside.

By day that room was a workshop where little bairns sewed sheeps' guts up into cundums for the more prudent of the town's venial sinners! Now though the day's work was done. There was no sign at all of the way the little family earned its bread. The coal fire blazed and the big black kettle was set singing on its hook. I put the demijohn of treacle down on the table. Mrs Bell sniffed and gave a nod.

"I've washed the poor lass's hurts and got her into clean linen… Given time she'll mend. But what 's worryin' the lass now is that she'll not be able to… to go to her work."

That was odd. Up to that moment I had almost forgotten that Hennrietta Bellis was a whore. It had been something I had recognised the moment I had clapped my eyes on her. Yet that thought had scarcely entered my mind at all. Of course the abuse she had suffered would prevent her from…" My thoughts echoed Mrs.Bell's careful words. '… going to her 'work'. Somewhere the same lass had a child to support. Also there would be a few fine gentlemen ' up the bank' who would have to forego their turns to grunt and sweat over Henrietta Bellis's young body. Though at the same time she might herself well worry that those poor lonely bastards might seek their pleasures elsewhere!

"Miss Ettie has information, Mrs. Bell… information for which I am willing to pay." I allowed my words to fall slowly.

"Then pay me… The voice was weak. "because it's my fancy that I came by this because of you!" I turned around.

Young Ettie Bellis stood in the lamplight, ghost pale and swaying on her feet. I caught her, gathering her up just as her legs buckled under her. But then as I turned to carry her to her cot I heard the ring of a coin dropping to the scrubbed floorboards. A bright flake of golden light caught my eye. It had fallen from her hand.

Mrs. Bell stooped to pick it up. She looked at it and frowned a little. She held it out for me to see. It was a new minted English guinea. His Majesty, George III was wearing his victor's laurels – and why ever not? But then I saw something else; it was a mark. At another time and at another place I had seen the like of it before.

The guinea bore an over strike. On the king's cheekbone the imprint of a steel punch showed clearly. At first sight the tiny indentation looked like the *Fleur de Lys.* . And to me at that moment especially that was a sight that looked damned odd. Indeed it was hard not to laugh. In France marks like that had been branded into the living flesh of convicted felons. It was an odd mark to bear for even a mad king. Slowly I turned the gold piece in the flickering gleam of the rushlight. Then I saw more clearly. The sign stamped into the metal was not the Lily of France. Instead it was the tiny emblem of the honeybee, a mark from the coat-of- arms of the Bonaparte family.

Of course to me all of this was old-fashioned nonsense! This sort of thing was more the property of the Italian secret societies. It is their agents who delight to be entrusted with all manner of esoteric signs, with the halves of a coin cut zig-a-zag so those pieces needed to be matched. I found myself smiling. I was reminded of Antwerp in the year '09. We had raided *La Rossignal* a common wine shop. To gain access I remember I had had to have a tailor alter the lapels of my best coat so that they formed the pattern of an arrowhead. That was the night Fouche's own men had been ordered to throw a net over the nightingales. Mostly we caught merchants who were dealing illegally in German copper. Within minutes we had every man stripped to the buff for a search. We lifted every rogue who had a stamped coin very like this one on the fob of his timepiece. The stamped coin was to be a signal of recognition serving to identify whoever presented it. Perhaps though this explained why D'Oeuys had reacted so viciously. When the mood was on him I knew that the same rogue could be lavish with his gifts. And while in his cups he had given Ettie Bellis a present of money. Probably it had been only later that he had discovered his loss. I could guess that the Frenchman had then – and rather suddenly - become a very badly frightened man.

But now I would have to wait until Ettie Bellis was able to speak to me again. Meanwhile however I supposed that I would get a partial account of events from her Uncle Jacob. I asked Mrs. Bell where he was. Her look soured.

"Oh, aye, you're his good friend, right enough; an' you're the feckless bugger who gave him money for drink!" It was an accusation. "You should know well enough what gin will do to him!" She pointed to a covered plate by the fire. "That's his dinner on the hob there. But if that feckless little beggar isn't here in half an hour, I'll be eatin' it m'self. Vittles is too scarce to waste in this house. That's best cow-heel, that is, stewed in milk – bought special - for a poor bugger wi'a smashed up face..."

I would leave the sack of odds and ends that I had bought at the apothecary's shop. Though in my judgement now only time could mend Ettie Bellis, time and rest. Her skin had been badly scraped. Soon too her pretty face would show all the rainbow colours of a hard knuckling. Perhaps there would be a concussion. The vicious blows from D'Oeuy's riding crop had driven the lass's senses from her. He surely had marred her beauty; though that perhaps would last for only for a few weeks.

Now however I reckoned that I, or say rather *The British Linen Bank* owed Miss Henrietta Bellis a debt. It had been she who had brought to me the stamped guinea. We had profited simply because no honest whore will ever stand to be robbed of her due. It is a fact I have often noticed! But almost certainly her squabble with D'Oeuys had provided me with proof positive that already there was at least one Imperial agent at work in Newcastle. And that was news I would have to get to Talaeus Dekker - that as quickly as I could.

However I would freely own that on my personal account I would have felt easier to see D'Oeuys arrested and safely in the town's lock-up. Though, I fancied that some ingenuity would have to be shown in framing any charges. For I knew that no magistrate would issue a warrant against a gentleman for the *mere* castigation of a thieving young whore!

"Will five-to-one in gold serve?" I spoke suddenly as I took out the money and held it out to Mrs. Bell. It was an offer I had to make. But I saw at once that there was no way that the stout woman who owned this little back-lane cundum manufactory was going to allow me to walk away unchallenged with Ettie Bellis's coin. She was too clever by half for that!

"Five to one, Sir, will *not* serve!" And there was no doubt that Mrs. Bell meant what she said.

"For from what young Ettie has told me the Godless bastard who did that to the lass won't be satisfied until he gets his guinea back." She thrust a thumb back over her shoulder." Aaah've been expectin' *that* same tub o' French shite to come bangin' on that door. And you'd have to admit that any howkin' of the like that lass has had won't be paid for by any five bright jimmy o' goblins!" I nodded. I understood.

"You'll give it up to the Frenchman when he comes a' knockin'?

Mrs. Bell reached down to the side of her chair. She pulled out a long knife – it was of the kind that we in the North call a gully. "My doorstep has the best bit of sharpenin' stone in this lane… An' aah'll slice the bastard's twiddle-diddles clean off his lousy body if he dares to step over my threshold wi' out at least ten pound in gold ready in his hand to offer."

To Mrs. Bell it was simply reasonable. Life did not offer a choice of options to poor women like Eadie. Ten pounds was what it would take to feed and shelter Ettie Bellis until she was well enough to resume her trade. That was the best that could be either expected or hoped for. Honour did not signify.

For myself now the best I could do would be to report at once to my own employers. But getting a message to Richard Grainger might take time.

"Can I beg a can of tea off you, Mrs Bell?" It was a request that no decent woman on Tyneside would have refused. While she let down the kettle on its hook I used the opportunity to spill out the bundles I had brought on to the table.

At once the crimson and gold painted canister took Eadie Bell's fancy. There was no mistaking it. And the little parcel of snuff disappeared into her apron pocket with a single sweep of a big hand. Odd indeed! That it can take no more than a pinch or two of powdered tobacco to dispel the world's misery! But I did not get my tea. What warned Mrs. Bell I never knew for I heard no sound. Nonetheless she stood up suddenly, listening.

"They're coming here!" Still I heard nothing. But that was all she said before grabbing my arm and shoving me bodily in through a curtain. Our Eadie was a big strong lass!

The rapping on the door was the knob of a gentleman's cane. I stood there a pace back from the curtain in a darkness that was warmed by the soft breaths of the sleeping children behind me. Mrs. Bell' chair creaked as she rose to her feet. She went to the door - but I heard her make no move to open it.

"Who is it, then?" There was a pause. "Folks are all a'bed here…"

"Eadie Bell? It's Mattie Crowley…" I heard the woman's breath sob softly. "Aaah've come to have a bit crack with y', m' Pet… it's about a matter o' weight." It was a harsh voice; yet now it whined like a door that wanted oil. "So open up, m' Hinny."

And Mrs. Bell knew the voice too. Crowley was obviously a power along Newcastle's Quayside. Though that she knew it was clearly no comfort to her. She turned and looked towards the curtain. She was asking my leave. I nodded, stepped back a pace and pulled the curtains closed behind me.

From where I stood in the darkness I could see that the big man had been hurriedly summoned from a ball or *soiree* of some sort. He was wearing the new English fashion in gentlemen's evening clothes: a black tailcoat with wide lapels and trowsers with straps that went under instep of his polished boots. I caught a glimpse of an ivory skull with big lobed ears. The man suffered from *alopaecia totalis*. As bald as a goose egg he was. The eyes too were remarkable. So heavy lidded were they that Crowly might almost have been on the verge of sleep. Though, knew at once that I would have been a fool to act on that assumption. The man's profile was that of a Caesar. Moreover this was a chap rising in the world, and he damned well knew it too. But clearly someone yet had power enough over him enough to get him to brave the filth of the streets and make his way down to this poor eastern ward of the city.

"I'll not try to gammon you, Mrs. Bell..." Now the voice was low; it growled up from within him. Crowley was a local man. And I sensed at once too that he was also a man who had become well accustomed to being obeyed by common folk. "Sometime early this morning a sorry business took place." His silver topped cane clattered as he dropped it onto the table. "A certain young lady was accused - mistakenly as it happens - of theft. What took place then was a happening which is... deeply to be regretted." His words fell slowly one after the other. It was a fair job of acting.

"Oh, aye... the poor lass certainly has had cause to be sorry for it, right enough! Aa'h doubt she ever be able to look in a mirror again without she's reminded. " Eadie Bell too was herself no mean performer. Big as Crowley was, she was not a woman to allow the man to overawe her entirely. She went on. "But what's done is *done*... and that scarce to be mended. Young Ettie Bellis was punched and kicked and dragged along on the street's cobbles. And she'll be tae keep for a month or more!"

"Ahh! Well aah've always known you for a woman of sound sense, Eadie, a lass with no time for nonsense." Mattie Crowley was already close to a chuckle. "And as you so rightly say, what 's done is done and can't be mended." There was the stir of silken cloth as the big man reached into his coat. "But *amends,* my dear, are a different matter altogether." He was coming quickly to the point. "Ten guineas is what I am authorised to pay, ten golden guineas with the fair understanding that she'll not lay any complaint against my friend. That *and* delivering up to me a certain gold piece that was the unfortunate cause of this tragic misunderstanding."

"You've a poor notion of what it costs poor folk to live, Mr. Crowley. Not every master pays as well as the King! That poor lass won't be able to stir for a week... and then there'll be a doctor to pay. "

"Twelve guineas... that much given for the sake of friendship." Even from where I stood I could tell that this was the sum that Crowley was going to pay; that and not a penny's piece more. He was a man well used to dealing with poor souls who have no counters left to play with in Life's dirty games.

Edith Bell said nothing. I heard the chink of money on the table boards and felt the chill draught and heard the fire roar up in the hearth as the door was opened again to let the visitor out. There was a little silence. Then I heard the woman draw breath. She began to swear, to blaspheme, with a terrible intensity. "Jesus Christ but aah did what aa' could to make it right for y', Ettie, ma' lamb ... you've my sworn oath upon that..."

I left Mrs. Bell with her head resting on her arms at the table. She was waiting for me to leave. Of course I already knew who Mr. Matthew Crowley was. When I had left England he had been young in the crimping trade. He secured seamen for ships that had difficulty in filling their berths. But the war had made him the chief agent of the port's regulating officer. Mattie Crowley sold men to the Navy's press-gangs!

My hope had been that D'Oeuys would have been waiting for the big man in the closed carriage that stood waiting at the corner. But there was no other passenger in the carriage. Fortunately however the driver was inclined to spare his horse so it was no great struggle to keep up with the carriage as it climbed up towards the streets of the upper town. Crowley was dropped at Buchanan's coffee rooms at the bottom of Newgate Street. I was glad to follow him into the warmth and cosiness of the place. He looked to be a regular visitor there because without a word being said a waiter hurried forward with a tray. I took a booth across the way from him and ordered a *café au rhum*. Damn me but Newcastle had become a sight more sophisticated in the last twelve years! The coffee served at Buchanan's proved to be remarkably good. I ordered a Havana cigar and sat smoking, a man pensive with many problems. Yet I conrived to watch the late business of the day going on around me, from behind a newspaper.

The scut of D'Oeuys's red hair blazed in the doorway as he hurried in. There was no mistaking him. The last time I had seen him he had been smart in the uniform of a lieutenant of *douaniers*. I was bent forward, trying to look intent upon filling my coffee cup as he walked by my booth. The suit of clothes he was wearing was brand new. From where I sat I could still smell the tailor's shop on them. But there was no mistaking that he'd been in a fight the night before. Nor had the battle been with any man. The bastard's face did indeed look as though he had tumbled headlong into a den of wildcats! Damn me but Ettie Bellis had truly scored her mark across the Frenchman's pale chops.

I could not risk trying to listen too closely on what passed between them. But I would, I decided, follow D'Oeuys when he left. From where I sat with my face well down into a copy the last week's *Tyne Mercury* I reckoned that I was safe enough. Around me and over the clatter of cups and dishes the comfortable merchants of Newcastle greeted on another.

All about us the air was heady with the perfume of roasting coffee.

I suppose that like the others I heard the distant roar of shouting and thought nothing of it. I had been expecting a riot in the city for some days now; so too of course had the town's magistrates. There were plenty of redcoats garrisoned in the town to keep the streets peaceful. But suddenly I realised that what I was hearing was not the anger of hungry men. These were cheers! A respectably dressed young lad pelted past the window, teetered at the entrance then grabbed at the doorpost to steady himself. It was almost as though to pay for his disturbance of the coffee house's customers that he thrust his head into the room. His breath failed him for a few seconds. Then we all knew!

Chapter Ten

"The Beast is loose!" The squeaky shout that rang out across the coffee rooms had a touch of hysteria in it. "Napoleon has landed in France... He's got an army and he's marchin' on Paris!" The young lad stopped to catch his breath back. Then he stuttered out the rest of his news.

"The mail... coach... has j'...just come in with the news!" There was an instant of shocked silence. But in that same instant Mattie Crowley was on his feet. His forearm stretched out like a man selecting a pippin from a basket as he took the young fellow by his coat's collar. With his mouth close to the lad's ear Crowley asked a few questions. Each time the lad nodded an affirmative. Without a word to his companion Crowley crushed his beaver hat down on to his shiny skull and strode off into the crowded street. D'Oeuy's might not have been there at all.

But this was news that had also given me much to think about. Not least that my own situation was now changed – and that as suddenly as everyone else's in Newcastle, in all Europe! Napoleon had been my master. And now he had returned. Nor was Joseph Fouche a man who could be lightly deserted! Now I too had to make up my mind. Aye, that, and to be damned sure about the way I was now to jump! Already the dice were rattling loudly in my cup. At this moment there might be no real decision to make; but in my heart I knew better than that! I reminded myself of the complete *dossier* on myself that I had been given to read. Yes; if the Emperor were to be victorious…well that might change much. But first there would be great battles to be fought. At least that would give me a few days to think over the matter!

Now though, at that moment, I had an even greater reason to find some way to get word to Richard Grainger. Simply it had become necessary, at least to show, some evidence of my own loyalty! At a remove *The British Linen Bank* had hired me. Promises had been made me! And above all I knew that the banks had always been a damned sight better at making good on their promises than ever Fouche had!

Before I moved however I had to allow the Frenchman to quit the coffee-house. But even before he stood up, and if I had seen one thing for certain sure, it was that the news of Napoleon's return had come as no great surprise to our Monsieur Charles D'Oeuys. Indeed it looked to be much more of an expectation suddenly fulfilled.

Following two fellows hurrying off through a crowd is an easy task. And it was made easier because all around us the streets were already now loudly a' buzz with the news. Moreover like every other soul in the city both D'Oeuys and Matthew Crowley had much to discuss, themselves. Yet the day's news it seemed was not hot enough to be distract the two men from their pleasures. I followed them up the hill to the top of Newgate Street. There I watched them push through the crowd milling about in front of the *Sun Inn*.

Here there was no mystery about their business. The crudely printed wall posters made that plain: ' *To be fought for in Mr. Isaac Fleming's Pit at the Sun Inn on Friday 10th March for £75…by cocks, stag ,and blenkards.* The men I had followed were going to nothing more sinister than a cockfight.

But this it seemed was not the ordinary run of match. Attendance at the string of fights was being hedged about by a shilling's door charge. For the moment however I saw that the crowd was made up mostly of the 'feeders', those fellows, pitmen they were mostly, who reared and trained the fighting birds in their own cottages. When I got closer too I could see the cock birds moving inside their stout linen bags.

For the sake of appearances I bought a printed 'list o' mains' for a sixpence. Over and above the price of the list my entrance to the sit among 'The Gentlemen of the Sod' cost me another half-crown. That day there were to be all of thirty 'mains' or pairs of cock birds set at one another to fight. But it was the names of the owners printed on the list that interested me. Dr. Mudie, was a name that appeared no less than seven times; while Mr. Mathew Crowley himself was entering two cocks and a blenkster. Severus Mudie, I recalled, was the name of the physician for whom the apothecary at Gilby's had ordered the big flasks of embalming fluid from London.

I could see now that the pieces of this puzzle were still set as far apart as ever they had been. Yet by now enough of them were already plainly set out on the board for me.

It had been years since that I had seen a cockfight. But the first click of needle sharp steel spurs brought it all quickly back to me. I heard the crowd's roar rise as the first feathers began to fly. In Newcastle town that day the parlour at the <u>Sun</u> was offering the <u>clientele</u> a very superior cockpit. Chairs had been arranged in three tiers. Wooden boards raised at the front row to form the fighting pit. Already the sawdust on the floor was brightly bespattered with fowl's blood. But then I was not there to watch fighting cockerels spur one another to death. I wanted to know what D'Oeuys was about, and above all who it was he would be meeting.

And almost at once that was something I knew. Across the drifting tobacco smoke I recognised the man who offered the Frenchman his hand. I had a link! It was Dr. Mudie. His girth was a deal wider than I remembered it but I recognised him. At once too however I noted that there was a distinct difference between the standings of D'Oeuys and Crowley. To the crimp Dr. Mudie had merely nodded. And that I think he did with a grace that was as close to churlish as made no difference.

Mudie however had offered D'Oeuys his hand – and that very warmly.

It is not too difficult to sit within a few feet of your prey and yet stay unseen. I yelled and swore with the best of them – but not too loudly. I even called a few bets of my own to a cross-eyed old fellow. While he, without so much as a scrap of paper to make a note, appeared to recall shouted wagers by the dozen. He would make no error. For almost an hour, long enough to see five brace of cocks crippled, I watched the fighting mains. Custom decreed that the heavier birds were to be fought last. Now the cocks entered were listed at above four pounds weight and the excitement was growing intense. Twice I saw two blenkards, cocks with an eye already spurred out in previous matches, full blinded. Mercifully their necks were wrung at once; their blood caked bodies went into the their feeder's sacks. By nightfall I supposed the birds would have become so much chicken broth! But at every shift of my gaze I was watching the three men who sat across the cockpit from me.

There was a dispute. An owner protested that his opponent's bird was protected by too great a thickness of ruff feathers. The wizened old chap in a suit of white corduroy who was the 'Teller of the Law' was summoned. He deliberated. He ruled that it was so. There was a delay while the setter-to kneeling at the pit's edge razored off more of the ruff feathers. I think that was my undoing. I looked up and saw Dr. Mudie's face. He was a man not best pleased with the decision. His fleshy hands clenched as he glowered around the tiered seats. It was then that I realised that for once I had been just too damned eager. Mudie's yellow pebble eyes caught, and then they settled on to me. Of course you never meet a man's gaze direct in such circumstances. You off-eye him as though he was not there at all. I waved to an imaginary acquaintance and raised my tankard to him. But it was too late. I hadn't been fast enough to off-eye him. Dr. Samuel Mudie was already trying to think from where it was he knew me.

When you're watching your prey you have to keep your eyes focussed. That was what had compounded my fault. In trying to look as though I had never seen Mudie in my life I took my eyes off D'Oeuys. It could hardly have been above a few seconds but it was enough. It was about as much time, I told myself, as I myself would have needed! I had seen him stand to raise his hand to order another round of the brandy they'd been drinking. I heard him shout his order over the hubbub of the crowd. When I looked again the bastard was gone. It was then that I knew that the Frenchman had both seen me and put a name to my face.

So D'Oeuys had slipped away - and damned handsomely he'd done it. Always give credit where that is plainly due! There would be no profit now in trying to follow him. He could already have quit the *Sun Inn* by way of any one of five separate doors. However Matthew Crowley was still there, and the rogue looked to be winning handsomely. From one main alone he'd won thirty guineas. It might be useful to learn more about the bald man. But then I changed my mind. One failure for that day was enough. Decidedly now it was time to leave.

Outside the town's streets were still busy. It looked as though the news from France had stirred up all Newcastle's trade. As if by a stroke of magic the merchants were busy again. In front of every shop there was at least one torch ablaze. However, now Bob Shafto had wounds to his pride to lick. I would go back to my lodging and see what Dick Triphook had for me to eat. Then I would settle down to write both Grainger and Dekker a full report. I had much to write about.

I should not have turned up the little street they call the Darn Crook. It was not that it was not busy. It was. Perhaps that was the trouble. To avoid the crowd I cut into the narrow lane that ran alongside the inside of the city's walls. I think it was the fact that it was unlit attracted me. I plunged into the darkness and began at once to hurry. I was perhaps ten paces along that lane before I realised that I had made a serious error.

A sword's blade comes from its scabbard with a little skir. The steel sings out and the song of it carries far. Once again I felt that warning bristle from the hairs at the nape of my neck. There were two of them. They were running after me. Footsteps echoed in the darkness behind me. One of the men kicked a pebble and sent it clattering. I reached into my coat for my pistol. Yet even as I did that I knew that this was no place to loose off a barker. Nonetheless it was a risk I had to take. I turned, levelled the weapon and drew a fair bead on the foremost runner. I squeezed the trigger, heard the clash of the hammer against the frizzen. The spark struck was bright and clear. The priming flashed. But that was all. There was no bang, no reassuring kick against my hand. I turned and ran again.

Within five strides I had shrugged off my greatcoat. It was a knife fighter's trick. The thick woollen cloth tight wrapped around my left forearm would shield me. The blade of my 'Jackie legs' gritted against my teeth as I pulled it open. I was as ready as ever I was going to be.

Behind me, close, there was a sudden footfall. One of the bastards had gained fast. I heard the flap of the shoulder capes on his coat as he raised his arm to strike. It was Matthew Crowley. In his great fist he had a naval cutlass. The bald man was hungry for blood. I knew then that if I tried to outrun him I would get my skull slashed open. I stopped dead, my boots skidding over the cobblestones. It took him by surprise. I spun about and put up my padded arm to fend off his blow. But at the last instant some animal instinct made me leap aside. I pressed my back hard against the stones of the city's wall. With a *thwrtt* the blade of Crowley's cutlass arced before my face. My nose felt the breeze off it.

But Mattie Crowley was a heavy limbed fellow and he had wagered all his strength on that one slash. The stroke had missed and now he paid for his error. As he tried to recover my stance, the long blade of my Jackie-legs pricked him deep in the forearm. I heard the shocked sob of his breath. But I knew then that I would not wound him again if I gave him the chance to lift his cutlass even once more. With my right hand I reached out to grab at him where I could. I touched his sleeve and slipped my hand down until my fingers were on the cold iron of his cutlass's guard. I found his thumb and used all my strength to bend it back. I badly wanted to feel the bastard's ligaments snap. All I heard was his gasp in agony. But with his free hand he could still jab punches at my head. My ears were ringing. But close cutlass play was not Crowley's forte. It had been more is style to wave his blade while he herded drunken sailors towards his own gang's flailing clubs.

For a few seconds it felt as though the bastard was going to rip my fingers away. Now too my bundled greatcoat was setting me at a disadvantage. It was hindering my movements. Nor could I drop it. All I could do was hold fast and thrust my shielded arm up at his snarling mask of a face. Crowley was swinging me round. He took a sharp side step. I heard his growl of triumph as the sudden lurch tore his cutlass hilt from my grip. Then he missed his footing. I heard the wet slither of his boots on the lane's cobbles. As he tried to recover I launched my self at him two handed. Elegant it was not; but it surely worked. The thump of his fat body against the city wall drove the wind out of him. Crowley's mouth opened to roar his rage but his breath was gone. I had been given a few seconds of time. I used them. Short and sharp again and again my fist's jab took him under the heart. His grip on the cutlass slackened. I eased it from his grasp to mine.

But by then my time too was spent. The other killer was on me. It was Charles D'Oeuys. The coarse woollen cloth of my folded coat took the force of his vicious down-slash. By God I felt it! I even heard the little click as his blade's edge struck against a horn button. I also heard the sharp in-suck of sheer frustration through the bastard's front teeth.

Now I fancied that I had always been much the better man with a blade than D'Oeuys. And I think he knew that! So sight of Crowley's cutlass in my hand was not to his taste at all.

He drew back back. It was just a posture. The fellow pranced about like a dandyprat; he feinted to left and right. Indeed we might have been two gentlemen facing one another across the floor of a *salle d' armes*.

"Well, Monsieur Shaft-toe… this perhaps is the one little scene we had to come to…in the end."

D'Oeuys had assumed the stance of a dandy on the *Rue de Rivoli*. He stood with his blade down. His choice of weapon was a light cavalry sabre. But he had forgotten that once before I had seen him stand like that. At Bruge in '08 I had seen him take the same position. That had been just minutes before he cut down a young lieutenant. D'Oeuys had goaded the lad into uttering the challenge. It had been simple murder. Then quite suddenly I realised what he was about. He had been running – I could see the heave of his chest. It was D'Oeuys who needed the time. And only a fool would have given him it. I went at him. I lunged down at him with my point, over arm like a cavalryman. Almost I had him. I thrust again and again. Each time I thrust he fell back. Then he countered. I parried two slashing down strokes. Our blades clashed. Red sparks flew in the darkness.

For all of a minute we went at one another. Then, and just in time, D'Oeuys was able to turn aside a low flanking cut. He evaded it; but by then I had seen the look on his face. This Fox was frightened! He was sweating. And that was from something more than the exercise. My last flurry of slashes had brought a stark realisation to him. He fell back panting. There was blood on his coat. Somewhere I had pinked the bastard. Yes, now Charles D'Oeuys knew. This could well be the night when he did not rifle his victim's pockets and walk away laughing. And by Christ I would not spare him. It was time for him to answer for what he had done to young Ettie Bellis. The dog was infected with a madness, was he? Well, Doctor Shafto had a specific cure for that. I would not waste any words in mocking Charles D'Oeuys. I raised my blade. I had chosen the place where I would open his lousy corpus to

118

the moonlight. Then behind me I heard the soft scrape of a boot on stone. Suddenly there was a great crimson flash. Some bastard had touched off a carronade inside my skull!

Chapter Eleven

It was the foul reek out of the bilges had told me I was afloat; that even before I heard the gurgle of the tidewater along the boat's sides. Beyond that sound however all I knew for a long minute's wait was that I lay in darkness. It was warm and oddly moist. Then, and this too I realised without being able to see a thing, my senses told me that I was among sleeping men. They lay on all sides of me, snoring and groaning. Now I heard them clearly as they began to stir themselves. Then a single foul oath, long drawn out and ending with the sharp spit of bitterness cut at the foul air. Tight packed we were. Like the corpses collected together on a battlefield we had been laid out on the filth caked deck planks. Then another man near to me gagged noisily. And at once I knew its cause. Already the air in that ship's hold was foul beyond words. Indeed what had woken me was my own fight for breath. So many drunken seamen in such a small space had all but consumed the natural vitality of the atmosphere. My own lungs it seemed had sensed their desperate need for fresh air. By then the noxious vapours - well tinged with the stink of strong tobacco and unwashed bodies - were sinking down low against the deck. Then as I tried to move my own body a sudden spasm of intense pain around my jaw reminded me that I myself had other troubles – and these were all of my own making. Memory returned.

Clearly I had not hit Crowley nearly hard near enough to crack that bastard's polished skull. And indeed in spite of it that damned hound had managed to struggle to his feet. Then the whoremonger had staggered hard at me. He had swung at me with his 'pacifier'. One vicious welt was all it had taken. The leather bag filled with lead swan-shot had damned near taken my head off. I had gone down like a pole-axed bullock. When I had been lying on my back and through all the dancing blur of my vision I had seen the devil's smirks on both their faces. Smart as you damned well please, the two bastards had me! But I remembered too that it had been D'Oeuys who had finally doused my lamps for me. Before his boot swung the bloody swine had laughed; and then with vicious deliberation he had kicked me in the face. I touched at my jaw. Under my fingertips the flesh was badly swollen. In the darkness I heard a man groan. It was me.

Of course I had been stripped. In place of my decent suit of clothes and good linen I now had on a torn canvas shirt and ragged fustian breeks. My feet were in a pair of 'hoggers', the footless stockings of a man who worked underground. This was the workaday dress of any Geordie coal-hewer. Both garments were stiff with dried-on mud; the shirt had been made for a man twice my size. From the feel of it too some thoughtful bastard had also smeared a stinking handful of gritty mud over my face and neck.

Without moving I struggled to take in more of my surroundings. My shoulder cushioned a man's head. Under my touch the tousled mop of his hair was greasy. The brandy on the fellow's breath made me turn my head away sharply. Gently, cautiously, I eased myself free of him. He began to mumble obscenities. Then another voice came wavering across the dark.

"Wor Jimmy... Jimmy Dixon... are y' there, lad?" No man answered. Again: "Did anybody see what happened to wor kid?"

"Aye… aah did." No further information was offered. The voice itself subsided into a long drawn out moan and ended with a piece of choicest blasphemy.

"What? For Christ's sake shipmate… tell us what 's become o' the lad?"

"No; he's not been pressed, Kidda! When them shit-lickers rushed us the foot of the Dog Leap Stairs aa'h saw Mr. Lieutenant – 'Fuck-face' Frazier stottin' a belayin' pin off your Jimmy's pigtail. The poor lad hit the cobbles like a bag o' hammers. But then that lassie, young Dolly Jemison it was, hikes up her clouts an' she kicks that Frazier straight in the ballocks. Aa'h hord the bugger scream like a kittiwake. Then that same sheep shagger folds at his knees an' falls… face to the for'ad like a virgin in a faint." The man's joy in his telling was plain. "An' aa'h can swear tae y' now… that's one bonny sea-officer what won't walk straight for a month." Little pools of laughter bubbled up around me. "An' then that same canny lass took her finger nails an' furrowed up the fat chops o' Hicks, that big hairy arsed bosun's mate off the *Lotus*! The last I saw of it… bonny Dolly had your kid on her back an' she was carryin' the poor lad away."

"Thank Christ for that! Wi' the both of us pressed wor mother would be in the poor hoose within a month."

"Please…" It was a plaintive, a wavering cry. "Where am aa'h?" Nobody answered for a moment. Then a response came from close by me. And almost it was jovial.

"Why *you*, ma' bonny lad, you're headed straight for Glory an' a hat filled brimful wi' prize money! This here is the *Jenny Howlet*. She's by way o' bein' a pleasure yacht wot's been hired by certain patriotic Newcastle merchants to take all us lads off on a jolly jaunt down the river. That's all of us gallant lads here who've expressed a loyal wish to serve in the fleet of His Majesty… God Bless Him!" The man's grim bitterness was scarcely hidden at all. "You'll be taken aboard the *H.M.S. Lyra*.

*P*resently that fine man-o-war is ridin' at anchor off down by Peggy's Hole off North Shields."

"But a caa'nit dee that…aaam't be wed… th' day… at St. Andrew's, 'leven o'clock. Why man, we've twenty folk comin' down on the cart from Spittal Tongues…We've even hired a fiddler." Laughter rumbled back and forth around the hold.

"Well, never mind, ma' bonny lad. Maybe Captain Charleton… who's a real gentleman… will be lettin' y' kiss the gunner's daughter instead…" This time the laughter was cut short.

"Aa'm Jesse Rae." It was clear that the name was known. And there was that in the man's voice that made the others listen. "Twice already aah've been pressed. Once into the *Euralyus*, frigate, off Flambr'o Head in '09…and then again by the *Hussar*, last year that was, just as aa'h was taking a drink after a four month's voyage to Quebec." The man's grievance was an easy one to share.

"This mornin' aa' was given the second mate's berth aboard the new collier, *Countess of R aby*. So some dirty bastard must ha' paid to have me lifted." Rae's story was not an uncommon one. Paying out money to have a man snatched by the press gang had long been an arrange-able fate in most British seaports.

"But aah'll find out. All ah 'll hev tae ask is 'who gets the profit?' An' then by Christ I'll have the bastard! There was a pause; the prisoners were still listening "Remember this, lads, we're still w' own men before the law until we stand wi' wor feet on the deck of a man o' war and some sneerin' little shit-peddlar reads his Book o' Words over us. An' aah may tell y's aa'l now: *aa'h* diven't mean t' serve aboard any fuckin' King's ship this trip!"

"Easy said, bonny lad, easy said!" There was no mockery. It was an older man's statement of a fact, a soft- spoken oracle uttered out on to the darkness of the hold. It was then that

Jesse Rae's sharp answer dropped among us with the seed of its sedition already sprouting:

"Sallie the whore, lads! Make this nail-sick old bitch rock until the bastards know we'll not be pressed!"

Whoever shouted 'Aye' I never knew. But within the next minute I was learning what it meant to *sallie* a vessel. Two dozen men, some still staggering drunk, struggled to their feet. In that hold there was scarce enough headroom for us to stand upright. But within a few heartbeats all of us, sailors and landsmen alike, were lined up against the one side of the hull.

Then it began. We acted together in a terrible unison. The men linked arms and began to waddle towards the opposite side of the hold. Slowly at first, back and forth we sallied. As we moved men slipped and cursed as they staggered on their own drunken vomit, but we moved. It was like some macabre dance.

It was on our third sallie that the ridiculous irony in all this business occurred to me: I was here aboard this floating privy-stall only because of the most amazing *good* fortune! True! At that moment Robert Shafto was *alive* at all only because of Matthew Crowely's greed – that and nothing else. Almost certainly D'Oeuys would have hacked me to death. But Matthew Crowley's business was man-selling. With my throat cut I would have represented the dead loss of an easy profit. With my feet forced on to a man-o'-war's deck I would be rated as a fit landsman. As such I would be worth three pounds to the Royal Navy. And Matthew Crowley was a man o' business! Had he obeyed the Frenchman I would already be dead meat - in the Tyne not on it.

For a few minutes there was no change in the vessel's movement. Then even I felt it. Slowly the *Jenny Howlet*'s hull had taken on a different motion.

All I could hear was the horny scrape of bare feet on the planks. There was a single cry of glee from the snatched bridegroom. Then he yelped like a puppy as the man next to him side-kicked him hard up the arse for it. For of a sudden ours had become the discipline of desperate men.

Back and forth we sallied; now more quickly. But still there was an order to our motion, a slow rhythm. I felt the vessel's rolling movement increase. A man began to hum the tune of a sea-shanty. We all took it up: *"Leave her Johnny, Leave Her"* And the more she rocked the more the *Jenny Howlet* did rock. And as she rolled we began to hear the slop and splash of the foul water in her bilges.

"Stop that at once you... you rag-arsed, Geordie vermin!" It was an educated voice, young, southern. From all around me that insult drew a growl like that from a cage of trapped tigers. I could almost see the bared teeth.

"Belay that I say! Or by God I'll put a musket ball among ye!" We heard the thud of a firelock's butt against the wedges that closed the hatch above us.

Without a word Jesse Rae left the line. With hardly a sound he ran aft. The hatch was lifted. There was yellow lantern light. I felt the fresh waft of freezing air. I saw the loom of a shadow, heard the harsh *snick-snack* as the lock of a musket was cocked. There was the sudden sharp click and the bright flash of priming. In that short instant all around me I saw the whole cargo of damned souls – seamen all ready to be shipped-out for Hell. In the thunderclap of the musket's bang we all clapped our hands to our ears.

But by then Jesse Rae had already made his wild leap. An eye's blink before the smoking muzzle could be pulled clear Jesse had his hands gripped on it. I heard a frightened squeak. But the lad was too slow by a whole heartbeat. I felt myself give an involuntary wince at the hideous thud as his head hit the hold's bottom. Quite distinctly I had heard one of the boy's neck vertebrae snap. He wore the white lapel patches of a midshipman.

The *Jenny Howlet* had become a floating madhouse. Wild cheers rang through the hold. Boots thudded over our heads.

For a moment it looked as though the men on the deck were going to be able to get their hatch down. But an iron musket barrel makes a powerful lever. With it Jesse Rae held the hatch until his mates had rushed aft to bear a hand. Then shoulder muscles strained and cracked. Slowly that hatch was pushed open again. It was all over. The two petty officers fled aft. With a wild flailing of arms and legs they struggled with one another to tumble down into the *Jenny Howlet*'s tiny stern cabin. We heard door bars hammered home. The two men were battening themselves in. Though to save some shred of honour for the King's Navy's a pistol cracked out. A single ball whined spitefully over our heads.

"Belay that or by Christ aa'l scuttle this fuckin' bumboat under y's!" There were no more shots. And Jesse Rae was our leader.

Without a helmsman at her tiller the *Jenny Howlet* drifted down the Tyne on the tide. But she drifted blind. Around us the rolling banks of river fog closed in. It was strange. Suddenly it was as though each man was for himself again. Already that unity of purpose that had held us together as pressed-men was going. With the vessel in their hands all these men wanted now was to be ashore and away. But which way to go? Where between Newcastle and the North Sea were we?

That could not go on. Without a word being said Jesse Rae had taken up leadership again. Though I knew then, as probably he did himself, that if ever it came to a trial these same desperate men would point the finger at him. They would, I knew for certain, betray the lad as the ringleader who had first incited them to revolt. Yet now when he held up his hand even the wharf-rat crouching over to pillage the dead midshipman's body looked up.

"Lads, you'll all know that after tonight it's goin' tae be a case of *run as far as you're able... as fast as you can!* This night we've killed a King's officer." The silence was absolute. "That's the yardarm haul for *every* last one of us if we're caught. You

126

don't need me to tell you that..." I could see by the gaunt faces that every man knew it. Jesse Rae offered them a way out:

"M' self... aa'm goin' to lay this bloody biscuit barge against the rocks across at Pelaw. Then it really *is* every man for his self!" There was a rumble of agreement. "An' aah do know that you'll all of y's have the plain savvy never to go back to anywhere near tae Newcastle until this bloody war is long over!

How he did it I never knew, but inside ten minutes with Jesse Rae at the helm the *Jenny Howlet*'s strakes were scraping along a ledge of rock under the south bank of the river. And as soon as she touched ground the men were over the side, scrambling like madmen to get ashore. I watched them disappear up the bank and into fields above. The bridegroom from Spittal Tongues was well to the fore.

But not all of them fled. One man looked undecided. He had jumped up on to the bulwark but then stopped, hovering almost with his arms outstretched. Jesse Rae gave a sharp nod to one of his mates. The seaman picked up a capstan bar and swung it. It smashed the poor sod's ankles out from under him. With a scream he slipped sideways and fell, scrabbling as he went, down between the boat's side and the rock.

"Judas sheep!" The man with the capstan bar spat the words. "What sailor ever manages to keep so much as a penny's piece on him when Crowley's Crowd gets its hands on him?" He was right. I too had heard the chink of coin. The fellow had been placed in with the prisoners to watch for signs of mutiny. He had failed.

But it was plain now that Jesse Rae had plans of his own. And he had four shipmates who were standing firm with him. As soon as the last fugitive was out of sight they manned the tender's long sweeps to fend her off into the current again.

"Ye're not away then...*Mr*?" Jesse Rae was reloading the midshipman's musket. He paused while he bit the end off a cartridge." Aa'h could see that y' were a bit too soft-handed to be the usual fare for Crowley's Crowd. There was the tap-tap of his calloused forefinger against greased paper. I even heard the siffle as the gunpowder grains went down the barrel. He was giving me time to think of an answer. "Though now o' course if you're taken you'll swing just as high as the rest of us..."

I could not help myself. I found that I was smiling. It was sour. "Shall we say that I too have business with Crowley... and there's another man in Newcastle I've yet to have dealing with... Neither is a matter that'll wait over."

"Aye," he said. "that 's about the way it is wi' me an' the lads..."

We drifted ashore on the north bank of the Tyne, landing within a stone's throw of the village of Wallsend. But this time no men fled into the fog. At Jesse Rae's order his mates unshipped the tender's big tiller bar. They heaved it over the side. I watched it swirl away on a fast falling tide. A knife was found and a seaman who looked to know his business clambered about the vessel cutting through her stays. The *Jenny Howlet* would need to be re-rigged entire before she shipped any more impressed men down the Tyne. We fended off the hulk and let the river take her.

I had thought that I faced a long walk barefoot through snow. And against the prospect I'd had the wit to snatch up a couple of rags of sailcloth and contrived to wrap and tie my feet into them. Already my toes were numbed. But Jesse Rae was a resourceful sailor: ' I know a cross-eyed young widder wi' the biggest arse in Wallsend'. His men laughed.

We stood, orphans o' the storm, while Jesse banged at the window shutters to rouse his light o' love. Only after a deal of shouting and in the glimmer of a rushlight was a piebald pony backed in between the shafts of a cart. That cart's last load of the day had been stable muck - steaming fresh!

It was a damned rough passage. We lay huddled together for warmth on that stinking cart. Nonetheless within the hour we were back – and on the empty streets of Newcastle.

I suppose that I might have jumped down and simply disappeared. What I needed now was a poultice for my jaw, a few drops of laudanum, soft food and a bed with a hot brick wrapped in flannel in it. But the man who had sold me to the Press-gang had been in Charles D'Oeuy's pay, acting under his orders. He would likely know where the Frenchman was. So through him I might yet find that fox-headed bastard.

But first I had the bald Mattie Crowley to find. And when I did so, this would not be entirely a matter of revenge. First there would be some small exchange of words between us. Questions had arisen. And, by Christ, I would have the answers to those questions – would I not!

Chapter Twelve

But for the rest of that night I was made aware that in this business Robert Shafto could to be little more than a passenger. That much was soon made clear enough to me. I was obliged to go wherever Jesse Rae and his mates took me. Though to be sure those lads had no doubt at all about where their first port of call would be. They knew well enough the names of all the men they sought and - better than that still - they knew exactly where the bastards were to be found.

The Press Room for Newcastle was in a wooden hut. It stood in the yard behind the *Plough Inn*, down at the end of Spicer Lane. Softly, like so many wolves gathering for a kill, we all closed in on that single lit window. Yet from beginning to end I was sure that the work of retribution took us no longer than ten minutes, that all told. Nor, and I must own this freely, at any time did I have so much as one qualm about the business. Truly those bloody scoundrels deserved what was done to them.

There were four of the crimping swine sitting in that hut. But as I shielded my eyes with my hand to peer in through the window I saw that the odds were about to be reduced further. A chair scraped; a man stood up. The door opened, spilling a smoky glow of lamplight out on to the trodden snow. As he stood there,

yawning his breath clouded on the freezing night air. He put his head down to fumble at his buttons. The man's last piss on this earth steamed - and was cut short. Nemesis descended.

There was a swish through the air; it ended abruptly with a sound like a blunt axe hitting a green log. I had always thought of such weapons as woman's toys. And to be sure I had thought nothing of it when I had heard Jesse Rae beg a pair of her brown stockings from his light o' love at Wallsend. Nor had it signified much to me when I had seen him stuff one inside the other. What had smashed in the crimpster's skull like a crushed egg was the big whinstone pebble he had tucked into that stocking's toe.

Drunk as they were the remaining three men were left with just wit enough to recognise Death's grimace when they saw it coming at them. That much I could see in the glaze it put on their eyeballs. One fellow began to blubber; the other two to gabble like crazed Bedlamites.

"I'd like to beg the favour of a word with the man who is wearing my boots..." I asked Rae's leave in as level a voice as I could manage.

"Y've a minute – no longer..." And I knew that Jesse Rae meant what he was saying. "These are the whore-masters who have made a fortune sellin' honest family lads to the King's Navy... and that's something they've done for years wi'out ever the once settin' foot on to a man-o'-war's deck themselves... These are the Hell-hounds who've left hundreds o' decent lasses and their bairns damned to the mercies o' the Parish."

I stepped forward, thrusting the man hard against the wall. He had my own *jackie legs in* his waistband. I think that at any other time he would have had it out and been slashing at me. Now with the lightest touch I relieved him of it. For by then he was gibbering with terror. My face was close to his. "Tell me..." I said quietly. Then the man shat himself. I heard him - plain! I heard the fellow's bowels slop out loose into his breeks. "Where will I find D'Oeuys...the *Frenchman*?" My whisper was vicious. Yet still the eyes showed no understanding. "You know him... the fellow with the red hair... earlier tonight?"

"He...he's with Crowley up at Mrs. Gomer's..." He got no further. I'd used up all the time he had been allowed. One of the sailors reached beyond me and grabbed at the wretch by the scruff of his neck.

"Willie Pape..." It was a voice with the sharp crack of Doom in it. "D' ye remember a young journeyman carpenter called Cuthbert Donaldson?" A knifepoint pricked blood from the man's throat. Pape nodded – almost eagerly. "Well, kidda, this is from Cuttie's ma!" The soft skitter of blood over a floor's planking is a curious sound.

Men will hold on to the belief that they are not going to die. Until their hearts stop they can never believe it. Almost it was as though these fellows stood to watch themselves being butchered like sheep. For now neither Rae nor his men cared. Nor did I. For what had any of us to loose now? We all knew that we had stood as condemned men from the instant aboard the *Jenny Howlet* when that young midshipman's neck had snapped.

It was with an odd formality that the four corpses were laid out on the floor. The wonder to me was that every man of them had been armed. One of them had even had a loaded pistol hooked into his belt.

I had a job to pull my boots off the man Pape's corpse. They had been just a little too small for him. It was only as I stamped into them that I realised that they were still pleasantly warm from the dead man's feet. Nor I think did that greatly bother me.

Jesse Rae spared his crew a minute or two longer for looting. By God, those lads had little enough to learn from the Emperor's Old Guard. Cold sausages and peas-pudding left in a dish were snatched up and crammed into hungry gobs; a half bottle of brandy was passed around. For myself I snatched up a tattered watch coat from a peg. Buttoned up tight it more or less covered my coal-hewer's rags.

But then I found what for me the real prize of the night. On a shelf there was a little beer-stained ledger. One glance at the columns of the names and the payments made told me what I had. Hurriedly I stuffed it into my coat's breast. With this book I had come by the means to level deadly threat!

It was Rae himself who disposed of the corpses. There was a deal table and half a dozen chairs. He piled them around the bodies and then soused everything with oil from a little keg. He turned at the door and hurled in the lamp. Only once did I look back at the blazing hut.

Mrs. Gomer's was a brothel. Or to say the word more politely, it was a House of Assignation. And as such its clientele might expect – and the more stupid of them might even believe it – that they were cloaked by a discretion that was near to absolute. But as I myself knew only too well, Newcastle folk are too fond of honest gossip for that ever to be true! Indeed I doubted that there would be a soul in the city who could not readily point out the Quality's own whorehouse to any enquiring stranger. Though to be sure, no establishment like Mrs. Gomer's would ever have been allowed to open its doors in the upper part of the town. It was in an old Jacobean house along The Close, above the Bridge.

In their wisdom the city's justices had licensed the lower floor of this discrete *Casa* for the sale of wines, ales, and spirits. A poker work board over the door declared as much. Only at the top of the beautifully carved oak stairway did it become a proper bordello. Carriages were allowed to set-down at the door. But they were never allowed to wait!

"We've picked ourselves a fortress to attack here. Mr Rae. It had seemed suddenly appropriate to address Jesse Rae in this fashion. In the Emperor's service a man like him would long since have been an officer.

"Nowt like it, man... it's still just a sty-full o' drunken pigs and whores. Just you do as I say, Mr. and before this night is over we'll both be paid what's owin' us."

And this proved no idle boast. There was an alley with a side door. From the rich smells of roasting meats hanging on the cold air it let into the brothel's kitchen. Knuckles rapped gently at the door.

"Hello… are y' there, Hinny?" This was sheer pantomime and I found it damned hard not to laugh out loud. The castrato tones were from a bearded A.B. who stood more than a fathom tall in his bare feet. Then again: "Hello, there, pet… it's yor friend, Meggie. Let's be in, love… ahhm not drunk…honest aah'm not…" Now the tone had slipped into a pathetic whine.

By clock time I don't suppose that it was more than couple of minutes before the door was unbolted. The old woman was at once gathered up into the sailor's arms.

"Now your goin' t' keep nice an' quiet, aren't y' m' Darlin' duck? A nice clean-livin' old body like you wants no truck wi' villains the likes of us… does she? She'll surely want to live to dandle her grandbairns on her knee. Won't she, Mistress?" The old woman said nothing. Though under her white mobcap she nodded and kept on nodding like a zany while the big sailor eased her gently into a cupboard. As we passed through that kitchen seamen snatched up knives and slashed great pieces off the waiting joints of cooked meat laid out on silver buffet trays.

As in all the whorehouses of my experience the luxury always ends abruptly. Turkey carpets and India rugs lay underfoot – but that was only where the business of the house began. We stepped into a hallway lit pink with shaded candles.

Here passion was being noisily spent in every room. As we walked down the corridor you could smell the men's lust hanging on the air. We heard the grunts and moans, slaps and giggles. And I knew at once that an exact half of it all was as false as a Dutchman's wooden nutmeg. An elderly waiter in a footman's livery turned a corner, saw us, and froze stiff in his tracks, The tray of empty glasses in his hands tinkled as his hands shook.

"Crowley... where's Mattie Crowley?" The question was whispered. Very gently Jesse Rae took the tray of glasses from the old man's hands. His smile was as warm as new bread. With a forefinger that wavered in the air the old man pointed to the end of the corridor. The bearded seaman with the contralto voice led the old man quietly away downstairs.

For all of a minute Jesse Rae listened at the door. Then very gently he knocked. But before he turned the door handle he allowed the tray of glasses to shake a little. I heard them tinkle and chime as the door swung open.

We might have burst into that whorehouse bedroom with the massed drums of a French line regiment rattling out the *pas de charge*. We were too late. Mathew Crowley was already well beyond any revenge of ours. The fellow lay stark naked on a bed with gilded cherubs carved into its posts. The starched whiteness of the bed linen was spattered over crimson with his life's blood. He was lying on his side. His sagging chins and his blue tinged jowls lay flattened under his bull's neck. The polished ivory of his head lay as though it had been served up on a platter of clotting blood. Oddly enough I found myself thinking of a painting of John the Baptist I'd seen in Milan. The Crowley's eyes were open. Like wet olive pebbles they stared away at some distant wonder. I put a hand to his shoulder. He was not long dead: the flabby flesh was still very warm. For me at that moment though no doubts remained. Whoever had slashed Eneas Knox's gizzard had surely been at work again here.

Of a sudden something stirred under the bloodied linen. I reached forward and pulled back the sheet. Lying at Crowley's side and snoring softly was a fat blonde girl. She lay with her chubby arms folded. Spilling up over them were quite the most enormous breasts I had ever seen on a woman. Truly the lass could easily have slung those boobies of hers over her shoulders. She stirred again, broke wind musically and turned over to expose what we lewd fellows would truly have called Blind Cupid's smile. Our grimaces were of the purest lechery.

The face of every man standing around that bed showed the Old Adam that lived within him.

However Jesse Rae was still a man thwarted. He was biting his lip hard as he looked down on Crowley's gross corpse. Yet even in his anger the man could see how pointless it was to rave at a corpse.

"Jesus Christ! The pity of it is that he couldn't have known what was happening to him." He hawked loudly and spat a fat green gullet-oyster down on to the face of the man who for years had led the worst gang of man-snatchers along the Tyneside.

" D' y know... I'd ha' given a year's pay to strangle the life out of that bastard! Why man, aa'h could even feel ma' fingers rivin' at his flabby throat..." Then he shrugged.

"Aa'h well... now he's a dead 'un and so that 's done. First come; first served! Right, m' lads, we'd best be away." Jesse Rae was not a man to waste his time on helpless anger.

But before we could turn from the corpse there was a desperate sobbing gasp. The blonde lass sat bolt upright. Like a woman crazed she was holding up splayed fingers before her face. They dripped with Crowley's blood. Slowly, her big, soft mouth o' ed itself small. I watched as it began to widen for a scream. That scream was stillborn. All it took to choke her cry off was one hard look from Jesse Rae. His decision was made.

"Get y'r clouts on, m' darlin'..." He spoke softly. "And then move y' r lovely arse! Go – quietly – rouse out your Mrs. Gomer... You tell that old bitch what 's happened. Tell her it'll soon be high water at the bridge... so if she hurries her sel' along she'll get this pig's carcass into the river before daybreak."

As I have mentioned before, in the year 1811 my service for the Emperor had required me to play the part of manager in a rather grand brothel in Brussels. So I knew the way things would be done here. Crowley may have been rich, but he was far from being what passed for 'gentry'. Within a week I knew that some new pack of rats would be busy seizing men for the Navy. Nor would his sudden disappearance give rise to over many enquiries. Only those to whom he owned money might ask. What was certain was that no whisper of scandal would ever be allowed to attach itself to the House on the Close. Gentlemen, even what passes for it in Newcastle, will always demand discretion. And whether they got it or no Mrs. Gomer's business was at least supposed to be based upon that premise. The corpse would be bundled up in its bloodied bed linen and dumped in the Tyne. Nor would it be found floating – not with the weight of ballast stone that would be tied to its feet. Before that day was ended the room would have been well scrubbed, re-painted even. No brothel-keeper could ever afford to miss even the smallest detail. Not a word would be said. And although she didn't know it yet, this blonde lassie with the big tits was due a holiday. She would be exchanged for a girl from a sister-house up in Edinburgh or down at York.

But the bloodied corpse aside there were still a few pickings to compensate us. Crowley's purse lay on a bedside table. It bulged. Again the assassin seemed to have had no interest in money at all. When Jesse Rae spilled out the gold and silver coinage he also picked up a fat roll of white paper. To my surprise he looked about to fling it away with disgust. I clicked my tongue and with a courteous inclination of my head I plucked the banknotes gently from his fingers. "By y'r leave, sir..." I smiled.

"Them there's banker's flymsys! Try to pass them, lad, and they'll likely put a noose around your neck..." It was a friendly enough warning. "Though you'll know best yourself..."

"Oh, but I do *that*, my friend, I surely do!" I winked at him.

The bunch of keys had lain hidden under the purse. I don't think for one moment that that Jesse Rae missed my scooping them up. But he said nothing. Probably he didn't care.

So we had done at Mrs. Gomer's. But I knew better than to try simply to walk away from Rae and his mates. I was not of that class of men who could be more or less lawfully taken up by the press gang. Though dressed as I was at that moment I might have difficulty proving it. I knew I still needed these fellows.

"No offence meant, Mister, but ye'll see how it is. I'll need to keep my eye upon you till we're safe off the Tyne. Though I will undertake to put you aboard the first fishin' cobble we come up with."

We exchanged sour little grins. For me now though there was no help for it. We both knew that. Of course I would have to sail down river with him. Jesse was too careful of his own neck to allow me any chance to slip away before he and his lads were well out the reach of the magistrates. Only too well this lad knew that a frightened man might think of turning King's Evidence, of selling his accomplices for a pardon. It was a small enough risk but it was not one that Rae was inclined to take.

We left Mrs. Gomer's brothel while the gentlemen 'all-nighters' still snored away in their private rooms. That was as well for them. For any face that had peeped out would, I knew, surely have got a seaman's fist smashed into it.

Curiously enough I was not surprised at all to find myself aboard the *Countess of Raby* when she slipped her moorings. I sat in her filthy after-cabin trying to bring round the man Jesse Rae had felled as he had stepped aboard off the head of the gangplank. A good swing of the fist had been, I supposed, as good a way as any other to get a second mate's berth aboard a Geordie collier. Nor did I have to spend long on the fellow. His jaw was not broken - though he probably felt otherwise. My own thoughts were now racing. The *Countess of Raby,* number 197, was the same vessel I had seen off Gateshead's North Shore just a few days before. I had followed the seaman from Eneas Knox's room directly to this ship. But he wasn't aboard now.

Discretely I rummaged through the after-cabin. Both the elderly master and his mate were sleeping off their night before's drunk. There was not much to find. Aboard such a ship there never *would* be. Nonetheless even a Tyne collier must carry a logbook. She had been in the Tyne for a week. Her last voyage had been to Norwich, nine days - a quick passage. But the one before that she had carried coals to Whitbread's Brewery in London. That round trip had taken all of nineteen days. 'Contrary winds... three days sheltered in Yarmouth Roads', the log read. My nautical knowledge was slight enough but I noted the dates. So far it was simply a few casually gathered facts. Grainger could seek more precise information himself from his ship-owning friends.

Now to say fair and give the lad his due Jesse Rae had either nerves of tempered steel or the brass faced cheek of the Devil himself. Or - more like - he was blessed with both. At North Shields he steered that collier brig to within hailing distance of the receiving ship **Lyra.** The *Jenny Howlet*'s hulk was tied alongside her. Rae's sole concession to disguise was that he wore the master's battered tarpaulin hat.

And then, true to his given word, a mile off the Marsden Rocks Jesse hailed a fishing coble. I had to help the collier's quondam second mate stumble down the ladder into the boat. There could be no gold for the Emperor carried aboard the *Countess of Raby* this trip.

However just one of Crowley's guineas between them persuaded the two Shields fishermen to take us into their boat.

What progress we made was slow enough, but by putting his arm over my shoulder I was able to steer my patient's still groggy steps towards the office of Robinson the Carrier on Farrier Street. There I paid for two rides for us through to Newcastle on the afternoon wagon. The second mate looked deathly pale but he would live. I would see to it. His name he told me through a twisted corner of his mouth was Ernie Hodgson. What he didn't tell me, but what I was sure of, was that he had been a small part of some plan.

"Wait till m'ee Uncle Ralphie hears o' this..." Three times that was what he'd said. Plainly this was more than some mere piece of Geordie nepotism. Someone had arranged to have Hodgson take Jesse Rae's berth aboard the *Countess of Raby*. That was a name I wanted. It wasn't much to work upon but it might be another thread to unravel. I left him asleep on a bench in the carrier's office.

What I most needed then was clothes. For in the harsh light of day I knew that I must have looked a proper Jimmy Queernabs to anyone who cast eyes on me. The rags I wore might well have fallen out an old clothes wife's basket down on the Sandgate Market! The watchcoat had worn thin and I was soon damned near to juddering with the cold. Besides which a man respectably dressed was not like to be snatched-up by any beady eyed naval lieutenant out a' roving with his shore-party.

Isabel Bone's shop stood on the corner of the Market Square at South Shields. Both she, and it, might have been put there for my purposes. She was a big woman with a great frizzy mop of ginger hair and with a pair of freckled forearms on her that made her look as though she could easily tear the living pluck out of a man's body. Our Isabel dealt in seaman's slops and second-hand clothes. I stood at the doorway with the coats of dark cloth hooked above me like so many hanging bats. She had seen me, of course she had, but she went on running her thumbnail speculatively along the seams of a pair of seaman's canvas trowsers.

"How can aa' h sarve y'i... sir?". Isabel Bone had come to a decision. My fustian breeks and the torn blue shirt were being ignored. For like any woman in her trade she would have to have a pair of eyes keener than any privy-stall rat's. So she had noted my good boots and, I suspected, even the neat cut of my hair. It was enough. Eyes, pale blue North Sea eyes, brightened with interest, and a proper caution.

"I need suit of plain of clothes, Mistress, clean linen and a hat of some sort... for cash down. Quickly!" There was no point here in fabricating a tale. Isabel Bone had heard all the stories, many years since. She just nodded and looked me up and down slowly, squinting a little as her eyes moved. I had been measured up without the need for a tailor's tape

" I have coat, breeks, and waistcoat of grey tweed cloth – the' would last you many years. Such garments, mebbe, as would suit say... a farm bailiff or a..." She shrugged. "Or what you will... sir." She was searching; very subtly.

"I need to be dressed respectably enough to escape the attentions of some fellows who might just desire me to take service in the King's Navy." We laughed; though both laughs had the same hollow ring to them. Mistress Bone nodded.

"Well... what aa' hve got have here a trunk. It contains the entire wardrobe of a priest, a minister of religion. The poor bas...soul died at sea two months ago on the way home from Hamburg. It might serve." She winked: "For aa've observed that His Majesty's Navy mostly has parsons enough aboard their ships..." Mrs. Bone fumbled behind her sackcloth apron for a key and unlocked the trunk.

The late Mr. Josiah Aycliffe had been what in England is called a Dissenter. In many people's reckoning he had hardly been a clergyman at all. Nonetheless he had worn the heavy black broadcloth favoured by men of God. Better than that, his breeches, although cut a little deep in the seat, fitted me well enough. This was no time to chaffer. A bill for five pounds drawn on Chapman's Bank at Newcastle secured for me the remaining worldly possessions of the Reverend Aycliffe. The worn banknote I laid before the woman was one from Crowley's roll. Something told me that it would be some time before the paper would be presented for honouring. Isabel Bone of course would have liked payment in gold, as who would not? Her broad shoulders turned this way and that when I offered her the white paper. But in the end her raw red hands had grasped at it. Likely she would know how better than most folk how to pass a stolen banknote – just as I knew that she would have made the proper allowances for that risk in her price.

"Aye, ma' Hinny…" I thought to myself. "Life is like to be terrible hard for a poor woman who has her living to make in South Shields!

We returned to Newcastle slowly on one of Robinson's big carrier wains. The shadow of the brim of my new black shovel hat did something to hide the bruise on my jaw. The fact that a dissenting minister smoked a cheroot and generously shared his square faced bottle of gin with Ernie Hodgson aroused no comment. Once in Newcastle I took him straightway to his lodgings up by the Barras Bridge. At sight of him his landlady threw her up her arms. Between us we got him directly into his bed. Questions would keep. Next morning I might visit poor Ernie - as surely a Good Samaritan should.

I realised very quickly that the garb of a non-conformist minister confers upon man a special state. In Newcastle town there had to be a dozen or more different sects of Christian dissenter; and each one was ready to cast the others into outer darkness with a venom that was equal and reciprocal. So I walked all the way down from the Haymarket to the foot of the Westgate hill like a man invisible. It was a market day and the streets were thronged with strangers. Drunks, men and women both, veered away from me. Other clergymen I met with a certain contrived ease. Quite simply our mutual glances failed to meet. I decided that I would keep to a minister's black broadcloth for a day or two.

It was when I had stopped at the corner of Monk Street that the little lad tugged at my coat tails. He looked up at me. I recognised him. It was Dick Triphook's son. And at once I realised that even among the crowds of the town that bairn had found me. So much for the cloak of the Cloth!

"Me Daa' says that you're not t' come t' the house… There's a man, some sort of soldier, he says, waitin' there now… he's been askin' about y'."

Chapter Thirteen

Down every bone in my spinal vertibrae I felt the slow sweating trickle of my own cold fear. And as it fell it drew itself together into a knotted fist that seemed to reach far through from my spine to grip tight at my bowels. A powerful urge to cut and run plucked at my limbs. Almost I twitched. Yet at the same time all my years of experience were shrieking at me.

'Calm yourself, man! H'aad y'r watter! This could be no more than a momentary spasm of simple line-o'-battle fear. I'd known it before; doubtless I would know it again. What I needed most to fettle the mood was nothing more than a decent night's sleep in a soft bed. Nonetheless the little lad's early forewarning had smitten me hard. What I really needed to do at that moment was to flee away from Newcastle, from the damned country altogether.

"A festering pox fall on Major flaming Farquahar! May the good Lord hurl the rogue down to the hottest hobs o' Hell!" A curse of my father's escaped my lips. Unfortunately its utterance struck the ears of a lady who with her maid was looking at the lace displayed in a shop window. Two pairs of eyes widened. Yet only the servant gave a little cry of shocked alarm. With a face like stone I doffed my clergyman's shovel hat to them both and hurried on.

This, I admonished myself sharply, would not do! How could I be expected to uncover the gang which had already bled millions of pounds of the country's coined gold away to her enemies. The more so when I myself had this great slobbering hound Farquahar snarling at my backside? To be effective as an agent a man needs to be to at his ease. I could hardly be a hunter and yet be hunted myself!

Suddenly I was filling my lungs, breathing, clearing away the smell of crowded humanity that came gusting at me on the breeze. I struggled to will all my numbing fears to flow around me, over me, through me. Then quite suddenly the spasm was gone, past, and I was cursing myself again for a damned fool. And then too I knew that I would not run. I was reminded that I still had access to a power to which I could appeal. Against an alarm such as this surely The British Linen Bank in Edinburgh must have the influence, power sufficient to clip short Farquahar's wings! At least now that the major had been actually seen in Newcastle it would be prudent and proper just to let Richard Grainger know now exactly how things stood. That was something I would do as soon as I could. Surely, I told myself, the fellow owed me that much.

As I drew another slow breath I reminded myself once more that whatever notional power his military rank might give him Farquehar would still have to present a civil court with strong evidence. And that was what he would have to get before he was ever likely to persuade the town's magistrates to detain me - that much at least, in whatever guise I was taken. Then I had to stifle a laugh. I was looking down at myself and I remembered. Recent realities were thrusting themselves at me. And the jab of those facts was painfully sharp. How the Hell could I be Mr.Egerton Keir any longer! All that cleverly fabricated identity, all those carefully assembled documents that maintained the same old lie were gone. D'Oeuys and the late Matthew Crowley had stripped more from me than my fine clothes. Now I was wearing the black broadcloth and plain Geneva bands of a non-conformist preacher. Though surely, dressed as I was, I would pass without remark in most parts of the three kingdoms. It was not however a disguise that I would care to risk on Major George Ninnian Farquahar. Moving with the flow of the crowd I began to drift towards my lodging.

It was one of Newcastle's market days. Markets are much the same wherever you go. Beasts for slaughter were being driven into the city. Folk must eat. But now the streets were crowded, milling, tight packed with country people. Stall-fattened bullocks, small flocks of winter thin sheep, geese, carts piled high with baskets full of live fowl were being driven all together up towards the town's Flesh Market. It is an easy place for a man to lose himself in.

Then from behind me, somewhere higher up on the Westgate Hill, I heard a long roll of drums and the crash of cymbals. There was a silence. Then the air shivered again under the brazen blare of a military band. Folk stopped, their heads turning towards the fanfare. That gave me the excuse I needed. I too, along with hundreds of other folk stopped and stood to gawp by the road's edge.

For in that winter of 1815 much of the city's garrison was drawn from the men of the North Yorkshire Regiment – the Black Cuffs. I watched. The cover that the band's appearance provided at that moment was surely a Godsend to me. For nothing draws a crowd like a military band. The drums beat out their quick-march behind a bandmaster who truly was as fat as Granny Brewis's pig. Behind him with their long bayonets gleaming marched the scarlet-coated infantry. Those were dapper lads. Their cross belts were fresh whitened with pipeclay; their shako badges glistened bright. But then at the tail of the column I recognised a squad of quite another kind. It was their new issued accoutrements that betrayed them. These fellows were veterans. Their hard-bitten faces marked them apart from young recruits fresh from the plough's tail. I'd seen such fellows before. This was what colonel's of regiments were pleased to call 'the leavening'. Every army in Europe carries a company or two of such bastards. These were the iron hard fellows who without a thought would thrust their bayonet deep into a striking keelman's belly. These troops wouldn't be sent to Canada to fight the Yankees. No; these dogs were the licenced felons. Yet, as I reminded myself, all this was just another part of the machinery of State. These rogues would be kept at home to maintain the King's Peace. It was a minor matter - but some alderman had heeded the nod and arranged for it. Extra rum was all it would cost. The English gentry would not easily forget what had happened in France in 1793. Over port and walnuts in the mansions of the upper town the presence of these brutes would be coyly referred to as the 'need to maintain decent civil order'. Napoleon too used such men.

The last of the Black Cuffs marched by me. At their passing I lifted my eyes piously on high and raised my hand in a supposed non-Conformist benediction. To passers-by I must have looked to be a loyal minister praying for a Divine blessing for the arms of His Majesty's soldiers. The same pose also allowed me to watch the windows across the street. But then my mock piety was interrupted. One of the mounted officers bringing up the rear raised a hand smartly to salute a young Miss in the crowd. It was the prettiest thing to see. The lass fluttered her eyes. Demurely she dropped a slow curtsey. That same moment however the drunken old biddie behind me dropped her bottle. There was the crash of glass on cobbles followed by gasp of disbelief. That cry gurgled into a plaintive shriek. A spilled pint of Muir's Best Newcastle Gin was burning its way into the trampled snow. And of course the harpie's filthy blasphemies were heartily cheered on by her bottle-kin. There and then there was damned near a riot! The drunken roar made the officer's charger to give a frightened tittup. That drew sharp squeals of alarm from the massed watchers. The crowd began press backwards. It was then that across the street I saw Dick Triphook swing open the front door. His face was creased up into a real turd-chewer's grin. Truly that look would have done credit to a Dijon lawyer. And at that very moment Farquahar chose to look across to where I stood.

God Almighty, how I blessed that preacher's black shovel hat. It was that – I was convinced of it - saved me. With my head down I could hope that the brim hid my face. Yet I had been ready for him. I'd picked the place where the crowd was gathered thickest. At the bastard's first yell I had been ready to launch myself forward with a desperate shout of 'Why that scoundrel has stolen my watch!' A crowd will always turn, milling inwards to follow where a fleeing man runs. And that always hinders pursuit.

But there was no challenge. When I dared to look up I saw Farquehar spin a shilling at Dick. As he pulled on his gloves I saw the Major smile. Something he'd heard had made Farquahar look uncommon pleased with him self.

But a little curiosity is a much more dangerous thing than a little knowledge. Quickly I bent my neck again so that my face was hidden. As though I too were being forced to yield to the crowd I allowed myself to sink backwards into the press of bodies. It was only then that I saw that the little lad who had brought me the warning was watching me. Without a word passing between us the offer was made. And I understood it. I tapped my nose with a finger and squinted sidelong at the lad. I knew then that Farquahar and his two bullies would be followed wherever they went.

Dick paled with alarm when he recognised me. I put up my hand to shield my face as I eased my way past him and in through the door. Then I heard him chortle. He shot home the bolts behind us.

"Eeee... Mr! B' God, Sir, you fooled me there... for a minute or two." In spite of the grin that twisted Dick's face I could see that Farquahar's visit had frightened the man badly.

"Tell me exactly what 's what, Dick!" I raised an eyebrow at him. "Tell me every damned thing that the bastard said from the first rap on the door onward. Try to remember. A man's neck may well depend upon it!"

Suddenly I was exhausted. I slumped down into a chair and held out a glass for Dick to fill. His visitors had been good enough to accept a hospitable dram. Good servant that he was he had even broached a bottle of his master's brandy for them. Though I could well guess that it was likely to have been Jottie

Stokoe's standing instruction for his servant to get drink into any strangers who called with enquiries.

"Major George Ninnian Farquahar wi' a special warrant to arrest some fellow called Eggerton Keir..." As soon as I had heard the word warrant I was prepared for what followed. When I held out my glass and raised my eyes to Dick Triphook I think I must have had the look of a martyred saint on my face. But nonetheless this was news that I would have to think about carefully. Farquahar must also have braved a savage winter coach journey. He had travelled all the way up to Tyneside to serve a warrant, not on Dr. Robert Shafto but on Eggerton Keir. That meant that he knew a deal more than I had realised. Someone, it told me, had to be paying for all this. Law officers seldom lay out ready cash. And whoever it was must surely have been able to name Eggerton Keir - directly. Few people, damned few, should even have known of the identity created for me.

Squires Taylor I think I still trusted. Richard Grainger surely was unlikely to betray his own man. Why create a new persona only to betray it? Yet, for certain, somewhere our pot had to have a leak in it!

"And the two bruisers with him?" Now Dick's face lit. Here he knew the tale.

"Both of them are good Gateshead lads!" The man's pride was plain to see. "Lemuel and Salathiel Coneybeare...twins they are, like as two peas in a pod. Fist fighters the pair o' them are." Dick took up the stance of the pugilist. He waved his knuckles in the air.

"Champions, both, they are, sir. They've been hired at a sovereign a day by this army chap to bide close by him and keep their maulies handy while he's in the city."

So Farquahar wasn't on such safe ground that he could afford to walk Newcastle's streets unguarded. That wasn't at all his style. But the news was welcome. Nonetheless I would still have to be careful. I could not allow Farquahar to get his hands on me.

"Aah have given the gallant major a couple or three names o' knowin' sorts of chaps he should be sure to look up along the Quayside. When he asks to speak to any one of those names there'll be plenty of clever lads down there'll be all ready to take his money and lead him a right dance. It's a wee ploy Mr. Stokoe has had set up to fettle such nosy chaps."

"But what was Farquahar doing here? How did the bugger know to come to this address?"

"That's something aa'h was wondrin' m'self…Sir."

I made up my mind. Now I surely would have to have words with Richard Grainger. He was going to have to stir himself. The Edinburgh Bank itself would have to use its influence to get Farquahar off my back. But how exactly I was going to communicate with Grainger I did not know.

"I'll have to go out again, at once." I drained my glass. "There's a man I'll have to make this business known to. I'll not be long, Dick."

The coaching office was quiet so that I was able to trace Jackie Nesbitt's snores to a bench beside the iron stove. He was awake and alert at first touch.

"Where the Hell ha' y' been, Mister?" I was pleased to see that for a few seconds the man had not recognised me at all. "There's been a lady here, a proper lady… in a carriage, seekin' you. She's been here three times already today. Here's the note she left for you!"

I spalled off the wax seal with my thumbnail and opened the folded note. As I read the few lines I found myself smiling – as who would not?

"Dear Mr. Keir,
Be so kind as to wait upon me at the Quayside landing place of the steam-vessel Perseverence – tomorrow morning, Wednesday, at 10 o'clock.

Mrs. Rachel Brydon

Chapter Fourteen

That morning there was a spring to my step. I could feel it. As I hurried on my way down the Tuthill Stairs I took a deep breath, filling my lungs with what passes for fresh air up in our Black Indies. It was mornings such as these that I remembered so very well. The banked fog that was swelling up below me would rise like new kneaded dough. Yes, soon enough too, it would thicken. By noon it would be as though a roof of glass had been drawn over the valley of the Tyne. Beneath that roof the coal smoke from Newcastle's thousands of hearths, not to speak of the chimneys of hundreds of vitriol works, soap boilers and alum houses, would lie trapped under it. Then like some drunken old granny huddled under her dirty blanket - the city would begin to choke on its own *efflatus*! Though to be sure, the old bitch was used to it. For once I found myself strangely elated. Another meeting with the beautiful Mrs. Rachel Brydon was surely something to look forward to.

While I stood waiting at the quay's edge I listened as the most tardy of the town's church clocks chimed out the hour. I clicked open the case of my watch. It wanted but a few minutes to ten o'clock. I was on time. In front of me by the jetty's edge a chalked board announced that the steam vessel *Perseverance* was due on the hour.

And while I waited I could not help seeing the sidelong glances I got from the young washer lasses hurrying by me with their baskets on their heads. I found myself smiling idiotically. Indeed I was quite unable to curb the twist that had got into the side of my mouth. For, it was certain sure, that those lasses had looked at me as a natural man and not a cleric. At that moment too I think I fancied myself to be quite the most dapper non-conformist minister who'd ever walked the Newcastle Quayside. And, to be sure, hadn't I a good right to my pride? I'd taken a great deal of care that it should be so. My broadcloth had been carefully brushed, my linen was fresh ironed; though by noon I knew it would be filthy with smoke grime. Dick Triphook had shaved me close. And, bless the fellow, he had waxed a gloss on to my boots that would have been the envy of any London dandy. But better than that I'd slept long and warm - and breakfasted well. So I was in better fettle than I had been for a long time. A copy of the Testament tucked firmly under my arm had been a last minute touch of Dick's. Truly that morning Bob Shaftoe felt like the Lord's own messenger.

But I was far from alone on the quay. Already there were some dozens of folk waiting to travel down river aboard the *Perseverance*. For in the year 1815 a steam vessel was one of the wonders of the age. From their fustian jackets and the tool bags they carried I saw that most of the morning passengers were craftsmen. These lads had not been slow to grasp the advantages the new steamboat offered. It spared their legs and carried them down to their work quickly – and they could work farther afield. But there were others: visiting gentry. That too was plain. For a while I stood listening to their host's impromptu lecture:

"With the tide behind her, ladies, she'll come up from Shields to Newcastle in less than *one* hour!"

The steamship, I learned, had been built just across the river at Gateshead and launched the year before in the February of 1814.

We had not long to wait. Though we all of us both heard and smelled the *Perseverance* well before we saw her. The steady threshing of paddle wheels echoed back from under the arches of the Bridge. Then the smell of the machinery came to us. I sniffed at heated metal and warm oil. The rotten-egg reek of quenched ashes had the young ladies twisting their faces at one another in distaste. We all, as I knew only too well, might as well get used to it - for this was the smell of the New Age that men spoke of. A thrill of excitement rippled through the crowd. The steamboat loomed up at us out of the fog.

But I must say that at first sight the vessel looked to me like nothing so much as a haywain afire! But by God she did move - and that, I could see, comfortably *against* both tide and current. There was a smart briskness too about the way the vessel was steered alongside the quay's timbers. Nor, as I was also soon to see, was there any doubt that this *Perseverance* was being run stage-to-stage like any mail coach on the land. At the gangplank's head a ruddy faced fellow in a blue coat with brass buttons stood waiting - his hand was out. Already the leather satchel that hung from his shoulder was sag-bellied from the weight of coin he had collected. I was the last passenger to step aboard.

For a few moments I had the thought that I was to be disappointed. On the open deck there was no sight of Rachel Brydon. But then when I turned about she stepped out of a cloud of steam and was before me. Beautiful as ever she was and – draped about with a black pelisse of *Gross de Milano*. Why was it, I wondered, that I should still think of Rachel Brydon as the Dark Widow?

Damn it all but I should have known better than to entertain such thoughts. Yet at that moment I felt myself gulp like any shy young schoolboy. She was dressed with the simplicity that only plentiful money spent without stint can buy. At once however the grey eyes flashed. The lift of those dark eyebrows was a signal to me. Slowly she took a hand from her huge sable muff. She raised her forearm across her bosom, touched her lips and then pointed the outstretched finger directly back over her shoulder. Rachel Brydon did not wish to be greeted.

So it remained that all the way down the river to Wallsend. I moved slowly among the passengers who were now packed aboard the steamship. All the whiles too I took good care to avoid Mrs Brydon. Though I must own that somehow I felt desperately cheated! However it took me no time at all to pick out the fellow who was following her.

It was not difficult. Indeed by simple default I could hardly have missed the stoat faced little snot. No other passenger aboard could so well have fitted the bill. He was a common taproom-idler. That he was out in broad daylight at all was almost proof enough. Once, the clothes on his back had been decent. Though, not a stitch of them fitted either his body or his class. Now every rag was filthy. The front of what had once been a good velveteen weskit was glazed shiny from the wipe of his greasy fingers. If ever I had seen it then surely this man was gaol bait!

I watched him. Not one of the craftsman who sat clustered aft, smoking their clay pipes, returned his over-hearty "What-cheer, m' lads?" And of course he kept himself well away from the better-off folk who were now standing well forward. Soon enough they'd been driven there. Already their silks and fine cashmere shawls were showing the greasy smuts of soot that tumbled like black snowflakes from the smoke belching out of the steamer's funnel.

Even on short inspection it was soon clear to me that the stoat faced tout had been hired a'-sudden for the job. Whatever his regular business was clearly _this_ wasn't it! There was a distinct want of ease in the fellow's manner. He was too active. Someone had simply paid him to follow Rachel Brydon. And I knew too that whoever they were they would get no more for their money than a bald report that told of every step she had taken, but just that – and nothing more. It takes experience to know what it is you're seeing… and what you might do about it!

Indeed so intent had I been on keeping an eye on the fellow that I did not hear the stout old man as he came up behind me and leaned on the rail. To get my attention he had spat noisily over the side. When I looked at him he cocked an eye and shifted his quid of chewing tobacco to the other side of his mouth. Before he spoke he paused to wipe away a trickle of brown juice.

"Mistress's compliment's, sir..." He sniffed noisily. "She says that if you would be good enough to step ashore at the Wallsend Landing... I'm to take good care o' yon chap!" It was only then that I saw that under his plain greatcoat of heavy *fearnaught* cloth the old fellow was in coachman's livery.

A few moments later I was trying to do as I had been bidden. When I moved down the gangplank however I found myself being borne along among the brown fustians and corduroys of the crowding artificers. I had taken no more than a few steps before I realised that among these fellows my black coat and white bands gave me some respect. Caps were touched to me as the men hurried by. I smiled and mouthed what might have been a blessing for the day. By God that was a damned odd feeling... even for Bob Shaftoe.

A dark green carriage waited on the bank's side above the wharf. The young footman who held the horses' heads saw me coming. He nodded for me get in. But I was not to be alone. A maid in a black straw bonnet and a dark grey cape was sitting there. I recognised her. She was young Mary Dolan . I remembered that she was from Limerick. At sight of me she blinked, raised a finger as though to point, then touched her lips. She was amazed.

"Yes, Mary… it is me…to be sure it is." I brogued at her and she dimpled a little smile. So that was it. The maid had been brought along to defend Rachel Brydon's reputation. And very proper too!

For perhaps two further minutes I was allowed the comfort of cordovan upholstery. Then with the mischief still on her face Rachel Brydon was handed up into the carriage. Again she was a girl: a young Miss who was trying hard not to laugh at a prank played.

"There will be a short delay, er..." She put a hand to her cheek...*Reverend*. My coachman, Joe Skinner is helping see to a poor fellow who sadly has just pitched himself headlong down some stairs aboard the steamboat..." As she spoke the carriage went well down on its springs. Joe Skinner it seemed had been every bit as good as his word. We moved off. "That wretched fellow has been following me about the city since yesterday. Partly this morning's trip has been to devise a way to shed that odious little man..." Just in time I smothered an old French proverb about lice not living in clean shirts.

"And have you been able to throw off the woman too, the limping washerwoman who was following you? Of course it was a lie, a mere fabrication to irritate the girl. "It seemed to me that the stoat faced fellow was moving about too much, making himself just too easy to see." I kept my face straight and at once I was rewarded for it. Rachel Brydon gave a little flounce. With a gloved hand she wiped at the misting on the glass and looked out of the carriage window.

Now while I must own that I had gone aboard the *Perseverence* eager to meet the widow Brydon again, I had also told myself that after all she was but a woman. And I had known dozens of women all over Europe. Years since I had ascertained for myself that save what their petticoats are made from there is scant difference betwixt noble and common. If nothing else the Revolution had showed that much - a thousand times over. But now that I was brought sharp to it I found myself keeping matters between us entirely formal. Of course it was simple failure of Will – nothing more! And I knew it. The whole of Polite Society stood firmly between Rachel Brydon and me. And I was, I reminded myself sharply, a man who lay under present threat of arrest as a traitor. Doctor Robert Shafto was still a hostage to Fortune.

My verbal report was delivered to her with all the care that I would have taken had I been standing before Talaeus Dekker himself. And save for not mentioning Ettie Bellis by name I told Rachel Brydon everything. Truly, beyond that, I withheld nothing at all from her. Some might even say that perhaps I had rather *spared* the lady nothing.

Nonetheless Mrs. Brydon listened attentively. She began to take notes, writing with a silver pencil on an ivory tablet. Sometimes she nodded; sometimes too I saw that what I had said struck a chord with her.

"Be assured," She murmured, "I will certainly see to it that Richard Grainger does something about that wretched man, Major Farquahar...and that very soon!" As she made that promise she smiled. "But now there is important work for you, Mr?" Her gaze scanned slowly up and down my preacher's black.

"These clothes belonged to a Mr. Aycliffe, a clergyman... er... now sadly," I paused and gestured heavenwards with a hand. "Gone to his Reward..." Rachel Brydon was not inclined to question me further on *this* particular matter.

"While I think on..." She was ready to discuss business. "It would be better, Doctor, indeed safer for us if for the next few moments our discourse were in French..." Her grey eyes flicked sharply at Mary Dolan. I nodded my approval.

"Your information about strong local sentiment against the gentleman who manages the Grand Lottery was of interest to us all... and also to our superiors in Edinburgh." As I had noted before Rachel Brydon's French was good, indeed almost good enough. It was clear that from an early age she had enjoyed the attentions of a French governess. To be sure her syntax was perhaps a little over-punctilious for a native speaker.

I sat up, bracing myself against the roll of the carriage. "Yes," I said quietly, "...the prizes he pays out are certainly corrupting the city's servant girls." I glanced across at Mary Dolan. "But more to the point the Grand Lottery is sucking gold coin out of the area. More than that fresh gold must always to be brought in quickly from elsewhere to replace it. Coal-hewers who sweat for their wages in narrow seams don't care to be paid in banker's paper." Rachel Brydon nodded slowly. It was something she had not thought of.

"However, all that our immediate enquiry indicates is that George Humble is a very astute fellow... indeed it seems that his fortune has quite doubled in the last three years. That original wealth he *married* - only five years ago. However, what we have also been able to discover is that he keeps the company of certain other gentlemen who *themselves* have recently come under our notice." Without warning she began to speak English again. "So much so that it has been decided that *you...*" She looked down at the ivory tablet." *Mr Wilfred Nettles*, are to take service as Humble's valet."

Now, and as demure-seeming as any convent novice, Mrs. Brydon was looking at me from under her eyelashes.

So my new role was to be that of Wilfie Nettles, a gentleman's valet. I waited, keeping my face clear of any expression that might be taken as either yea or a nay. For whether I liked it or not I knew I would have to do as I was directed.

"I... that is *we* have put ourselves to some trouble to secure this appointment for you. The position was first advertised in the Newcastle newspapers. One of Richard's clerks picked it up. On your behalf that young man has been in correspondence with a *Mrs.* Flavia Humble. Indeed in a number of ways we have all been very active on your behalf these last days: the *lady* of the house expects to receive you at Higham Place at a little before eleven o'clock tomorrow morning." Rachel Brydon handed me a sheaf of papers. They were copies of all the letters that were supposed to have passed between *Mrs* Flavia Humble and Nettles the unemployed valet. Madame, it was plain from the letters, took to herself the hiring of all the household servants.

I would, I read, be 'treated with consideration in all appropriate respects'. Now *that* was truly as grim a phrase as any fellow could ever wish to read – no matter in what language! More particularly I would be required to 'ensure that your master was at all times presented to the world in a proper and gentlemanly fashion'. Well that was something that I ought to be able to do!

Nonetheless I had to admire someone's efficiency. Again the Bank was providing me with an entirely new identity. And for sure I was supplied with the most impressive references. Though, Rachel Brydon was close to a smirk as she handed me the testimonial which read that I had been second-valet to a Marquis.

"From what we have learned of Mrs. Humble, that reference alone ought to secure the position for you. The lady has… ambitions."

While we talked the carriage took us back along the road to Newcastle. It took us a deal longer than had our trip together on the *Perseverance*.

The town house in Higham Place looked pleasant enough as we drove past it. I suppose it ought to have been. It was well within what amounted to the city's *enclave*. These were the streets where the town's quality resided. There were no fences or palings to mark off its limits, but beyond certain corners and street ends a man might just notice that he not bothered by beggars; and that few drunks ever strayed there. This was where little lads with heather besoms kept the pavements and road crossings well swept of snow. Here was a place where the horse droppings were shovelled up before they could cool on the cobbles. This was genteel Newcastle. This was where the Money lived.

Mrs. Brydon's carriage stopped to set me down at the corner of George Street. There was the chink of coin. "Here are sufficient funds to buy whatever you need to present yourself convincingly for the work." My hand closed on a leather bag. "Do what you have to do…Doctor Shafto, but don't be there longer than you need. Three days at the most should be time enough for you to learn whether George Humble is our man."

"I expect to be somewhat active, Mrs. Brydon." I looked directly into her dark eyes. "That means that I may have to leave

George Humble's house without ceremony... in something of a hurry." What I was saying was dawning on the girl. I pressed my point; though it was a greatly exaggerated one. "And it may even be that there will be those there who will be trying very strenuously to...detain me." I cocked a quizzical eyebrow at her. "My dear, if there are any cries for the town's night watch to come out at the run, then it surely will be *me* who is being chased... "

It was plain that such an eventuality had not even occurred to her. "For that reason I shall of course need to have two reliable fellows, one at the front and one at the back – unobtrusively. They must of course be there all night and all day."

She gave me no excuse to linger. I had been given my orders. However, the beautiful Mrs. Brydon was not *quite* done with me. As I stepped down past the footman he coughed and hefted to me a hide trunk studded with brass nails. There were the beginnings of a grin on the dog's chops. I wiped it off with a sharp glance. "This man will do very nicely... for the night's middle watch." I called lightly over my shoulder.

"Oh, Mr... Nettles" Rachel faltered. "Please do try to bring those things away with you when you... when you leave." She called from within the carriage where I could not see her face. "I have had to borrow the full *equipage* of a quite excellent valet... Richard's man." This time I had no doubt: the minx was laughing at me.

However, I had a day to spare before I faced Mrs. Humble. It was time to visit my outposts, my own people. I needed badly to speak to Jacob Storey. Anything that was known at all about the Humble household he doubtless would know it. Or he could soon find someone who did. What Rachel Brydon had told me could only be a start. I would need to know a damned sight more if this mission was to be profitable. Besides which, and I will own it freely, the state of young Ettie Bellis's health had crossed my mind more than once.

First I would steal the time to visit Mrs. Bell's cumdum factory. The oddity of that idea brought a smile to my lips. On my way down through the Groat Market I bought a basket, a fine strong osier basket. Into it I put three bottles of Canarie wine and two dozen of new-laid eggs. These I told myself would mix to a good restorative for young Ettie. Only as an afterthought did I add a half bottle of rum. Then my nose dragged me into Yellowley's cook-shop. There I called for a good parcel of beef to be sliced straight off the spit. In the same shop I had the oven man fill me a stoneware pot with the rich brown drippings from his sizzling meat trays. That would be the stuff to put a gloss on the little faces of Eadie Bell's bairns. As I walked down past Amen Corner it occurred to me: I must really have looked like a curate bearing a charitable basket of comforts to the needy of his flock. Three stray dogs followed me every foot of the way.

Stone cold sober and with his bruised face ripening lushly Jacob Storey was a terrible sight to behold. More than that, the old bastard was sitting under the jaundiced eye of Big Eadie Bell. Here Poor Jacob was a man brought at last to a full knowledge of his sins. When I stepped into that room he looked up at me from the fireside as though I were the Saviour come. I was not. He got a single short tot of rum as a stir-y'r-heart. And that was all.

"Who I want to know about, Jacob, are the Humbles of Higham Place... *all* about them, especially *him*!" The battered face licked its split lips and brightened.

"Well..." He began." She's an Errington from Warkworth way. *Her* money came off a great aunt who was distantly related to the Delavals. Now... *that* lady was sadly crossed-in-love... in the year 1780 that was..." Storey was relishing his tale like any old hen-wife on her doorstep. Nor was there any doubt that Jacob knew the whole history of Mrs. Flavia Humble's side of the family. But for all his store of gossip it was clear that the old villain knew little enough about George Humble himself. That man was still a mystery.

"Get out and about, Jacob... Find out more" I spun a half sovereign in the air and then handed it to Eadie Bell. It was a cruel trick I know but I needed to keep my hound both hungry and cold sober.

Eadie however would let me take no more than a peep at young Ettie. She was asleep on a truckle bed with a patchwork quilt over her. In daylight there was no doubt that the poor lass was a badly trodden blossom. After the beating she had taken she was lucky to be alive. She would need care, yet there were already a few signs that she would mend. But a single glance was what Eadie Bell had said - and that was what the woman meant. The hand that drew me back from the frieze curtain did it with an ease that would not be easily resisted. But then I knew too that Eadie had a purpose of her own. Her grip held firm.

"Was it you?" Her whisper hissed at me like a scythe blade along a whetstone. "Did 'y? Now the woman was intense, bright eyed. But still I could not understand what she was asking. Then it came: "Was it you who cut Mattie Crowley's throat the other night?" She was so eager to know. With pinched lips and a slow, grave shake of my head I denied it. But I might have saved my breath. For then Eadie Bell smiled like sunshine and patted my cheek as though I had been a bairn who had recited his catechism without fault. I knew then that nothing I could have said would ever have convinced her otherwise. An old score had been settled and Bob Shafto was drawing full credit for it.

Many times in my career have I had occasion to be thankful that I had never been *obliged* to be a work-a-day servant in another man's household. Always, and no matter what lowly station I had occupied I had always had that inner smirk of confidence that an Emperor's commission bestows. Nonetheless, eleven o'clock sharp the next morning found me knocking at the servants' entrance of the house in Higham Place.

Chapter Fifteen

That I was expected was plain enough. But from the moment his eyes lit upon me I could see that the Humble's butler was a fellow far from best pleased. With a practised sneer gathering slowly over his narrow face that old snot gobbler looked me up and down. It's in the nature of things that an upper servant will always try to put down a new comer into the establishment. But then I saw that this sour greeting of his was only towards me. To the young lad squeezing past us into the yard the old rogue's face changed at once. It was like warm sunlight glancing across a summer's meadow.

"The mistress says aa'm tae take the dog for its walk, Mr. Wanless…" The young servant's speech was light and pleasant. He would be I guessed about fifteen and he stood all trim and slim in his new undress livery. And at once I was cued to all the signs. Here there was no mistaking any of them at all.

"Oh, aye, yes … you do that m' bonny lad!" It was as though Wilfred Nettles had never existed. Seldom indeed does an agent get such a gift! The cause of the butler's mooncalf gaze after that young footman was beyond any doubt. Certain sure: the old fellow was besotted! No lover could have looked after his lass the way that old sodomite gazed after young Alexander. All my experience was telling me that whatever future he might have planned for himself this fresh-faced youngster himself was going to have damn all say at all in the matter. That poor little fellow's doom, I fancied, was set! Already his choice lay between, for a young servant, a pampered life, or, if he were as wholesome a bairn as his parents would have wished, a veritable Hell on this Earth. At best I could only hope that the lad was a born-to-it Ganymede!

But, as I reminded myself, before English law Wanless's tastes were still a hanging matter. Even in France we had sniggered and hooted at the cases printed in the London newspapers. I smiled. So here, even before I had fairly arrived at Higham Place, this Isaac Wanless was a gift in my hands. Soon enough, I knew, his appetites would betray him - and for sure if I had cause to I would use that squalid fact to my profit. In my work such things as this had to be mere grist to my mill.

But the kitchen maids and the cook addressed him as *Mr. Wanless*. So if I were to be employed here I too would need to remember my place. He however, dirty bastard that he was, did not see fit to introduce me to the other servants as other than: "This here's the chap what wants to be the new valet." I followed him up the backstairs to see Mrs. Humble.

It has been said that the eyes are the windows into the soul. In Mrs. Flavia Humble the blinds were drawn close. There truly was little natural animation in the woman at all. What little outward show was there was, truly, was counterfeit. That very morning the woman had had her hair coiffeured. I could smell the scorch of the hot curling tongs on her. The dress she wore had come direct from Paris. But that could scarce amend the fact that the poor woman had a face that was as plain as the bottom of a chamber pot. While on that same face a childhood attack of the common small pox had left its mark. On both her cheeks there was a spangle of pocks. Though, her visitation had been mercifully light. White lead and talc did a lot to hide her marring - but even that would not completely cover the scars. I stood before her and bowed from the waist. And as I inclined my head it occurred to me that perhaps George Humble had taken a pretty penny to marry poor Miss Flavia.

But if the Almighty had seen fit to afflict the woman in her face He had at least left her a sweet voice. The soft roll of her Northumbrian r's was combined with a slight lisp to bestow upon her voice a charm all of its own. I remembered too that Jacob Storey had told me that she was an Errington.

"Well, Nettles, you have expressed a desire to be considered for the position of my husband's valet..."

From beginning to end every word of our dialogue - on both sides – had been lifted, entire, from pages of *The Lady's Polite Repository*. And to be sure our Mrs. Humble had learned her part very well indeed. I had long known mine. Within twenty minutes she announced that "I am inclined, Nettles, to give you a month's trial..."

Nor was there any doubt that Mrs. Brydon's prediction had been right. It had been the forged letter of reference from a marquis that did it. Flavia Humble read the crest headed sheet twice while I stood before her. With a bow that would have passed muster at the Palace of Versailles, I accepted: "Thank you, mad'aaam... I hope that I shall always give perfect satisfaction!" Very graciously *madame* also inclined her head, a little.

From the outset and above all else a valet needs to make an impression on his master. Like few other servants he will be wise if he quickly becomes his employer's *confidant*. That is the one thing he must do without fail.

Within the hour my trunk and valise were delivered to the back door of the house in Higham Place. Joe Skinner was driving the cart.

"As you asked, Sir, there'll be a man at both front and the back... day and night."

"There's a young footman..." I wanted information about the object of the butler's passions.

"Aye, yon bonny butterfly 's out takin' the woman's little spaniel to have its shite on the green..." Joe Fletcher was matter o' fact but it showed me that he had been alert to all that was going on!

"Scrape acquaintance with the lad, Joe... listen to what his crack is about. Find out for me how he thinks he stands with the butler here. I winked at Joe. My investigations had started!

I had three hours of daylight to go through George Humble's wardrobes and cupboards. From even first appearances the man was certainly no dandy. His clothes were well enough made and the materials were of the best; but both the style and cut were barely second rate. As a cover and to give a first impression of honest industry I laid out all of Humble's outdoor clothes and began to search through them very carefully.

"So you're Nettles are you?" I had heard him on the stairs and when he appeared in the doorway I was busy brushing the velvet lapels of a dark grey shooting coat. I bowed to him, slightly. "Mr Humble, Sir..." I got no further.

"Just make yourself busy, Nettles; but you keep your hands off my women servants unless you've a mind to wed. Don't try to steal my cigars or my brandy. That's what the last fellow was loosed for! And don't you throw out so much as a rag without my express leave." He raised his voice. Now the whole house was meant to hear him. "But above all ... *Mr* Wilfie Nettles you take good care that you mind yourself with that sneaking, creeping shitehound, Wanless! Clear?" He was gone.

Damn my eyes but flying away with him went most of the suspicions I had held about the man. Almost. For at first sight this George Humble was as bluff a fellow as you could wish to meet. He was the sort of English chap I could like! Below me I heard Mrs. Humble call out his name. It was followed at once by a bang as the front door was slammed shut.

By the time that it was getting dark I had been through every stitch in Humble's wardrobes. I could find nothing, nothing at all that was untoward. At a little before five o'clock I lit a candle and stood before the window for a few moments. Across the street a face looked up at me. Joe Skinner grinned.

But as I had to remind myself a household servant's duties last from first rising until bedtime. There could be no going out into the town this night for Nettles the valet. That was not what respectable servants did. I had been promised a half day for walking out every other week. I heard myself sigh as I took out a dozen of my new master's fine dress shirts. The spirit lamp, the set of the tiny flat irons and crimping irons which I had found in the valet's chest were the tools of a master craftsman. I went down the backstairs to the kitchen. It was time to establish my credentials with the other servants.

I introduced myself first to the elderly cook. Mrs. Porritt would be my ally. That much I knew within minutes. She would be my friend because like her master she hated Wanless, the butler. From the way she glared at the back of the fellow's neck alone that had been easy to see. As I came in the old sod grunted, stood up, and left the kitchen. That was his right of course. A butler can be as sullen as ever he pleases with the other servants. It's always best to know where you stand.

The ironing of the frills on a gentleman's shirtfront to perfection is an art. Either you possess it, or you don't. So it was that under the admiring eyes of both Bains and Jeavons, the two maids, that I demonstrated my skills. It was a necessary exercise. For it was a safe guess that Mrs. Flavia Humble would lose no time in quizzing her servant girls about me. But then that gave me my chance. From the first hiss of the little silver smoothing iron I knew that so far as the other servants were concerned Wilfie Nettles was everything he claimed to be.

So it was that I almost forced myself to fall into the daily round of petty nit-pickery that defines the work of a valet in a gentleman's household. I was confident. What man who had satisfied the fastidious tastes of the Monsieur le Baron Peyrusse would not be? Apart from a careful attention to my master's clothes my other duties could always be somewhat loosely interpreted. What I had to remember was that it pays always to *look* busy. And of course I had to keep myself just a little remote from the other servants. Indeed to that end the valet's place at the servants' table had long been fixed by custom. In a gentleman's household the valet occupies a distinctive position.

He has always an appeal to his master's personal comfort. He can always get hot water upon demand! Beyond that… well it is a mean spirited fellow who lets himself be put upon! I reckoned that I was well worth the thirty pounds a year that had been agreed upon as my wages.

The valet's chest that Mrs. Brydon had supplied answered all my needs. The neat boxes and coloured bottles inside it had been refilled. I had Milanese soap wafers and perfumes from Provence; I had cachets, powders and even pastilles for the breath. With these I could send George Humble out entirely fitted to enter provincial Newcastle's scurrying little world. Certainly his linen would not have disgraced the Prince of Wales. So I settled in easily.

Of course there was curiosity. As I had expected there would be. Before my second day was over I knew that Wanless had been through my chest. I had left it unlocked for just that reason. A fine sprinkling of talc on the floor around it betrayed him.

However I soon began to collect intelligence. By the afternoon of that same second day I had been at Humble's dressing room with a stiff brush and a magnifying glass. If the man had been in any untoward places I would know of it! What I found on three of his suits of clothes were the fibres of common hemp. There was no mistaking that. At some recent time my employer had been in a rope-walk or in a warehouse that stored the stuff. It was something - I supposed.

However and all told George Humble was not at all a difficult man to satisfy. For the mornings I laid out what he ordered. And what he ordered, I knew, had always been determined beforehand by *madame*. For those few moments of the day when I had to shave and dress him he was almost silent. Once or twice he did ask me of my former employers. But these were obviously questions passed on from his wife. Without doubt Flavia Humble was indeed a lady very anxious to rise in Society. Wishing her well of it I even invented a few tales of the doings of the nobility. Nonetheless, throughout the whole business I moved myself with a canny caution. I made a good beginning too by preparing a pomatum for my master's thinning hair. Even Mrs. Humble herself was moved to ask what the pervading perfume in it was. Well she might! It was Richard Grainger's own and the label on the crystal vial declared that it had come from the shop of Daru in the *Rue Sainte Valerie.*

Nor did I forget how important it is to make yourself popular with your fellow servants. The first thing I learned was that George Humble himself had warned his servants that they would be dismissed upon the instant if any one of them bought so much as a shilling's share in any ticket of the Grand Lottery. But of course like servants everywhere they all loved a gamble. So it was not difficult to get myself a name for being a handy sort of chap – a fellow who knows his fighting cocks and his racing whippets. This served a double purpose. It made it easier for Joe Skinner to reach me. He put on a beaver hat and posed as one of the sporty old dodgers who turn up at the town's backdoors to take servant's bets. On my second morning at Higham Place I had made show of tucking a thin wedge of white bank notes into my coat. A wink and a grin was all it took. Within the hour Joe Fletcher was taking penny bets for the maids. Nor indeed did it take much guile between us to see to it that each day one or other of the lasses won enough to put a happy smile on her face.

But for all my efforts there was damn little I discovered that advanced my enquiries at Higham Place by so much as a hairsbreadth. Though as ever I learned much else. Mrs. Porritt confided to me that Isaac Wanless had started life as a gamekeeper up at Wark.

"He shot a lad, he did. It was for poachin', so *he* said! But from that day not a soul thereabouts would speak to the man… even poor folk wouldn't take the gift of a rabbit from him! In the end the family had to send him down here. That'll tell y'!" Indeed it did.

But all that the other servants could tell me was about George Humble was that their master managed the Grand Lottery from his office on Mosely Street. Yet my own wits alone told me how improbable it was that the man himself owned the enterprise. Even so it could hardly be that he did not know either the sole owner or any of the principal shareholders in the venture. But exactly who they were I would have to leave to Richard Grainger to find out for himself. His friends down at the Exchange who would surely tell him all he needed to know.

By the end of the second day I was already more than half convinced that I would find no trace of anything untoward. So far as Higham Place was concerned that was very much *that*. Mrs Brydon had been right. Moreover the truth of it all was that I was bored!

And indeed little at all happened until I had been an ornament to the establishment for four days.

It was the night of the thaw. With a crash that near took the back door from its hinges Wanless burst into the kitchen. There were six of us servants siting around the lamp after supper. We looked up startled. There was no doubt about it, the sour faced old bugger was blind, staggering drunk. More than that, from the state he was in he looked to have just tumbled headlong into the muck and slush of the back lane. He stood there in the doorway swaying, his clothes all slathered with filth. His bloodshot eyes glared about him. He had the look of a wild boar ready to charge. I recognised the signs. And that made me joyful! It really did. Here he was, just another sour old toss-pot looking for someone to hammer with his fists. That much I could see from the evil glint in his eye. And I told myself then that if this old bum fancier moved towards me I would fell him where he stood. That at least would serve to get me conveniently out of my employment at a minute's notice. For, suddenly, I had decided. This line of enquiry was yielding no results: the rat was a dead-un and I badly wanted to drop it.

"Isaac Wanless! Have you no shame? Man, you've disgraced yourself! Now get to your bed... directly!"

To my surprise it was Mrs. Humble. There was no doubting it: the woman was genuinely angry. And with her hair in curl papers that impression was oddly enhanced. But with her own bold Isaac, this woman was obviously holding back. Indeed for what might be expected of a mistress's dealings with her own servants, Flavia Humble was being damned forbearing!

"Nettles..." She turned to look at me. It was then I saw. The woman was as much frightened as she was angry. Her lower lip trembled. "Nettles! You will help Mr. Wanless up the stairs... He's been taken poorly. Get him to his bed!"

"Yes, ma'am..." I said obediently and with quite the straightest face in that kitchen. Nonetheless as I hoisted the old piss-bucket over my shoulder I put a wrestler's grip on him. At that moment I had decided that if the old fart gave me half an excuse I would smash his collarbone! Wanless was not going to get any chance to lash out at me. However, as I soon discovered, from the heft of his weight the man had to be more than three parts belly-wind. Under his clothes he was an over-boiled chicken carcass; there was scarce a picking on him.

It was only when I saw the tall dance of her shadow against the candlelight at the turn of the stairs that I realised that Mrs. Humble herself was following me up.

From the smell of Wanless it was gin he had been drinking. It was also quite the cheapest gin; it was the poisonous filth that the pitmen call 'Blue Jackie'. And damned well steeped in that muck he was. It was also my certain guess that come the morning this old sodomite would not be fit for his duties. I threw him on his bed and began to get him out of his soaking clothes.

"Take his keys, Nettles..." Mrs. Humble was standing close. She gave her order in a short clipped tone. "You'll be needed to wait up for the master tonight. Then you will have to lock up for the night as soon as Mr. Humble is safely home..." Suddenly I realised that I was being asked, not ordered. At that moment Flavia Humble had seen Wilfie Nettles as the only able bodied man in the house. And at that moment too I knew that l had I slipped into my role so well that I found myself thinking how easily it would be for a smart lad like me to work Wanless quite out of his place altogether!

"Yes, ma'am." I said smartly. This was the chance I had been waiting for.

Wilfie Nettles was left alone in charge of the house.

Mrs. Humble returned immediately down to the kitchen. From there and ringing clear up the stairwell I heard her orders. Everyone, even old Mrs. Porritt, the cook, was being ordered off to their beds. It was to be an early night for the folk at Higham Place. That is except of course for Nettles, the valet.

Now I had the household keys in my hands. Years before, in Strasbourg, I'd been taught by a master thief how to copy keys. However the question I was asking myself at that moment was would Humble be fool enough to keep any quantity of gold coin on his own premises. I could hardly believe that he would. But then old habits die very hard. It was odd, but at that that moment I found that at least one part of my mind was still in the Emperor's service.

In my pocket I had a sheet copper box. The box was packed with beeswax blended with fine china clay. It was a composition that the man at Strasbourg had found would always take and hold the sharpest of impressions. There were eleven keys on the ring: everything from the big front door key down to the tiny key to the kitchen tea caddy. Three however were obviously for the house's fine clocks. With great care I pressed the head of each remaining key into the wax. The trick with such things is not to warp your mould by handling it too much. Grainger would have to find a locksmith who asked no questions. Later that night I would pass that box out to one of Rachel Brydon's fellows. Every hour on the hour a man paused as he walked under the light of the post lamp that burned across the street.

It was when the ormolu clock in the dining room was chiming out midnight that I heard a loud tattoo on the door's knocker. There were voices. Boots were being scraped. I hurried downstairs.

Humble was surprised. Clearly my employer had been taken aback. As I stood aside for him he turned his head sharply to glance into my face. But, thank God, the gentlemen with him were talking to one another. As I took their hats I bowed my head and kept my neck bent. I was just a servant. They all brushed past me in the gloom. My master's guests were Monsieur Charles D'Oeuys and Dr. Severus Mudie. But both men I saw at once had stood aside and given precedence to the third guest. And there it took only the merest flicker of candlelight to tell me who that was. It was the fellow who in the carriage along the London Road had looked so close to death. It was the same intelligent fellow who had been identified to me as the honourable Arthur Hetherington .

When Humble had showed his guests into the parlour he returned and looked at me.

"Where is that slimy, key-hole peeping blackguard, Wanless?" The venom in his words was real.

"Taken very badly, I fear, Sir…" My voice was deeply hushed. I made it sound as though the Almighty Himself had taken to his bed. That however was all I could say before I saw that Humble's fat mouth had folded itself into a distinct expression of pleasure.

"Excellent!" He snarled. "Damned good! That's a piece of news to cap my night!" I proffered the bunched keys. He left them in my hand. " I have keys…Nettles. You get yourself off to bed, man!"

It came without warning. Dame Fortune had smiled upon me. And I suppose too that at that selfsame instant the same Goddess had begun to frown down darkly at the Grand Lottery's syndicate. I stood forward to relieve George Humble of his heavy coat. But to my surprise he actually resisted me, indeed he actually fended me off. "No, leave that; I'll see to m'self." His instruction had come out as a bark! Then as my master turned sharply away whatever he carried under the skirts of his coat nudged against my thigh. And it was a buffet with real weight to it! I knew. For what sound is there in this whole world that is quite like the chink of golden guineas in a leather sack! Even had there not been the creak of new leather I think that I should easily have guessed what it was. As the man walked away from me I saw his silhouette against the candlelight. The burden he carried swelled out his high waisted greatcoat. I couldn't help myself. I smiled. So, Geordie Humble had come home that night all harnessed up like a sutler's mule. Under his coat's skirts the man had to be carrying at least a thousand pounds. That one thought struck me like a blow. Christ! Were all four of them carrying sacks of gold?"

Chapter Sixteen

So after all - and rather easily at that - I had clapped eyes on what I had come to Higham Place to find. Moreover, now I could be pretty certain that both Talaeus Dekker and The British Linen Bank at Edinburgh would have to accept my testimony. Now, through their agency, the machinery of state would have to move. Official eyes would be turned to scrutinise the affairs of George Humble and his Grand Lottery. And, however discretely spoken, the words of that ancient magic spell 'In the name of the King' might safely be whispered. Among most folk in England those words were usually enough to loosen tongues. But with that, and I realised it at once, the traitor, Robert Shafto, might well find that he had suddenly reached the full extent of his usefulness. Perhaps!

But for the moment I reminded myself that I still had no actual evidence of crime. It was in no way unlawful for any man to possess so much gold coin, nor indeed a hundred times what had been in those bags. It was not even unlawful, if that were his whimsy, for Humble to carry his hoard about on his person. No, the law would only be broken if and when the man placed his guineas in the hold of any ship cleared to leave a British port. That and that only would be a clear felony! And of course the sum hanging harnessed about George Humble's waist would have to be but a tiny fraction of the whole hoard. Somewhere inside this ordinary Newcastle townhouse there might already be a hundred thousand golden guineas. That was a thought to dizzy a man. But nothing was surer to me now than that I had better start making shift for Bob Shafto's own continuing well being! The gratitude of princes was a goblet from which I had already supped!

Perhaps I should have left then. Probably I could simply have walked out into the street and been gone. But I did not. For by then the fatal clink of all that gold was ringing loud in my ears!

However, as I also reminded myself, at that same moment the whole house was listening. You may send your servants scurrying off to their beds like naughty bairns. But not even your servant lass on five pounds a year can be ordered off to dreamland. Above me in the attic's darkness I could sense them all lying there at the top of the house. Every one of them - except the drunken Wanless - would have their lugs cocked sharp. Tonight for sure the poor beggars would be giggling into their chaff filled pillows. And who could blame them? I smiled to myself. Disturbance must make for change! That night at least I would not be kept awake by the moans of mutual pleasuring from the maids, Sarah and young Effie. Nor, for once, should I be startled from my own sleep by the clatter of the chamber pot's lid from Mrs. Porritt's little room under the eaves. Tonight the servant's attic would be silent; like as not all its folk would fall asleep still listening.

As a good manservant should however I did look-in on Wanless. Though there would be no tears from me if the dirty bugger had choked on his own vomit. He was alive. And almost as a matter of course I found my fingers creeping their way through his soaked clothes. There was nothing save a crumpled letter. By the shielded light of my candle I read it. At once I knew the cause of the butler's disfavour with his master. Wanless had been a wedding gift who had come, or been sent, with the bride. He was, it seemed, Mrs. Flavia Humble's own servant, and all that would mean to a widespread family of canny landowners up in Northumberland. The Erringtons it seemed had never trusted their kinswoman's choice of a husband. It was a demand for more information about George Humble's expenditures. I noted the address. Richard Grainger would know how and where to make the proper enquiries.

I had been about to leave when I saw that the drawer in the bedside cupboard had a keyhole. That drawer was locked. But even on a second search I had found no key in Wanless's clothes. It was one of two he carried around his neck on a cord. Gently I slipped a hand under his head and lifted them. Shielding the candle flame's light with my body I went through the drawer. There was a bottle of malt whisky, opened, and a bundle of letters from someone who signed himself 'Pyramus'. I read just one of them. That was enough. Truly the twisted passions of some souls are beyond any understanding. That however is as may be. Yet without the leverage that such curiosities of human Love provided us with an agent's work would indeed be a damned difficult business! I pocketed the whole bundle. The second key opened the small trunk that lay under Wanless's bed. In England a household the servant's 'box' is almost all the privacy the poor creature is allowed. Though as a butler Mr. Wanless's box was large, and it was uncommon heavy. But I found little in it that interested me. Save what I had already half expected: a couple of fine silken gauze nightgowns and a pretty little lace edged cap. Doubtless Wanless had procured them for when he was to have his wicked way with young Alexander. Then I lifted out the man's Sabbath suit. In one pocket there was a badger's-head purse. It was heavy and I had almost meant to leave it quite untouched. It is perhaps an odd sentiment but I had always felt that when you mean to blackmail the living tripes out of a fellow you should not beforehand stoop to thieving from him. I was about to spill out the coins into my hand when I heard the Frenchman's laugh echoing up through the house:

"Yes, laugh you bastard…" This time my breath scarcely soughed out the whisper. "Laugh while you may!

For half an hour I lay on my cot. Briefly, very briefly, I entertained the notion that I might creep back down the stairs and try to eavesdrop. For sure that would have given me something worth hearing. Prudence however re-asserted itself. At one against the four of them downstairs the odds a sight longer, even than those offered by the Grand Lottery!

To pass time I began to read the pocket book that I had snatched up in from the press-room on the Quayside. Jesus! Those pages showed me the rotten inner core of a city's soul. That night in Newcastle there were poor fellows thinking themselves safe in their beds. But their names had already been marked down for lifting! Though for sure now their fate had at least been deferred. Yet I knew that Matthew Crowley's pitch would not lie empty for long. For now with the Emperor loose in Europe the British Navy was likely to be in desperate need of seamen. The fragrance of the guest's tobacco drifting up the stairs began to torture me. To the servants the smoking of tobacco was strictly forbidden within the house. I sought for something to take my mind off my craving. In the candlelight's flicker I ran a finger down the list of the names of those worthies who had sold their fellow townsmen to the Navy's press-gangs. One entry was new written. The name penned in was Rae, Jesse Rae, 'prime seaman'. My finger moved across the entry. The name of the man who had actually paid out five pounds in gold to expedite the impressment was one R. Hodges. Surely this had to be the deposed second-mate's 'Uncle Ralphie.' As soon as I was able I might visit the lad who had enjoyed a brief promotion to second-mate aboard the collier, Countess of Raby. The lad would tell me where I could find this Ralph Hodgson. Sometimes it can be most satisfying to do a good deed in an entirely disinterested fashion. I would think on it!

Outside in the street now there was the patter and drip of melting snow. From time to time the snow slid and rumbled from the slates. One of Rachel Brydon's fellows had stood under the lamplight across the street for a few moments. I had allowed him to move on again. For, suddenly I had decided. Now I had something to stay for. I would wait until I could get at least some indication as to the whereabouts of the coffer or strong room that had to be in his house. Of a sudden a daft thought struck me. There was of course one way in which I could discover where the treasure was hid. Once in Ulm I had done it to get my hands on some stolen maps. All I needed to do was set alight Wanless's room -then to jump up and shout 'Fire' at the top of my voice.

At two o'clock by the town's clocks Humble's three guests left the house. From the steadiness of their voices the men had not done much drinking. Moreover I was more than surprised at the apparent cordiality between them all. I listened at the stair head in an attempt to hear what was said. But that not too boldly. With D'Oeuys present that would have been a fool's risk. We had both learned our trade at the same ecole! Now however Humble was alone downstairs.

The clanging thud that a plate iron door being banged shut makes is quite distinctive. There could be no mistake. It was at that precise moment when I was finally convinced that at least some thousands of the Grand Lottery's guineas were down there: three floors below me in the big front parlour room of the house in Higham Place.

But my long experience warned me that it would have been damned foolish to go sneaking about in the dark. Men like Humble seldom rely upon locks alone. Before I acted I would need to get some fair idea of exactly where the gold was kept.

That morning I was up and about even before the cockroaches had fled the kitchen. As ever our own Wilfie Nettles was truly a real treasure of a man. Young Effie, the skivvie, blessed me loudly for getting her kitchen fires well ablaze and the water kettles filled well before she was down.

"Y'r a 'reel gent' Mr.Nettles! Not like some as aah could name..." This was a lass who would gladly tell me whatever she knew... but later perhaps.

As the chief manservant in such a small household it was part of Wanless's duties to prepare the parlour for the serving of breakfast. But that morning I could see that the fellow was lying like a dead man. He might yet rise - but not I fancied much before noon. And when he did he would surely, as vulgar fellows say, have a head like a firkin o' piss! This was the chance I needed. I drew open the heavy velvet curtains to let in the light. It was a fine bright morning.

From down in the kitchen I ran up the stairs with a shovel of burning coals to set the parlour fire away. That gave me exactly the excuse I needed. I suppose that I had expected the hiding place to be somewhere about the fireplace. It was not. When I had set the sheet iron 'bleezer' against the hearth to set the flames roaring up the chimney I began to make a careful search. There was neither a false hearthstone nor a hinged mantleshelf. Then I saw the two finely lacquered Chinese cabinets. They were luxury items such as are brought home by the captains of East Indiamen. One of them was unlocked and I saw at once that it was where the silverware for the table was kept. When I had laid the table for breakfast for two I stepped over to examine the twin cabinet. And damned cunning it was! That the black and gold cabinet stood on such lender legs was what at first deceived me. How could such a frippery piece of furniture hold any weight of gold? But some part of a man's brain seems sometimes to think thoughts apart from the workings of mere intellect. Gently I tried to move the cabinet. It would not budge. The thing was fixed; its top rested securely on forged iron brackets set into the wall behind it. The creak of a foot on the stairway made me move away quickly. Mrs. Humble found me holding up a polished silver fork to the morning's sunlight.

"Good morning, Nettles…" Flavia Humble looked as though she had spent a restless night.

"Good morning, ma'am…" I murmured softly. There was nothing else for a servant to say.

"Mr. Wanless…he is er..?" It was not a question she had wanted to ask; though clearly she did want an answer to it.

"Mr. Wanless appeared to be sleeping soundly, ma'am…" For a second or two I had dallied with the idea that I might make some sort of lame excuse for the old bastard; but that fancy left me. The woman might have thought that I was mocking her pet. Gratuitous humour in a servant is a commodity that should always to be proffered with care.

"Thank you, Nettles… The maid will wait upon me for breakfast. You may go. The master left the house early this morning so I shall be eating alone…"

Christ! The anger that boiled up behind my blasphemy all but forced itself from my lips. I had blundered; I must have dozed off. Just when the lottery manager had become marked as a man to be followed I had let him slip out of his house. Damn me! I had been so sure that he would have slept late. More than that, the valet in me protested, he must have left the house dressed in yesterday's clothes and linen. It was as well that Flavia Humble had looked up as the maid who was bringing in a laden tray. I could not have helped myself. The emotion that had twisted across my face had been nothing better than simple ill-natured annoyance! And Mrs. Humble could scarcely have missed seeing it.

"May I return the household keys, ma'am?" I held them out before me. Mrs. Humble nodded and with a finger she tapped at the precise point on the polished mahogany of the breakfast table where I was to lay them. No matter, before the day was out I would have the exact copies of them in my hand.

"Since the master is not at home today, ma'am… I would beg leave to go out into the city this morning: there are a few small purchases that I will need to make…" I ventured the request softly. "… to replenish our wardrobe's requisites. 'Our' With valets of course it had to be 'our'. It was what 'we' needed in order to maintain our master's appearances. Almost it was the 'we' of kings.

"Why yes… do that Nettles…buy whatever you feel is needed. Mr. Humble has a increasingly important position to maintain." Before I turned away I put a hand to my breast and gave a little bow.

I was loose, free. Though, I knew the shortness of its extent. No limit had been set but two hours at most was what had been granted me. Servants could seldom expect to be allowed any longer leave of absence!

There may well be some truth in the statement that if you eat like a servant you're very like to come to think like one! I strode straight along to one of the chophouses on the Haymarket and yelled out an order for a platter of grilled meats and a tankard of porter's ale. Hard on my heels Joe Fletcher came in. I must have been moving fast: the old fellow was panting. At once I handed him the box containing the impressions of the keys for the Humble house.

"Tell Mrs Brydon that it would be very useful to us if she could have those made up as quickly as ever is possible. The truth was that I wanted rid of him. There were other things that I needed to do. It was then that I saw that he was hesitating.   "I won't be able to do that, Sir... It's Mrs. Brydon, Sir... she hasn't been seen since last night."   At that news the noises of the chop-house all around us seemed to fall away. My thoughts were magnified inside my head. "Take a drink, Joe..." Fletcher was not a man to be flustered but now he really did look worried. I waved for a mug and poured ale for him from my jug. "Now, Joe," I spoke softly. "... just you tell me what has happened."

Chapter Seventeen

"**D**amn the woman!" My teeth clicked against the rim of my beer pot. "But by God I'll eat the meal I've ordered first. Nor, Joe Fletcher, will I offer to move my arse the distance of one Scotch ell before I do it!"

Of course this was all mere posturing. Of a sudden I was not very hungry. For I would have to admit that as such things go the Humbles fed their servants better than most. Which is not to say much at all. But oatmeal porridge for breakfast, nor even Mrs. Porritt's fresh baked baps piled up on the table at dinner, will still leave a fellow with a draught blowing through his bowels. Truly it is not provender to do sharp thinking on. A man needs meat! And for sure old Seppie Gallon's chophouse was a place where a man could fill his belly. When I had been an apprentice physician – and could afford the price - I had often eaten there. And for sure at the splutter and hiss off the griddle my mouth began to water. Within minutes I had before me a chipped brown platter loaded with a bloody cut of steak, a couple of fat links of sausage, Newcastle black pudding, and all garnished round with a great pile of golden fried onions.

Until I had cleared my platter I said nothing. Then with a last deft wipe with a flat wedge of oven cake I asked Joe to tell me what he knew. I listened, paid my score and walked out into the Haymarket. Damn her eyes! Already I could feel that whole mess of good food lying on my guts like so much sauerkraut and rye bread. Rachel Brydon's plight did concern me. That was why my innards were balking at their task! I was worried.

"She was lifted, Sir. Of that we're certain sure. The town's watch found the empty curricle abandoned – and my two greys were chilled the bone.

"The house?" I had supposed that Rachel Brydon would have been staying with family friends somewhere well outside of Newcastle.

"Mr. Grainger's town house, sir. *Old* Mr. Grainger's house that is... up at Gosforth."

"Then you'd better take me to your master, Joe." I said quietly. This game was warming up. Whoever our enemy was he, they, were on to us. And the rogues had become bold! For we could suspect what we liked but without any evidence we could prove we were helpless. For just so long as the guinea smugglers did nothing which could be said to break the law it was <u>we</u> , not they, who would have to tread with caution. Yet again I found myself damning the woman. Just once too often the young widow Brydon had ridden her high hobby horse. Doubtless the wilful bitch had assumed that her social position would unfailingly save her from any consequences of her actions, no matter how stupid they were.

Sitting up on the box of a carriage is a grand place to observe what goes on along a city's streets. With a rug over my knees and my face muffled in a scarf I might have been invisible. As we moved slowly through the town's traffic I scanned the crowded pavements for any face I might recognise. I saw no one.

Nonetheless it was plain enough then that already the mood of the city itself had changed. The excitement at the news of Napoleon's escape from Elba was growing. War with all its bounties had returned.

A little to my surprise a footman ushered me directly into the house on Brunswick Place. Nor could I help observing at once that it was a grand establishment. When I was shown into the room Richard Grainger strode forward. His hand was outstretched in greeting but he looked grim.

"Bloody woman!" His forced smile was suddenly rueful. Nonetheless he put a friendly hand to my shoulder and guided me over to the fire. He poured wine for us. "Well, Doctor. I have been reading your reports with the greatest interest. Yours, unlike many of the others I receive, have substance to them; something that can actually be verified." Praise indeed!

"My next report, Mr. Grainger, concerns the man Humble." I was making it plain to him at once that my business was immediate. "For the last four days I have been employed as valet to this man. The situation was secured for me by Mrs. Brydon..."

"That it was!" Grainger did not look exactly irritated. "Though I will say that she did so quite entirely without my leave or permission! Mrs.Brydon was taking my name very much in vain when she used one of my own clerks to write certain letters. My valet too is much put out!" Grainger smiled his whimsical smile. "Look upon it as a holiday Doctor. Get out of there with as little ceremony as you're able... as soon as you like. Don't even go back! Mr. George Humble has been cleared of suspicion by reference to a gentleman who stands at... at the highest levels of our society."

I was staggered. Was Grainger being serious, or merely blasé? It was just so unlike the man. Grim faced I looked at him until I held his gaze. "Not so, sir!" Richard Grainger's mouth opened. He was a amiable sort of fellow but I rather think that at that moment I had made him remember his rank. Nonetheless I went on. "I!" Richard Grainger's mouth opened.

"Indeed, sir, I would say, quite as forcefully as good manners allow, that it would be a folly for us not to examine this gentleman's doings further." When I spoke my voice had risen higher than I had intended. My words brought him up short. His response was to raise a quizzical eyebrow. Slowly and with a careful deliberation I began to outline what I had learned at Higham Place. But then with a lift of his hand he stopped me dead. He turned quickly and tugged at a silk tassel that hung at the side of the marble fireplace. Within half a minute I heard the click of the curtained door behind me. The man was a clerk, elderly, dressed in black satin knee breeches and a swallowtail coat with satin covered buttons. He carried a writing tablet and had a goose quill tucked behind his ear.

"Take this down Martindale…" Silent on his soft leather pumps the clerk moved to the seat where Grainger pointed. He began at once to scratch a preliminary note. From the speed with which he wrote I realised that he was writing in Gurney's shorthand. This man was, or had been, a civil servant. Few mercantile houses did the sort of business that called for the use of Gurney's system. . It was said that it that took years to learn; but that a man trained in it was able to take absolutely accurate verbatim reports.

And the report I made that morning was detailed. For I took pains to remember every significant happening. When I had finished Richard Grainger held up three fingers to the show the clerk how many copies he wanted.

"Speaking of copies…" I said slowly. "I have given the coachman, Skinner, a box of key impressions from Humble's house. Would it be possible to have the keys themselves made up… soon?" I had thought it unlikely that I would get help from Richard Grainger. I was wrong. He cocked his head on one side. "You'll have the keys by this evening… my word upon it!"

I must have shown my surprise. " That will not present us with any difficulties at all, be assured." Now Grainger had looked away so that I could not see his face. "This present war alone has lasted – on and off- for more than twenty years, Dr. Shafto. We've had the time to learn all the skills we need to have on ready call!" His smile turned into what was an undoubted grin. "We have here an odd little fellow in our service, a second footman I believe. When we first found him he too was in a state of er… slight embarrassment!

"Mr. Grainger…" I allowed a little formality to creep into my voice. "My own position…?"

"Is as safe now as it is has been possible for me to make it…" Grainger tilted the decanter and refilled our glasses. "Find the men… stop the loss overseas of whatever gold is being collected in this city. And I will undertake to secure for you…" He looked at me across the table. "… either a full pardon from his Majesty, or at the very least a new identity that no man in this world will be able to break." There was a silence for a moment. Outside in the yard I could hear a man's voice coaxing a horse to back into the shafts of a carriage. "Does that satisfy you, Dr. Shafto?" I chose not to answer directly.

"Major Farquahar… still pursues me, sir. Were I my own man I suppose I could make light of him. But his appearance here in Newcastle at this crucial time…" I knew I could allow Grainger to draw his own conclusions.

"Major George Farquahar was with Wellington in Spain. The report I have on him from Talaeus Dekker is that the fellow served… without especial distinction as some sort of wagon-master." I was listening intently. "However, so far my further enquiries indicate that the three officers who claimed to know him well have confided that his own rank-and-file did not regard him highly. The fellow is said to have left under some suspicion of… shall we say, sleight-of-wagon regarding certain stores entrusted to him. The wretch also is said to be too damned fortunate at cards. Our supposed allies, the little brass gods at Horseguard's Yard, indicate merely that the officer has been granted special extended leave. They are however quite unable to say exactly what he is doing."

I had already decided not to ask anything about the name Arthur Hetherington. If need be I could 'discover' it later. For the moment my common caution told me that this was an item to be sat upon for the moment."

Already Grainger was shrugging. "Simply, we will have to cope with even more uncertainty… though just a little." He smiled. "The only way you will find answers to your questions, my friend, is to solve our current riddle. Find the gold, Doctor Shafto, and all other questions will be answered. And that can hardly take more than a few more days." He took out his watch and thumbed open the case. Of a sudden he seemed to have picked up and tugged at a loose thread of his thoughts. "It was in my mind to haul you out of Humble's house straight away. For we could certainly do with your help in finding Rachel... Mrs. Brydon." I saw that his fingers curled into a grasp. " But from what you have said my wits tell me that for a while longer you should stay as close to the Lottery Man as you can."

"On the question of Mrs. Brydon..." I allowed my words to fall slowly. "Perhaps I can offer my advice..." I watched Grainger's clenched fingers straighten and stretch. He was listening.

"Yes, Doctor Shafto...I should be glad of it..."

"Lifting a man at night, even in the street, is no difficult task." I smiled at him. "After all that is what happened to me in Paris. But abducting a gentlewoman like Mrs. Brydon is something very much more difficult to do... discretely." Grainger nodded.

"Indeed I would have said that *whoever* wanted it done would certainly have had to *pay*, and pay very well, to have it done." I did not say it but it had already occurred to me that Charles D'Oeuys was just the chap to put such a jaunt in train; though he himself would have been far too slippery to take any direct part in the venture. I went on. "Newcastle, sir, is much as any other city. Certain kinds of crime are done by certain types of criminal - and by those fellows *alone*. A dog thief, sir, steals dogs; he does not pick pockets. For that would soon lead to a cracked head for his poaching on another man's preserves." I looked at Grainger. "Among villains there is an order to things. That order quite is as rigid as... as the ranks and stations of our own Society." I paused. "So I would suggest that what you are looking for here is a common brothel keeper... Find him, or *her*, and you just might find out who *paid* to have Mrs. Brydon abducted. And if you are really lucky you might discover exactly to which of the town's brothels she was delivered. Look for fellows who have money to splash about…"

"But why, Shafto… Why?" Now for the first time Grainger was showing just how anxious he really was.

"Why, sir?" I was now oddly certain that my answer was the correct one. "Because our friends have learned, or been *told* that we are close on their heels. From the very beginning I have suspected that someone among us has been working what you might call *both ends against the middle*." It was my turn to look directly at Grainger. "There has always been a smell about this business. It begins to remind me a little of how *we* acted as 'the preparers of the way'. We agents went to our work just before the Emperor's own eagles swooped. "

But Richard Grainger was slowly shaking his head. "Only fools heed vague rumours, Doctor. Nonetheless I will deal in them here; though only so far as to impart to you one particularly silly tale. It is going the rounds in a few of the London clubs. It is that the Admiralty itself had privy instruction to *allow* Napoleon Bonaparte and his officers to escape from Elba; that Captain Ayde of the sloop *Partridge* had been given special orders… that, appearances aside, his proper vigilance was perhaps… tempered."

I think I felt my eyes widen. It was possible. I supposed. This was the higher politics of Europe. "Someone wants a definite… *conclusion* to be reached. They want the whole business finished!" I had spoken before I realised it. I went on. There was no point in holding back. "The rulers of Europe, the money men too perhaps, want the Emperor finally destroyed!" Grainger might, or might not, have been nodding.

I went back to my room by the Westgate. The chance to pick up news of anything that had happened while I was away was too important to miss. Again I was surprised. My friend Jonathan Stokoe had returned. His news too was that all Europe was indeed in a turmoil. Some ship's passage home must have been swift for he tossed me a copy of *Le Moniteur*.

The newspaper was no more than four days old. I remembered then that Jottie had spoken of an offer to buy a shipload of French army muskets. Events must surely have overtaken that enterprise. Though to my surprise my friend was not at all downcast.

"Between greedy men, Doctor, there might have been some bad blood." Jottie spread his hands. "But good sense has prevailed and I fancy I won much goodwill with the French for the future – whichever way the battles go - by putting two thousand stand o' new muskets back on to the quay. Moreover the immediate terms I won were damned good." He grinned a little. "So I'll be offerin' His Majesty's Commissioners in Whitehall a whole shipload o' salted horse hides. They'll make boots enough to keep a whole army marchin!"

This was an insane world. I found myself reflecting that in the person of Jonathan Stokoe the cruel whim of a sea-officer had lost the British cause the loyalty of a damned sharp fellow. For a short moment I even found myself wondering about my own case. It had never been my intention to serve Napoleon. Indeed at the beginning I had not even suspected who my master was. Abandoned, I had been left to sink or swim among the English *detenues* at Verdun. After all had I not merely followed where the grip of an empty belly had pulled me? Only later and when I had begun habitually to frame my thoughts in the French tongue did I serve the Emperor as readily as - I suppose - I might have served King George. I admit it! Would I so easily have sold the muskets that would undoubtedly soon be used against my fellow countrymen? But then I remembered, saw again, stark in my mind's eye, how the living flesh on Jonathan Stokoe's back had been clawed to bloody rawness by the Navy's cat-o-nine tails. Yes, it stood to reason, given cause almost any man will change his loyalties.

We talked long, and on the strength of our old friendship I trusted him with much. The end of it was that he promised me that if by evening I had not got my hands on some news that Richard Grainger had not come by then I would have a right to be disappointed.

Comfortably before noon I was back at Higham Place. With my green baize apron protecting my clothes I stood hard at work putting boot varnish and wax on George Humble's footwear. The house too was all a' bustle. The brightness of the day had moved Mrs Humble to order a general cleaning. She herself had been driven into the city 'for the shopping'. So I flirted with the maids on the stairs, though with caution. It was not a time when Wilfred Nettles could afford to have… affections. However I contented myself by singing a quite obscene peasant song - in Italian – loudly, as I worked. And though I say so myself, in a not bad tenor voice. Though had the lasses understood the words I had no doubt that they would have thrown their pinnies over their heads and run off screaming!

Suddenly I decided. It was time to stir up Isaac Wanless. At two o'clock I went upstairs and roused him. Nor was I gentle about it. The cheap gin had damned near poisoned the rogue. The signs of it were obvious. His skin had an awful slate colour to it; his shoulders and hands trembled; the whites of his eyes were yellowed. Without doubt Mrs. Humble's own *major domo* was in a damned parlous state. The wretch was ill. And *that* too answered my purpose. With a bounce I sat down at his bedside. I smiled down at him.

"Hector Wanless… stir yourself man…" I made to sound solicitous. "The cart will be here in just a minute or two…" He goggled at me. I patted at his hand. "Aye lad, they've come for you! You'll be hauled up the road to Town's Moor." He was squinting at me.

"The *Mercury* says that there's expected to be four or five thousand folk there…

"What the devil are y' gabblin… y' crazed gowk!" His anger was gathering fast. He tried to sit up. My hand to his chest forced him down again.

"Why bonny lad… they've come to take you up to the gallows." I chuckled with mock jollity." The crowd 's gatherin' already! All the little lads are ready to run behind your cart a' jeerin' at you every step o' the way." Alarm showed under his pallor. I think that at that moment I might have walked away and left the dog thinking he was suffering a nightmare. I went on. "O' course after they've stretched your dirty neck they'll let your body hang for a season or two, all drippin' green like a well jugged hare. Then the hangman's apprentice will paint Stockholm tar on what the hoodie crows have left!" Wanless opened his mouth to roar. But I shut him up again. "The Higham Place Buggerer… Isaac… That's what they'll call y'. Understanding dawned. The mouth clapped itself shut.

"Why aah've done nothin'…" By then the fellow's fear was almost palpable.

"That's not what *we*'ve heard…Isaac." I leant closer. "Ye' unnatural shite pokin' old bastard!" It always pays to multiply the number of souls who are supposed to know of a perversion. I had to swell the ranks of the man's foes. "An' you've only yourself to blame! Who was it made such a rare bloody *spectacle* of his self, last night? I jabbed a finger into his ribs. "And by Christ *that* so plainly before a dozen honest serving men – an' in a common alehouse!" Then I mimicked: 'O' Alexander, me'ee darlin' lad… How aa'h do love y'!'" Wanless closed his eyes; white knuckled he clutched at his blankets.

"Man, did you leave go of your senses? If that sort of thing 's your pleasure why the Hell didn't y' get yourself down to the back rooms at the *Three Indian Kings*… there's catamites a' plenty foregather there every night… Mistress Fannie Feggelthwaite and all her Jolly Maids." The fellow damned near turned green.

It was not so much of a risk. A man who had been as drunk as Wanless had been would naturally have lapses of memory. Though truly, as the Bible says, the guilty man flees where no man pursueth! I left him alone to catch at what memories of past sins he cared to. The man needed time to recover. He also had yet to find that his passionate love letters were gone. However, I had decided, this was work that would be better furthered by someone else. I would be surprised if Richard Grainger did not have somebody on his staff who would be able to put enough fear into this old sinner to make him eager to do our bidding. At least Wanless would not get in my way now, that for certain sure.

Joe Fletcher the coachman arrived as we were eating. His ready-money knock on the kitchen door made the servants look up from their mutton and neaps. I could not help thinking what a good choice the old fellow had been. Old Joe knew naturally the proper etiquette that prevailed among below-stairs servants. Very civilly he had stood first in the doorway to wait until Mrs. Porritt had nodded her leave for him to enter her kitchen. Then the rogue set one of the maids squealing with delight as he dropped two new half crown pieces in winnings on to her plate. While her friends were gathering around her Joe bent towards my ear to whisper. I was looking for him to deliver the forged keys to the house. He had brought none. Instead he whispered:

"Up, bonny lad, you're to get out of here now...this minute That 's the word and them 's the orders. Leave all your traps here at Ellison Place and come wi' me... Word is that your master has had his throat cut!"

Chapter Eighteen

Severus Mudie's house was down on Silver Street. I remembered it well. And to be sure these days some of the other folk who lived along Silver Street were no longer short of a florin or two. Even though that could scarce he said of all of them. In my time that quarter of the town had long been dedicated to little one-room schools of dancing and deportment; teachers of music struggled for existence there. Yet there had been a few changes. I saw one bright polished plate that brassily proclaimed the presence of an 'Academie de Francaise'. So even some of the middling sorts of folk must have done well out of the French wars. Sure signs of the fact came down the street with a fluttering bevy of young girls – all carefully chaperoned – sent there, I had to suppose, to be turned into ladies.

Jonathan Stokoe's 'runners' were following a stout little fellow who struggled to lug a heavy basket up the bank. At first sight he looked to be nothing more than a seller of 'yellow clay', the bricks of ochre that house-proud women use to colour their hearthstones and doorsteps. And indeed under his ragged coat and Scotch bonnet he might have escaped notice altogether. However that morning it was his misfortune that one of Stokoe's lads knew him. Amidst his mates' sniggers he confessed that he had recently 'enjoyed commerce wi' the man'. His day's work it seemed was collecting for an Orchard Street moneylender.

'Yallah Cla'yyyyyeee!" Ordinarily it is a sound fit to set a man's teeth on edge. But I found myself exchanging grins with Jottie Stokoe. For with that one half strangled call the man's disguise was destroyed. Even I could remember all the cries of the town's hawkers. And this day the poor fellow had failed lamentably to catch the rising lilt that always comes at the end of a clay seller's street cry. More to the point he went like an arrow across to number eighteen Silver Street.

There we were in time to watch the little drama that took place. The impostor had to stand all on tip-toe to grab at the polished brass knocker on Mudie's front door: rat-tat…a-tat-tat! Jesus! I saw the look on that face. Truly this was one errand the beggar was doing under protest. The thick lips were twisted with all the raw belligerence of a bum-bailiff's dog!

However at his third fusillade an elderly servant swung open the door. For half a breath the poor woman could scarce comprehend at all what manner o' wight stood before her. Then our *soi disant* yellow clayman held out the note. I saw the flash of white paper. But no note was passed. The fellow stood there brazen still. Of course, he wanted paying. Here we saw a meeting of two worlds! The prim servant's mouth fell all a' gape. Clearly the poor woman was shocked. Her gob began to flap like a privy door in a gale. It was indeed a damned odd day when such as he knocked on Doctor Severus Mudie's front door. For a few seconds she was remained speechless. Then she then began to gabble, jabbing a finger at a carriage being reined up at the kerbside. The smart young coachman who had been about to jump down from the box paused. The lad could see well enough what was happening. And to be sure he tried hard to keep his face straight – and failed, lamentably. But then from within the house I heard a full roar of anger. The servant was clearly terrified. She turned her head at the sound and shrank aside. Mudie rushed to the doorway; and there he stood like a goaded bullock. The man's jowls were the colour of raw sheep's liver – indeed I feared from the bulge of his eyeballs that our good physician was about to suffer an apoplexy. Nonetheless, and between bobbing his little bows to the two elderly ladies within the carriage, he struggled to thrust his fingers into the pocket of his waistcoat.

I could appreciate his predicament. While it surely was unwise not to show the courtesy his genteel patients warranted; yet nonetheless the man who brought the message would have to be paid – paid cash down on the drumhead. However with the reckoning paid the spectacle show was soon over. Like a hound at a tossed scrap the hawker snatched the coin out of the air. He ran off leaving his heavy basket at the doorstep.

"Doctor…this is no job for us." Jonathan Stokoe was obviously alarmed." That 's Doctor Mudie's house… and that particular gentleman has too many powerful friends in this city, men that we, you, would be damned stupid to cross!" I could see that Jottie was deadly serious. "I've helped you all I can this far; but don't ask me to take any more risks with my own freedom. If that house over there is broken into there'll be a cry of riot and we'll have the Black Cuffs out on the streets! Those same bastards will have the poor wards of this town rummaged inside and out at bayonet point - until they do find out who's guilty. My lads won't dare do it. They've all families, Doctor. That I know even before I ask them. Besides which," Jonathan Stokoe turned to face me. "in a few more days I'll be sailin' for Copenhagen… an' I'll not soon be back on the Tyneside! Y' do understand that, Doctor?"

I was neither angry nor surprised. Already I had already asked a lot of Stokoe and he'd given it without stint.

"That I do, Jonathan, that I do… And I tell you freely that already you've done all a man could ask of a friend." I thrust out my hand. His grip was hard. But for just a second he held on. He had something else to say:

"Three days more is all I reckon to be safe in this town. Whispered word of who I am filters slow, but nonetheless it does filter." He let my hand fall. Now there was a different kind of earnestness to his voice.

"By this time tomorrow, Doctor, I'll be down the coast at Wearmouth. There's a Danish brig, the Heirje, there. She's at the jetty's end now - loadin' still... but ready or not she's all ready to let her lines slip at my word. Let me book passage for you... Unless I bid her master otherwise she's due to sail on Saturday night's tide." He took hold of my sleeve and bunched the cloth tight.

"Leave these bastards Doctor... all o' them! This isn't your fight... it isn't even a fight at all. It's a bloody scramble! They're all no better than kittiwakes screechin' around floatin' turds! Take my word for it, man. Where gold is concerned there'll be no such thing as honour. For when all is said and done your precious Bank is nought but a gang o' graspin' bastards just like the rest of us. Oh, they're out to stop the Emperor's agents from getting their hands on the gold all right. But when they do that... d'y think that one piece of it will it go into the Government's coffers? Will it lighten a poor man's taxes? No, Sir! It bloody well won't! Instead it'll go tae line the pockets o' some dandyprat of a marquise or a duke. Lad, haven't such men already betrayed you once? Will such silk-tongued thieves think twice about doin' the same thing again? Good Christ, they'll bloody well see to it that you're hanged - that much if only to snip off a loose end o' spun yarn! Man haven't you learned yet that is no such beast as a gentleman... never so long as they've a hole in their fundaments!"

"You know!" Almost it sounded as though I were accusing him. "You damned well know about the gold!"

"Aaah know!" Jottie Stokoe stood there, incredulous. " Kidda'..." He shook his head like a woman over her bairn's foolishness. "The old biddie who sells lemons down on the Sandgate knows it; the tinker who mends pots at the end of Friar's Chare knows; the one-eyed old bugger who waters his ginger beer at the Sandhill pant will retail the whole story to you for a half a groat... Why man have y' forgotten? This is Newcastle! Folk hereabouts might be treated just like the slaves in the Black Indies ...but we all of us live too close in one others' pockets for there ever to be any secret long kept! The only trouble now is that so many tales about the smuggled gold are goin' the rounds that no bugger really knows who or what to believe! Why man the whole town has known about the shower o' silver since the night o' the big explosion!"

"The night of the explosion?" I levelled my gaze at him. "Tell me… Jonathan, tell about that, tell me what you know about it!"

Jonathan Stokoe laughed sourly. For, I had made my ignorance obvious.

"Sometime last November it was. There was an explosion in an old lead factory up by the Shield Field. Three men were blown to pieces and lumps of half melted silver were thrown far and wide. One way and another it was reckoned that better than two thousand pounds worth of silver was scattered about that night. The stuff was all left there to be freely snatched up by any poor soul who found it." Stokoe's face broke into a smile. "Why, man, the bairns in the street were pickin' up the stuff and carryin' it to their ma's their pinnies. He made a circle between his thumb and forefinger: "Dickie Triphook's own laddie fetched home thirteen thick cowpats of pure silver."

This was fascinating. And I began to wonder just how much of the tale Richard Grainger knew.

"And did the coroner find out what caused the explosion? Surely with dead bodies found there would have to have been a Coroner's Court."

"Oh, aye, there was no mystery there. The old furnace and chimney were to be blasted. And, freely told, a lad by the name of Ernie Dixon who worked up at the Todd's Nook Pit was paid by the owners to fire off the shots o' gunpowder. It was the manager himself who had left a powder box and fuse straws - for safe-keeping - all ready in the flue o' the chimney. The pitman was to have come down the next day to lay the charges. But whoever was there that night didn't know that… they'd fired up the furnace to melt their silver. Now the only mystery that remains is who it was got blown to smithereens, or I should say was blasted full of lump silver. For sure there's never been a soul come forward either to claim or even to name the three corpses." It was the end of the story. Again though, Stokoe put out his hand to me.

"Come away, bonny lad! Have the fuckin' sense you were born with! It doesn't matter. By next this time week you could be in Copenhagen… clear and free and sittin' suppin' coffee out of a porcelain cup. Why Doctor, man, you could be stuffin' y'r face wi' cream cakes in one of the little cafés on the Kongens Nytorv! " And of course I knew that the man was right.

"Keep a berth handy for me, Jonathan," I said, softly,"but don't you delay your sailing for me by so much as a minute. If I'm there… why then, I'll be there!"

Now I could not deny to myself that the business with Doctor Mudie was something that I would have to lay before Richard Grainger. This, I told myself, was no more than plain common sense – it was not because I lacked the bowels to do the work. Even if it were possible to break into the house of one of the town's leading physicians it would be a job that called for something more than just a delicate touch. For all I knew a man as well connected as Grainger might even be able to get a magistrate's warrant-to-search. And plainly too our Mrs. Brydon was a considerable person in her own right. Surely it would serve the town's reputation ill if report reached the London newspapers that a gentlewoman could be kidnapped on Newcastle's streets. Besides, I told myself, having a house in Silver Street broken into and searched should a trivial matter for a man of wealth to have done.

But I knew that getting to talk to Richard Grainger again might take time. He might not even be in the city. So I decided that the prudent thing would be to get a word or two with Joe Fletcher first. Crossing the to the further side of Pilgrim Street I began to make my way up the bank. It was a market day again. Both highway and pavements were crowded.

Papa Dimnet had always said that even as spiritual beings Guardian Angels were notoriously unreliable; yet he swore that sometimes where simple alertness failed, the unsleeping sentinel within a man's mind would sometimes sound a timely alarm. He was right. I didn't know why but first thing that warned me was the heavy click of a loose boot copper on the pavement behind me. I realised that I had been hearing it for a while. Ahead of me a press of bodies blocked the way. It was a chattering and fluttering crush of well-dressed matrons and their daughters. They were crowding excitedly around the windows of an emporium. What attracted them was a display of newly imported Venetian mirrors. Just a blink before the crowding-in of bonnets blocked my vision what I saw reflected in the bright silvered glass made me catch my breath.

I'd seen the man before. Or say rather that it was the bastard's size alone that caught my attention. I was being followed by one of the Coneybeare brothers, either Lemuel or Salathiel, one of the matched brace of prize-fighters that Major Farquahar had hired to protect him.

At once I pulled a trick that I had first learned on the streets of Rome. I turned sharp face about and walked straight at the fellow. All he could do was gawp. The batterings he had taken in the ring had slowed the bastard's wits. As I squeezed past him I had just time to take in a heavy jaw with a three days' growth of ginger stubble on it, a pair of piggy blue eyes; aye, and as short stumped a set of teeth as ever graced a gob. Like the philosopher Plato of old, this Coneybeare had obviously sprung syphilitic from his mother's womb.

Women gathered in a crowd can be savage creatures. Treat them always with caution. Three steps back and I was again at the shop's double bow windows. With many cheery 'By y'r leave, ma'am's, a few winning smiles and a little handful of 'Thank you kindly m' dear's I was able to squeeze my way through the crush. Coneynbeare, ignorant bastard that he was, knew no better. He swung about sharply and tried to lunge headlong through massed satin skirts and fur lined capotes. I heard the women, or say rather the ladies, shriek out almost as one angered she-beast! It is no difficult thing to cause a street riot!

But I had to put distance between Coneybeare and myself, and that damned quickly! Somewhere up ahead I heard yells, the crash of iron and the splintering of timbers. From the sound of it a loaded wagon had smashed a wheel. Already the stream of market traffic was slowing, drawing to a halt. I stepped into it. Before my feet had left the kerb I had looked back. I saw Major Farquahar. Twenty yards away he was leaning out of the window of a hired hackney carriage. The fellow had seen me. But he had tried to stand up too quickly and hit his head on the cab's roof. I heard him raving after me at the top of his voice.

It is an observed fact that even a man in fear of his life will sometimes do things that he will later consider whimsical. At that a moment a daft fancy took me. I put a hand to my heart and bowed to the bastard. There was no resisting it! Then like a chased street urchin I ran headlong into the traffic. Skitter-scattering among the piles of fresh horse dung I breasted my way up the street between the columns of wagons and cuddie carts. Ahead of me for a hundred yards or more all the street's traffic stood there, stalled and steaming.

I had guessed aright: a loaded wain had shed a wheel. And, as ever, the spill had drawn a crowd. Without provoking so much as a murmur I squeezed my way through it.

A hurried passage through two narrow lanes and I could walk unchallenged to Brunswick Place. It was not until I had was passed under the arch that led into Grainger's stable yard that I realised just how bloody angry I was.

"Choke it off, Mr... an' swallie it..." Joe Skinner had been watching me. He was sitting on the shafts of a carriage. His mouth moved slowly as he shifted his quid of tobacco across to the left side of his mouth. He spat the brown juice on to the cobbles and wiped his sleeve across his gob. "He's got a magistrate an' two lawyers wi' im... they've been there for an hour...a' shoutin' the odds"

"Joe, I think I've found out where Mrs. Brydon is. So perhaps that will that serve to get me an entree to see your master?"

"That I doubt, sir. You see, Mr Richard reckons he already knows where she is…"

At that moment Joe was cut off by a shout of fury that shook the windows of the house.

"The gutless bastards! Simple lily livered cowardice that's what it is – no better than common foul-your-breeks funk! I tell you, Sir, these last years a weeping, rotten canker has eaten into the very heart of this city. Where some damned traitor has the power to have two sworn justices stand pale faced before me… and then have the damned impertinence to dissemble to me in the matter of issuing a simple warrant o' search against a known scoundrel!"

For a few seconds I had thought I was hearing Richard Grainger giving vent to his anger. But when he came to the window and saw me below I knew it wasn't.

"That's the Master, sir… old Sir John that is…" Joe Fletcher was chuckling. The coachman had sat listening to every word. He had enjoyed hearing it. "He's been a' roastin' yon mealie-mouthed beggars for a good hour, sir."

"But to no good end." Richard Grainger had stepped up behind us. Plainly the man's anger was burning within him too. I could sense it. "My father is right but the world has changed a deal more than he supposes these last years…" He stopped; his ire was already reined up tight. "And what have you to report, my friend?"

"I've learned that Mrs. Brydon is being held in a Doctor Mudie's house on Silver Street."

With all the grim mouthed briefness I could contrive I gave my report. And indeed truth to tell I was more than a little pleased with myself. But then to my surprise I saw that Richard Grainger did not seem at all impressed.

Chapter Nineteen

"**S**urely you mean off All-Hallows Green...Doctor."
Grainger spoke quietly. "That is what I hear...
from my own friends." For a moment I was about to ask who
had given him that information. I stopped myself. Grainger
would be unlikely to tell me anything about his own source
of information. The upper town and the gentlefolk who lived
there were his exclusive concern, his own province. And
damned annoying to me that was. Though, to be sure, I could
well do without being snubbed in front of his coachman.

I heard Joe Fletcher's quid of tobacco shift in his
mouth:"The one backs on to t' other, sir."

"Perhaps then, the best thing would be for us to go down
there and look over the ground." Richard Grainger was clearly
a man who at this moment hungered after action.

At his orders Joe Fletcher hurried to put a steady little mare
between the shafts of a light carriage. We made our way down
through the city's busy streets. Though with my morning's near
meeting with Major Farquahar still much on my mind I sat
with my hat pulled well down and my greatcoat's wide collar
turned up. Twice I was tempted to speak to Grainger but from
the set of his jaw I knew that this was clearly not a good time
to broach the matter of my own protection. Men like Richard
Grainger, I knew, will seldom take kindly to being reminded of
their promises. To me however the matter had already become
more than pressing. I could hardly help reflecting that had I
been just a bit less slippery an hour before I could well now be

in a cell. And as a man charged with high treason I doubted very much that any civil authority in Newcastle would care to argue with the military about my legal status. For that same reason I doubted very much too that Grainger would wish to test his influence with the authorities.

Joe Fletcher was right. The front of Mudie's house was on Silver Street, but it also backed close on to the pleasant green square that lay around the church of All Saints. Here there was another dwelling. Whitewash smeared on the inside of its windows told us at once that it was untenanted. But I soon saw too that access to the backyards of both houses was through a narrow arched passageway. Looked at professionally it should not have been a difficult place to get into. Grainger tapped for the carriage to halt.

With something of the mien of a gentleman and his clerk looking to buy properties, Grainger and I made a short tour around the square. I made show of pointing here and there. And to be fair the man had the wit to take a good part. Sometimes he nodded; sometimes he shook is head and sucked pensively at his fist. Though to be sure, much of our play-acting might well have been wasted. There were a few street traders. A man was selling vinegar from a barrel on a barrow; an old woman was taking a bairn for a walk. Across the way a sexton was spading up the black churchyard earth for a new grave. From within the church of All-Saints' itself we could hear a choir at practice. So far as I could see we had drawn small attention to ourselves.

But while we had walked the ground Joe had pulled in the carriage so that it masked the entrance to the passageway. Neat as you please we slipped in under the archway. At the end of the alley there were two yard-doors. Grainger squinted between a seam in the timbers. But at a rumbling snarl and the scratch of claws against the wood he swore and flung himself backwards. From the heavy pad of paws I guessed that there had to be at least two watchdogs in that yard. We listened. Within the house I could hear insistent yelping. Doctor Mudie had obviously had the good sense to keep another dog, probably a small terrier, indoors. It was an old trick. We'd seen and heard all we could hope to.

"We'll need help if we're to break into that place…lots of help." Richard Grainger's gloved fist hit the palm of his hand with a thud."

"No, Sir… not *we*! This night you are not to come within a furlong of this place…" Visibly the man bristled. An imperious eyebrow lifted itself. But then almost as quickly the anger was gone. Richard Grainger was listening to me.

"This morning, Sir, your father applied to the town's justices for a warrant to search these same premises. It was refused. So, for you, now, to be seen anywhere near that house would bode damned ill for you if anything goes… amiss! Moreover, Mr. Grainger, housebreaking is a plain felony, a matter o' transportation - at the least - for any man 'found on enclosed premises'." It was clear to me then that the idea that he *himself* should stand in such danger came as a shock to Richard Grainger. He was going to say something but then he changed his mind.

"What do you suggest, Doctor Shafto?" The question was asked quietly. "How are we to get my… *Mrs* Brydon out of that house?"

"You must leave it to me, Mr Grainger… After all, sir, isn't *this* is precisely the work for which the bank rescued me from Major Farquahar?" Once again the stupid grit of heroism was in my voice. Yet even as I spoke the words I was already damning myself into heaps for my own folly. Nonetheless, I had said the words. Pride and vainglory will break a man's neck for him - every time! So daft Bob Shafto had gone and enlisted himself into the forlorn hope!

"But what we have to remember, now, is that this must be a win-all or lose-all business. If we break into Mudie's house and *don't* find Mrs. Brydon, why then we've risked our necks for nothing."

"But by God if we *should* find her there…"

Now I saw that what was behind Grainger's tight lips was plain. What he had in his mind now was simple bloody murder. His hand gripped at the hilt of an imaginary sword. At that moment I had just the merest glimpse of the same tall fellow who in Spain had hacked French dragoons out of their saddles. "Why then for sure it's the kidnapping... of a *gentlewoman*. We ourselves could even arrest this Mudie fellow on the spot... and *anyone* else he cares to name as his accomplice." I could see that it was an idea that appealed greatly to Richard Grainger.

"I shall need cash, gold coin, to pay whatever people I need hire." Grainger nodded. He put a hand into his coat and brought out a purse. It dropped heavily into my hand.

"Joe will bring you more this afternoon. What else will you need?"

This was my chance.

"On Pilgrim Street this morning one of Major Farquahar's hired prize-fighters damned near got his hands on me. And I may tell you, sir, that I had to dance pretty lively to get away from him." Now was the time to make no bones about what I needed Grainger to do: "Left or right, my friend, just one hook from either of those fellows' maulies and Bob Shafto wouldn't wake up until his feet were on the gallows' trap." As a message it needed no more elaboration. Clearly Richard Grainger understood.

"Within two hours, Doctor... You have my word upon it!"

"Then also I must ask that you find for us an old lady. Moreover it would us serve better if she were one who is well known to be wealthy; she should perhaps be some old dowager o' the County who has been taken of a sudden with spasms of, shall we say, a most painful colic. This worthy dame will need the urgent attentions of a highly regarded physician! It might be better too if that same lady lived some little way outside of the town."

This time Grainger smiled. "As it happens I do know *just* such a lady."

I stepped down from the carriage at the head of the Dog Bank. From there I went from shop to shop buying what I knew I would need. At an ironmonger's I bought a tinned-iron candle lantern with a shutter. If a man needs a light on a break-in job then he must take it with him. And in the same shop I saw the sign, chalked on a barrel: Birdlime – Fresh-made'. Now birdlime is always a nuisance to spread. But where a fellow needs to smash in a window with the least possible noise then your ordinary gardener's stickum is excactly what you need. At a butcher's stall I had the fellow cut some thick pieces of sirloin beefsteak for me. When I had finished my shopping I went back to my lodgings at Westgate Street. There, one after another, I slid ten of Grainger's bright guineas across the table at Dick Triphook.

"What sort of a street riot will that buy me, Dick?

With a wink and a grin the old sailor swept up my gold. "Any time o' the night or day, Sir, and at any place you say, these ten beauties will see twenty lumps o' really prime gallows bait *and* their doxies turned out all ready to go a' riotin' on the streets. Aa'h know a publican not a mile from here who for this kind of money would cheerfully have the whole toon bornt doon … an' that t' the bloody ground!" I gave him the rest of my instructions.

Some folk of course might well have thought that ten guineas was a damned steep fee to have the town's drunken scum break honest folks' windows. But for me that night anything that kept the harsh skirr of the watchmen's rattles well way from All-Hallows Green had to be well worth the cost.

As the clocks began to chime out eight o'clock I was in position at the corner of Silver Street. Above me the night sky was spangled bright with hard burning stars. I watched from the shadows as a smart carriage drew up at Severus Mudie's house. And I couldn't help being amused. For it looked very much as though Richard Grainger was doing me proud. A footman in plum velvet livery strutted up to the front door of number eighteen. His rap at the front door knocker echoed across to me. I saw the flicker of light as the door was opened. The footman handed a long envelope to the woman servant and waited. There was no delay. It took Doctor Oliver Mudie no more than five minutes to answer the summons. With his coat-tails flying free the physician was helped up into the carriage. The footman handed in his bag and they were away.

If your common English householder knew just how unsafe his home's little castle must always be against the skills of the accomplished housebreaker the poor beggar would throw away his keys. Thought to be sure Mudie's property was well enough defended.

I slipped into the alley and walked quickly to the yard door. Before I had paced out three steps the watchdogs were snarling; as I came closer the snarls grew to the full alarm. I whistled softly as I knelt, holding one of my bloodied pieces of steak to the gap under the door. It is best first to allow the animals only to lick at the bait. There was a lot more snarling but soon enough the barking ceased. Those poor beasts were ravenous. When I had teased them enough I threw the meat one piece after another over the wall. The clash of teeth told me that each of the beasts had caught and bolted down his three pennyworth of prime steak. The three fifty grain pills of Wilkiman's opium I had sewn into the meat would, I reckoned, have toppled a big pitman like a felled oak. But even Bengal opium takes time to work its powers. I walked back up the bank, took a gill of ale and got a light for my lantern at the *Black House* on Pilgrim Street. Patience pays. It was a good hour before I came back to the alley. By then all I could hear was the crunch of my own footsteps.

One brick wall standing alone will always present difficulties; two backyard walls standing scarce three feet apart are a joke. A man has but to brace his body between the two and walk upward. A grunt and a heave and I had got myself over the wall and into the yard. Two dark shapes lay still and stark on the snow. I listened. From within Mudie's house I heard the sharp yelp of a little terrier. Then there was a sudden burst of shrieking female anger. I heard one drawn out whine and then there was peace. Again my heart's blood was pounding against the silence. The timing was perfect. From down the bank towards the river I heard the first harsh corncrake of a watchman's rattle.

It was the empty house that interested me. The snow between the back doors of the two houses carried a well-trodden track. Recently too, stout locks had been fitted to the backdoor. But unless you have a professional housebreaker's set of picklocks the locks on any outside doors are things best left alone. Sometimes you can be lucky; mostly you aren't. There was a window. That was why I had bought the birdlime. Honest men smear the stuff on to the twigs of the fruit bushes in their gardens. Before long, dozens of greedy little birds will be stuck fast there. However there is another use for birdlime. And it has nothing whatever to do with horticulture. With a sheet of stout brown paper well plastered with the stuff you can muffle the sound of a breaking window. Among certain fraternities that fact was well known. Indeed before today merest smear of the white stuff on a fellow's coat has served to hang him. So I was very careful as I spread my brown paper against the pane to smooth it down. Then I put my forearm to the glass and leaned against it. There was no more noise than the breaking of the ice of a frozen puddle. With delicate care I gathered up and folded the shards of window glass sticking to the paper. I was in.

The first thing I noticed was the reek of the oil of cedarwood used in embalming fluid. I risked a flick at my tin lantern's shutter. In that short blink of light I saw the coffin lying on its trestles. The embalming had been done. Brass syringes and the empty glass demijohns lay where they had been left. I was looking down at the corpse. And I had to admit that the work done was most artful. Obviously Wilkiman had taken my advice. Instead of a corpse's pallor the dead face had a pleasing pinkness to it. Perhaps the apothecary had been *just* a little too free handed with his Mexican cochineal. The mouth had been artistically stitched into an angelic smile; the cheeks too had been padded out and rouged. Indeed the fellow looked live enough to sit us and greet me. Someone had also gone to the trouble of dressing the body. It wore an of old fashioned suit of black velvet court clothes. There was a sprigged waistcoat of lavender silk; the buttons were set with brilliants. At both throat and cuffs lace frothed. The right hand bore a signet ring and clutched at the jewelled hilt of a dress sword.

This had to be the deceased French nobleman that Wilkiman had spoken of. Yet even on short inspection I sensed that things here were not as they were presented. Though quite exactly what for the moment I could not say. Dead men always look much alike. Yet somehow this fellow did not have quite the face of a French nobleman of the *ancient regime*. But I was risking my neck just by being here, I reminded myself. I had come to find Mrs. Rachel Brydon. And that alone was what I had to do. Nonetheless I bent forward and opened my lantern's shutter a little next to the hands. Perhaps the crest on the ring would tell me something. Save that the ring was not gold at all, I deduced nothing at all.

It was the coldness of the coffin's edge against my fingertips that made me linger. Wood never gets that cold. My boot toe kicked against the ornate lid that lay against the side of the trestles. I stooped to try to lift it. And at once I knew that this particular corpse box had been cast solid throughout from pure metal. I felt the cold shiver of excitement - my short hairs began to bristle. I'd found the gold!

It was an old smuggler's trick, perhaps the oldest. In my time I had seen gold bullion cast into anchors, into chains, and, once, even formed into the lacquered pan of a lady's travelling commode! Quickly I knelt and with my knife blade I shaved away the thinnest spiral from the soft metal. In the seam of light showing at the edge of my lantern's shutter I

209

peered at the fragment. No matter which way I turned the tiny shaving between thumb and forefinger it was always the same. The bright glance of the metal was still silver-blue – for all its ornateness that coffin lid had been cast from nothing more precious than Alston lead. A man should surely try hard to avoid the game of what-might-have-been.

The rest of the ground floor contained machinery: gears and cog wheels. The device had been half dismantled so there was no telling what it had been. But then up on the second floor I heard a little moan. It came from under a great heap of carded hemp fibre that had been piled in a corner. I remembered the hemp I had found on George Humble's clothes. In three steps I was across the room and on my knees before her. She was almost naked. At the first sliding touch of my hands I knew that. I widened the lantern shutter to a finger's width. All the girl was wearing was a thin shift. And from neck to navel the cambric had been ripped open. I looked into the face. Above the gag her eyes stared; wild they were like those of a ewe caught in a thorn bush.

Chapter Twenty

"**B**e still, Mrs. Brydon, ma'am…" I shushed her as I would a hysterical child. "I'll soon have you free… But please, m'dear… I beg of you… try not to cry out!"

I reached forward to undo the gag. Her mouth was bound across with a strip torn from her petticoats. I eased the knot. But still the girl was fighting for breath, writhing about. What gagged her still was whatever had been hard stuffed into her mouth. I cradled the lass's head and with the crook of my finger I drew out the soft wetness. It was a lady's glove rolled up tight. The girl's lips mouth appeared to have been widened hideously by the blue dye that she had sucked out of the Russia leather. For a moment she lay there among the carded hemp gasping in deep breaths.

"Now, ma'am if you would just allow me to untie you…" I stopped. I felt my lower jaw fall - I was gaping at her. The light escaping between the lantern's shutter was the merest glimmer, but it was enough. Whoever this lass was she was not Mrs. Rachel Brydon.

"What 's your name, girl?" I was careful not to sound unkind. Whoever she was this lass would have a story she could tell me. And even then I was almost certain that her tale would have some bearing on the kidnapping of Rachel Brydon.

"Martha Dolan, sor…" I remembered the name. This was Mrs. Brydon's own serving maid. And with that realisation I came quickly to a very fair idea of what had happened.

"Aagh well now, Miss Martha Dolan..." I smiled at her as I brogued. "You know what they do say, me darlin': 'The pitcher that goes too oft to the well...' So you took your mistress's place ag'in did y' not?"

The Irish girl nodded. Gently I took her by the arms and turned her over. There was no struggle. Though, by God, what a fine white body she had on her! But as soon as I had turned her over I knew exactly who it was who had tied the knot. What told me that was the sight of the poor child's thumbs. They had been bound together with a piece of cord no thicker than grocer's string. But that of itself was a very distinct touch. The knot was what in the Paris underworld the thieves call the *cabriolette*: they call it that because the man who holds the string may drive his prisoner wherever he will. It is a torture under which even a strong man will scream. With care I cut the string and then all the other cords that bound her.

"Now Martha, my dear, what you must do - straightway - is to pop those thumbs of yours into your lovely mouth!" I smiled at her and patted at her cheek. "Suck at them, child... like a wee babbie... That's it. You'll need to keep them there for a while." Already the circulation was returning. I saw young Martha begin to sway. The young lass was ready to scream with agony. The moan that came from her as she rocked her body back and forth against the pain sounded like a dirge at a wake. I sat silent by her until she stopped.

"It was Charlie D'Oeuys who tied you up that way - wasn't it... the French fellow, the man with the red hair?

Young Martha Dolan nodded and then clenched her eyes shut at the memory. It was an easy guess too that for this lass her coveted service as Mrs Brydon's personal maid had clearly not been the grand adventure she had thought it would be. I put a hand to her wrist and gripped at it.

"Martha... the Frenchman... did he?" I had to ask. Though the reason for my question was altogether unworthy of the gentleman I was supposed to be. But I knew Charles D'Oeuys' past sins only too well. I knew the crimes that had first sent him to the galleys at Toulon. Where a rape was accused, and the matter properly pursued before the courts, the magistrates would be obliged to bring D'Oeuys to answer. The young lass shook her head. There was no need to press the question further.

"No, sir... But the devil tore the clothes off me and... he...he looked and he touched and promised me that he would be comin' back for me here... tonight." Her tears broke like a storm. And for long minutes I let her weep.

"Well then, we must get you out of here...away from this place – back to where we'll both be safe among our friends."

Modesty will soon enough reassert itself. It was at that moment that the lass realised that all she wore between herself and nakedness was a shift that had been ripped to the waist. I began to unbutton my coat. With a sob she shrank back from me, bringing up her knees and crossing her arms over her breasts.

"Put this on, child..." I whispered softly as I draped the heavy greatcoat round her shoulders. She was lost in it. "Is that how they brought you here? Near to naked? Have you no shoes?"

"The foreign woman at the... at that *place* made me strip to m' skin... that was when she let all the drunken men come into the room to look at me." I touched her lips with my fingers.

"No more for now, Martha..." The rest of her tale needed little guessing. "Nonetheless, you be sure to tell your mistress all that happened... every last thing!"

'Yes,' I thought, 'by all means, young Martha Dolan, you should do that. Tell Milady Hoity-Toity what pain her stupid tricks have caused you. Keep back not one bare detail of it, my dear. Let that flighty bitch know how in her wilfulness she's let her young servant be lifted off the street; describe to her how you were dragged to some stinking back street whorehouse.'

Though of course I realised at once that there'd been one man, or woman, who'd seen at once that they hadn't got the goods they'd paid for. 'Tell your mistress too how the bastards had got their money's worth; let her know how they'd stripped you and made you - an untouched virgin - stand mother naked before a roomful of smirking, leering drunken lechers.' I could guess what had happened. Martha Dolan had been used to encourage the lust of the brothel's regular customers. The scene of it was not difficult to imagine. 'Yes, young Martha,' I thought, 'you be sure you let your Mistress see exactly what her charade has...' I stopped. This was no time for emotion. Already my anger had cost me ten wasted seconds of time. And for want of that space of time we could both be dead!

I carried the lass down the stairs and set her down bare footed on the boards. At once I heard her draw a breath. Her wavering sob echoed across the room. In the play of the moonlight she had seen the coffin. With a frantic suddenness the girl crossed herself, twice. How quickly we forget. In France, of course, such a thing would have been no surprise to me at all; but here among the Protestant English a young lass crossing herself would be a rare enough sight. Though done by an Irish servant girl it was something that was would draw no more than a look.

"You take no heed o' that old fella, Martha Dolan... for hasn't y'r own priest told you that the same body contained the Holy Spirit and for that reason is to be revered?" She nodded her head like a creature in a dream; though while we walked past that coffin her wide eyes never left the old man's face.

But we did have one piece of luck. The front door was not secured with locks. There were three heavy bolts but it was easy enough to draw them.

Over the way in the darkness I heard the sharp click of Joe Fletcher's tongue. Only the jingle of harness told me he had been waiting for me all along in the shadow of All-Hallows' wall. I carried the lass out to the carriage and laid her along the seat. At once too I sensed that there was someone already in the darkness. Whoever it was I felt them take hold of Martha Dolan's body and draw her along the leather cushions.

"Take her home, Joe. " I whispered. "I've more business here tonight. But this poor lass has been sadly ill-used. So you'd better get Grainger's house-keeper to look to her!"

"Yes, indeed, sir. But my orders are that you are to come in straightaway. It would be better if you were to climb up here with me…"

"No…" The sharp voice cut out from the darkness. "The Doctor is to sit in here with me…"

My own anger at Rachel Brydon boiled up. There were things that needed to be said; now matter who the flighty bitch was. I had been put to sore trouble because of her silly whim. This time the woman would hear me! However it was only when she had finished speaking that I realised again that Rachel Brydon's was not the voice I had heard. I suppose that my expectation had been that any woman's voice from within the dark of the carriage would be hers. It was not. At that moment I saw all profit from my nights work fade. My time had been wasted; I had risked my neck for nothing. Save perhaps that I had rescued young Martha Dolan. No; not quite. I had also found the mummified corpse. Though what significance it would have, if any, was unclear. And within a couple of hours at most I had prospect of getting my hands on a man who was, or had been, one of Fouche's chief agents in England. I heard myself give a little snort of self-derision. Damn it all what a bald lie that was; and I knew damned well it was. What I really wanted was some simple but solid *revenge*. That much I admitted to myself. Yes, very badly I wanted to put the terror of an agonised death into one sneering little pimp. For in my heart I knew that the true score that needed to be settled was for what Charles D'Oeuys had done to Ettie Bellis. Already I could taste the savour of that. I had wanted to step out of the darkness and hit the bastard. I wanted to hear the crack of my fist against his jaw; I wanted to hear his teeth spill out rattling across the floorboards! It was something I twitched to do. And then, before *Monsieur's* so-innocent blue eyes were opened again I would have that same piece of grocer's string around the bastard's ballocks! And then it would be Bob Shafto's turn to drive the *cabriolette*! By Christ I'd have D'Oeuys screaming into his gag! He *would* tell me everything. And then I would know all of this business through and through to its furthermost end.

"Yes… Doctor Shafto…climb in here beside us, quickly if you please. The sooner we're away from here the better it will be for us all. And that, sir, is Mr. Grainger's own order…" Now I knew the voice. The last time I had heard it had been in the house in Charlotte Square. It was Lady Donkin, Rachel Brydon's paid companion.

At that moment I was as near to anger as I was to surprise. Just in time I was able to bite off the oath gathering in my throat. It was simple prudence made me kill it. That and, as the carriage turned into a street with a few torches burning, the sight of what I saw for the first time had once been a damned handsome profile.

"Yes, ma'am…" It was the intensity of my curiosity that stifled the anger seething inside me.

" Lady Donkin," My voice was level. "You are in good health, I trust?"

As she moved to settle herself I heard again the rustle of satin. The old woman wore her skirts a deal wider than had been the fashion these last twenty years. In the old style she had filled them out with many petticoats. It was at that moment that it occurred to me. I had scarce given the old woman a thought. At the time I had dismissed her from mind completely. I allowed my questions to fade on my lips. Of a sudden I knew that to attempt to enter into conversation with this woman was sure to invite a terse rebuff. For whatever else the silly old woman was, in England at least, she was still 'Lady' Donkin. Though indeed that was _all_ she was! Without the money to back it that frail title was the last tattered shred of dignity remaining to her. Without it the old bitch would be just another lady's companion, a quivering creature with nothing save her gentility between her and the poor house.

Besides from her first glance at me I had known that the old bitch had regarded me as being little better than some village bonesetter.

"Well enough... I thank you, Doctor Shafto...well enough!"

I supposed it was something. These I realised then were more words than I had ever had from the woman. Though it was also plain enough that they were as many as I was going to get! No matter, Nicolo, Mrs.Brydon's man-servant would soon tell me what I wanted to know.

The odd silence that lay between us was maintained as the carriage carried us up to Brunswick Place. Of course, and even more, I had wanted to ask her if there was yet any news of Rachel Brydon. But I would be damned if I would ask her now. Nor would I tell her what I had been doing that night. Though to give the old bitch credit she sat cradling young Martha's head on her lap. Perhaps she had herself once been one of those poor creatures. The fancy took me: had she been crossed-in-love, soured against men.

Richard Grainger came down the steps into the yard at the run to greet us.

"Well done, Doctor, bloody well done..." He thrust out his hand at me. His grip was hearty. He waved a couple of footmen forward to wrap Martha Dolan in a blanket and carry her into the house, "Just you leave Mrs...er Lady Donkin... to take care of the youngster. Come you in man, take a glass..."

From that first instant I knew that something was amiss. That was obvious to me. I could smell it! The greeting had been sincere; Richard Grainger gave all the appearances of a man well pleased. But then I found myself fancying that perhaps he had been just a little *too* sincere. With all the gravity I could muster I thanked him.

But we did not go into the dining room. From the roar of noise that came from behind those heavy rosewood doors it was obvious that a dinner party was on-going. Indeed it was only then that I saw that Grainger was wearing the black satin knee

217

breeches that such a formal evening occasion still demanded. He led the way to down the hall to a heavily curtained door.

"There's a fellow at my table tonight whom you will doubtless remember, Doctor. He too has been busy hereabouts these last days…"

Grainger poured sherry and handed me a glass. Then he stood warming his backside at the coal fire roaring in the hearth.

"If I could ask you just step up to yon Velasquez." He pointed a finger at a new oil painting. When I went to it I saw that its gilded frame was hinged to the wall. At Grainger's urging I swung it open. It was what I had suspected. I found that I was looking at the back of another painting. Through a neat peep-hole in that canavas I could look down into a dining room bright with the blaze of wax candles.

"I've so arranged the seating that those fellows who are of interest to us can been seen from that butler's squint."

Almost directly across from me, quite magnificent in his crimson coat and bullion thread epaulets, sat George Ninnian Farquahar. Already the major's fat face was deep flushed with good port. Then Grainger was at my side.

"As something of a gambit, Doctor, this evening I asked my father to invite a number of the garrison's officers down to a dinner. At my behest the guv'nor suggested to his friend, the colonel, that Major Farquahar would be a particularly welcome guest." I could sense rather than hear Grainger's amusement. "Though *quite* what we are to do about the major yet awhile I really don't know. However thus far I want you to see what a sound fellow I've just said 'sic'em! to. You'll recognise him – there, two places along."

I looked. And for what seemed an age I saw nothing. It was an infantry officer with an eyepatch and his left arm held up in a black sling. He was talking, and the company present was listening intently to what looked to be a wounded hero.

"So then Wellesley shouted… at the very top of his voice mark you…'Why then Sir, you should return there at once and ask your colonel for the loan of *his* umbrella!'" At the great roar of laughter that the officer's anecdote drew from the company I felt the stretched oil painting before my nose vibrate. It was only when he picked up his glass to return the toasts that it began slowly to dawn in upon me who it was.

"God Almighty!" Awed I truly was. Again the fellow had created a perfect new *persona*. Only a certain something about those eyes allowed my recognition to crystallise. Indeed it was still damned hard to accept at all that this was the same fellow who had greeted me at the *Bull and Mouth* in London..

Through that small hole pierced in an oil painting I looked down and across at the agent whose skill had in a few short hours transformed me from a shabby unemployed French officer into the acute semblance of a gentleman from the comfortable middles classes of English life. And now here again I was seeing the consummate skill of the man's art. I remembered too that the cutlass slash under that sling had still to be real enough.

"Taylor has been given his instructions. Until this business is entirely settled he is not to let Farquahar out of his sight. Those are my orders to him. And for this night at least he looks to be fulfilling his guarantees that the major will stagger drunk to bed. Though be assured, Doctor, should the worst come to the worst…" Grainger looked me in he face when he spoke. "Our friend won't hesitate to…*do* whatever he finds it necessary to *do*. Does that satisfy you Doctor?"

What was there I could say?

"It does, Mr. Grainger; with the man I know as Squires Taylor watching my back I rather think it would have to!"

I sat with a glass in my hand as I delivered to Richard Grainger a simple report of the evening's happenings. The only exaggeration I made in the amount of the sum I had paid out to have a minor riot keep the rattles of the ward's night watchmen clacking merrily for a few hours.

" An old man embalmed, you say; an' my cousin's Irish maid lyin' upstairs above him – near to naked and her bound up like a trussed goose'!" Grainger was suddenly pensive. "So what are we to do, eh?" He was talking to himself and for a moment he might have been alone in the room. I put my suggestion:

"If you could get a magistrate out of his bed at this time o' night… Mrs. Brydon's girl was brazenly kidnapped. She was rescued from premises owned by Severus Mudie…"

"By whom…Doctor, by whom?" Grainger looked at me directly. "*You* yourself are hardly in a position to…" Yes; it was an awkward question. Clearly that had been a wrong move. But then and at once I saw from the look that fled across his face that the whole plan of campaign for Richard Grainger had changed. That something had happened to change it. Of course I could see that the courts would simply not treat the case of young Martha Dolan in the same way as a complaint from the lawyers acting for the rich widow Brydon. Rarely indeed did anyone have magistrates' warrants sworn out on behalf of their own servant lasses!

Grainger stood up. " I fear that for the next few hours duty demands that I return to entertain my guests. Pray, Doctor, stay in this room. I've already given orders that you are not to be disturbed. It is late, I know; but nonetheless I will ask you to write a full report of all your doings this evening." Grainger winked. "I too have masters to serve."

It was at that moment that I began to suspect that Richard Grainger was trying to buy me off.

Chapter Twenty-one

The only exaggeration I made to my report lay in the amount of the sum I had paid out to have a minor riot keep the rattles of the ward's night watchmen clacking merrily for a few hours.

As he read my tale I saw that Richard Grainger was again inclined to amusement. "And with Mrs Brydon's own girl lyin' upstairs above it – near to naked and her trussed up like a Christmas goose'!" Grainger was suddenly pensive. "So what to do, eh?" For a little space he seemed to be talking to himself. He might have been alone in the room. I put my suggestion:

"If you could get a magistrate out of his bed at this time o' night… clearly young Mary Dolan *was* abducted. And I rescued her from premises owned by Doctor Mudie…"

"Abducted by whom… my friend?" Grainger looked at me directly. "You yourself are hardly in a position to swear anything before a town's bench!"

Yes; Grainger had a point. I had tried the stroke – but clearly my move had been in the wrong direction. But then and at once I saw from the look that fled across the man's face that what I was suggesting was not being accepted. For Richard Grainger his whole plan of campaign looked to have changed. Moreover something important really had happened to change his view. Of course I could see what local society might make of the case if the *Newcastle Mercury* printed the story.

Grainger stretched out his arms. "But for the next few hours at least plain duty demands that I return to entertain my guests. Pray, Doctor, stay in this room. I've already given orders that you are not to be disturbed." He motioned to an escritoire. "There are paper and quills. It is late, I know; but nonetheless I will ask you to write a formal report of all your doings this evening. Colonel Dekker will be pleased to receive them." He winked. "We both have a master to serve. But then the comfort from that is that the sooner your intelligence is received in Edinburgh, why then, as I should have said, the sooner I can get a further disbursement of cash authorised."

Again I caught Grainger's point. But again, and now more surely, I realised that the man was trying to buy me off. But exactly off what I could not guess. Though I was able to conjecture that a least I would know soon enough.

Within half an hour I was shaking the sand from the last page of that report for Dekker. While I had been writing a footman had come silently in and set down a tray. It was the escaping waft of savoury steam twitching at my nostrils that made me realise how near to famished I was. I lifted the silver plate cover's edge to see both boiled potatoes and green cabbage; both piled up to guard the flanks of one of those wonderful confections of beefsteak and oysters the English call a 'saddlebag'!

But then just as I was tucking in my napkin there was a loud roar from the dining room next door. It was so loud that it had me on my feet at once and across to the squint hole. I swung open the oil painting and tried to focus. Clearly the story had to have been a good one. All along the dining table men lay among their plates and glasses, banging their heads against the table linen; unashamed tears of mirth were running down whiskered faces. Except, that is, for Major Farquahar. Down through the squint hole I could see him clearly. Whoever was sitting directly across from him had his entire attention. The major was not sharing in the company's mirth. Far from it! His mouth opened then snapped shut. Whatever had been said to him had not left Farquahar a happy man!

While I took breakfast with Grainger next morning I realised again that I was being fobbed off. His very mood told me that. The man was detached, worried. And surely with Richard Grainger such a thing had to be a rarity? Something was now sadly amiss. Though whatever it was Bob Shafto was not going to be allowed to be privy to it. The first thing that had alarmed me had been the way that Grainger had obviously balked at a clear opportunity for us to get our hands on Charles D'Oeuys. I remembered what my own old spy-master, Major Dimnet, had once said about a man who procrastinates – he has always some other hidden motive. With a sworn statement from Rachel Brydon's maid set before them the city's magistrates could scarce have refused to issue a search warrant for Dr. Severus Mudie's premises. D'Oeuys would have been in our hands. There was much I wanted to ask of the red headed man. Nor would all my questions have been to do with the smuggling of guineas.

"So you have decided not to apply to the magistrates for a warrant, Mr.Grainger." I asked that question as the lightest of asides.

"Not prudent, old fellow… nothing to gain by it, now." As he mumbled his answer Grainger had looked vacantly out of the window. The room was warm and bright with daffodils flowering in blue and white chinaware pots. Their yellow glow added a distinct richness to pale sunlight. He took a sip from his coffee cup. I watched him. For whatever reasons of his own Grainger clearly did not want the town's Watch to raid that house by All-Hallows Green. I felt it; I knew it. Very gently but nonetheless very firmly Richard Grainger was now tightening his leash on me - his sleuthhound. The night before he had even insisted that a cot be made up for me in Joe Fletcher's quarters above the stables. It had been plain enough then that the old coachman had been set to watch me. Even Joe had been embarrassed.

But, as they say, if a man is marching… why he is not fighting! Moreover Grainger had airily waved aside my offer to return what was left in the purse he had given me.

"Well, sir, if that is your *considered* opinion…" I was the very soul of deference. I needed no reminding of my own position. No matter how courteous Grainger always was, for so long as I was anywhere in the British Islands I would be, first Talaeus Dekker's dog, then Grainger's. My masters' worries were mine - they would have to be. And for a certainty this was no time for me to go poking any idle fingers into the cogs of the powerful machine we both served. Put it whichever way you cared to, at his merest whim Grainger could jerk at the noose that was around my neck! if that was what he chose to do. Again the insistent voice within was warning me that I could not feel truly safe again until my own vulnerable backside was out the country – altogether!.

"Something happened yesterday…" Richard Grainger had come to a decision. The light o' battle that had gleamed so brightly the day before had been dulled. Though nonetheless, and I had no doubt at all, whatever it was still smouldered on. Quite simply Richard Grainger had himself been suddenly bridled. Moreover the curb iron had hurt his soft mouth. And the recent events still sat very ill with him.

"With all due respect, Doctor Shafto, I will say this." Grainger was choosing his words with care - his discomfort was written plain on his face. "To be frank with you… we brought you into this enterprise to…er, to look into the doings of the merest pawns in this game." His faint smile was almost wistful. " Also perhaps, too, to follow the moves of a few of the lesser knights on this chessboard of ours. But always the kings, queens, and bishops, so to speak, in this game were to be left to… others." I nodded slowly, shifted back a little in my chair, looked at Grainger directly, but still saying nothing.

Of course what he said was quite true. But then, and no matter which way Grainger had said them – the words came to me clearly enough! In my time I had hunted down, aye, and then heard the slam of the dungeon doors on quite a few of the highest officials in Europe. But then, and after all, this was the North of England. So of course even Richard Grainger might wish to put a clothes peg on his nostrils against the stench coming off certain very private local dunghills. Moreover I suppose too that by his own lights Grainger had already sailed close enough to the wind by telling me as much as he had. Certainly I had been brought to Newcastle to search; but never to meddle. For, I knew only too well that the landed classes stick together – as the old saying has it - 'Like the folks of Shields'. They tend to know one another; or at the least and if they need bother to stir themselves they can usually find out what they want to know about anyone who interests them. Nor was it that the man was being a snob; say rather it was simply that Richard Grainger had made the assumption that *he* would always know his own kind better than any outsider ever could. But then yesterday something had happened to prove him wrong.

"Your servants had to carry Major Farquahar out to his carriage last night." Deliberately I had changed the subject.

"Hmm?" Grainger seemed to shake himself. "Oh, yes… yes…" He spared me one of his whimsical little smiles. "But he still has Squires Taylor sticking to him like a burr on a sheep's back. Or as I should rather say Captain Sebastian Tolliver…" We both smiled.

It was a name I would need to remember.

"Mr. Grainger… are you able to tell me the name of the guest who sat almost directly across the dining table from Major Farquahar last evening?"

A'ha! A hit…a damned palpable hit! If there was surprise there then Richard Grainger had contrived to suppress it wonderfully well. But I had seen how the broad shoulders had stiffened under the China silk of his dressing gown. That alone was enough to tell me something.

"Er…No; 'fraid I can't do that, Doctor…guest o' my father's, I suppose…"

He should have asked me why I had asked. He hadn't. His tone had been oddly remote. Grainger was still trying to feign that his wits were busy elsewhere. He had failed; moreover, I rather think we both knew that.

"Resume your searching, Doctor…" The instruction had come suddenly. My polite enquiry was being ignored. "You will still need to get yourself out and about into the streets of Newcastle. Find out anything you can. Note particularly," The eyes turned keenly upon me. "I am giving you *no* specific directions." I watched his afterthoughts gather. "Save that unless you are ordered by me – word o' mouth – that you should stay away altogether from that house by All-Hallows." As he spoke Grainger tapped his fingers slowly one after another on to the table linen.

I left the house in Brunswick Place like a hound loosed! Something, someone, was restraining Richard Grainger. But for all that the gentleman was allowing me to run free, free to go on doing what he, what the *British Linen Bank*, had first hired me to do.

"Arrange with Fletcher that he is to pick you up from somewhere at some small distance from this house in two days from now… at say two o'clock" I was being given my orders and, without doubt, Bob Shaftoe was being dismissed.

But what I had realised by then was that whatever intelligence my employer had come by the night before it had clearly forced his hand. Something had happened to cause Grainger to refer back to his own superiors, probably to Talaeus Dekker. That was what the counting taps of his fingers had been about. Richard Grainger had been working out just how long it would take to get a message to, and an answer from, Edinburgh. This was why I had been loosed for two days. So for at least two days I had to assume that what Talaeus Dekker had called his *Black Indies Enterprise* was being suspended.

I suppose that I might have idled. When I had served the Emperor there had been a few rare times when I had been able to make holiday. In the year 05' at Venice during such a furlough I had enjoyed a phenomenal winning streak at the pasteboards. That game had been just too profitable to quit. Truly, for a day and a night Dame Fortune herself had stood by me rubbing her nipples against my shoulder. More than that, during the last hour at the cards I came by a mere scrap of new information. That little snatch of information however proved to be vital to quite another case altogether. But for today, I decided, I would dedicate some time to a little gentle twitching at a few of Newcastle's loose ends.

The name I chose from the entries in Mattie Crowley's brown book was Ralph Hodgson. This fellow had to be that same Hodgson who had arranged to have his own nephew, Ernie, signed on as second mate aboard the collier, *Countess of Raby*. The entry on the stained page showed clearly that the 'Rph H'gsn' had paid the late Matthew Crowley all of five pounds. It had been a simple fee to have the seaman, Jesse Rae, lifted by Crowley's gang. Now I could have been persuaded that the whole matter was no more than a grand piece of old-fashioned Geordie nepotism: 'a berth for the sister's laddie.' Perhaps it had been. Equally too I was curious. For upon more thought I had to allow that I myself also had cause to be grateful to this Hodgson. However indirectly it came about, this same tangled chain seemed to connect events. Throughout, the whole turn of affairs had been determined the mystical power of money. Instead of leaving me in the alleyway with a smashed skull Matthew Crowley had stooped to take a small profit. He'd had me stripped and put aboard the *Jenny Howlet*. But then aboard that same transport tender there had been a rare leader o' men. Again, had Jesse Rae and his mates not been taken up by the pressgang that same night, why then Bob Shaftoe might well at that moment have been scrambling about rigging of a British man-o-war. Fate!

But even so there were still too many other fragmented links in this same twisted chain that I had yet to find and forge together. About the *Countess of Raby_* I was almost certain.

Beyond the fall of any chance that ship had come into the picture too often. It had been to that vessel that I had followed the seaman who had looted Knox's tenement room. If illegal gold was to be carried by sea, then surely that collier brig had to have a part in the business. But I knew too that she could only be the merest cartoon of a full-finished picture. So far, I still knew almost nothing but the scarcely connected pieces of the puzzle. Grainger had been right. Bob Shaftoe had indeed been just a fellow they had employed to spy among the lowly folk of the town, among the tradesmen, and the servants below stairs. Indeed, and the thought struck at me sharply, in the end it might prove dangerous for me to find out too much anyway. Thus far, though, nothing had happened to overthrow my original notion that Newcastle's guinea smuggling game was in the hands of only one man, or at most, perhaps, a tight little syndicate. Almost by definition only a few very rich men could mount such a venture. And in such dealings these adventurers would have to keep their own hands tight on *their* gold at all times. Above all they would know better than any man that bright gold will always take a grip on the human soul. Just as they would also know that the only instrument which would hold all the parties together was simple terror of death. I thought of the attempted killing of George Humble

The rich smell of oak smoked hams drifted out on to the pavement. Ralph Hodgson's shop stood up at the fashionable north end of Northumberland Street. I had found his name prominent in the *Newcastle Directory* in the column devoted to 'Purveyors of Fine Provisions'. One glance into the fairyland displayed within the shop was enough to tell me that this Hodgson already had his hands on a good deal of the County's carriage trade. As I went in I was met by the waft off smoked hams and the perfumes from dried herbs.

The upper servants of a nobleman's household will always strive their hardest to reflect their masters' rank and wealth. Indeed they will often go to some ends to display a fair counterfeit of that same aura. You can see it in every step they take. That much I should know; for twenty odd years my own father had been steward to a coal-owning lord. And that morning was no different. At those long, polished counters three such men and one woman stood. These were the sorts of people I had moved among all my boyhood. They were dressed in good but sombre clothes. But that scarcely masked the pointed fact that for so long as they stood in Hodgson's shop every one of them enjoyed a brief moment of power. For, this was one of the few places where such folk as these could - at their slightest whim - bestow or withhold the gift of custom and patronage. So at the farther side of the counter no fewer than six young fellows in green aprons were hopping about like frogs in their eagerness to serve. Even so I knew well enough that the whole show was part of a time-honoured game:

"And I'll take a full ounce of saffron…if you please." The woman's enunciation was slow and precise. Indeed it was every bit as careful as the step of a chambermaid carrying a brimming piss-pot down the back stairs.

But then the lad's response too when it came had the detectable slick of easy insolence to it: "Livorno, ma'am … or superior Greek? Then in the faintest of most confidential whispers: "Of course, Mrs. Hart, ma'am, we do keep the slightly cheaper…" Good lad! I thought. One day you'll be the mayor o' Newcastle! That wicked little stab of his had pieced her dignity to the quick. Yet it still worked. The housekeeper froze the offer of the cheaper spice on to the fellow's lips.

"And may we do anything for *you*, Sir." The voice was as unctuous as the soft glug-glug of olive oil out of a keg. Without a sound the youth had come up from behind me. When I turned he was at my elbow. He stood there, a superior counter jumper in a green tailcoat and tight strapped yellow pantaloons. Here too though I knew the signs. Of course I could hardly have taken even the slightest exception to *what* he had said. Nonetheless from the way that he had said it and the greasy curl of his fat lower lip I might as well have been holding out pauper's soup ticket.

Chapter Twenty Two

"**L**addie..." my drawl was like a panther purring over its fresh killed prey. I poked a forefinger hard against one of his pearl shell waistcoat buttons. "Take me to the owner of this establishment ...and you be damned sharp about it!"

There are many ways I might have dealt with this young fart catcher. At other times, in other places, I might have used them. But not, I thought, today. Master pantaloons was all swollen tight with the pride and ignorance he had been born to. It would be no difficult job to prick his soul's inflated bladder for him. As always, however, sinister is, as sinister does:

"Young man... if you would to save yourself from a deal of trouble...." I looked away from him deliberately, squinting sidelong down the shop and talking to him over my shoulder. "Then you should take me to your master without a moment's delay... it might save you some sorrow!" As I had meant it to the whole shop heard me. There was a sudden silence. It was broken only by the crash of a dropped scale weight skittering through the floor's sawdust. For a few seconds I sensed his pride resist me. Then he broke. "I'll see if Mr. Hodgson is in...sir."

At first sight I knew that I had already seen Ralph Hodgson twice before. He had been with his friends in the theatre. He had also been at the cockfight in the back room at the *Sun Inn*. It was the fellow with a face like a pug dog. And from those same face bones I saw too that young Sir Pantaloons had to be

Ralph Hodgson's son. The 'Da' himself sat at his desk by the window merrily ticking off the items on a bill of invoice with a quill pen. A half smile was flickering about at the corner of a wide mouth. This surely was a man doing what he liked best to do.

"Aye, Rupert...what is it? " Slowly he looked up. Then, and without pause for breath he rasped out: "Have you tendered his Lordship's bill to Mrs.Hart, yet?" From the dismayed look on his face Rupert clearly had not.

"Then move your idle backside and do so, y' useless bloody article...Do it!

Suddenly disconcerted the heir to the House of Hodgson turned about and fled. But even then I knew that every bit of Hodgson's performance had been for me and me alone. "Now, Sir, what business is it you have you with me?" His manner had to it the firm *snappety-snap* of the new British Commerce. Though well before he had spoken Hodgson had looked me up and down and I fancied had already valued my estate to within a penny's piece. And I knew that with the same speed that the fellow had not been much impressed.

"Matthew Crowley..." I began. The mouth clapped shut. Hodgson glanced up at me. Then with slow deliberation he picked up a cloth and wiped the ink from his goose quill. He strained as he reached forward to thrust the pen's tip into a little bowl of birdshot. His chair creaked. As he took a breath I heard his chest wheeze; I also heard his stomach rumble. Oh, yes, this master grocer needed some time to think.

"Dead," he said shortly. "...dead as a drowned sheep, or so aah've read in the *Mercury*...throat slashed and tossed into the river...cast up on the south shore just above the brick kilns at Redheaugh."

"Yes; indeed, *sad* it was." I allowed my voice to fall. "But then Mr Crowley had foolishly seen fit to make light of a certain er...serious proposal." Deliberately I flicked up a single eyebrow at him. "... a very handsome offer made to him by the... *Glasgow Man*." I allowed all this information to fall and settle like dust.

Ha! It seldom fails. Phantoms served up smoking hot off the griddle! Gothyck names will always carry their own uncanny power. Five years before in Rotterdam I had fabricated '*De Vlaming*', The Fleming. Mythical entire he'd been. And even at its most tangible my invention had been scarcely cost me more than the retailing of a few gruesome anecdotes. Yet for the whole of the winter of 1810 that phantom, my own invented bogeyman, had stalked from corpse to corpse along that port's wharves. From beginning to end, it had all been a pure ruse. Here a similar phantom came readily to hand again.

"Which Sir, is why I have been sent here to see you today." Briskly I pulled five new minted guinea pieces out of my purse and spread them in a line on the desk before Ralph Hodgson.

"We failed... or say rather that our predecessor failed. The seaman Jesse Rae was not taken aboard the tender *Lyra* - *w*hich was what Crowley undertook to do. And accordingly I am instructed here to return to you your fee... with our sincere apologies."

This little piece of play-acting of course amazed Hodgson. Though, not so much that he failed to scoop up the ready cash from the table.

"However..." I allowed myself a pause that also verged upon the theatrical. " My er... associates, being now in possession of the late Mr. Crowley's ledgers, are of the opinion that you, Mr. Hodgson, and indeed some of your more discrete business associates, might yet give us an opportunity to prove our worth... in some other cases."

My smile became suddenly very knowing.

"If, for example, are there any *radicals* that you happen to be aware of in your employment..." I held up an admonitory finger. "Like the clever young men who meet in the backrooms of the *Cauld Lad* across at Gateshead. Those fellows who of a

Wednesday evening eat toasted cheese together and discuss the sheer sedition they are pleased to call… *philosophy!*"

But so-called working men's clubs disguising unlawful assemblies and even trades unions were clearly of no interest to this prosperous grocer. I turned over my hand in the air to display that I was spilling out the topic.

"Well, then, Mr. Hodgson… I think that this re-payment has concluded our business, on this occasion." I stood up and offered him my hand. After a split second of hesitation he took it. I applied the quick double thumb press of an Italian freemason's grip. I had seen the talisman he wore on his watch chain. But he gave no response that I could recognise.

"Though if it should be that you have further need of *our* services…" I caught his gaze and held it until it dropped away. "Just ask for Jacob Storey in the taproom of the *Rose* down on the Pudding Chare." The warm flicker of my own humour licked at him. "You should however not be deceived by the fellow's appearance. He is our trusted servant. Give him no more than a shilling and tell him that you wish to speak to 'Mr. Farrow about the newly shipped goods'." I waited until Hodgson had nodded. "Shortly thereafter I, or one of our agents, will call upon you."

Damn me but this was turning into such a good tale that I near believed it myself! I turned at the door and gave the merest ghost of a bow. Hodgson had already picked up his quill and was back at his papers.

"Wait!" Hurriedly the grocer softened the harsh hiss of his order to a request: "If you would be so obliging…" Mr. Ralph Hodgson poured wine; and he rose to his feet to hand me the crystal glass. It was supposed to be a *manzanilla* – not quite it wasn't! Though, it was certainly good enough to offer to a man wearing non-conformist minister's black broadcloth. "It may be, sir, now that I turn my mind to it, that I am, after all, in a position to offer a you a proposal… a very, very discrete piece of business."

I spread my hands apart very slowly and raised my eyes; if not to Heaven itself then at least to the rows of dark smoked hams hanging from iron beam hooks overhead.

"You will understand that this is not work that I would ever have offered Matthew Crowley. Certainly this is no job for street hooligans." For a few seconds Hodgson chewed at his lower lip. It was plain enough that he badly needed to have something done; but it was just as clear that he was nervous about the doing of it. This was indeed a big cock salmon, fresh run, so I would need to play him very cannily. I sat down again.

"With *us*, Sir, discretion, *absolute* discretion, is always the prime watchword." I gave him a restrained smile that I hoped was reassuring. "But, if you would allow me to make a suggestion. *We* always find it useful to speak of any transaction in a form of code." I puffed out my cheeks and blew softly. "That is to say from first to last we always prefer to couch our discussions in the terms of Euclid, of common Geometry..."

Hodgson goggled at me as though I had gone mad. Naturally enough! But I hastened to explain.

"You, Sir, in any further discussion, will always be referred to only as '*A*'; *I* as '*B*'... and the individual with whom we are to have some..." I allowed my tongue to lick around my lips. "*business* dealings... we will always label as '*C*'..."

Once made clear to him Hodgson was clearly delighted with the whole idea. The lawyers' cleverness of it all intrigued him. Nor did he need to be reminded, though I did mention the fact to him, that upon the matter of whatever words passed between us he could with a pure heart swear on the 'Testament' that he had never *mentioned* any man's name to me.

It took him a minute or two to get his intellect applied to what I had suggested. But when he did there was no doubt as to what he wanted.

"There's a young chap who is part owner of a warehouse in which I have an interest. And in the ordinary course o' business this is a state that aa'h can just about abide." A child of five could have told that the fellow was busy mincing-up the truth finely as he went. "What aa'h want is for the three of them to be away for two full days... him and the two labourers who work for him. But mind ye, aa'h won't have any harm come to any of them."

"You wish for these good fellows to be spirited away, so to speak; you want them kept secure... nothing more, nothing less. Ralph Hodgson was clearly delighted at my insight. After all it was all a matter of mere description, a way of describing in other gentler words the kidnapping and unlawful imprisonment of three honest men.

"For which service the fee will be fifty guineas - in gold – to be paid immediately... upon the successful completion of the work." That reined the greedy bastard up sharply enough. At once I put a hard edge on my voice. Men like Hodgson never do appreciate anything that they had not paid for through the nose. And to be sure his pain was scarcely feigned at all. But I pressed straight on.

"Two rolls of English guineas are to be parcelled securely. They will be well packed in, say, a small cigar box." I shaped the air with my hands. "Fill any free space with oat bran or lentils – we find them both admirable for preventing coin from chinking." Detail always adds veracity. "That sum will then be held in waiting until our agent collects it from your shop downstairs." I looked at him again. Yes; he was accepting what I said. "At that time, without question or comment of any kind, one of your apprentices will hand the package to the messenger... He will simply ask for a parcel for Mr Farrow. That is all."

"But fifty guineas is..." I cut him off.

"When you paid Crowley to lift the *Countess of Raby*'s newly appointed second mate, that fellow was able to count also on getting a good sum in head-money." I smiled bleakly. "That of course would have been from the port captain down at the *Lyra*..." I wanted Ralph Hodgson to know that I was familiar with all the workings of the man-snatching trade along the Tyneside. "Also that same payment was drawn at the North Shields regulating room, down near the *Wooden Dolly* by the Customs House Quay. We however will be able to seek no extra payment!"

"Fifty guineas it is." His collapse had been sudden. Indeed I rather fancied that I had convinced him fully that I, *we,* whoever we were, had come into the entire goodwill of Matthew Crowley's crimping business.

"You have made a wise decision Mr. Hodgson," I was full of mellow approval. "And you may have no fear that for fully two days these men will be kept in darkness and in silence. Yet you can be assured that they will not suffer the slightest injury from their abduction." I frowned at my own fingernails. "That is to say provided that they are all reasonable fellows and do behave themselves."

Slowly Hodgson nodded back at me. His hand reached for the decanter again but at the last moment it stayed itself.

"So then, sir... I will need to know exactly when you wish us to proceed with our... our little commission?" I watched the disquiet sweep through the grocer's frame. This was a man who making a pact with a Devil he didn't know. At that moment too I could see that he might well lose courage and withdraw from the whole business. Yet all of sudden he seemed to recover his nerve.

"Until the day after tomorrow, at...."

My left arm swept up and I drew two fingers diagonally across my mouth. He was instantly silent.

"Discretion, Mr. Hodgson!" I admonished as slowly I let my fingers fall away. "In *all* things dis-cret-ion rules! At this particular moment, sir, all you need do is to tell me the day." He looked puzzled. "Only on the morning of that day you will be asked to supply us with the names of the men and where they can be found. Until then you should keep the venue secret to yourself alone!" I took Matthew Crowley's book from my pocket and thumbed it open. A page showed that a certain Mr. Josiah Barras with a shop on the Side had paid three pounds to get a journeyman saddler called Bainbridge lifted by the press gang. I tore it out and handed it to Hodgson. He was not a man likely to leave alone the secret of the transaction it betrayed. I remembered the bewildered young bridegroom who had been battened down with us in the hold of the *Jenny Howlet*.

"Write, print, on that paper *only* those things which we will need to know. Seal it securely. Then on the morning of the day, send a messenger down to the *Rose*. Have the instructions left with the landlord. Our man will communicate with us and within that same hour our people will act!" My face's expression bore, I was convinced, the very artifice of reassurance." We have found in the past that our methods make us quite untraceable... any of us, Mr.Hodgson, any of us - whomsoever!"

Chapter Twenty Three

As I walked towards the street door I could feel the curious eyes boring into the flesh between my shoulder blades. Three proud butlers and a housekeeper, and every other soul standing in the shop were all stricken dumb. This was something to bring a smirk to my face. I couldn't help myself! Because I knew well enough about the speed with which a wild and juicy tale runs among the town's upper servants. Any tale about the doings of the Hodgson family was one that would travel fast. They had all heard the man's roar; and they'd certainly seen young Rupert scuttle down the stairway. Yet what none of them could suspect even for an instant was that I had left behind me a Ralphie Hodgson who was swelling with pleasure at his own cunning. And a sentiment like that would surely deliver the man as a safe hostage to Dame Fortune. For from first sight I had marked him well. This Hodgson was one of the grasping swine the Paris shopkeepers had begun to call 'un aigrefin Anglais'. Though, I had fancied that this would be one deal where our friend would find his own acumen so sharp that he slashed a vein with it. Indeed I would try to see to it that he did!

An agent however must improvise. That is an axiom of the trade. I had! But it's always gently as does it. As always, I had begun by building up the scoundrel's trust; his belief in the existence of an organisation captained by the fictional *Glasgow Man*. And it had been remarkable how readily Hodgson had swallowed the whole fable. He had accepted at once that my invented entities were the natural successors to Matthew Crowley. Here, yet again, the dead crimp's little account book had proved invaluable.

To be sure, from the outset I had been damned careful. Throughout I had stuck religiously to the methods I had been taught at the *Hotel d' Arcol*. Moreover there had been – I have to say it – a pleasing thrill to that interview. As I walked past the shop's coffee grinder all my senses were telling me that I ought to have been sniffing at prime Mocha. But instead what I could smell to the point of tasting it was the bitterness of that foul-tasting infusion of burnt acorns and chicory they had used to serve us at Reims. Yes, give the dog his due, at Fouche's little *academie* on the *Rue de Lyon* I had learned the bones of all the lesser villainies. And that morning I had proved at least that much to myself. Had Hodgson been asked to advance so much as a penny's piece? He had not. Indeed I had opened the game by returning <u>his</u> gold to him! That had been a wrench! My mouth became crooked again as my old mentor's teachings echoed in my head.

"Remember this, Robert. The world-at-large may think that only a twittering fool ever returns moneys paid. So do that. For it gives the impression that you have superabundant funds to hand. But that very often will pay huge dividends in the commodity you most desire – *confidence!*"

And it was so. I was quite sure that I had drawn Ralph Hodgson into compromising himself. The smug bastard had sat back in his chair convinced that he had not given away one jot of information. And I suppose that in his own mind he had not. Of course I could still be wrong. Yet, for all that, my firm suspicion was that in this grocer had to be one of the links in the golden chain…though to be sure one of the thinner links!

I suppose that I might have gone on with my vain conjectures; but of a sudden my whole urge was to act. I needed to see some progress. Indeed I knew that what I wanted most at that moment to have this whole festering boil of a business brought to a good ripe head. There was much poisonous suppuration swelling up within and it surely begged for a sharp lancing. It needed to be drained. And Bob Shafto, I told myself, was just the lad who would do that! That itself was only a step on my road. What I wanted most of all was to get myself somewhere well beyond the grasp of Talaeus Dekker. Only too well I knew that what Jonathan Stokoe had warned me about was probably right. Or at least it was well worth bearing in mind.

But for now I had again to drag the fine teeth of my nit comb through all the chares and entries of Newcastle. Hodgson might be as cunning as a bare-arsed Barbary ape. But from now on that same scheming bastard would hide nothing from me. Besides which this little enterprise of mine was being done on free time. For whatever reason, and that was something I would certainly think on, Richard Grainger had given me a leave-of-absence. For two days I was free to root around as the fancy took me. My first thoughts turned to the lass who lodged down by the Pandon Gate.

But when I got down there I was disappointed. I found Eadie Bell's door shut. But Storey was sitting on the cold stone step at the head of the stairway. It was comical. From the look on the fellow's face it was so obvious that poor Jacob had been barred from the house!

"What chee'or, wor' Jacob?" I was in good humour. I had intended to stand the disgraced butler a pot of porter's ale and a slice off a roasting joint. For it had occurred to me that for a few days I might need him. I had thought that at least I could trust the rogue to wait in the *Rose*'s taproom until Hodgson's note arrived. But even at twenty paces off I could see that Jacob had about him the sorry look of a bum-bailiff's dog.

"Ah've betrayed the lass, Mr." He raised his head. To my surprise the washed out blue of Jacob Storey's eyes was salt bleared from his tears. And I knew straightaway that this was more than any melancholia born of cheap gin.

"You've betrayed *who*, y' daft beggar?" I gripped his arm and lifted him to his feet.

"Why man, young Ettie. She's set off walkin' tae Sunderland, t' see that bairn o' hers…" This was a man wretched with his own guilt. That was when I began to feel the black bile of foreboding stir and rise in my guts.

"And then what, Jacob; what happened then?" I spoke very softly; though my fingers were ripping at the seams of his shirt. Like a terrier with a rat I found myself shaking him. I think that just in time I was able to remind myself that Jacob was an old man.

"She's bein' followed by two creeping buggers from some lawyer's office up in the town. Word along the Quay is that they've been askin' after her for a couple of days now… offerin' money for the right news." He looked up at me pathetically. "Christ Almighty, sir, but them bastards was clever! Aah' thought that they were just two good-hearted chaps offerin' me a glass… "Storey put his head into his hands.".… An' ah' had tae be the stupid slaverin' gob-shite that ah' am!" I felt my fist curl and tighten. Then, of a sudden, coolness settled about me. This wasn't the way.

"Aye, Jacob… Newcastle town looks to be just full to bursting with prime liberal handed fellows these days…" He seemed to have missed my sarcasm entirely. I loosed my grip. The wretched man sagged like a bag-pudding.

"And these er… good-hearted chaps, Jacob, did they by any chance drop a name?" Surely, I thought, the man must have had the common gumption to remember that much. Like a child at play Jacob Storey clenched his eyes shut and flicked them open again.

"The big 'un was called Archie… He's the one who has got a great lump on the side of his nose…He motioned with a forefinger, "and he's bearin' a rare green crop o' ringworms. Y' can see them plain on his shaved scalp."

I stared hard at the old man until he had recalled the other fellow's name. "<u>Mr</u>. Cattermole…" It came with a jump. "He's the gaffer o' the pair…slim built, talks like gentry… Oh, aye." He remembered. "He wears a pair o' square specs wi' green tinted glass in them." It was enough. There was no need to drag Ettie's story out of old Jacob. Already I had had the bones of the tale from Dick Triphook. It was an old story and one I had often heard before.

By now the parents of Lieutenant Crozier would be desperate to get their hands on their dead son's bastard child. I could imagine that two years before these same comfortable burghers o' the town would have died o' shame before they acknowledged the poor fatherless bairn. But - as it will - a stray French chain shot had changed the game. The wild oat had been conjured suddenly into a little rosebud. Probably it had dawned on these decent Christian folk that Ettie Bellis's come-b'-chance was become a different creature altogether. Now he was their darling grandson. Indeed now that little mite was all the blood kin they had left in this world – their sole lease on the future. That it had been their son's casual lusts that had thrust a little lassie of fifteen headlong into whoredom was something they had forgotten. What a pox-blinded thing is this human nature of ours!

Even as I shoved Jacob Storey aside I already knew that I would have to follow that girl, Miss Henrietta Bellis, along the road to Sunderland. For that was the moment I realised what was in my heart. Simply I could not bear to see the young lass abused again. For the next few hours my dealings with Ralphie Hodgson would have to be set aside to simmer on the hob of my affairs.

I pushed my way through the crowds milling about at the bottom of the Sandgate. Only the once I paused. At the stall of an old gypsy besom seller I lifted a blackthorn stick from the dozen she offered for sale.

"That'll keep y' safe, m' Hinny. Aa'h cut it m' self on Blanchland Moor, aa'h did; it 's been laid tae dry slow for two seasons…" She'd watched me and I fancied she had seen the hard set of my jaw. "That knob root on the end o' it will crack open any villain's skull, it surely will!"

A hand like a squirrel's claw caught my sixpence. I winked at her. Yes, I fancied she had seen the glint in my eye.

"Why, then Mistress… I'll test its virtue out on a couple o' chaps I'll be meeting up with" I called over my shoulder as I turned away. I could even hear the brittle snarl in my own voice. "An' next market day I'll come and let y' know for sure!"

Her cackling laugh followed me into the crowd.

I was making for Manley's by the Tyne Bridge. I would need a horse. Besides which I knew that such a stable was one place where I could safely unload a few pounds worth of Mattie Crowley's banknotes. For I knew well enough that as a stranger I would not get any decent piece of horseflesh without I put down security close to the full value of the beast itself. But I'd forgotten it was a market day. Hours before all the best mounts had been hired out.

So it was that I set out along the road to Sunderland on the back of a twelve-year old bag o' bones that looked to be but a short trot from the knacker's yard.

But that little mare had still some heart left in her and we made very fair progress. Moreover the road to Sunderland was not the hard going I remembered. For part of the way at least it was new metalled with crushed limestone. To my surprise, too, the way was busy. Both coming and going there was a fair traffic of wagons and driven livestock. But I had ridden as far as the White Mare Pool before I realised exactly what was different about it. It was only then that I realised that I was in a country that fought all its wars elsewhere. Few highways in Europe would be like this one today. Here folk still greeted one another along the way. I dismounted to beg a light for my cigar from an old man puffing at a clay pipe. He gave it with a smile.

Chapter Twenty- Four

I came up with the lawyer's men at the far side of Boldon village. The two rogues had pulled in to give their beast a breather after it had pulled them up the hill. They were in a light gig with a leather hood. Then under the spatter of mud I saw the cart's colour. At once the significance of it struck me. Recently it had been roughly repainted – in a garish canary yellow. Though for any working cart that I had ever seen yellow was, by far, too gay a colour. This might be a coincidence. Probably it was. Nonetheless for fellows of this ilk there just might just be a significance in it.

And to be sure today this particular brace of quirk-merchants were lording it high. An empty brandy bottle was flung out of the cart. It smashed on the road behind them. Yes, for sure, there could be no mistaking their trade. Though doubtless they would be down on their employer's books as clerks.

The driver had come out well enough protected against the weather. He sat like a dark hump hidden in the folds of a thick wrap-rascal coat. That would be Big Archie. He wore a tabby cat's skin cap with earflaps. It served to hide most of his face. From the lopsided set of the gig's springs I judged too that he was a heavy beggar. However the skinny Mr. Cattermole had not been near so provident. He sat huddled, having to make shift with the poor nag's blanket draped over his knees. However the fellow did cling to a few shreds of gentility. He shielded himself with a green umbrella and he had a knitted scarf wrapped around his head to secure his hat. Though to be sure his ginger coloured beaver was gone sadly into moult.

For a time I held back, dismounting and leading my mare. By then the poor beast needed the rest. It was at the next bend in the road that I caught sight of Ettie. She was hurrying along with her head was well down and holding her shawl tight against a bitter east wind. By God but that lass had a living form to her that would be a fair match for any Grecian marble! Sight of her, with her skirts all wind pressed into the hollow of her belly, would have stirred any man's loins. And I for one could not help myself! The bundle she carried too added an extra sway to those hips of hers. Then all unchecked the daft lovesick words escaped my lips. Damn me for a fool what came out was something that had a song in it somewhere.

"She 's aye seventeen but she's sae bonny!" I let the freezing breeze carry away my words.

Few men I suppose can ever choose the time they'll be smitten. But at that precise moment I knew that I had been. At that moment by her walk alone I could have picked that Ettie Bellis from among a hundred other lasses. Hurriedly I reminded myself of the old adage: when a man feels the weight of himself his wits are already scattered asunder.

"Keep to the game in hand…Monsieur Sertillanges." Quite deliberately I addressed myself by one of the many names I had masqueraded under. "Grip hard at events…before you, yourself, are gripped!"

I forced my attention back to the two bravos who were following her. These lads I saw were not altogether devoid of caution. They had some slight notion of their business. Probably they had been promised a bonus - but I fancied only if they came home with Ettie's bairn.

Darkness was drawing in when down the road ahead of me I saw the red glare of two burning tar barrels. I remembered. Those lights marked the bridge that spanned the Wear gorge. Sunderland folk are rightly proud of what they called their 'Stupendous Iron Bridge'. Though there were a few wags,

Newcastle folk mostly, who have said that it was a bridge that led 'from little to nowt.'

Until then I had kept my distance. But then as we approached the bridge I saw that young Ettie's pace was quickening. And clearly Cattermole had seen it too. He whipped up the pony and the yellow gig began to rattle along. But at the north end of the Sunderland Bridge all travellers had to stop to pay the toll. It was there that I overtook them. While Cattermole was fumbling to find coppers enough I leaned from the saddle and tossed my own pennies into the bridge-keeper's basket. A little nudge with my spurs and I was out ahead of them.

Then it happened. And straight away I knew that the blame could only be mine. Fool that I was, I had underestimated young Ettie. My error had been to forget that the lass had a keen pair of eyes in her head. Some where along the way Ettie had seen that she was being followed. At the farther side of the bridge I saw her turn about. Dainty as a porcelain shepherdess she was. For a few heartbeats she stood in the bright circle of torchlight. At that moment she might have been on a theatre's stage. Then like a fawn disappearing into the forest she was gone.

I reined up and listened. From far below me came a ghost yawn echoing up out of the swirling fog, I heard deck orders being bawled out on an outward bound collier.

But I wasn't lost. Presently the little gig rattled past me at a smart trot. Yet it seemed that even then the lawyer's bullies were not in any hot pursuit. All I could do was follow them. And since Sunderland is a small town I had not far to go. Not a hundred yards away a smoky whale-oil torch lit up a board with a rough blue anchor daubed upon it. The gig had drawn up at an alehouse. As I watched, Big Archie jumped down and stamped his way inside. Within half a minute the lout was out again. Close at his heels there shambled a tavern idler. Before the swirl of the fog took them both I heard the rumble of dirty laughter. Cattermole clicked his tongue; the gig followed them down the lane.

At the bank's foot by the waterside I saw the gig reined up. I saw their informer point the Judas finger at one of the whitewashed cottage that stood a little apart from the other dwellings. Quietly I dismounted and tethered the mare to a hawthorn bush.

Within a minute I had cause to bless that old woman who sold her broom besoms down the Sandhill market. There was a soothing ease to the way my grip curled around that blackthorn stick. Yet nonetheless I knew that this night's business would call for more caution than went with any lover's passion. All about me Sunderland lay silent. Out on the harbour bar a bell buoy clanged in the fog. And a damned mournful noise it sounded. But for all that I knew that within easy earshot of where I stood there had to be better than a hundred households. On winter nights poor folk who work hard all day commonly seek their beds early. Then I heard him. The informer panted white breath as he came up the pathway. The wharf rat would be hurrying off to guzzle his fee at the *Blue Anchor*.

"Here's to you…my little gob-shite! My words hissed at him out of the darkness. Just in time to meet my swing the sneaking little bastard looked up. The knob end of my blackthorn stick hit him. I heard the gristle in his nose go. With a choking gurgle the maggot went down. His hands went to his face. By Christ it had been a blow to wipe the grin off that Judas's face. That was one fellow who would stay down. I left him writhing where he lay.

Ahead of me in the drifting wraiths of sea-fret I heard a man's grunt of exertion. He was putting his shoulder to a door. I felt the muscles of my face crease. For, odd as it may seem, there was within me a sudden burst of glee – glee, mind you, no mirth. Then I heard the splintering of timbers and I began to run. A woman screamed. From inside the cottage came a burst of raucous laughter. It was answered by a wavering scream of outrage. And at once I knew the voice.

I swept out of the fog and fell on to that bastard. Cattermole was stepping down from the gig. His boots had scarcely hit the flagstones before my blackthorn swung at him. The knob of it hit him squarely on the point of his chin. Neat as you please it was. The lawyer's clerk collapsed with a groan. But the hired pony took fright, whinnied, and reared up in the shafts. I even heard the clatter of shoe iron as its hooves flailed against the stones. For all I knew they might have been pulping Cattermole's brains. But by then Bob Shafto was beyond giving an honest God-damn about anything!

When I stepped into that cottage I truly did find a fair Hell's Bedlam in full play. A driftwood fire blazed high in the hearth. The light of its flames sent the tall shadows dancing like demons across whitewashed walls. At once I saw that the fisherman's wife had been brutally felled. She lay with her head bent to the sanded floor. She was sobbing. Blood ran from her nose and down on to her apron. But Ettie Bellis was on her feet. There was a fire iron ready in her hand as she stood before her sleeping child's cot. But I could already see that Big Archie was in truculent mood and the same whore-monger was ready for sport. He had paused. His thumbs were hooked into his weskit pockets. With no man in the house to worry about this arrogant swine thought he had found easy prey.

"Aah've come tae tak the babbie! Giz'im here, y' bliddy whore…or by Christ aah'll sarve ye wi' two broken arms!" Damn his eyes! To offer such a threat to Ettie Bellis at that moment he must scarce have had the wits he was born with. And indeed his words were scarce out of his fat mouth before Ettie Bellis went for him with the poker. By then our young Ettie was nearer to a she-wolf than a woman.

But accidents will befall. It was the scrape of my boots on the floor's flagstones that saved Big Archie's hide. He had heard me. Had he not then the flesh on his face would have been seared to the living bone. For at the same instant the fisherman's wife staggered forward. She snatched up a cauldron from the hearth. Like a sailor hurling a bucket of slops to leeward she swilled the bastard. Only by his sharp turn about did the hog miss his scalding! Boiling the stuff was; and from the smell of it, crabs! Had he faced the old woman the animal would have taken the whole seething mess full in his face. As it was it was only the thick wool of his wrap-rascal coat that shielded him. But it didn't save him entire. For then I stepped forward thrusting bayonet fashion at the bastard with my blackthorn. The knob head took him in the Adam's apple. I recovered from my attack and stepped back. The fleshy mouth fell open. The unshaven face blanched. His gasping for breath was a terrible sound. Gnarled hands with blue tattoos on their backs gripped up at his throat. The fellow looked like a lunatic trying to throttle himself. Then like a terrified horse the bulging eyes began to roll. In the firelight I saw the gleam of their whites. The game needed to be ended quickly. Again I drew back a step. This time I meant to finish the bastard with a good hard crack along the side of the head. No need. I heard the thud and smelled the stink of scorching cat fur. Ettie Bellis had struck. The lass had brought the poker down – red-hot and with her full weight behind it. Like a man falling to his prayers Big Archie dropped to his knees. Slowly, very slowly, he keeled over sideways. Save for the hiss and spit of burning driftwood the cottage was quiet.

"We'll go, m' Dear…" That was all I said; that was all I needed to say. Nor did Ettie Bellis dally. This lass had led too hard a life to entertain any female fits or fancies. She hugged the old woman, lifted her son out of his crib, and handed me her bundle.

Then at a thought she turned back to the fisherman's wife:

"Aggie, m' love, you know what'll need to be done?"

The fisherman's wife wiped blood from her mouth. Her nod was grim. " Oh aye! Ettie…that aa'h do! It's wor turn now, Pet!" It was an inner smile. The woman lifted a forefinger to me. "So, aa'll thank you for a hand in getting' this big bugger's boots off. They'll need t' be hoyed straight on to the fire – then ah'll run among the cottages beatin' on ma' big pan wi' a ladle… that'll bring all the neighbours out." This was a woman

249

set to enjoy herself, "So there's no need for you two to stop. We've big fisher lads a' plenty hereabouts. Enough t' see this great pillar o' shite bubblin' for his mam!"

But as I stepped though the cottage door I was brought up short. I could hardly believe it! Some zany bastard was screaming a shrill *"Hola!"* at me. I turned in time to take the blade's point into the bundle I was carrying.

I think that had it not been so damned dangerous I might well have laughed out loud. Even so without a thought between I had shouted back: *"Hola* ...my arse!"

It was Cattermole. And what I was astonished to see was that this streak-o'-snot had a sword-cane in his hand. With the swordsman's cry of triumph loud on his lips the skinny slimy bolus had made his lunge at me. But the thrust sadly miscarried. So now he stood there like a man who realises that he's broken wet wind loud in mixed company. Cattermole had thrust *tierce.* So elegant it was. His sword arm was extended still; he stood there fixed in the classic pose taught by all the best two-penny Bell's Court fencing masters. Yes, this same dog looked to have taken instruction! Perhaps indeed it had learned a few tricks! For certain his sword cane's three-cornered blade *might* have gone into my throat. But at that instant my unsleeping psyche had been standing to its duty. Like a shield I had brought up Ettie Bellis's bundle. The thin steel had pierced deep into the black and grey plaid. There was a pause. We looked at one another. Behind the green tinted spectacles I saw Cattermole's eyes widen. He knew; and by God I knew too!. This quill-rider had seen his chance to be a gentleman killer and taken it. Now he was looking squarely into Death's own face - and I rather think he had seen it grin at him. Though for sure all this ninny could do was goggle at me. Then I felt his wrist flex. This hopeful rag-arse was actually trying to wrench his blade free. Now I have always held that the Goddess Fortuna will sometimes grant even the most luckless of sods *one* chance. But ever to expect two bites at the same toffee apple is surely a gross impertinence! I let the bundle go and grabbed out to clutch at the fellow's sword arm. His wrist was a thin as a girl's. I twisted it viciously and jerked him sharply towards me. With a yelp like a trodden puppy Cattermole dropped his blade. With a wicked smile on my face I gave him a brisk bow. My forehead butted him square him in the mouth. Then I stepped back and swung my stick. It seemed only to tap at Cattermole's forearm. But I heard his *ulna* snap like a chicken bone. With a little soft wiffle of breath the lawyer's clerk fainted clean away. I couldn't help myself. I leant over him and said very clearly: "*Hola, Monsieur* Cattermole, *Hola!*"

Of a sudden all the excitement had fled away. We could take our time. But first and as always in my work there would be something to learn from the body of the man sprawled at my feet. From his watchcase I discovered that his full name was Cyrus Cattermole. From a letter I found on him I learned that he was in the employ of Swinbanks & Needler of Low Friar Street at Newcastle. That was an odd address for any respectable firm of solicitors. But for now it was all I needed to know. I left Cattermole both his purse and his pocket book. We could well do without the bastard raising a hue and cry for robbery. But we did need the little gig. Moreover I would have to hinder Cattermole from following us for a few hours at least. Though I will own that some folk might think what I did then was a damned miserable trick. I stooped and grabbed at Cattermole's waistband. He moaned. Then I took up his own blade and began to slice at the cloth. Delicately, almost, I cut away the entire square flap of his breeches' broadfall. Behind me I heard Ettie Bellis giggle.

"Cyrus Cattermole!" The pig was conscious but feigning. "Listen to me, sir." The eyes opened. The agony of a broken forearm was already beginning to reach him. Very soon the fellow might swoon in earnest. "You, Sirrah, are to inform your employers that this lady is now married." His mouth opened. "And her child is now under the legal guardianship of a gentleman ... a gentleman, I may say, of some *considerable* influence." This was language Cattermole would understand. "So that… and as a matter of <u>Law</u> … they would be wise to inform their clients that any further attempts at this clearly *criminal* abduction will result in an immediate recourse to the Courts!" He understood. "And, Mr. Cattermole…" I sounded almost solicitous. "Surely it would be a sad business to find yourself supping gruel in Newcastle's Bridewell for the sake of Messrs Swinbanks and Needler, would it not?"

Cattermole gave no answer. Although I allowed that he was likely to be dazed from his pain. Yet I had to impress fear upon him with an object lesson of some kind. It would be a kindness in disguise – one that might yet save the fools' life. I raised his sword cane and swished it through the air. Flinching he shied away from me. It was then that I realised that the dog was mumbling a prayer. With the sudden 'whitt…' of a savage slash I brought the blade down on one of the gig's iron tyres. The cheap steel shattered like glass and tinkled down on to the stones.

A long weary way we had of it back to Newcastle. The weather had turned. At long last winter's claws showed some small signs of slacking. Though as yet there was no whisper of any certain Spring that I could hear. Snow and ice had merely been commuted to a hard pelting rain. In the swaying light of our little lantern I watched the raindrops explode against the tarred leather of the cart's hood and apron. That and the pony's backside were all I could see. Under our gig's wheels the track was a morass of black muck. Spared the weight of a rider my own little hired mare trotted behind us.

And yet all in all I found myself strangely happy. Sheltered by the drape of my greatcoat around our shoulders and with a horse blanket over our knees it was as pleasant a time as I had enjoyed since I had come from France. Moreover by the time we were passing the Fulwell Windmill the warmth of Ettie's thigh had begun to strike through her skirts.

"Miss Bellis…" I had been silent for long minutes and now that I had opened my mouth I knew that that particular polite mode of address sounded ridiculous. Then I realised what it was. To me, at that moment, this girl simply *had* to be *Miss Bellis*

For 'Ettie' was the name of a seventeen-year old prostitute. Henrietta was a nice enough name, I supposed. But for all that it was now one I could scarce bring myself to use. In time, I fancied, she might allow me to give her another name. Would she consent to become Henriette, in the French fashion? Even before that daft notion had formed itself I had felt myself swallow - hard. What a fool I was being! How far would we both need to run to escape our own histories.

At last however I did manage to speak. Yet I had known at once that in broad daylight my face would have cruelly betrayed me. I was flushed. I could feel the heat of it. What in the Devil's name was this! Was I some daft lad at his first courting? Was Ettie Bellis a virgin pure? Were we sitting together blushing in some Saville Row parlour with a watchful chaperone busy at her embroidery in the corner? The Hell of it all, I supposed, was that I could not help thinking how things might have been: had the fall of the dice allowed me to go into practice as a physician! Then with a sudden start the silliness of my own daft notions sprang back to mock at me. My jaw tightened as I strove to smash that cosy image, to tear it apart and scatter its sharp fragments. Wronged or not, we both had to be simply what we were: the prostitute and a traitor. Almost it might all have been foreordained. For us there could be no going back. My road had been set for me on that day in 1803 when Napoleon had revoked the Treaty of Amiens. Great events destroy little folk!

A perverse oddity of thought had me trying to recall just how many women over the years I myself had enjoyed – and that in half the cities of Europe. Though some I could hardly include in the reckoning. Could I count the women I had seduced, under government orders? Was I getting old? How many had there been? Had I sons, children I knew nothing of? From time to time a man must surely wonder! Where now was…Gianina? I plucked her name out of the ragbag of my past. That had been at Milan. I had to suppress a little smile. That girl had been the quite clumsiest card sharper I had ever seen at work. I had not minded. No one had minded! Another fluke of mind brought the picture of the bean shaped mole on her hip. For two months Gianina and I had loved one another to distraction, and damned often to soreness. Then one night during a thunderstorm there had been the thud of gendarmes' musket butts at the door. An order signed by Fouche himself was thrust at me. I had slipped from the warmth of Gianina's bed and by sunrise I had been on the road to Cracow. By the time I returned to Milan I found the girl heavily pregnant and married to one of Marat's young cavalry majors. Ha!

"Doctor Shafto…" Ettie had been silent for a long moment before she had answered me. Her little son stirred in his sleep and she began to rock him on her knee. Then with a start I realised. The girl had used my name, my real name. I blinked against the darkness. Yet I was really a lot less surprised than I might have been; indeed I was scarcely angry at all.

"You know!" I struggled to blunt the sharp edge on my whisper. Slowly the girl nodded her head.

"About three days ago Nannie Watt heard you going down the Butcher Bank. You strode past her doorway. The widow-woman misses little. Near to blind she is now but for all that, Doctor, she recognised your tread…straightway! It was only in the way of gossip that old Nan told Eadie Bell of it." I felt myself draw a long slow breath. Use all the guile you like there'll be no way that anything you say or do will ever escape gossiping womenfolk. I found myself wondering if there might not be some goodwife somewhere in Newcastle town who would willingly tell all I cared to ask about the smuggling of golden guineas!

"The old woman recalls very kindly how in the year '02 you cured her of a bad dose of the quinsy."

And to my surprise I remembered that too. I had, I recalled, dosed the prattling old witch with a decoction of crushed black currants rendered mystical with the sharp bite of cayenne pepper. It had worked. Her throat had been better in a few days. I could even remember that she had paid me with a much-clipped Spanish dollar.

"Christ", I swore. "So my life hangs by the taut stretched thread of some old woman's chatter!"

"Not so very tight, Doctor..." Ettie's cheek was turned away but I sensed that the girl's eyes were dancing. "No man who douses Mattie Crowley's lamp for him is going to be betrayed by any woman anywhere along the North Shore... nor by any man who wants to keep a whole skin."

"But I..." I fumbled to catch and strangle my own denial. I stopped and thought. Even now, I could suppose, it might still be no bad thing for Newcastle's poor folk to think of me as the man who had done for Crowley.

Her laugh was musical. "But, Doctor Shafto, Eadie Bell *thinks* that it was you who did for Mattie Crowley, and surely that is all that matters." She reached for my hand and squeezed at it. "Don't you know by now that along the town's Quayside you'd be offered a can of tea in any woman's kitchen!"

For want of anywhere else to go it was back to Mrs. Bell's little cundum manufactory by the old Pandon Gate that I took Ettie and her bairn. For that night at least they would be safe there. Even if Cyrus Cattermole escaped the Sunderland mob it was going to take him some time to carry the news back to his employers.

Truth to tell, I had thought to do some more courting that same night. But the flow of Eadie Bell's tears of relief was more than I could stand. With regret and more than a slight feeling of martyrdom I left Henrietta Bellis with her friend and pleaded press of business elsewhere. As I made for the door I knew that I should have known better than to have asked the whereabouts of Jacob Storey.

"*That* drunken little piss-kettle..." Mrs. Bell had cat-spat the words." Is *not* welcome in *my* house!" Eadie's hands went to her broad hips. Foursquare she stood before me. This, I saw, was a woman who had swept her fancy man clean off her hearthstone! Indeed at that moment I could not help but feel sorry for poor Jacob.

"I see." I said. "Though to be sure, Mrs. Bell, that is truly both a pity... and an inconvenience to me." I caught Ettie's eye. Did she know yet about her Uncle Jacob's loose mouth? Probably she did. "For it was my intention to offer the man some days of ...well paid employment. So I would be grateful if you could tell me where he might be found. Or perhaps, if word could be sent to have him meet me at... "

There was no mistaking the look on Eadie's face. This woman was adamant. She sniffed long and hard. Yes, I knew then that it might indeed be a damned long time before Jacob Storey would sit again on his little cracket stool before Mrs. Bell's cheery fire.

However as I lifted the door latch I felt a touch to my arm. I turned to find Ettie standing close. She put her hands to the lapels of my coat and went a' tiptoe to kiss my cheek. For just an instant our eyes met. Even through her bruises she had that same lively mischievous look I had caught the first time that I had ever seen her. Yes, Miss Henrietta Bellis was a lass this world would never beat. A man might do worse. – if she'd have him!

"Allowing that he has the coppers for a jug my Uncle Jacob will be in the *Unicorn*." She whispered, "They bake potatoes for the regular customers tonight. If he hasn't, why then you'll still likely find him hanging about in the lane outside..."

I had been about to put my arms about her: to draw her to me. But Henrietta Bellis was like quicksilver. As I reached out for her she skipped back.

"I'm sure we'll all see you again very soon, Doctor Shafto." She laid her head on one side and gave me a look that not even the cruel bruises could hide.

When I left Mrs. Bell's I was reminded that I had still to take the mare back to Manley's stables. What I would do with Cattermole's gig I did not quite know. But I had little need to worry. As I drove into the yard the lad who was working the after-guard ran out and took the horse's head. I saw at once that the gig was one of at least four others owned by the stable. The thick yellow paint was Manley's way of marking his cheaper hire carts. I suppose I was disappointed. The chance that Rachel Brydon had been carried off in a hired cart had seemed slender enough. Somehow the style of the business was all wrong.

"I fancy that Mr. Cattermole will be along to collect what he's owed – probably tomorrow."

"Oh, that's alright, sir..." The lad grinned. "Mr. Cattermole's employers have an account here."

I suppose I might have walked away. But the three other yellow carts all in a row had to be a gift that only a fool would have spurned.

"Here, lad... bring me a lantern, will you?" A penny's piece worked its magic. He was back in a minute with a candle lantern.

I found what I was looking for on the floor of the second gig. It wasn't much. But it served. It was a clipping, a thin strip of woollen cloth cut from a man's coat. What I was holding had come from what in he North we call a 'hookie' mat. Had Mrs. Brydon been rolled up in just such a rag mat?

I looked at the youngster. He couldn't have been more than twelve. The eyes, however, were going on thirty. This was business. It called for a straight offer simply made.

"For a new sixpence, son... "I turned the bright coin between thumb and forefinger in the lamplight. Tell me who hired this cart last... Wednesday, or maybe it wasTuesday?" There was no hesitation.

"It was a Wednesday, sir. That I know because the cart was damaged when it was brought back. It hasn't been out since.

An' the fellah what took it out wasn't the same chap as brought it back" I looked keenly at him.

"But for the full bounty… what I really need, bonny lad, is a name…"

"Mr. Oliver Garvie." The answer came pat and the lad sounded so certain. I raised an eyebrow at him.

"Garvie was the name of the gentleman who brought the gig back, sir… I know that because the master and him had words about the damage to the gig. He tried to pass hisself off as Redmond but Mr.Manley told him to his face that he knew his real name was Garvie and that it didn't matter who he was… there was still seven shillun' to pay."

"But what manner o' man was he?" Almost I was asking myself.

"Garvie, Sir? Why that's somethin' aah can hardly say. The man had a tall hat on and a big knitted scarf wrapped around his chin an'…"

"Aye, lad," I said as I dropped the sixpence into his hand. "I suppose he would have done, at that…"

Jacob Storey's pockets must have been empty. For, I found him hopping from one broken boot to the other in the street's filth outside the *Unicorn*. Damned near blue with the cold the poor bastard was, and close to fainting for want of something to put into his belly. Truly this Jacob's misery had curdled in its bowl. Coming up behind I clamped my hand on to his shoulder. He jumped.

"Beef bones, Jacob," Like the Serpent in Eden I hissed my words into his ear. "Devilled ox bones, served piping hot and that with plenty of crusty new bread to soak up all that rich marrow." I made a hearty sucking sound. The old rogue looked at me as through those rheumy blue eyes of his. I think I might have been the Tempter himself. So I put an arm around Jacob's bony shoulders and squeezed him with feigned affection. "What would you say to that, my friend? And also… let ' s say a couple o' tankards o' porter's ale, dark and with a good head on it." Jacob Storey stood there like an orphanage waif bidden to the Lord Mayor's feast."

We went again to the *Rose*,down on the Pudding Chare> And as I had promised we sat before a roaring coal fire in the taproom and sucked at our devilled bones.

"Did you…" I knew what his question would be.

"The lass is back at Eadie Bell's… which, my friend," I squinted at him sidelong. "is a sight more than *you* are like to do for many a long day… " I relented. "Young Ettie has her bairn safe…" But then I gave him no time to rejoice.

"Now, Jacob, this is what I want you to do." Like a hound he licked around the marrow juice on his chops. His rheumy eyes were fixed on my face. Now I had the old man's entire attention. "Find someone for me who can tell me all about Hodgin's, the big Grocer on Northumberland Street…" Storey was beginning to swell. "Once I used to put in my orders for…"

"No." I cut him off, sharply. " I don't want to know how much oat flour the bastard uses to spike his white pepper. What I need to know - by tonight - is all about Ralphie Hodgin's warehousin', where he keeps his bulk goods… where he ships his stuff *out* of the Tyne!"

Storey was thinking hard. I had set him a puzzle that he could not answer straight off. "Well, aah s'pose we might ask old Toby Catcheside…but he's locked up in the St. Andrew's lunatic asylum…"

"Jacob!" I narrowed my eyes at him and put an edge on my voice. I was in no mood for jokes. "What I need is a creature who is *compus menti̱s*, entire – a fellow whose wits are all of a piece!"

Chapter Twenty Five

Storey's grin was a thing comical to see. "Why man, sir, you'll find no chap in this town wi' a keener brain than wor 'Tickin' Toby... an' that either *outside* the St Andrew's Asylum - or in it! Because I'll tell you now that the only reason wor Toby 's in that place at all is that the vittles served in there are a wee bit better than at the Poor House... Though mind you, right up to last Michaelmass that old chap kept the ledgers for Ralphie Hodgin'. Though, o' course he'll be all locked up for the night now."

"I'll see him, first thing in the morning... I suppose I might just do worse than seek help from the insights of some madman!"

"Make sure you take three shilling pieces wi' y'...that's what Jimmy Shadforth, the keeper there, charges. The Quality have always to pay high for the privilege of viewin' the loonies...he's very strict on that."

"I think I'll be able to manage that, Jacob... "

I knew the ways of such places. But then I was reminded of Jacob Storey's own case. Until Mrs. Bell relented – if indeed Big Eadie ever did - he would need somewhere to lay his head that night. I turned and looked at him.

"Now, Jacob, this is what I want you to do... Tonight you'll stay here...I'll arrange that with the landlord. You're to sleep on this bench by the fire." I signalled for two more tankards. "You're to do the selfsame thing *all* day tomorrow... and if need be the next day. You'll get the *Rose*'s ordinary for your dinner, a twist o' baccy and a couple o' gills of small beer to drink. I'll already have told the landlord here what 's like to happen." I raised an eyebrow at him. "So now, Jacob Storey just you cock back your lugs and listen hard! His head went to one side as he strove to attend to me.

"A lad will bring a letter addressed to a Mr. Farrow." I fixed him with a hard gaze. "Remember that name... *Mr Farrow.*" Storey's mouth formed the words. "You will bring that letter to me... at once." For a moment he looked puzzled.

"But where?

"Down by the Quayside... somewhere. I'll not be hard to find!"

Of a sudden the buzz and babble of the drinkers in the *Rose's* crowded tap room seemed to grow louder. The roar of it felt to be bearing in upon me. I knew that it was a warning and one that I would be wise to heed. I knew then that, at that moment,I myself was close to exhaustion. Moreover porter's black beer is damned heady stuff. I drew a long breath and looked around me, yawning. Almost at my elbow two Dumfries cattle drovers, both men stumbling drunk, were trying to break up a fight between their dogs. Then coming from the corner of the inglenook I heard an eerie drone. I turned my head back. An old fellow in a grey plaid and bonnet was gently working at the bellows of a set of Northumbrian small-pipes. Set before him on a stool lay both an empty glass and a wooden bowl. His fingers would stay at rest on the polished ebony of his chaunter until there was either a drink in his glass or a coin in his bowl. A fancy took me. I was of a mind to hear a tune. I caught the potman's eye and pointed to the inglenook's corner.

The piper's fingers began to work their elf-magic. I could not have chosen a

better tune. *Alnwick Fair* was what he was playing. It had been a favourite of my mother's. Now, I had heard bagpipes a' plenty in France and elsewhere but none had ever been played like this. By his magic the whole company was quieted. Even the drover's dogs stopped their fighting and lay still. At that moment too I felt a great weariness creeping in upon me. I had good right! It had been a long day. Tonight, I decided, I would risk seeking a bed at Mrs.Dilkes' house.

Lodgings there had been arranged for me there when first I had come off the mail coach. However for the sake of my own safety I had slept there only the one night. Nonetheless, and if I knew anything about it, the old woman would follow her instructions to the letter until she was told otherwise. She would have been paid to do that. So if I knew ought else about it then every single night there would have been a dinner hot on the table for me. Indeed I would count myself much mistaken if Mrs. Dilkes had not already put a hot brick wrapped in flannel into my bed.

But sweet as the pipe tune was there were still a few insistent questions gnawing along the raw edges of my thoughts. Very soon now I would need a new identity. After today's business at Sunderland it would be only prudent. Cyrus Cattermole had seen my face and would not soon forget it. It would not do to be challenged in the street. The preacher's broadcloth had served me well – but I knew that I had been leaning hard on my luck. Too many folk about the town had already clapped eyes on the black suit and shovel hat. Moreover I'd already been seen about in much the wrong places for most clergymen. Soon, next day for preference, I would have to do something about my appearance. Even a city's streets can become straight and narrow when men are out looking for you.

It was the burst of clapping that brought me out of my reverie. Damn my eyes but I had been too busy with my own worries to enjoy the other haunting tunes. Belatedly I added to the cheers and sought for a coin.

"It's been many a year since I heard that tune, and even longer since I've heard it played so well." Even as I spoke I admitted to myself that my words were mere 'French' courtesy. But to my surprise the piper looked up at me.

"That's most kindly o' ye, Sir...most kindly..." He looked up into my face. "Though mind you, it's not every man sittin' here tonight who 's taken all the pleasure he might from the music o' my small pipes. There's one snipe-nosed beggar over there by the door there, his eyes have never left your back... not for one blink."

"I'm obliged to you, my friend, uncommonly obliged. " I spilled coins into his bowl. "But so that I don't need to turn about to look at him would you just give me with a hint or two more as to the chap's lineament and likeness?"

"He's the glum faced lad who's warming his hands at the candle...no need for me to say more."

The piper was right. Like a man amused by a clever joke I turned about with a noisy laugh. A face well creased with mirth can scan about a room without seeming to have an interest in anything at all. He was quick but not quick enough. His head went down. But I had seen who it was. He was sitting far out on the edge of the taproom's firelight, holding hands to the flame of a candle. Before him on the bench there was a bare gill of ale. The last time I had clapped eyes on this fellow he had been sprawled on the floor of a government carriage. One of Rachel Brydon's men had just made his skull ring out with a crack from his cudgel. It was Lieutenant Cable.

Sometimes you have to take a chance. My immediate fear was that Cable would clap a whistle to his lips and blow a blast that would bring in a file of militia at the double-step. Yet if for no other reason than the simple wretchedness of the man's mien I knew that this at least was unlikely.

My shadow fell over him. He looked up at me slowly. His mouth peeled open a little.

"Join us, Mr. Cable!" I said holding out a welcoming hand. "Come, Sir... take a glass with me..."

As Cable eased himself past me he staggered a little. I heard him suck in the pain. If Lieutenant Cable were playing a part then he was playing it damned well.

"Rum, Sir! That's what's what is needed to restore the life to a chilled body." Well before I had got Cable across to our table I knew he really was wounded. I made a clenched fist to sign for the potman to bring us a bottle.

"Here, just you get this into you, Mr Cable! It'll do you a damned sight more good than any apothecary's wintergreen lozenges. Eh? Come now, sir; no heeltaps now... D'y hear." A triple tot of neat Jamaica rum will ease the soreness out of most wounds. Two glasses of the same treacly brown spirit was my prescription. Before I went any further I had to see to it that our Mr Lieutenant Cable was drunk enough to be far beyond doing me any mischief. And before many minutes had passed his thin face did show the beginnings of mellowness. I lit a cigar at the candle and breathed blue smoke across the empty dishes that still lay on the table. And I waited.

"Was it a blade or a ball, Mr. Cable?" I had looked across the candle flame and seen the pain in his eyes. Already the dark Jamaica was having its effect. He was unwise enough to move a hand to point to his wound. His wince was real enough. I reached across and gently pulled open his coat. The shirt had been of white linen. Now it was scarlet and plastered fast to his ribs.

"Scored across the brisket..." His hand patted gently at his left side. "Not deep but long... and damnably sore." His laugh came out as a feverish giggle. "My very first sword cut! Though, the bleeding does seem to have stopped." I reached out to re-charge his pot of rum.

"When and where?" It was at that precise instant that what I saw changed my entire perception of Mr. Lieutenant Cable. The fellow I had first known in Paris as Farquahar's witless minion was no longer on the stage. That man had gone. Pain had wiped him clear away. Then for just an instant I caught the eye-glint of a thinking man. And that mistake too I had seen. It had been no more than the quickest flash but I had seen it. This fellow was one of us! With a liberal seeming disregard I splashed more rum into his pot. This was a fellow I wanted rendered mortal drunk just as soon ever as might be.

"Where then is your Major Farquahar...are you no longer in his company?" Cable took a gulp of neat spirit before he answered.

"The written orders given to us in Paris were that we were to hand you over to the civil authorities at Bow Street. Mine - specifically - were to assist George Farquahar in that commission until it was done. Wherever he went, Yours Obediently, was obliged to follow..." Cable looked up at me. "Mr...Doctor Shafto, I had no choice in the matter. I'm a serving officer...it's all the living I have." The rum was doing its task. "When you made your escape Farquahar behaved like a madman. And yet the day after he had made his report to the Horse Guards in London everything seemed to change. All was well! And it seemed suddenly that he had no shortage of money! When we got to Newcastle we both stayed at the new *Turf Hotel* on Mosely Street. Until yesterday that was how it was. My own instructions were to search this city until I found you..." His grin was wry. "So I did. Then, without any warning, Farquahar announced that the warrant of arrest issued against Dr. Robert Shafto had been withdrawn. Brusque as you please the wretched fellow ups and orders me to return to my regimental depot at Bedford." Cable lifted his shoulders to shrug but then just in time he remembered his wound. He settled for a wry little smile. "I suppose that I tarried in Newcastle when I should not have done so. I'm pretty sure that it was Farquahar who sent his bullies to attack me! "

"Describe these fellows to me...what were they like?" I began to wish that I had been more sparing with my own rum.

"One, the tall fellow, looked for all the world like a prize fighter. That clod handled his blade as though it were a loom-beam..."

"That Mr. Cable would have been Salathiel Coneybeare. You're lucky to have escaped his fists! And what can you tell me of your other attacker?"

"Oh, there can be no doubt at all about it! He was a Frenchman…"

Another half tot of my rum set Lieutenant Cable swaying on his feet. I put a supporting arm under his good side and eased him towards the door.

I would have to give Mrs. Dilkes this much : the old servant woman did not turn one curl papered hair when she saw who stood at her door. Without one word she lifted her candlestick up high and shuffled aside. With a nod to her I steered Cable past her and into the blessed warmth of the kitchen. By then the lieutenant had become even more unsteady on his feet. Though I think by then most of that was owed to his loss of blood rather than to the rum I had poured into him.

"Sit there, my dear fellow…" I said quietly." We'll have your coat off… and what's left of your shirt!" As the old woman looked over my shoulder I heard the sharp suck of her breath as she thrust her knuckles to her mouth. From armpit to hip Cable's white shirt was soaked bloody. He had not lied. It was a damned long cut – probably, I saw, delivered from behind. Also I judged that when that blade had cut at him his own right arm had been raised to deliver his own slash at another adversary. Altogether it looked very much as though Cable had been had been in something of a close grunt and heave fight. Also I could guess that his swordplay had been against more than one man.

Yet in spite of her reaction Mrs Dilkes soon showed that she was no stranger to the dressing of wounds. Without a word she took a razor from a drawer and began to cut away the shirt. Carefully she peeled back the blood stuck linen. The wound itself cut ran from his left shoulder blade down deep into his brisket meat. He'd been moving fast to avoid a down slash could well have taken his arm off. Yes, there was no doubt about it – that night our Lieutenant Cable had surely clashed his steel! And if a man will but look carefully at a wound he can divine much. What I did see was that since it was his shirt alone that had blood on it and not his coat I might be safe to guess the set-to had been within-doors. There was more. As Cable said this might have been his first sword cut. However it was not his first wound. A tell-a-tale dimple around a button of scar-tissue in the flesh near the base of his spine betrayed another story. At some time in the past Cable had taken a small calibre pistol ball. Personally, I should have said that he'd been damned lucky! Another thumb's breadth to the right that time and the fellow would surely have been a cripple.

I washed Cable's wound with hot water and drew together its edges. Like most cuts caused by a curved blade the wound was not deep along its entire length. But flesh will always mend the quicker for being stitched. Mrs. Dilkes hurried to bring me an embroidery needle ready threaded with silk. As I took it she drew a ribbed bottle of dark blue glass from her apron's pocket. It was an apothecary's phial of Godfrey's Cordial, the same household potion that the French call 'the killer of dreams'. I winked at her as I allowed a heavy dose of the opiate to drip into a tumbler.

"Bite on the ball, Mr. Cable. You'll need a stout heart for this business." I poured the last of the rum over the Godfrey's and stirred the draught with an apostle spoon. Cable looked into the glass for a second before he gulped at the draught. Before I had tied the third suture he was snoring.

"This man is to be kept a close prisoner, Mrs Dilkes…" It sounded an odd thing to be saying among all the burnished copper jugs and blue Delftware that made the kitchen so cheery. "Though I do think it will now be some hours before this lad moves." The old servant woman simply nodded. "That nephew of yours, the big lad, Cuthbert, is he about?" I would sleep easier for knowing that Cable was held secure. Perhaps he had come to me all too easily for it to be just Luck!

"He can be roused out, sir…" Prospect of work for her nephew obviously pleased Mrs Dilkes. I nodded and in mid-nod my mouth fell open in a yawn.

"Then send word for him if you would oblige me, Mrs Dilkes… But for me, m' Dear, it's been a damned long day and I'm for my bed!"

While I was out of my bed bright and early the next morning it was a damned sure thing that I knew better than to arrive at the asylum too early. Any fool who strayed into that den while its denizens were being fed looked for trouble. Bitter experience told me that like as not some raving old biddie would gob out her gruel over my coat. Or worse! So for an hour I walked the town. Truth to tell, I was diverting myself - stealing the time. What I was looking for was a present that would brighten the eyes of Miss Henrietta Bellis. For a time a pair of embroidered slippers in crimson Morocco leather displayed in Mortimer's shop window occupied my fancy.

The rain had cleared. Above me the sky was high and the few clouds wispy. Cobblestones glistened wetly bright and the soot blackened walls of the houses steamed in the sunlight. Newcastle is a grand old town when she's had her face washed! But I knew that all this was a mere chimera. It was still March. This patch of fair weather could still be a false herald. As my father would have said, it was a bright sun but too full of water! And anyway before long the chimney smoke would soon smother the sunlight like an unwanted bastard! I decided I would allow the crimson slippers to stand until I knew the size of Ettie Bellis's feet.

The town's charitable establishments lay up by the Gallowgate just outside the old walls. I knew all three well. As a young doctor I had treated the poor creatures there. The work had paid me tenpence a visit and often I'd been damned glad to get it. So it was that the bell-pull at the side of the green door came readily to my hand. Strange, I never had discovered where that cracked bell that clanged out was hung. Presently however I heard the shuffle of leather slippers on worn sandstone flags.

The face was what I would have called truly skeletal. The fellow was almost a scientific curiosity. With such an emaciated body he could easily have earned his ale money by stripping himself naked before any class of medical students. His musculature I guessed would surely be a sight to see! But what first drew my gaze was the rare fine bunch of wens that dangled where they grew on his neck.

"James Shadforth!" I growled at him. Eyes, muddy green, goggled up at me from their pits. Skin and bone he might be – but at first sight I flattered myself that I knew both his kind and his character. In response to my guess I assumed the brass-bold sneer of Authority and thrust my paper at him. That morning I had taken Richard Grainger's name most criminally in vain. I had penned a note of introduction for myself. I have always found that a fine set of swirls and curlicues added to a strict legal hand will make a simple note look much like a royal warrant.

"So…You're the keeper here, then?"

"Aaahm the *manager*, Sir! The man's face took on the expression of a small dignity much offended. James Shadforth was clearly a dog who guarded his own manger. My own position however was the more elevated one. Though to be sure it owed a deal to the greatcoat and hat I had borrowed from Nicholas Cable. And Shadforth, to be sure, would already have realised that my visit was not going to bring him any fee!

"You will kindly conduct me at once to the inmate entered on to your books as Tobias Catcheside…" Never, ever, give any petty official time to think. As I spoke I stepped in forcefully over the threshold.

It is a curiosity of asylums. Though every scrap of woodwork in that place was scrubbed with lye, even though the limewash on the walls was new, the faint smell of the madhouse alone would have served to tell me where I was even in pitch darkness. Years before I had pondered upon how it could be that the lunatics had a stink about them that differed so markedly from the wretched creatures next door, those who were merely destitute.

"We keep Ticky in here, sir. He's not given to violence… he's just a plain, ordinary daftie wi' a half rotted brain."

The reason for the old man's nickname was obvious at sight. On the waistcoat of workhouse brown shoddy-hodden were pinned a dozen or more pocket watches. Every one was broken; there was not a tick to be heard. But I was not deceived. Quickly I came to the conclusion that this Tobias Catcheside might be no more insane than I was myself. His eyes were lively and the tone of his skin was healthy enough.

"Leave us if you will, Shadforth…This is private business." I allowed the order to fall back over my shoulder. "Though if I might beg a candle: I may need to affix a seal to a document."

Go wherever you will! Across all of Europe the faintest whiff of melting sealing wax is the incense that will never fail you! Shadforth's interest kindled and then blazed!

"Tobias… Catch…eee…side…" I puffed my cigar at the candle's flame and then blew the smoke upward. "You kept the books for Ralph Hodgson…"

"For nigh on twenty three year…sir." The old man's attention however was not on my question - it was on the smoke of my cigar. He watched it spiral upward into a beam of sunlight. It hung there above us swirling blue among the dust motes. Tobacco is not a commodity that the city fathers of Newcastle dispensed to their madmen. Tobias Catcheside sat there watching. This fellow, I knew, would willingly sell his immortal soul for a smoke. It was a hunger I knew well. I smiled as I opened my shagreen case and held it out to him. He took out four cigars and stuffed three of them into the leg of his workhouse breeches. Damn me but for a supposed madman Catcheside sat there and smoked his cigar like a prince at his ease! With his eyes closed and a look on his face like a saint in an ecstasy He blew out three quite perfect smoke rings. Then he put his head on one side and cocked an eye at me. Without a word passing between us we had entered into an agreement. And I judged then that I would probably be able to trust anything the old man told me.

"Until that little bastard…though no, not bastard…for wor young Rupert is indeed his father's son, true to the seed of the miserable loins he sprang from!"

While I smoked I allowed Catcheside to spew out his every last woe. For men must go through their rituals. It was like listening to a prisoner in the cell. So very patiently did I listen; I enjoyed my cigar the whiles and sat there knowing full well that the man would have to be allowed to tell his tale. Only then would the old fellow be ready to tell me what I wanted to know. And, as I had expected, when all was told it was only another sad little tale. Like many another and after all his years of honest service poor Tobias had been accused of a minor peculation. But then he had been fool enough to both prove and show that ' pantaloons' was the real thief. Of course in the face of an accusation against his own son Ralph Hodgson had flown into a rage and discharged his book-keeper on the spot. What the Hell had he expected?

"That mean-hearted bastard was saving himself from havin' to pay an old chap a couple of shillin' a week in pension!" He had done. The tale was spent. I allowed the column of ash to fall from my cigar.

"What I want to know, Mr Catcheside, is what properties and warehouses Ralph Hodgson owns in Newcastle and elsewhere - every single one."

For a supposed lunatic Tobias Catcheside was possessed of an excellent memory. His many timepieces might have been stopped but his fingers could still tick off Hodgson's properties easily enough. "There's where he cures his hams and tongues…that's at Paul Street, under the Ballast Hill…" I nodded him on. "Then there's the little place he used to take his whores – to hide from his wife. Though, since his Annie died he sometimes offers hospitality there to other gentlemen. Merchants who…"

"Where is that, Tobias?" I pressed gently.

"Fenwick's Entry…though mostly that place is barred and locked up like a gaol."

"Somewhere closer to the river… perhaps some place that Ralphie Hodgson doesn't own outright; but maybe still somewhere that he has an interest in…?"

Catcheside's reaction was immediate. His mouth split wide. This question plainly touched upon a matter that had significance for him. And then too for the first time I saw that after all there might have been just a streak of unreason in his expression.

"Clartie Mitchison's…there's where you'll be thinkin' of… by Burdon's Staith." He leaned closer to confide. "D'y see… the trouble there is that both those bloody rogues have their shit-sticky fingers on different copies of the same old woman's last will and testament…"

But at that instant the supposed lunatic stopped. He stared at me. Suddenly he poked a finger into the air. It was a preacher's gesture. Then I too heard the slow creep of muffled footsteps. I stood up and leaped forward. An eavesdropper should always remember to walk *towards* any door he is surprised at! It may avert suspicion. I grabbed out at Shadforth. It was like trying to get a hold on a bag of eels. Lord High Muck-a-Muck among his charges this Mr Shadforth might be. But taken with his lugs flapping at a keyhole the skinny bugger was but a greasy rasher o' nowt. And in any event I now had what I had come for.

"Ah! Mr. Manager…" I hauled Shadforth upright until his ear was close up to my mouth. "A word to the wise!" I tightened my grip until he winced with pain. "Within a very few weeks this model establishment of yours is to undergo a most rigorous 'special' inspection." Shadforth's eyes widened. "There will be some *most* important visitors …up from London. Gentlemen whom our own Board of Guardians themselves will be exceedingly anxious to impress…" I stared into his pale face with the steel edged gaze of a Provost's corporal. "So a man who valued his position would see to it that his scale of provisions here was correct to the last pinch of oatmeal…" I reached down and squeezed the bulge in his coat pocket. "And if I were you, Mr Shadforth, I would burn this wee doggie whip o' yours before this day is out…the Christian sentiments among decent folk are turning against the use of such things on poor creatures whom The Almighty has already seen fit to afflict!"

There was no help for it. I would have to get word to Grainger. For now I was sure. The whisper of Reason had become insistent. If there was anywhere on the Tyne where the gold coins from the Grand Lottery were to be shipped out of the country had to be from the warehouse owned by this Clartie Mitchison. Why else, the last piece clicked into place, had Hodgson hired me to abduct the same fellow, Mitchison? I, or say rather the fiction of the 'The Glasgow Man', had been contracted to arrange just that. First of all though, it would be as well for me to go down to the riverside.

Mitchisons' Warehouse, it turned out, was well known. The first man I asked pointed out to me the narrow frontage backing on to the river. This morning the big iron braced gate lay wide open. At the further end of a wooden building I saw a square of daylight. The patched brown mainsail of a coasting lugger was slipping across it. Excellent to its purpose: in at one end and out at the other!

I spent a profitable half-hour walking up and down, breasting both ways against a hurrying press of working folk. At my third passage I heard a wagon driver address a tall black bearded young man in a calfskin waistcoat. So this was Mr. Mitchison. And as if to oblige me he turned about and shouted to two fellows. They would be the other two men to be lifted. I studied them all for a long time.

I was about ready to go back to Mrs. Dilkes' house. I would look at Cable's wound, and ask him some pointed questions.

273

Thus far I had let him off lightly. That was something I had soon realised. Today the same man would be damned miserable. His wound would be smarting badly; his head too would be thick from the rum and opium I had plied him with. I knew that I would get groaned answers to whatever questions I cared to ask. For my own satisfaction I would begin by quizzing him about every move he had made since the London Road. I wanted to know everything up until the njght before when he had warmed his fingers at a candle in the *Rose* down on the Pudding Chare.

The warm perfume of a bakery carrying on the breeze reminded me also that I was promised steak and kidney pie in Mrs Dilkes' kitchen. For a long moment I stood dilly-dallying between prospect of Mrs. Dilkes'cooking and looking in on Henrietta Bellis at the cundum factory. Then in middle of my own short snort of self-derision I heard the clatter of hooves and the jingle of harness. Bearing down on me was a handsome pair of dappled grey horses pulling a brewer's dray. It was a team to catch any man's eye. But as I hurried to step aside the thought struck me. A brewer's dray is built to carry great weight, twenty or more full beer barrels. Indeed such a cart is made for nothing else. So what had at once caught my attention was that this brewer's dray was loaded with ship ropes. Like thick plaits of blond hair the great hawsers lay coiled on the wagon bed. The mind is a wondrous mechanism. An incandescent spark of insight had been struck. It lit my intellect. Then bright illumination flared. Mitchison's warehouse was about to take delivery of a load of hemp ropes... new hempen ropes. Scenes began to dance before my mind's eye. There had been a twist of combed brown hemp in Eneas Knox's Bible. I had brushed hemp fibres from George Humble's clothing. And when I had found Rachel Brydon's young servant lass she had been left lying stripped near naked on a pile of the same stuff. Suddenly those disparate events, taken together, had summoned up quite another memory altogether.

In the May of 1806 I had been in Genoa. On a wharf, just landed, there had been piled a thousand baskets of fresh cabbages. The cabbages were real enough. One of my lads had sliced through one with his sword. But then I'd seen a little smile had creased the veteran's scar puckered cheek. The man's name bat-flittered up from my memory's depths: 'Pisser' Jacquard! He had put down his musket and knelt. That had surprised me. Then like a dog at a lantern's post the old corporal had sniffed at one of the baskets. His smile up at me became a crooked grin. Over the hand wringing and fat salt tears of the fat Ligurian consignee we had turned out every one of those thousand baskets. Every basket was woven from tobacco stalks; and every basket had also a thick cushion of green uncured tobacco leaf lining its base. An officer who looked only at cabbages would have seen nothing! And this, I knew, had to be a kindred notion! It was as I watched the new rope being unloaded and coiled down on to the floor of Clartie Mitchison's warehouse that the idea began to form itself. The last few pieces of the puzzle began to slip into place. The piled hemp and the pieces of machinery in the house beside All Saints church. I began to see how it might be that the gold coins gathered in by the Grand Lottery could secretly both reach and leave Newcastle Quayside.

However mere fancy is no evidence. That much I knew only too well. The English courts would always be inclined to protect Property. Moreover before the King's Excise would arrest anyone they would have to take the smugglers _with_ the guineas hidden aboard a ship and cleared ready for sea. Only in that way would the prize fall to the Crown. That, I suspected too, was also what would most please the *British Linen Bank*...perhaps would best dispose them to their humble servant Robert Shafto.

But as I walked back along the Quay all my plans were thrown into confusion. For on my way I overtook the procession following the town's dead wagon. A corpse on display always draws a crowd. And this day the mob of folk was as big as it was noisy. There was, I soon heard, a 'gentleman' under the canvas. That the cadaver still had its boots on told me that the body was newly discovered. That the cart did not leave a trail of water suggested that the body had not been taken from the Tyne. Nor did I have to ask where he was being taken. Discovered dead bodies are taken to the Coroner's Court. I asked and was told that the hearing would be held down at the Moot Hall. I began to step out, striding along to get ahead of the crowd. I was there well before the wagon. And a couple of cigars to the usher got me a corner place on one of the public benches.

I had almost forgotten how much the English, *we* English, love our ceremony. The swearings-in and proclamations took close to a full hour. But at last and before a well- packed courtroom the proceedings got under way. As it happened it was well worth the wait. When the Coroner motioned for the town's constable to lift the canvas a great sigh went up over the court. The last time I had seen a face like that it had been a Polish lancer caught in a blast of grapeshot! The face was quite gone. Someone had used a pistol to blow away the jawbone. And that had taken more than one shot. Such skin as remained was seared and blackened with powder grains. It was an expert piece of work. Certainly it was expert enough to cause a fair number of the idly curious to retch their guts and scramble for the door.

But the young surgeon who had examined the body surely knew his trade. There was no quarrelling with his findings. The shots had been the prime cause of death. That sabre wounds had been inflicted earlier was incidental. Another groan swept the court as against the onset of *rigor mortis* the doctor used his knee to force upright a blue tinged arm. All around me I saw the rictus of bared teeth. I heard the sharp suck of spittle. What caused that was sight of the raw ends where two fingers had been clean severed. Like fresh cleaved beef they were. Another frisson of horror scampered around the hall. But I had seen something else. The sheer size of the corpse told me who the

276

man was; sight of a couple of stumpy syphilitic's teeth in what remained of his upper gums confirmed it. This had to be one of the Coneybeare twins, either Salathiel or Lemuel. Which one it was exactly had now to be academic.

I followed the proceedings through almost to their end. The body was identified by a Mrs. Hannah Spargo. A respectable looking body she was, in a plain bonnet and a light grey cape. Plainly she was much affected by sight of the thing under the canvas. Nonetheless Mrs. Spargo was confident when she identified Lemuel Coneybeare: "His twin brother, Your Worships, having gone to York by the stage coach two day's ago..." She drew herself up and gave her head a little toss. "For a hundred pound bout wi' the Black Turk!" There were muffled cheers from the benches

In the end the Coroner's verdict was all it could have been: "Unlawful killing by a person or persons unknown..." When I got back to the house on the Butcher bank that same unknown person would have a great many questions to answer.

But when I got to Mrs Dilkes' house I saw that she had a visitor. And I recognised both the carriage at the door and the driver up on its box. It was Joe Fletcher. I came up to him on the carriage's off side.

"Mornin', Joe...What cheeor?"

The coachman shifted his quid of his tobacco to the other cheek before he answered.

"As ever, Sir. Little enough cheer...an' vexation a' plenty."

"What news o'Mrs. Brydon is there them?"

"By all accounts the lass is away... visitin' her Aunt, a Mrs. Ayres, up at Morpeth, for a couple of days...at least that's what Mrs. Frankis, the housekeeper, says. And that's all I know." The coachman was not best pleased." Though, how she got there I don't know. It wasn't me who drove her!" She went last night... in all that rain!"

I was relieved, pleased even. Naturally I wanted to hear more of her story. But I knew that all I would learn is what

Rachel Brydon wanted me to know. Like everybody else I would have to wait until *madame* deigned the time fitting to tell us.

"So who is it who is calling on Mrs Dilkes?" I motioned to the front door with a sharp nod of my head. Joe Fletcher winked.

"Aaa've just been instructed - special - to bring Lady Donkin down to call on Meggie Dilkes…" It was plain to me that Joe had been surprised.

"Instructed, Joe?"

"Mr. Richard himself, Sir! A lad came with a message. Straight away it was shouted down to me that I was to put old Philomena here into the shafts."

It might well be nothing; it might be mere woman's business, fripperies and furbelows that had nothing to do with guinea smuggling at all. But at the same time something told me that this was unlikely. Besides, the presence of the carriage alone offered me an excuse to beg a ride up to Brunswick Place. Whatever Richard Grainger's orders had been I was sure enough now that I had a good excuse to set them aside.

When I entered the kitchen I found Nicholas Cable sitting on a stool. His back was to me. He was stripped to the waist. Lady Donkin had just finished knotting fresh bandages around his ribs. For a long moment I stood looking at them both. Then Lady Donkin looked up. Very slowly she lifted an eyebrow. That old woman was demonstrating the skills of a mistress! The only woman I had ever known who could quite show contempt like Lady Donkin had been a Paris whore who drew a widow's pension for a full colonel of artillery. The woman looked at me as though I were a second footman

"You…Doctor… should not be here…Go away!" It was only then that I saw the heavy double-barrelled pistol that lay on the table at her side. "This gentleman is vouched for. Mr Grainger knows all about him. He is in… much the same employment as your own."

She might have got away with it. She might. But not today, ma' bonny Lass! I felt myself bristle. All along, through this whole damned enterprise I alone had been the one who had done the work, who had discovered exactly what was what. I supposed that Richard Grainger could use me as he liked; and I had had to put us with the schoolgirl pranks of Rachel Brydon. But I did not need to allow this spavined old hag to ride me one yard further.

"I have just come from the Coroner's Court at the Moot Hall…Milady. The Justices will be looking for whoever it was blew the living face off a prize fighter called Lemuel Coneybeare." I saw Nicholas Cable's shoulders twitch. I took a step forward and took hold of the double-barrelled pistol by its muzzles. I lifted the weapon to my nose and sniffed at the lock. It had been reloaded but it had not been cleaned. There was no doubt in my mind that it had been fired off the night before. They say that revelation comes in a flash. And it did come to me – and in that fashion. Even as I spoke I knew that it might still have been no more than a lucky guess. However much more likely it was the sameness of their response that gave their game away. Even through his pain Cable tried to twist his face into an expression of denial. And in all her poe-faced pride Lady Donkin gave almost the same look.

"After all…" I said quietly, "What more natural than that a mother should do all she can to save the life of her son…"

Chapter Twenty Six

"Good morning, Doctor Shafto..." The newspaper crumpled down on to his lap. Talaeus Dekker inclined his head so that he could scan me over the tops of his spectacles. "Out and about the town early, as ever... I see."

I was more than surprised to find him in Newcastle. Somehow I had come to think of Dekker as an old spider sitting at the centre of his Edinburgh web. This was the man who for the present was my master, the old fellow to whom my written reports had gone. Yet it was odd to remind myself that in reality it had been no longer than a few days since I had talked with him in the house beside the Meat Market. Now he looked even wearier than he had been. But now too Dekker was dressed as a gentleman, almost as a dandy; someone who was wearing clothes that were without doubt in the height of London fashion. But I could also see that he had travelled, and travelled far. The weathered face was framed against a wide collar of rich black bearskin; it made him look oddly barbaric. Spatters of mud were drying on his highly polished boots. "Be a good fellow, Doctor, and tell your coachman to take us up to..." Dekker fished a scrap of paper from the fob pocket of his brocaded waistcoat and squinted at it. "A Mrs. Mortimer's at someplace called ... the Painter Haugh. A street is it?"

"It is a *street*, Sir... though I fear it is not one that stands in much favour with the... better classes of the town's people."

"Good! That's what's needed for this business... Are there any whorehouses in it?"

"Not that I know of, Sir." I kept a straight face. "Though there well may be… These last days I haven't been looking much for bordellos, Colonel. Though if you did happen to need…" It was only then that I knew that I had provoked a bright spark of humour in Dekker's eye. He was amused. "You do me credit, Doctor, truly you do me much credit indeed." Talaeus Dekker may not have had much of a heart - but perhaps, just perhaps, the same bastard still owned something of his own soul. "The truth is that I've a dozen hard-riding Bow Street Runners with me. They're all good lads. They serve me under a special warrant given me by the Home Secretary. The Bank has given me leave to hire the buggers for a week. So I'll need to see to it that this affair in Newcastle comes to term damned soon. That's why I want to keep every bastard of them out of whorehouses. At Bristol a few months ago two of those lecherous hounds missed an arrest and a haul of seventy thousand in gold coins because they were both fornicatin' when they should have been elsewhere!"

Mrs. Mortimer's was one of the narrow fronted old houses along the Haugh. Indeed the building looked to be held up only by the good fellowship of its drunken neighbours. Downstairs on the street front was the warped bull's eye window of a little shop. Above it and reached only by a narrow stairway were the rooms. One sharp rap from the handle of Dekker's riding crop was all it took to get us in. The hard-eyed bastard who stood in the doorway had a face that looked to have seen recent service as a butcher's chopping block. But at sight of Dekker he stiffened, knuckled his forehead and stood smartly aside. It was then that under his brown frieze coat I saw the edge of a robin redbreast waistcoat with the small gold buttons of his office. So this fellow was one of the famous mounted patrol of the Runners. I'd never clapped eyes on a Bow Street man before - though naturally enough even in France we'd heard about their spy catching. And as I stood at that moment I was not so sure that I welcomed this meeting. He led the way as we climbed up the narrow stairway. As we climbed the steps we rose upward into a near solid down draught of the clinging stink that comes from Shields kippers when they splutter in smoking blue of hot beef dripping.

The men lay on cots pulling at their clay pipes and idly rattling dice. Every man was in his stocking feet. One of them was pouring a brew of China tea into earthenware mugs. Today, it seemed, Talaeus Dekker was running a dry canteen. One of the men was busy about the lock of a cavalry carbine with an oiled rag. Another fellow lifted his eyes at me to show the haggard look of a man in dire need of a hair-of-the-dog that had bitten him.

"Well, my fighting cocks... are these accommodations to your liking?" Dekker had passed the men by before he growled his greeting. Nonetheless every man there responded. These fellows liked their leader; or else they feared him. And their accents too, I noted at once were mostly Cockney. "Rudman! The stabling out at the back will serve well enough – will it?" One of the Runners jumped up and grinned.

"I will pass on to Y'r Honour any complaints made by d' horses, sir!" There was a rumble of laughter.

I followed Dekker to a little back room. It had been scrubbed clean no later than that morning but it was sparsely furnished. On one wall hung a recent map of the city. Behind us Rudman hurried in with two steaming mugs of tea. He said nothing as he put them down. But then as he laid a stack of greasy notebooks on the table he said: "Yesterday's occurrence books for all the riders, Colonel, sir!" At that moment I realised that in all probability these men had already been at work in Newcastle for some days. That was something I didn't like – not at all!

Dekker pulled out a silver flask that must have held a pint. The fragrance of good brandy hung on the air as he splashed spirit liberally into the teas and motioned for me to take up a mug.

"Sit down, sir... Now, from the twenty eighth day of February... from the very moment you got out of Mrs. Brydon's barouche before the 'Bull and Mouth', you tell me everything, *again:* tell me what you've found out; tell me who you've met and what you've done and then , and above all, tell me what you suspect!"

That I did. Already I knew that I would have to be careful here. In the French service they teach you how to make a proper report. It would be a damned fool thing to do any worse for this man.

"And so all you are waiting on now is for this fellow, Jacob Storey, to bring you the letter from the grocer, Hodgson?" Dekker had been listening to my report. But clearly enough his thoughts were already well out on the road ahead of me.

"Yes, sir… that's how the business stands."

And at that moment it dawned on me that what Dekker now intended to do was to take over this entire affair. Of course I understood. Senior officers will always garner the cream o' the credit for a success. Just as they will show themselves to have been set dead against a botched job from the outset! Be that as it may, what I knew then was that this affair was soon like to reach the point where Robert Shafto might no longer be needed; even, he might become an embarrassment, and inconvenience. I would have to watch for any signs. At the first sniff of any betrayal I would be a fool not to be away!

"So we might suppose that the guineas will be brought down to the wharf within hours of the proprietor and his two men being abducted."

I nodded. "An hour or two before high tide today, sir, was my supposition… I was about to call upon Mr. Grainger for his help."

"No, Laddie! Don't you do that!" It was obviously a command; he'd fairly snarled it at me. Talaeus Dekker's face was suddenly set grim. "From this moment we must leave poor Richard out of this own affairs… completely. He doesn't know it but he would seem to have a spy sitting in his very pocket! That spy must remain in ignorance of our doings." I saw that now Dekker's gaze was fixed on me. "While I have no need to remind *you*, Robert Shafto, that you are in *my* service - and no one else's. That much, I hope, is entirely clear?" The anger that had twitched at the corner of Dekker's mouth disappeared. He took out his watch and thumbed open the case.

"At two o' clock I am to meet with a Mr. Johnston down at the Customs House. Together we are to discuss an application for a licence to ship the corpse of a certain nobleman home to France. We have called for the corpse to be presented for a lawful inspection. And that licence *will* be freely issued. What happens then will depend upon the identity of the man who comes to collect the paper. That fellow of course will be followed..." Dekker looked at me again over the tops of his spectacles.

"What I want you to do, Doctor Shafto, is to find for me a brace of entirely reliable witness. One of them at least should be an eminently respectable person; a man or woman who will, if need be, swear before a whole bench o' beaks that the corpse in the coffin is a dearly beloved relative of theirs... You can do that?"

It was my turn to smile. "In Newcastle, sir, I could secure a dozen such honest folk... for ten pounds a head."

"Ten pounds!" That had been an error. My asking price had obviously taken Dekker aback. So I countered at once by pressing my case all the harder.

"Ten pounds in *gold*, that is... each?" Now it was my turn to raise an eyebrow and look at him sidelong. "After all, sir, even here in the North, perjury is a plain felony!" I should have known: in the matter of cash-in-hand Talaeus Dekker appeared to be distinctly tight fisted.

"Do it for five, Shafto... I know *I* could." As he took out his purse and began to count out the coins into my hand I was much reminded of some old farm wifie paying out her quarter's rent to the estate's steward.

It had been strange just how quickly the sour face of Hector Wanless had sprung into my mind. So after all I'd found a use for that old Sodomite. For an hour or two Mrs.

Flavia Humble would have to spare me the services of her butler. But first I had outposts of my own that I would need to inspect. Fortunately it is only a short step from the Painter Haugh up to the Pudding Chare.

I found Jacob Storey sitting by the fire in the *Rose's* taproom. Moreover, and more than a little to my surprise, I saw that he was stone cold sober. He sat there with the relish fading from his chops as he wiped up the last smears of mutton gravy from a tin plate.

"What chee'or, wor Jacob! I had let my shadow fall on him. "Have y' owt at all to report?" To my surprise the old man nodded eagerly enough.

"The letter is here, in m' coat pocket, sir…it was brought half an hour ago." A plaintive whine shivered in his throat.

"Then, Jacob…why the Hell weren't you out trying to find me?" I tried to rein-in my rising anger at Storey's apparent idleness.

"Because, sir… the same young chap who brought it here is still hanging about outside in the lane. Dougie Jamison, the landlord here, doesn't know the chap."

"And has this lad got yellow pantaloons on, Jacob?" I heard myself sigh.

"Aye, he has that…"

"Then you've done well… Y'r a damned smart fellow, Jacob Storey! I'm pleased. For this you shall have a pot of the best porter." I held up a finger. "Later though…"

It had been an easy guess. And I suppose that I ought to have been relieved that Ralph Hodgson hadn't been tempted to play any daft games with me. This was only what I might have expected. All that had happened was that the grocer had sent out his letter in the hands of his son. Keep it in the family! Nonetheless it was a minor annoyance. And it did occur to me then that the lad must have seen me come into the taproom. It was a small complication. It added merely to the number of things I had to think about.

But it was a problem soon solved. A word with the *Rose's* landlord was all it took. Though, if I needed one, it gave me an appreciation of what a treasure an inn-keeper who knows his business can be! All Big Dougie had to do was drop the whisper to his crippled potman. The poor lad nodded and hobbled away. Within minutes from outside on the busy Pudding Chare bank the ears of every man in the *Rose* were cringing under the harsh screech of hurled abuse and accusation. Across the lane a couple of big blowsy lasses were already closing in on young Rupert Hodgson.

"Why, Mary, m' darlin' here 'ee is! This is the selfsame dorty little beggar… bold as y' please… an' him wi' out the shame t' so much as blush for it!" They were both as brash as only a hunting pack of Bigg Market whores can be. Cautiously I stepped to the doorway to watch. That poor youth was foredoomed! Already they had young Hodgson trapped tight between them. With the thrust of broad hips and big bosoms they were mobbing the wretch. Both lasses were already the worse for their gin – though to be sure that had put them both in grand fettle for the business to hand.

"Well I'll be buggered by a blind billy goat… but it's right y' are, Aggie, Lass!" Their two screeches rising and falling one to the other gave a curiously musical counterpoint. "This is that selfsame young arse-wipe, him what ran off last night – brasss faced – an' owin' the pair of us… f' wor services…an' them was of a *most* speshul kind!" Mary glanced over her shoulder and nodded coyly as though to seek confirmation from the townsfolk hurrying by. Yet for certain, every passing soul knew better than to poke his face into this affair. "D'y think that any Christian body would even *believe* the Godless things this filthy … little… heathen had us do for him!"

By then the lad was little better than a sheep to the slaughter. At every slash of the girl's broken glass laughter he flinched. While the words that Mary was crooning at him from her side were so tender and solicitous: "Why, Aggie m' darlin', would you believe that this poor bairn's little bum is near t' froze off!" By then she had her hand thrust deep down the back of the yellow pantaloons. Under her nimble finger work the lad was squirming like an eel on a spear. Now the bold Aggie had Rupert's buttons loosed. She was hauling out fistfuls of white shirt from the front of the pantaloons. By then young Hodgson was blushing scarlet; his fat face was twisting. I couldn't help but laugh. He reminded me of nothing so much as a prissy maid being goosed frantic by a pack of village lads. Then suddenly young Rupert seemed gather himself. His elbows came out. He struggled hard. Suddenly like a Hercules casting off heavy shackles he was free. To be sure though, that was only because the two lasses had loosed him. Mary punted him hard with her knee; so hard was the blow that the lad went staggering forward. But already Aggie had her fingers into his pockets. Wide eyed as a calf in the shambles the lad pelted away up the lane. But of course he had left his purse behind him. Giggling like a pair of ninnies the two whores disappeared among the gathering crowd of their friends.

"Right…Jacob Storey…we'll away then!" I hauled him to his feet. "Today we've a bit of work up among the gentry…"

As we walked up through the town I looked at the letter. The grocer was being careful. The message was printed in grocers' pencil on the same leaf I had torn from Mattie Crowley's account book. It read simply: "Attend to the business we agreed upon at two o'clock" Yes, this grocer was being cautious.

Our luck was in. We overtook Wanless as he was walking down the lane behind Higham Place. It was only when I took hold of his arm and swung him around that I saw the changes the last few days had wrought in the man. May the good Lord bless Doctor Shafto for all his pious works! For it looked very much to me as though I myself might have been responsible for the man's apparent reform. For to be sure, Isaac Wanless was the very picture of the Sodomite who has turned away from his Wickedness. He was fresh shaved and his clothes were well brushed. Also the bastard was clutching a Bible. I've always found that to be a damned ominous sign.

"Do I find you well then, Mr. Wanless?" My smile shone like a polished brass collection plate. My expression however was barren of any friendship and the surly bastard knew it.

"You'll find me purified of all sin, Wilfred Nettles…" The voice was tomb-hollow. "Now in both my Body and my Soul I am wholly the Lord's." His fingers whitened around his Testament.

"Why then, sir, I'm most tremendous glad to hear of it!" I patted his shoulder until the dust lifted. But this new Wanless was truly pathetic. Several time before I had seen such a case. The truth is that all these buggers protest too much. Salvation among his kind is always a fragile thing. Fear of the rope and nothing else was what had driven Wanless's filthy appetites away into deep hiding. Soon enough though, the man's unclean passions would creep out again. This same fellow, I supposed, had to be exactly as his God had made him. And as always the Beast would come back ravening! Yet for the moment all I needed of Wanless was to have him come down to the Customs House and bear false witness in the matter of an embalmed corpse.

"So… a man so wonderfully saved then, friend Isaac," I said gravely' "would surely be ready to do his king a service…"

Of course I was right. For a man new saved from the wiles of the Evil One that filthy old shite poker needed little persuasion at all to condemn another poor soul. Indeed this particular creature was actually eager to perjure himself. I had my two witnesses down to the Customs House at the stroke of two. On the way I coached both Wanless and Jacob Storey in what they should say.

Talaeus Dekker was waiting. And as we walked across the cobblestones towards the Customs House he cocked knowing eye at Isaac Wanless. "And what precise manner o' tenterhook do you have skewered into this one's bowels, Doctor Shafto?"

"The man is a Sodomite, sir. I came to know of it." Brevity pays!

"Aye, the fellow has the look! Good, well done." Dekker stared at Wanless with a faint curiosity.

"However, Doctor Shafto, it also occurs to me that sodomy is an appetite that will usually secure a man tightly enough... and for sure too tight for us ever to have to pay for his perjury." Smiling wryly I dropped the five pounds in gold back into Dekker's waiting hand.

"Yes," I thought, "it will tie that wretch almost as securely as it does another poor bastard - one with a charge of treason held over him!" Naturally I said nothing of the kind.

Mr. John Turnbull was the official who was waited for us at the Customs House. He was a plump, smiling man who clearly was trying to make the most of a passing likeness to the Prince George. And for sure in the matter of his many chins that likeness was marked. With his coat tails lifted he toasted his breech's arse before a roaring fire while he looked upward, apparently engrossed in the intricacies of the high stucco ceiling. However it was also clear at once that Turnbull knew that, of the three of us present, he need treat only Dekker with respect, and even that was scant enough. The business overall however was obviously not exactly to the Collector's taste. We were not offered wine.

"As you requested I set the time for the appointment at a quarter past two...sharp! The license to take a body out of the kingdom has been drafted. Here it is..."

Dekker took it and unfolded the stiff paper. I watched his eyes scan the lines. He was satisfied. "Excellent, Mr. Turnbull..." His smile would have seduced an archangel. "The phrasing is so apt...superb!"

At Turnbull's suggestion Wanless and I were ushered into the clerks' annexe to wait. It was typical of such places. The office of the Collector was spacious and panelled throughout in oak. Its annexe was a cold and cheerless little rat-hole of a place. As soon as I stepped into it I caught the faint whiff from a leaking cess-pit somewhere close by. It would be a damned sight worse in the Summer. We pushed our way into the room between two desks piled with papers. Neither of the two clerks at work there were at all best pleased by our intrusion. They looked, scowled, and began to push their quills into motion again. They were copying documents. Both men I saw had developed the skill of making accurate copies in a clear copperplate while at the same time, still, being able to chatter to his fellow.

"Dickie… What will ahh do wi' a note from one of the lads workin' the Hendon Shore at Sunderland?"

"Consarnin' what?" The older clerk broke into a bored yawn.

"There's a tide-waiter called Smaile who says here that he's had a fella pointed out to him as a deserter from a king's ship… Jottie Stokoe is this fellah's name."

I stiffened and slowly turned about to look at the clerk who had spoken. That he held a man's life in his hands seemed not to concern him at all.

"Soaked in a poor sailor's blood, that is! Chuck it into yor basket, son. Forget you've ever seen it!" The older clerk looked pointedly at his assistant. Do it, young Sam! An' them 's my *instruction* t' you. This is the Customs Office. We're far too busy here to interfere with matters concernin' the damned Navy." The look on Dickie's face told me that he meant what he was saying.

"But the Regulations…"

"Bugger the regulation book! Listen, y' slushy headed little cah'cah!" The chief clerk was getting angry now. "D'y think that one of our own poxy tide-waiters won't know where he can pick up a canny little reward for layin' just such an information? Why man, that beggar will already have run tippy-lappy along to the Port Captain's office. All Jack Smailes is doin' with that letter is tryin' get twice-praised for the same piece o' arse lickin'."

That little exchange truly served to set my teeth a' grinding. I was plunged at once into a damned foul temper. I couldn't help myself; and yet that was something I should have been able to do. What did I owe Stokoe? All I had done was offer my help to an badly mauled British sailor taken from the sea off the Italian coast. Then I remembered the hideous sight of Jonathan's back. The living flesh had been clawed to raw meat with a hundred lashes from a heavy cat-o-nine tails. Hadn't I doctored him, saved him from certain death by *septicaemia*? So why had the wretched fellow dared ever to come back to Tyneside? Surely that had to be the cause of all his troubles now! I was fuming still when I heard the sharp rap of knuckle against the door to summon us back to Turnbull's office.

The room was crowded. Doctor Mudie had presented himself to swear the declaration. But he had had to employ four undertaker's men to bear the lead coffin. While for show Turnbull himself had called in two of his preventive men. Like a guard of honour they stood with their cutlasses drawn. Dekker sat apart and at his ease in a high-backed ebony chair by the window.

"This need not take us too long, Doctor Mudie..." Turnbull smiled roundly at all the men assembled. He had a quill already dipped and in his hand. "You have sworn a legal oath that this...er corpse is that of the late Marquis de Sebrincourt... a French gentleman..."

"I do... I have."

"Then I herewith grant you a licence to take from this kingdom..." The customs official's quill was raised over the license.

"A moment, if you please Mr. Turnbull..." I heard Dekker's footsteps on the polished floorboards. He looked at the undertaker's men: "Wait outside, if you would all be so good." Doctor Mudie's expression had changed but he was not yet alarmed. When they had gone Dekker turned to address himself to Turnbull. He waved a paper.

"In conformity to this warrant I require that the coffin to be opened at once, if you please, Mr. Turnbull." Dekker's words echoed up to the high ceiling over our heads. Turnbull's eyebrows were raised but he made a signal to his guard.

Vapour from the oil of cedar was at once heavy on the air. And I found myself wiping an errant trace of a grin off my face. To be sure I could scarcely help myself. In stark daylight I saw that after all the dead man's cheeks did perhaps look just a little too cheerily pink.

"Mr. Wanless… will you be so good as to step forward, Sir!" Oddly enough Talaeus Dekker also had the look of a man who was enjoying himself to the full. "Pray examine the corpse… closely if you please!" Wanless stepped forward. He shuffled up close to the coffin, looked into it, and then pronounced in a sepulchral tone. "Sir…this man has something of the look of my own dear brother… he who disappeared from his home in…" Jacob Storey stood by as silent as a mourning mute but he managed to nod his head gravely.

I saw that Doctor Mudie's cheeks had blanched. His fat mouth sprang open, then slowly closed again. Yes, the man was in still in control of himself.

"Thank you: that will do for now." Dekker cut Wanless off short by holding up a finger. "However, *Mr* Wanless, you will hold yourself in readiness. You may well be called to testify, elsewhere… in due course."

There were three of us left in the room. The only sound to be heard was a soft wheeze as Mudie drew a slow breath. Then to my surprise Dekker thrust a silver flask cup into the doctor's hand and waited until the brandy had been gulped down.

"Well, Doctor… we find ourselves in a damned sorry business… do we not?" I would describe Dekker's words as being emollient, indeed downright greasy! "You yourself will appreciate that there are so many offences – most of them felonies - tangled into this affair…" The voice lowered. "For any one of which you would certainly face the supreme penalty. Quite simply, sir, it doesn't bear thinking about."

Together they took three steps in silence. Then. "But come, it is certainly not my way to torture a professional man… " With his hand pushing against Mudie's shoulder he began to steer the physician away out of my hearing.

Why I should have stooped to look at the corpse in the coffin I do not know. Probably it was because I wished not to seen trying to overhear what Dekker was saying. Call it professional curiosity if you will, but I did. I had never had opportunity to examine an embalmed corpse at my leisure before. The first thing I noted was that in the stark revelation of daylight all this talk of life-likeness was mere apothecary's cant. That cadaver looked what it was - just so much preserved meat! The dead man's apparel too was tawdry stuff. Then I saw that one of the fingers had not been pushed into its glove. I suppose it was no more than a sense of neatness that made me roll it down and pull it off. But it was the harsh scrape of the calluses against the cotton of the glove that made me look closer. And almost at once I felt one of my eyebrows rise. What manner of work, I found myself asking, would a French nobleman have to do to put such heavy calluses on his palms and forefingers?

My own insight leaped. From link to link along the chain it went. I knew at once what the dead man had been. I would not have to cross the river to the ropewalk at New Deptford to take a look at workmen's hands. I knew. French marquise, my backside! The corpse in the coffin had been a ropemaker. This poor old fellow must have been hired for the work. Then when his job was done he had been murdered. That would have secured secrecy! I remembered the pieces of dismantled machinery in the house by All Saints. The dead man had worked there, alone, making something from hemp rope. And whatever that was it had been damned special. If I was right, and by God at that moment I knew I was, then thousands, perhaps hundreds of thousands, in gold coin had been worked into something like the core of a heavy hawser or mooring rope. Hemp again! In this game the fibres of *cannabis sativa*, the common hemp of commerce, blew everywhere. And from the beginning it had been lying about to be seen by anyone with the wit to realise. The fall of the footsteps signalled Dekker's return.

From the physician's face I saw that at least some sort of accommodation had been reached. Quickly I decided. Though in any attempt at false dealing with a man like Talaeus Dekker I knew the risk I took. Yet for a little time at least I would keep to myself what I had learned from the corpse in the coffin. The thrill of it went through me. As I stood there I knew where the guineas were, or would very soon be.

"Call your fellows, Doctor Mudie. Take your coffin and put it aboard the *Countess of Raby* " To my surprise he was offering Mudie his hand. Mudie wrung it hard. "Then go back and attend to your patients… Good day, t' you."

We watched from the window as Mudie followed the coffin out to the cart. The man was reassured. I saw that from the way he tapped his new beaver felt hat down jauntily down on to his head with his silver topped cane. But then when Talaeus Dekker turned I saw that the merest twitch was passing across his gaunt cheeks.

"Shafto, know me, sir!" The voice was like the splintering of bones. "You may well have heard me promise Mudie that he would practice medicine again. Doubtless he will. Has he not my given word upon it? However, you did not hear me utter any undertaking as to precisely… *where* he would tend the sick and needy!"

'As you say, sir." It sounded non-committal enough. The Emperor had been right: *Albion perfide* indeed! It was a thought that I could not stifle. Though Napoleon's error, I think, had been to assume that the English readily broke their word. They did not. Instead as a nation they were merely the great dissemblers. They always allowed you to *think* that they had promised. That was how Talaeus Dekker was deceiving Mudie.

Along the waterside the light of the lamps and torches glowed through the swirling fog like amber beads. With Jacob Storey close at my heels I followed Mudie's little entourage. And with a deal more speed than respect for the dead might demand we all got smartly along to Clartie Mitchison's warehouse. There I saw at once that two of Dekker's Bow-Street men were watching the place. One of them moved towards me. He looked out over the river like a man searching. When he spoke it was through lips that seemed not to be moving at all.

"The two labourers was lifted, that was ten minutes ago. Our lads have got them into a boat. They'll be kept moving about on the river until full dark…"

"What about Mitchison, the owner?" These hired Runners were said to be efficient fellows but still I was worried. This was no time for even the slightest mistake.

"He's too big a chap to bash on the head an' cart off. So half an hour ago one o' the Colonel's fellows strolls across there an', all civil like, offers Mitchison a rare proposition o' business. The fellow was ready enough to step out for a pot o' ale." The Runner's thin lips twisted. "I reckon they'll 'av 'im snorin' by now."

We waited. Fine drizzle sifted down through the grey swirl of chimney smoke to spangle on the wool of our coats. We listened. A man cleared his throat and hawked. Then somewhere up the bank we heard the heavy rumble of a dray's wheels – of more than one dray. All around me in the gloom I heard men stir, take breath. One after the other, here and there around me, there was the harsh click-a-clock of flintlocks being cocked. Somewhere to my left a blade was drawn. Across the road from me the gates of Mitchison's yard stood open; two tar barrels hung on poles had been lit in the yard. The sound of the flames spluttering against the rain came to me. The rumble of tyre iron on whinstone cobbles grew louder.

"Wait for the signal…" Dekker's voice was soft in my ear. He was holding a horn whistle on a cord. "I want no mistakes... the gold has to be put aboard that ship before we move at all."

I had been right. Two carts each drawn by a pair of fine big Clydesdales turned into the yard. Both had a gang of men aboard ready to do the unloading. And from the noise they made they were at merry lot. To my relief I saw that what both carts carried was indeed heavy ship rope. I watched as they picked up a loose end from the cart and began at once to haul the rope across the yard and towards the ship. I could hear the grunts and the rhythmic stamp of feet. Then Dekker put up his whistle to his lips. All around us in the gathering mist men stirred. One sharp blast cut at the air.

As a surprise attack it could not be faulted. The Emperor's own men could not have done it better. There had been no yells or shouting. The clatter of boot iron was the only sound. Then every man who had come on the carts stood boggle eyed at the muzzles of the firelocks, cocked and primed, that were levelled at him.

"Mr. Turnbull, sir... is that you?" The foreman in charge of the carts was on his feet. His hands were raised high; the face was as pale as wood ashes. But clearly enough, the man knew the Collector of Customs and it was obvious too that he fully expected to be recognised.

Chapter Twenty-seven

I'm very much afraid, Sir, that the Collector of Customs *himself* is willing to vouch for Tommy Slack, the foreman. And that man in his turn swears he can answer for every one of his own men. It seems that the Collector and he are fellow church wardens..."

I had already asked myself whether that of itself was a sufficient badge of probity. But then I saw that Dekker was nodding his head. I coughed loudly to clear my throat. The next item of my report was also a matter likely to chafe against a tender spot. "These ropes, Sir, there's a blue thread twisted into every lay: Navy stores. They've been made on contract at the New Deptford rope-walk across at Gateshead and consigned, direct, to His Majesty's Dockyard at Chatham..."

"T'cha..." Dekker's mouth twisted angrily to form a filthy oath.

"But there are, Sir, two other things which might signify. The man Hodgson, the second mate who was...er... punched out of his berth by the seaman, Rea, is on the wharf." I had already looked at the collier's log. Against the names of Rea and his mates who last trip had shipped out from Newcastle were inked in the words: 'Skinned out wilful. Sign'd aboard a Yankee...'

"I'm beginning to think, Doctor Shafto, that this time we've been very thoroughly humbugged... damn it all we've all been well hum-buggered! Three blessed hours we've spent here – and for every minute of it I've felt in my bones that we've all been let play Daft Jock! For sure we've been chasin' after naught that's tangible!" Dekker drew a weary breath. "Yet every step of it all has all been so cleverly done!"

For all that I saw that, and even angered, as Dekker was, it did not stop him from the task he had in hand. He was pouring brandy from a brown bottle into a polished silver flask. The flask was his; the bottle he'd found in one of the cabin's lockers. Frustration takes different men in different ways. Now I could see that the Colonel's expression was tinged with a growing sourness. Perhaps it would now be prudent for me to watch carefully and pay good mind to what I said. There was a slight tremor to his hand. He muffed his pour and a few drops of brandy spilled on to the deck. Now the old devil was forcing his words through teeth clenched in concentration:

"It occurs to me too, Doctor Shafto, that this Hetherington fellow, the cunning bastard, has neatly schemed it so as to get most of the Excise men along this river together and busied aboard this one ship." The flask was full to the neck. Dekker swigged off the remaining inch of spirit from the bottle. The old beggar had not offered me so much as a drop. "My own reluctant conclusion therefore is that the gold is to be shipped out... from elsewhere. Perhaps all of this game has been a carefully contrived piece of play acting."

The cabin was dank and chill. I stepped across to shut the stern window. For a few seconds I looked out, down over the collier's stern. Green water fouled with all kinds of filth and flotsam swirled past the rudder. I watched the flow of it break and swirl away in little whorls and whirlpools. Then I heard the steady beat of paddles. Beneath my feet the collier's hull began to lift and sway. As the steamboat *Perseverance* threshed her way by us our own moorings answered with creaks and groans. A glance out over the river told me that well before dark there would be a fog. Already the wisps and wraiths of white vapour were gathering.

"A full dozen of Turnbull's skilled rummagers have been through this ship - keel to truck." Dekker's fist began to pound softly on the tabletop. "But all they have found aboard is exactly what her manifest states: two hundred tons of best Tyne coals, twenty dozen of new woven hemp fenders, and two dozen ship ropes… and as you say, every strand, Admiralty ordered. Oh, aye, and now one mummified Frenchman. A damned odd collection it is, but without doubt every bit of it is just so God awful lawful it fair makes my teeth ache to think on it!" Dekker yawned like a dog and rubbed hard at his eyes. He had been weary when I had seen him that morning. Now I think the old man had to be close to exhaustion.

"I begin much to fear, Doctor, that there's no gold on her – nor ever has been…"

"But you'll want to keep men aboard her until she clears the Tyne?" It was an obvious precaution.

"More than that: as a matter o' common <u>nous</u> I have already made arrangements to have the *Countess of Raby* shadowed by a fast Revenue cutter once she leaves the Tyne. So be assured, Sir: this hooker is branded deep with the Mark of Cain! Wherever she sails, day or night she'll have a glass focussed on her…"

"Which is what I believe we ourselves have focussed on us at this very moment, Aye, Colonel, and that perhaps from two separate places" That I had picked up a spyglass from the bulkhead rack and focussed it on the Gateshead shore had been an act of sheer idleness.

For once Dekker's anger got the better of him. He was on his feet; his face was pale and twisted.

"Where man…where?" Dekker had snatched the glass from my hands and was pulling out the brass slides. "By God, I'll stretch the bastard's neck…"

"Stay seated, Sir… if you please!" I put my hand to Dekker's shoulder and bore him down. He subsided again into his chair. Suddenly he was just an old man who realised that his enterprise might be foundering under him.

"Where is the whore-monger?" His quiet hiss lashed out across the cabin.

"There's a chandler's warehouse across on the Gateshead side...'Munro & Son.' From where I stood I could read the tall white letters painted on to tarred timbers. "I've seen someone stir up there in the window at the gable's end... "

The rap of knuckles against the door interrupted us. It was Mr. Partis, the excise officer the Collector had assigned to us. He stood there balancing on the threshold, his tarpaulin hat resting on the crook of his elbow. But he did not enter the cabin. That I think may have been tradition.

"We've done. Sir..." That was all he said.

"Nothing?" Dekker asked quietly.

The Excise man lifted an unshaven chin. "Nothing, Sir... no contraband of any kind... An' aah've been the Chief Jerquer on this river for fifteen year... so aa'h think this far down the road aa'd know all the beggar's clever bloody tricks!"

"Very well then, thank you Mr. Partis. You may permit the crew come to come back aboard and make her ready for sea..." Dekker groaned and eased himself to his feet. But Partis stood still; he was looking askance at Dekker.

"She'll not be movin' now, Sir!" There was a rising, quizzical tone to the man's cry. "You've kept her here overlong for that! Why, man, her keel is on the mud – there's not enough water under her t' float her off. Aah 'd say she's has missed this tide altogether." His smile was thin and he looked directly at neither of us. Though I think I could detect that this fall of events had brought the revenue man a certain relish. "An' t' be sure that'll not please Sir Michael Geddes." The spark in his eye told me that the fellow was enjoying himself. " Doubtless y' ll ha' heard that since last week the *Countess* has a new owner. Though mind y's, gentlemen... it was none o' my duties t' stop the Mate from trippin' along the Quayside t' tell the new owner that w' we're doin' here." I heard Dekker swear bitterly under his breath. Partis was drumming his fingers on his tarred hat. He had still more to say.

"This new owner... gentlemen, he'll likely be the reason for the ship being made all trim and tiddly since the last time she was in the Tyne. A deal o' good money 's been laid out on her! " This time Partis was venturing his own ha'porth. "Just cast an eye over her if you will, gentlemen. Whenever did you see any Tyne collier that wasn't slidin' along on the bare bones of her arse! Whoever heard the like of it? Why man, since last trip her fore-topmast has been replaced, entire; there's two new spars aft. And this hull has been out of the water. She's had her seams new caulked. All in all, a'ah wud say, gentlemen, that this last week this vessel has had shipwrights swarming all over her." The man's face split into a sideways smirk. "For certain sure!"

"Thank you, Mr. Partis…" It was a dismissal. And the man had the wit to know it.

Dekker looked at me: "She's not been far: Hartlepool. According to her logbook she was there only four days. Use enough men and a lot can be done in that time…"

"Surely Sir, only men who were about trust a great quantity of gold to this ship's bottom would go to so much trouble."

"That's what the cunning bastards want us to think, Shafto… Well, Doctor, I won't swallow it. We must now search elsewhere"

"It's surely been a deal of trouble and expense to go to."

Dekker's smile soured even more. "Nowhere near it. A new Geordie collier straight off the stocks and with all her gear standing can be purchased outright for a little over seven hundred pounds. In the scale of this business that's mere chaff. The gentlemen o' this syndicate have been smuggling out hundreds of thousands of guineas a voyage. The margins o' profit must be enormous! Widen your vision, Doctor. To these rogues the cost of an old collier – along with a few murders thrown in - is mere coppers, small change from the petty-purse. Besides which where's the loss? That collier will ply at her honest trade for years with the work that's just been done on her!"

I looked at Dekker and raised my eyebrows so as to concede the point. Nonetheless, my bowels were giving me a fair warning. A nagging ache in my guts was shouting out at me that the crux of this business was closing in on me fast. I could feel a sharp narrowing in of all my options. And of course the chief squeeze of things now concerned my own safety. Yet there was more. Somehow I could not help the feeling that the whole damned city of Newcastle town had to be rolling about and laughing at our zany antics. It was as though every soul in the town knew the secret and that they were holding their breaths against the outcome. Almost I was convinced of it. Wasn't this our Geordie way? On the surface all would be calm. Underneath, and all through it, the maggots would be there busy at the cheese. Yes; time, my time, was spilling out fast. If Talaeus Dekker had misjudged – if word trickled back from the bank's other spies in France that more English guineas had come to fill up Napoleon's war chests - then soon enough there would be English officers of state whose business it would be to cast around for someone to blame. That was when some time serving crack-louse might recall a temporary stay of arrest issued in respect of a physician called Robert Shafto…who was a traitor.

"By your leave, Sir, I'll go out on deck…" Talaeus Dekker nodded. I needed time to think. So too I think did he.

And as I paced about that deck I began to shape my own rough calculus of probabilities, stacking my *pros* carefully against my *cons*. The Danish merchant vessel *Heirje* would still be down at Bishop's Wearmouth. I knew Stokoe's offer of a free passage would hold good. Moreover I still had hidden about my person over seventy pounds in local bank notes. It was the cash I had taken from Crowley's corpse. I might loose a few percent when I changed them into *rigsdalers* but I was sure that notes issued by a respectable Newcastle banking house would be accepted in Copenhagen. That would give me a start. There was also, I reminded myself, a fifty-guinea fee waiting for me to pick up at Hodgson's shop. After all, the service the grocer had contracted for had been fulfilled. Somewhere or other Dekker's men had Clartie Michison and his two labourers held safe. So by any fair reckoning that money was due to me! Yes; taken all in all, Bob Shafto's affairs were in a damned sight better case than they had been in Paris less than a fortnight before.

A shout of fury brought my head up. From behind me up on the wharf there was a great bellow of outrage. Hooves boomed on the dock's timbers. What I saw was a squire or gentleman farmer in a velvet-trimmed riding coat and button-up calfskin spatter-dashes. He was having difficulty getting his foot out of his stirrup. As I watched him hop about one-footed I was reminded of a bull pawing the ground. But as he came on the ship's crew waiting on the wharf they parted their ranks for him and forelocks were tugged at. He galloped charging up the gangplank. There was a water-guard. But that gormless ninny stood where he was with a naked cutlass gripped in his fist. He shuffled uncertainly. Then like some terrified lackey he jumped aside. I heard Partis swearing under his breath.

"What ignorant boot is in charge here? Where is this bloody Jack-in-Office, who claims that my vessel carries contraband!"

The new owner glowered at me, decided I could not be responsible, and strode below. As the stern cabin's door burst open I heard him bellow. As much for my own curiosity as anything else I wanted very much at that moment to know how Dekker would deal with this belligerent pig. But at once the cabin door was slammed shut. Then all I could hear was a voice that began high and angry. Then there was a long silence. The next sound was no more than the scrape of a chair's legs on the deck planks. The door opened again. Together the two men stepped out on to the deck.

"No, indeed, after *you*, Sir... And once again allow me to thank you for showing so much patriotic forbearance... only a true Englishman would do that! " It was hard not to laugh; and harder still to believe I was listening to Talaeus Dekker at all. For this was a role I'd not witnessed before. The hard mouth and the steely gaze had melted all away. Now clearly 'emolience' was the watchword of the day. Every word that fell from Dekker's mouth was slathered thick with oily blue unction. " You'll understand, Sir Michael... as any loyal subject must, that sometimes your vigilant Crown servant must perforce ride a little... shall we say ...roughshod over the honest rights of decent men!"

"Of course my dear fellow, of course, as you say! Rest assured of it!"

I was impressed. I watched Sir Michael Geddes step ashore like a lamb. Dekker stood at the gangplank and waved him off. But then I saw him raise a hand and stroke at his chin. One of his riders on the quay caught the signal and raised a forefinger to his hat brim. When Dekker turned to me again he was wearing the same old grim smile.

"Doctor, there may be no gold aboard this ship at this moment... but by the great Lord Jehovah, Sir, there *will* be before this ship leaves the river! It has a smell to it that is as strong as any billygoat's sweat. Why Sir... just now I do believe that I even heard the merry chink of it!" Dekker clapped his hands together with a bang. "And then we'll get our hands on the beggars!"

"It seems that your interview with Sir Michael Geddes has given you cause for cheer, Colonel?" If a dog fox can laugh then, at that moment, Talaeus Dekker was laughing. There was even a little colour in the old bastard's cheeks.

"I had no interview with any Sir Michael Geddes..." He took out his flask of filched brandy and unscrewed its stopper. He drank, belched, and drank again. This time he handed me the flask. As well he might. But I should have known. Spanish brandy pilfered from any collier's cabin could only be as raw and rough as any old badger's arse. And it was.

"For I tell you now, Doctor, that whoever the ranting fop was he was not Sir Michael Geddes... A gentleman maybe, perhaps, but he's not the Geddes I dined with last week at his house in Edinburgh!"

"Are you sure of that, Sir?" My own experience would have told me that enquiries were needed. Geddes was a common enough name in Newcastle.

"Sure enough to take a chance on it… and damned sure enough now to be certain of this venture!"

"It will likely be as you say, Sir. So then, have you further orders for me?

"Yes, Doctor…I have. I want you to stay by me… close as my skin until this business is resolved."

I suppose I must have shown my surprise because Dekker cocked a quizzical eye at me. "I will say that straight and open, Doctor Shafto, because I know that you are the only man in this town who knows enough to betray tonight's business."

Colonel Dekker stepped ashore. With a nod to Mr Partis standing at the gangplank's foot I followed him. But then I saw that the old man was moving slowly; his head was down and his shoulders hunched up. The thick fur at his greatcoat's collar gave him almost the look of a grief-stricken bear. Yet even then I could hardly suppress a stray smile. For at once I had realised. Dekker was feigning. Whatever else, I knew then that the old devil was far from beaten. What he needed was time to scheme. That was all. This whole elaborate act, I guessed, could only be to deceive whoever it was had a spyglass trained on us. And as I had suspected, his misery of defeat lasted only until we turned up into Dene Street. At that point I heard him give his sharp little laugh. For all his years Dekker was suddenly stepping out like an imperial grenadier.

"Seven and a half hours to ebb…four to the flow…" He mused aloud – though seemingly to no one in particular. Then with a blink Dekker came out of his reverie. "That's the times o' the tide at the Tyne Bridge, Doctor. According to yon Partis we have a little less than six hours to prepare. Because, and thanks to our visitation and rummage, that collier-brig won't be able to move until late tonight." An unholy glee swept across the saturnine face at the thought – Dekker wore a look that would have soured fresh cream.

"Now, Doctor," Dekker was scanning an entry in his pocket book. "We've a piece o' business to do which calls for the commercial confidence that can only be entrusted to a banker. And I do believe that this – convenient to hand - is the establishment. Good!" He pointed across Dene Street. "You, Doctor Shafto, will oblige me by giving the world the impression that you are my confidential clerk…God knows, y'r dressed right for the part!" He was right – in my suit of shabby, black broadcloth I was.

The atmosphere in Lambert's Bank was a match to any other banking house in Europe. As we stepped into the place the double doors guillotined off clean all the stinks and noises of the town behind us. The big room was light and airy, the bare walls were painted sage green and the panelling was of plain dark oak. There was a calm in there that was almost palpable. This was a holy place; it was the sacred grove where the priests of Mammon daily performed their rites. Here all business was transacted in hushed murmurs. To me at that moment however the most blessed thing was that the place was all so very pleasant. It smelled very faintly of wax. At either end of the hall a cheery fire blazed in a wide grate. Copper scuttles were piled with big knobs of coal. Every lump of it looked to have been polished beforehand.

Nonetheless and for all its gravity of manner Lambert's Bank was busy, quite crowded with people, both men and women it was. And all about me I could hear the chink of coin and the soft rustle of bank notes. Rents were being paid in. Old ladies wearing their best Sabbath satins had come to draw their dividends: the wholesome fruits of a life of prudence. Yet for a long moment it looked very much as though even Talaeus Dekker would have to wait his turn. But then he caught the vigilant eye of a clerk. Indeed I think the lad had actually sensed Dekker's scowl. The old man held up a long envelope. He was at pains to show the scab of crimson wax that sealed it. And it was that sight that worked the magic. The young man raised an arm; then he dipped his forefinger towards a curtained door. As we reached it there was the sharp snap of a heavy lock being sprung. We slipped through the green baize curtain.

The clerk inspected the seal. I saw his eyes brighten. Then like a hare he leaped away. Within seconds a more senior servant of the bank was in attendance. Thin fingers played pianoforte over his waistcoat's buttons as he hurried towards us. This man however was expecting us. Obviously the bank had received a forewarning. He tapped at the seal, turned the envelope over and looked at its front. Only then did he suck in an awed breath. After that, his manner towards us was close akin to reverence.

"Ahhh! Yes, gentlemen… if you would both kindly come through, I am sure that our director, Mr. Lambert, himself, will wish see you at once."

"Mr. Lambert…Sir." Even as he put his head around the door the warning was there in the clerk's tones. " I was quite <u>sure</u> that you would wish to welcome these gentlemen without…without a moment's *delay…*<u>Sir</u>!" The signal had been received and was at once acknowledged.

"Thank you, Rawlett… I'm sure I do."

We stepped into the inner sanctum. Here the severity of the bank's premises had been considerably relaxed. There was a Chinese silk carpet on the floor. On an inlaid tulip wood table at his side a silver samovar was coming to the boil. Might we be offered tea? The next thing I took in was that Mr. Lambert obviously employed a valet who was well worth his pay. I could scarce fault Lambert's cravat. I hoped the servant's efforts were as appreciated as he deserved. Lambert's fingers remained poised in the air until his clerk had shut the door behind him. Then he snatched up the letter. Crimson wax splinters crackled under his thumbnail. He sniffed as he raised the single sheet of paper to the window's light. There were I saw only two lines written in a legal hand. But then Lambert reached into a drawer and took out a matching sheet of embossed paper. For a few seconds he held the one sheet against the other, comparing both the signatures and joining the two halves of an intricate ink drawing. Satisfied, he bent his mouth into a smile. "You appear to be vouched for by lofty company, gentlemen...very lofty company, indeed!" The smile faded. "Now, Sir, how can Lambert's Bank of Newcastle serve you?" That too was a carefully chosen phrase. Moreover he had not stood up; he had not offered his hand. Nor it seemed did he expect to be given our names.

"What we ask of Lambert's Bank is that it charter, on our behalf, the use of the steam powered vessel *Perseverance* for a few hours... tonight from about seven o'clock." There was a drop in Dekker's voice. "What is important is that this entire business be conducted with the utmost discretion and...I use that word advisedly... secrecy! " Talaeus Dekker was obviously not disposed to explain any more than that. Nor did Lambert display either surprise or unease.

"That should not present a problem... Gentlemen." He sucked in his cheeks. "This banking house is well acquainted with at least one of that company's directors..." The smile was tight. "Work, Sir, is always welcome. So I fancy that they will be *very* glad to accommodate us." He reached towards a quill. Then he seemed to think better of it. "The terms will be agreed by us on behalf of ...your principals?

Dekker nodded his head. I understood. The device was simple enough. One banking house was making an accommodation for another. And plainly enough Lambert's Bank was honoured to fulfil that request! Moreover I guessed too that in this matter the secrecy really would be near absolute.

My little cough had in it all the discretion of a Viennese procurer. "It may also be worth specifying, Mr. Lambert, that the vessel will need to have sufficient coal put aboard her - and it will also be essential that the crew know their duties and are in every way.... reliable." I had found that when I came to think on it I had little idea at all about what a steam vessel might need. "And that everything else necessary for a safe passage down the Tyne is already aboard." From what I had heard of steam power it was a necessary point to make.

However, and I will own very much to my chagrin, Dekker had obviously meant what he had said about keeping me by him. I doubt he knew it but that double-proofed old bastard had thwarted all my plans to visit Miss Henrietta Bellis.

As soon as our business at the bank was done we walked straight back to the seedy lodging house in the Painter Haugh. There we waited for his men to return. And to my surprise while we sat Dekker did do me the memorable favour of accepting one of my cigars. Yet setting aside my own irritation I would have had to own that by that afternoon's end I had learned a good deal about the way the Colonel handled his own sack of hired wildcats. Of course at first sight I had recognised every man jack of them as a felon who had missed his own hanging. Nor had I any doubt at all that Talaeus Dekker knew enough about each of them to keep them all shackled tight. Yet there was no doubting too that these rogues served their master with a rough loyalty that was real enough.

Moreover I found myself paying careful heed as one-by-one Dekker's riders stepped up to him. Each man delivered his own report. And while they did that the old man sat listening. His eyes stayed shut, sometimes he nodded, sometimes smiled as he blew a smoke ring. Once he even grunted a terse 'guid'. Nor was there any missing of the way the praised man's shoulders had gone back. Whatever other means he might employ Dekker certainly knew how to catch at a man's pride.

"Soooo... Danglin' Bob Mc.Laughlin." Laughter rumbled about the room. This was the fellow I had seen cleaning a carbine. I had guessed that the crippled man was their quartermaster. He limped up to Dekker and put a crooked forefinger to his brow. "All flints changed, all blades whet staned an' oiled, Sir. An' aaah've made up thirty fresh cartridges for every..."

"Never mind that, Bob!" Suddenly Talaeus Dekker was in jocular mood. "What all your comrades here want to know is... Hae y' tupped oor landlady yet?"

"Aah'd hope tae know m' duty, Sir…" Danglin' Bob's grin had in it the living soul of lewdness." Aye, Sir, so that's one Geordie lassie who knows she's had Lanarkshire sausage frae her dinner. Can y' no hear her now, singing away down in the kitchen!"

Their officer had joked with them.

"Now lads, lend me an ear! What we're about this night is going to give us all a trip on one of these new-fangled steam boats…an' there'll be no charge for the ride!" Dekker stood up suddenly. And I could actually feel the ripple of excitement in that room.

By nine o'clock that night all of us were aboard the *Perseverence*. And the plan that Dekker had laid out to us all that afternoon was already under strict execution. It had begun at seven o'clock with a tin bowl of hot beef stew for every man. It was excellent! As almost an afterthought Dekker had also approved the issue of a – decent - tot of whisky.

When we had eaten each man took up a brace of double-barrelled pistols from the row of weapons laid out on the table. Two of the men however were chosen as marksmen. They were each handed a Bavarian *jaeger* rifle altered to take the new Forsythe percussion caps. Beyond that however Dekker allowed some play of personal fancy in the matter of blades. Number 3 British cavalry sabres looked to be the common choice.

The *Perseverence* lay lurking in the shadows below the Tyne Bridge. Her mooring ropes were singled up. Her lamps were low and seemingly the vessel had been laid up for the night. The only sound aboard her at all was the soft sigh as a safety valve lifted. By then the fog on the Tyne was drifting in as thick as that afternoon had promised. But that is not to say that Newcastle herself was fast asleep under it. This was a pay-day's night. The town's honest distillers had a great stock of gin they needed to be shot of! There would be few hours of that night when we could ever hope for quiet. Above us on the bridge heavy wains still rumbled by. That day too, many foreign ships had come into the river. Now all along the quays the new arrivals were tied up, waiting their turns to load the coals brought down from above the bridge in keelboats. Their crews would all be ashore; every man out looking for his liking. It was obvious that it would be a damned foolhardy naval lieutenant who would risk bringing his press gang into the city that night. The throb of it all reached out at us across the water.

"It's the waiting that's always hard..." In the dark I sensed that Mr. Partis was addressing me. "All these years at the jerquin' game and still it grips deep into a chap's belly puddin's." I could hear his steady sucking at a clay pipe, but I could see nothing. Partis was hiding his pipe's glow under his tarpaulin hat. The sucking stopped. "And here borne up on the floodtide the good news comes..."

At first I saw nothing. Then I heard the rhythmic creak of a sculling oar. Like a cockroach crawling out from under a mat a little foy boat jigged its way out from a wall of fog. Dekker stood in the bow waving a lantern. All around me I heard the men stir. There was scarce a splash as a sailor loosed our moorings.

"Follow her gently, Captain. Give her plenty of room. But when I order you to overtake that vessel... you do that! D'y hear me well?" On short acquaintance I had found the master of the *Perseverence* to be a man of few words.

"Aye, Sir! When you give the word!" His response was certain. I think by then even the steam boat's taciturn master had been caught up in the excitement. His heel stamped against the deck planks. From below us there was a ghostly "Aye?"

"Give her steam, Geordie... slow t' start... but stand by. Then when aah give y' the signal just ye' kick the bitch's arse!" Below us I heard a valve crack open and the slow *swush* of steam in a pipe. A warm moistness lifted up around us. The big paddle wheels began to turn.

When first we caught sight of her The *Countess of Raby* was already out in midstream. A bare rag of sail had been rigged forward to help her steerage. But it was plain that master was allowing the current to take his ship down the river.

"This'll be a slow business... for poor lads who've already done a hard day's work." It was the *Perseverence's* master who spoke. Nor was there any mistaking his intent: the bold captain was sniffing after a bonus. Though to be honest that was not something with which I could disagree. Such a ship was a damned good berth for a seaman. But nonetheless wives would be waiting, worrying. This was all extra time. I had wondered what payment the company would have agreed with Lambert's Bank.

"I'll give a guinea a man and five for the master." It was Talaeus Dekker who spoke. "That is of course if this night's... business... is entirely successful. Though mark you well, *Mr...* You'll get what we get. No purchase; then no prize!"

I couldn't help myself. This was gall bitter. Here we were chasing, probably, better than a hundred thousand guineas in British gold. And what was being offered? A maybe-so of a guinea apiece! Emperors and Banks have much in common!

Then for just a couple of eye-blinks we saw the *Countess* again. Her stern caught the flicker from the torches that marked the line of waterside taverns and gin-shops. Then she was gone, wafted away again into slow swirling river fog.

After that glimpse we saw nothing of her for all of ten minutes. Yet always she was there. For our Mr. Partis owned an eerie knack - always he could point to wherever she ran. His skill was close to uncanny.

"Low Glass House abeam... on the port side..." It was the merest ghost of a whisper. Then, as though to verify his claim, I caught the reek of bituminous coals and saw the dancing flames above a bottle kiln loom up at us through the fog. Against that hazed light I too caught sight of the *Countess* again, the black thread web of her rigging showing *en-silhouette*. Then she was gone.

"He's put her helm over..." All I had heard was the creak of straining ropes. But now Partis was as confident as ever. With a certain formality he turned to Dekker: "Sir…" It is my belief that that collier brig is being put alongside… there's a little staithe by the old Ballast Quay!" Dekker did not argue.

"Captain… stir this whurley-gig o' yours! Feed the beast wi' best steam. I want to take this lady while the bitch is still hot in her adultery!

The beat of the paddles quickened. Under me I felt a sudden surge in the steamer's power. Towards the bow there was a spark and splutter. Then light, brilliant glaring flame, lit-up all before us. We threshed out of the swirling fog with a pair Bengal lights flaring at our bows.

It was Mr. Partis who saw her. For him this triumph would be a personal matter. "Got ye'… Y' bliddy hoormongers!" The words were spat out harshly. Mr Partis was in on the kill.

But if I had thought for an instant that this was going to be any simple hands-up arrest I was wrong. And to my astonishment it was Talaeus Dekker himself who precipitated matters. He reached up and grabbed. The shrill scream from steam boat's whistle cut at the air. And we had no wait for an answer. A flash and a bang echoed back and forth across the water. From above on the staithe top a musket crashed out and the ball whined down at us. I felt a numbing shock. The bullet bit splinters from the rail by my hand.

Our return of fire was immediate. The vicious crack of one of the two jaeger rifles made me flinch. Nor was there any mistaking that the shot had struck home. From above us on the staithe top we all heard a man's wild scream, long drawn out and eerie it was. He stood spread-eagled in the glare of the light. His musket fell clattering against the staithe's timbers. He tumbled forwards after it. I had judged the man would hit the water. He did not: he fell short and struck the stones. That was when the collier's crew broke and scattered like a poked-up nest of rats.

"Forget those bastards! Up there's where we want to be…" At that moment Talaeus Dekker was a man fairly in his element. He had a sword in his hand. He leaped ashore.

Without waiting to see if he was followed his skinny figure went charging off across that wharf. Damn me but the old man was yelling like a daft young ensign in his first skirmish. That was when I was reminded that I too had pistols in my belt and a revenue cutlass in my hand. Yet I found that somehow I could not quite summon up Dekker's martial spirit.

A glance was enough for me to take in the smugglers' ruse. And truly attacking when we did we caught them all with their breeks fairly down around their ankles. The collier brig lay alongside with part of a hatch stripped. The canvas was rolled back and the boards stacked. The vessel had been put alongside directly under the staithe's chute. Had she been about her lawful occasion a wagonload of coals would have been tipped down the chute and into the hold. But this trip the *Countess of Raby* was not taking on coals.

Suddenly our wild rush was halted with a jerk. Our own men were pooled, halted at the bottom of the staithe's wooden steps. One of Dekker's men gave a grunt and staggered. He fell backwards like a felled log. I stooped to him. Just above the bridge of his nose there was a little hole in his skull. "Leave the poor bugger! He's a dead'yin, for sure!" Dekker snapped at me; then he roared over my head: "Up there, my lads, that's where the gold is!"

All he had to do was point with his sword blade. Without a man faltering, his felons charged. But these fellows all knew enough to hold their fire until they were at the head of the stairway. Only then did the ten pistols crash out raggedly in aimed shots. Again and again the bangs echoed back from the night. Then it was over.

Two bundles of bloodied rags lay on the boards under a pall of acrid white powder smoke. One man was sitting up. Oblivious to us all he was as he struggled to stem the blood gouting from a chest wound. Even as I watched him his eyes glazed. Willing to take on a fight these poor fellows may have been; yet so clearly too they had lacked the gross cunning that only the blood and snots of many battles can teach. The damned fools had all loosed off together! Our own considered volley had smashed into them as they had fumbled with their reloading.

We stood. I saw men's chests heave and forced breath condense on the cold air. Frightened men grinned at one another. And I fancied then too that I was sharing in the selfish realisation that – this time - I had survived unscathed.

Where the Hell?" Dekker was puzzled. The wooden staithe platform was now empty.

"That way, Sir!" Mr Partis pointed to a brick arch built into the hillside. "It's the wagon way tunnel - dug to serve the *Chance* and the *Virgin* pits. That's the way the buggers came; that's the way they'll ha' gone back."

As soon as we entered the tunnel the words to the old song came to mind: "Clap hands for Daddy coming down the wagon way... a pocket full of money and a bag full of hay!" Behind me a man swore as he slipped on wet iron rails. At my elbow I heard one of Mr. Partis's tide-watchers suck in sharply as he bit the end off a paper cartridge.

"Aye, lad," I thought, "The saltpetre does bite back a bit if a chap hasn't got sound teeth! Does it not?" But the lad was still eager. Very likely this was the first time he had been given leave to loose off his musket in hot blood.

Talaeus Dekker was well ahead of us up the tunnel and shouting loud. "Come on lads...run! Yon was just the piss pot slops o' an afterguard! We'll have the bastards. Take them an' there'll be a grand bounty for every m..." Dekker stopped. Up the tunnel before me I saw a flash centred with a stab of red flame. The spiteful crack of a rifled musket followed. The ball screamed twice as it ricocheted against the tunnel's walls. I winced as a chip of brick stung my cheek. My hand was still rubbing at the place when I heard a distant rumble. It was coming on and it was getting louder.

Then close beside me I heard a man gasp out a desperate whisper: "Good Christ!"

Chapter Twenty-eight

"**W**agon aaa' main!" That eerie cry, with its echo trailing far behind it, came wavering down the tunnel. And the warning it thrust at us was plain enough. Some murdering bastard had loosed a coal wagon on us. What I could hear were iron bogie wheels rolling, trundling fast, down the incline towards us. Already I could feel the rails shaking under the soles of my boots. Nor did any of Dekker's hooligans need a second warning! On either side of me his men were pressing their bellies hard up against the dripping walls. Then away up the tunnel in the darkness I saw the patch of red glare. It was travelling fast. Around me the tunnel's dank air began to sough past my ears as the on-coming wagon pushed at it. Then I saw the red sparks reflecting back from the shining wet bricks of the tunnel's arch. It was a fuse.

And that was all the time I had.

With a great crimson flash and the shattering crash of a striking thunderbolt the coal wagon was blasted into splinters. We were like men standing up within the barrel of some giant siege cannon. A swirling ball of fire and smoke swept down the tunnel at us. There was no escape. The flames of Hell engulfed us all. Plucked up we were, thrown headlong, dashed about like so many like so many rag dolls. For one endless instant I writhed amidst the flames with all the other damned souls. Men screamed. I felt the agony as the intense heat slipped between my spread fingers to sear at the skin if my face. I heard my own hair frizzle.

Someone was clubbing me about the head. But as each blow stuck my skull it seemed to ring out like the great bells of St. Nicholas's church. Then out of the white powder smoke I saw the shimmer of a man's shape staggering towards me. He paused twice to hawk out the sulphur fumes from his lungs. And as he advanced I heard him giving vent to some very elegant obscenities. By the flicker of burning debris I recognised Talaeus Dekker. Though, to be sure, only just!

Often I have heard it said that risk and danger will heighten some men's sense of the comic! And for sure at that moment I was damned hard put-to not to laugh out aloud myself. Dekker had been well within the flash of the exploding mine. And now close-to the old rogue showed it! His face looked, for all the world, like the arse of a goose, fresh plucked and singed! It would take him months to grow back those magnificent side-whiskers of his. But then I saw him stop in mid stride. He bent to shake at a huddled form lying across the rails. It moaned but it did not move.

"On your feet, ye crab louse!" I heard the hiss of a savage whisper. "Off y'r idle backside! Rise up, m' man: there's Philistines tae smite!" Dekker turned the body over.

"Colonel Dekker..." I called to him.

"A moment!" I heard the click-a-click as Dekker cocked one of his pistols. "Och, Jaimie, Laddie..." That was all he said.

My ears were still ringing from his shot as Talaeus Dekker hunkered himself down at my side. " Yon lad was thrown close to twenty yards - he had the wagon's axle blasted into his guts. His backbone was smashed. There was naught else I could do... That's three good men I've lost this night... But have no doubts, Doctor...their names are set down clear on my own muster rolls...and in a wee while all *will* be paid!"

I understood. It had been as a plain mercy that Dekker had shot one of his own lads. On this battlefield he was the triage – the Chooser of the Slain. Where there was no cure, for sure this Colonel asked no man to endure.

317

"Are y' hurt, Doctor?" Before I answered I found I had to give a little thought to his question. One side of my face and the backs of my hands were smarting, but only a little. I was not badly burned. Solely for the sake of appearances I think, I groaned. Then I looked at him.

"No, sir, My professional opinion is that my corporeal frame remains… more or less intact." Before I could stop myself my mouth had twisted up with the sour plums of sarcasm. My face paid in pain for my humour. "Though I am forced to wonder what cuddie kicked me!" I held up a thumb and a forefinger with a little space between them. "That much, sir… if those bastards had cut their fuse just another inch longer we'd all of us have been blown to smithereens…"

Dekker was in no mood for philosophical speculation. I felt him take a hold on my forearm.

"Smither y'r blather, Shafto! Move y 'r idle doup! After them! They've still a wagonload of guineas to haul… wi' that they'll move neither fast nor far. An' wi' the tunnel blasted yon treacherous hell-hounds will likely think they're safe from us. Go man… Here… take this lantern wi' ye. Leave the midden sweeping o' this business here tae me!" It was only then that I guessed that the old man was wounded.

At the very seat of the explosion great shards of the brickwork lining the tunnel had fallen in. Stumbling forward I squelched as I sank into a great bank of wet clay. I sank to the thigh. Its grip was hard. Nonetheless at the top of the bank there was a hole left under the arch of the roof. I was caked with stiff clay from head to foot but in the end I managed to squeeze my way sideways through it. Once through that gap I breathed easier. I could feel the waft of a chill breeze coming up from behind me. My head began to clear. But then too over the reek of fired gunpowder I recognised the stench of scorched human flesh. Now too I began to feel the backs of my hands. Their coat of wet clay soothed them so that now they tingled rather than smarted. That aside, the tip of my nose and my left cheek would both have benefited greatly from a good smear of Carron's oil. I had been lucky. These were minor hurts.

At the head of the incline I stopped. For long minutes I stood there panting like a blown cuddy. Before me all I could see was the steep sides of the open wagon way. Under pale moonlight the friction polished rails ran away like snail trails up the hillside.

I had to force myself to move. But still caution made me step light and keep to the shadows. All the whiles too I listened hard. Somewhere up the fellside I heard the slow shuff-click-hiss of a pit's pump engine. Then near me, too damned near, a man swore as he missed his footing. I heard the scrape of clout nailed pit boots on the stones. That stopped me dead in my tracks. I felt the trickle of my sweat. A dozen more steps and I would have stumbled into him. But then I realised. This fellow was not walking down the wagon way. He was crossing it. I saw his outline against the skyline. As he topped the rise he gave a little skip and a jump. A collier-lad out after a rabbit or two for the pot, was no danger to me. But still it had been a warning! For this was one night when Bob Shafto wanted badly to stay well back from the thick of any other bugger's fray! Above all - and I reminded myself of this stiffly – from the beginning I'd been instructed that it was no part of my business to get my hands on the gold. For sure at this stage of the game a musket ball in the bowels was not a mishap I could do with! These fellows I was chasing were well armed. That much I had seen! What, indeed all, I had to do now was to find out where the guineas had been taken. That, and only that! My work would be to produce whatever evidence would allow Talaeus Dekker to serve his warrant of arrest on Hetherington. Weren't we in hot pursuit of bold felons? The King's Excise had been fired upon, his servants killed. Moreover we had all witnessed a bold-faced attempt to smuggle gold aboard a vessel already cleared for sea. Every one of us had seen the woven rope fenders slide down the coal-chute into the collier's hold. I had heard the thumps as they had landed! So whatever else, the ship's master would have to answer. He had broken his sworn affidavit. There could be little doubt about that now. Moreover tonight that little turd-in-a-twist-o'-rag, the so-called Sir Michael Geddes, had lost his collier-brig, *Countess of Raby.*

But none of this, I told myself, could be my concern now. That much I had decided. The moment Dekker's words of arrest fell upon the honourable Arthur Hetherington, would also be the moment that Doctor Robert Fenwick Shafto was away, off, gone! Though for certain sure there would be no way that I could stand to swear an oath and offer my testimony before any English court. I could already see Major Farquahar and his file of redcoats - all white pipe clay and polish - waiting to arrest me. What price the word of a gentleman against that of a declared traitor?"

Movement betrayed them. They were darker shapes against the blue darkness. But it was enough. Four men at least there were. I saw the shift of their shadows in the moonlight.

What I had to admire was the clever ruse they were about. It was a trick to remember. On the one steep bank of the wagon way's cut a long ladder had been laid over the grass and whin bushes. Walking up that ladder was a man teeter-tottering with two heavy burdens. They had to be bags of gold coin. It was then that I recalled the notes that Squires Taylor had made for me on the torn flyleaf of Tate's Universal Cambist. A thousand English guineas weighs about twenty two pounds… Troy not Avoirdupois! Yes, though I think that was a weight I could cheerfully have borne by myself. Chance would be a fine thing! But it was what was being done on the opposite side of the cut that was so damnably clever. I heard the whinny of ponies. A train of perhaps a dozen of the little beasts was milling about, being herded at the gallop down the embankment's side, then up again.

That was the masterpiece. Whoever came up in the daylight looking for tracks would find them aplenty. The coal wagon they had used for the gold would be left overturned. The ground all about would be all roiled with hoof prints. And a well- marked trail would lead them away across the open fields - for miles. The guinea coins were already being carried away in quite another direction!

I moved no closer. All my experience was telling me that - no matter what - I had to wait a while before I moved. And I was right. After five minutes a man with a musket held in the crook of is arm rose up from among a clump of bushes. I watched him as he loped away after the ponies. Now I could follow the gold.

They had loaded a cart with broad wheels. One of the men was driving it; three others cantered along on horseback behind. These animals had been left waiting, tethered out of sight in a little copse of willow trees. That much at least I was able to satisfy myself of from their tracks. But then after another couple of hundred yards the gouge marks of the wheels showed where they had abruptly turned off the grass and on to a highroad.

And I suppose I might have lost their tracks there among a hundred other wheels ruts and hoof prints. But this night they were not driving any ordinary cart. This one was heavy laden! Several times I crouched down and opened the lantern shutter. Just a flicker was enough to show me the way they had taken. For the broad wheels of a loaded cart will squeeze the water out of the very road it moves over – and it takes only a little while for those ruts to fill again.

Though in the very end of things that I found them at all again was owed to nothing more than a pile of fresh dropped horse dung. Truth to tell I could scarce have missed it. A hot fresh animal stink carries far on the night air. And when at two o'clock in the morning your boots kick into a heap of the stuff steaming hot before you on the road… why then it's an event can scarcely be ignored! I examined my find. A captain of Guides had once claimed to me that he could tell whether hussars or dragoons had passed that way merely by examining their mount's droppings. Perhaps he could. Without doubt, here though these beasts had been fed on good Durham oats.

And while such a sign might not constitute actual proof, it was noteworthy. No tinker's donkey would yield such droppings. It was only then that I looked up.

Just in time I choked off my snort of self-disgust. Here I was, squatting like some lunatic, warming his hands at the steam off some nag's droppings while I was crouched before a pair of stone pillars. Sight of the carved bears that topped the pillars was all I needed. Now I knew exactly where I was. This was the gate to what had once been a mansion. As long as I could remember the town's folk had called it Conyer's Place. In my day it had been said that half of the bastards in the town had been sired among its park and ruins! But now it looked very much as though someone had again taken up residence.

At that point I suppose I should have turned about and hurried back to Talaeus Dekker. From what I had to report he would certainly be justified in mounting a raid. That perhaps might have served to mollify his scorched whiskers! But then through the bare branches of a tree I saw the loom of a light passing across a curtained widow. Excitement bubbled up within me. And I knew it would not be still. This was one terrier who would have to nip at the neck of his rat before he could be quieted!

Nonetheless I would still have to be careful. This was England and that old bitch was far from gentle with her children. Hereabouts, I knew, a trespasser could easily get his leg bones crushed between the steel jaws of a mantrap. The tingle of my powder burns began to irritate me.

As they say, good reconnaissance is seldom wasted. What I found was that the old wall of mortared rubble had been repaired. Now the way in could only be through a gate lodge that was being rebuilt. And I had seen at once that if an alarm were raised I could well find myself trapped like a ferret in a wine barrel.

But I soon found my way in. And I quickly saw too that most of the old outbuildings of the old Conyer's Place itself had already been pulled down. Whoever owned the place now was having most of his mansion re-built. There were stacks of bricks and barrels of lime everywhere. Nonetheless and even under its cage of ash pole scaffolding I could see that already the house outlined its fine classical proportions. Indeed I had to admire it. When the work was finished Conyer's Place would certainly offer its owner a comfortable residence. Clearly the honourable Arthur Hetherington was already every bit as rich a man as the townsfolk said he was – that perhaps even before he had smuggled a single guinea.

But more important to me at that moment was that there were no signs of either dogs or a watchman. Immediately in the yard of the new-built stables I found a broad-wheeled Scots cart. It had been unloaded. The drayhorse that had pulled it had been led into a stall. I heard it tearing hay from a manger. The riding horses, too, stood saddled still and steaming in the cold. Would they be needed tonight again?

I had enough. Surely all this would be enough for Dekker. There could be scant doubt about the facts. In this respectable house there had to be those selfsame bastards who an hour before had sent a keg of gunpowder at us down a wagon-way tunnel. They had attempted to blow us all to Hell and gone!

From within the house there was a sudden clatter of boots hurrying down wooden stairs. The reflex of my own response would not have disgraced the twitch of one of Professor Galvani's frogs! With scarce half a breath to spare I turned and took three long steps into the darkness within the stable. I was scarce hidden in the trussed hay before across the yard a door was kicked open. The rays of a swinging lantern lit the cobbles. At such moments your hard grip on the warmth of a walnut pistol butt becomes a real comfort. As the man stepped out into the yard I heard him chuckle. Though from where I stood the sound that rattled in the back of his throat reminded me more of the first growl of a suspicious watchdog. His companion however sounded querulous.

"So we'll be as far forward again by this time tomorrow night?"

This was a man seeking reassurance. Almost there was a plaintive note to his tone.

"We'll be as far forward and much more certain of success…depend upon it! You'll never have made a profit like this one! She's in the Tyne now and I'm certain sure there'll be none to step aboard her without leave! " The assurance ended with a little bark of a laugh.

As they crossed the yard fingers of yellow lantern light reached into the darkness where I stood. But by then I had seen them both. Two faces had been caught in the upward gleam. Shadows cast below the chin and nose and eyebrow can sometimes emphasise identity. The man who carried the lantern was Doctor Severus Mudie. The other man wore a tartan plaid rug over his shoulder. It was an odd garb for Charles D'Oeuys to wear. At sight of him I had I felt my teeth clamp and my lips part from them to shape an ugly grimace.

"Bye-the-by Doctor Mudie, sir…" For D'oeuys the voice was strangely mellow, full of good fellowship. Though of course, I knew my man too well for that. Wherever I could taste honey so much the more I would expect powdered glass! Mudie turned. He held up the lantern so that its light played across the fresh white stucco of the wall behind him. Almost the good doctor was at his ease. Then I heard D'Oeuys chuckle. It was a sour sound I had heard once before, in Toulon. But now his back was to me so I could not see what he took out from under the plaid. But Mudie had. The man's eyes rolled like those of a tethered bullock under the poleaxe. It seemed that the terrified man was staring towards me.

Then for just the thinnest shaving of a second I thought that D'Oeyus was about to suffer an assassin's ultimate nightmare: his gun had misfired! But it had not. It had not because there had been no powder in it to fire! There was no vicious crack from this gun. No white smoke hung on the air. Indeed all I could see was the aura of fine water vapour that now writhed about Severus Mudie's head. Before my eyes the man seemed to fold. I heard first his kneecaps and then his brow hit the stones. The sound of the shot had been no louder than a baby's sneeze. What D'Oeyus had used was what the Germans call a *windbuchs,* an air-gun. That was why it had been almost silent; why also there had been no smoke.

But the one thing I had to own was that D'Oeuys – as always when he killed a man - had been totally cool. It was uncanny. I watched as the hyena tore at his carrion. His hands rummaged in the dead man's clothing, snatching up Mudie's purse. But oddly enough, for the Frenchman, the bulging calfskin purse was all he seemed inclined to bother with. And that had surprised me more than a little. Surely the warm corpse of one of Newcastle's most successful physicians ought to have offered him altogether richer pickings than that? I knew that Mudie habitually carried a silver Nuremburg pulse-watch. It had to be worth at least eighty pounds. Then the slow treacle of my intellect flowed its way through and around this situation. It occurred to me – or at the least I guessed - why Doctor Mudie had been murdered. Stupidly the fellow had shown his hand. The night's venture had failed. His mistake had been to whine about it. Quite simply Severus Mudie had begun to make his partners nervous. They had come to doubt him! I imagined that he gone to them directly from the Customs House them and revealed what threats, what promises, Dekker had made to him that morning. Whatever had been said it not been quite enough to tip the balance of his terror. Put in simple terms Severus Mudie had feared Hetherington much more than ever he did Talaeus Dekker. In that I suppose he had been both right… and also it seemed now wrong!

"Leave him where he lies, Monsieur…" The order was in terse French. "…And pray oblige me: put the purse back!" There was a thin keen edge to Hetherington's voice. And I think that it had startled D'Oeuys quite as much as it had me. Nor indeed could either one of us know exactly how long the honourable Arthur Hetherington had been watching. He was no more than ten feet from where I stood.

"Arrangements already are well in hand. Before daylight a party of my most discrete servants… will see the good Doctor safely to where I want him to go." I heard no amusement but I sensed it was there. "A friend of ours has expressed a wish for this particular cadaver. He intends to use the earthly remains of Severus Mudie to make a… salutary end to another vulgar fellow. A man who has already been a sight more trouble to me than…" Hetherington's laughter was now full-bodied. He liked the notion. "…than all my money!"

I could scarcely help being amused. It had never been that carrion crow's custom to leave valuables on his victims. Wherever he'd had he chance he had always picked them to the white of their bones! Tonight I had the pleasure of watching while – under orders – *D'Oeuys* had been ordered to shun his own loot. As I watched him kneel to tuck the purse back into the corpse's coat I bore the pain of my burnt smile almost gladly.

"Now, my friend…" Hetherington's manner had again changed altogether. "I think we both deserve a handsome reward for all our labours. We'll take an early breakfast together at our old friend Mrs. Gower's establishment." I saw from the lift of his shoulders that Charlie D'Oeuys had been somewhat cheered. Hetherington was becoming expansive.

"Yesterday morning Old Madame Alum Pot herself sent me word that she has just bought-in some fresh young… bloodstock. She's been fattening them up for me. Both girls are warranted as virgins pure and not stitched goods!" Hetherington's relish was obvious." Two little maidens, sisters she says. It seems that they escaped last week from a Leeds orphanage." He snapped his fingers. "I've paid for first option, D'Oeuys. If I like 'em I shall retain both girls for the week. Mrs. 'G' suggests that I undertake their careful… schooling!" His afterthought was deliberate. " I'm sure my dear fellow that she will find a pleasant enough girl, or two, for you. "

Charlie D'Oeuys was a dog denied a morsel. Thirteen year old virgins it appeared were to be kept only for the gentry and nobility...not for the likes of him!

"Ordinarily I should of course have had the creatures brought up here. But as you know my own little schoolroom is...er...has a pupil at the moment." As he spoke the honourable Arthur lifted the plaid from D'Oeuys' shoulders." My fellows will see to all of this..." He wrapped the air-gun in thewoollen rug and stuffed it into a holly bush. "My fellows will deal with the Doctor too..."

The clatter of the hooves had faded. Though as I had waited I had been thinking hard. And to be sure I had much to think about. Surely the guineas had still to be in the house. Of that I was as certain as I could be about anything. But at the same time I could only marvel at how trusting this madman Hetherington seemed to be. And however could he trust the Frenchman?

However, as I reminded myself, before I could hurry back to fetch Dekker I had a use of my own for the fresh cadaver of Severus Mudie. For by then it had occurred to me that *I* myself might be that same troublesome fellow that Hetherington's friend had plans for. In any case I could not pass up this chance to discomfort Charles D'Oeuys. What had obviously been intended was that the body, with its purse bulging full and a fine German watch hung across its silken waistcoat might placed where some long nosed and curiously well-informed magistrate might find it. My lodgings at Mrs. Dilkes' house had come to mind. Well, two could play at that game.

At Rheims I had been taught that the true essence of a good round deception is economy of effort. Never overdo it! A little of Mudie's fresh gore was all I needed. His fine muslin neckcloth was already well soaked. As I bent to the corpse I saw at once that D'Oeuy's weapon had put a large calibre ball – pneumatically – into Mudie's heart. The blue edged hole was large. With a sparing hand I drew the bloodied wad along the fresh white stuccoed wall. The marks I made were those of a wounded man desperately seeking a way out. Only the once did I imprint a bloody hand mark full on to the plaster. That I hoped might serve. But the blood on the wrought iron gate was my own *chef d' ouvre*. Sight of blood, the sticky touch of it, and Hetherington would be led astray by the cleverness of his own deductions. Now, and manifestly, Doctor Mudie was *not* dead. Also, of course, it would appear that D'Oeuys had badly muffed his killing shot. What a gratifying assumption that was!

And with Mudie now supposedly running loose on Newcastle's streets the immediate situation had changed. They would go after him. Of course they would. So too I would have no need to lug his corpse very far. With a sharp jerk at his coat lapels I jerked the corpse upright. Even in death Mudie was a big man, and still damned heavy. But, and bearing in mind that I might yet need to 'discover' his body myself, I did not carry him very far into the grounds. There shielded by a holly bush I carefully laid broken pantiles from a demolished dairy shed over the corpse. First though I poured out seventeen sovereigns from Mudie's purse and with scarce a chink slipped them into my own. Prize o' war! Three guinea pieces and some loose silver I left – it was about the sum such a man would carry on him. For a long moment too I fought a rising desire to take the German timepiece. I resisted. That watch would yet hang a man.

As I slipped back through the trees to get to the gate I was struck of a sudden by the cheering thought that this game was now all but over. By midday we could, damn it all, we would, have taken Hetherington, and Monsieur Fouchet's own mangy dog, D'Oeuys, with him. It would be my pleasure to see the pair of them clapped both wrist and ankles into heavy irons. They would be locked up secure in the town's pesthole of a Bridewell. Once there too Talaeus Dekker would surely see to it that none of their genteel friends would get near to help them! By this day's end the city would have been scoured raw with a stiff bristled broom. What a thought that was! Now all the folk of Canny Newcastle would marvel as they saw some very well-respected faces become of a sudden all pasty pale and drawn. Patent manacles would chink merrily as soft hands trembled. Aye, I had seen it all before. Hither and yon the closed carriages would speed as men were arrested…or fled the town. The city's lawyers would think there were free Madeira cakes tumbling down their chimneys! And somewhere in all that confusion Bob Shafto would slip down to Eadie Bell's little cundum factory in the Pandon ward. There I would make Miss Hettie Bellis my honest offer. We were two of a kind and I think we both knew it. So, if she would come, why then, she was the girl for me. And if the lass did prove willing then together we would slip off quietly on the back of the carrier's cart to Bishop's Wearmouth. It was in my mind to spend a few months in Denmark. A prudent man would wait there drinking his coffee until he was again sure who was to rule in Europe.

The sharp squeal of a carriage's brake blocks started me out of what had been becoming a pleasant little reverie. In half the blink of an eye I was back into the world of the here and the now. The wrought iron gate was being swung open. It seemed that when the honourable Arthur Hetherington arranged for a killing then every part of the enterprise was connected together like the cogs in a clock. His 'most discrete' servants had come to pick up Mudie's corpse.

Chapter Twenty-nine

From first sight nothing could have disguised that carriage's trade. Plainly she was sinning-sister to one of the neat little berlinas we had used at the Antwerp brothel to bring in our discrete Sabbath trade! Under its white frosting of mist droplets this was a proper little whoring cart, gleaming brightly under her new coach varnish. She had a shine to her like that on a clumsily restored oil-painting!

And I saw at once that whoever these passengers were they seemed to have no inkling at all of their whereabouts. All I heard from within that carriage was lusty singing. Tonight this berlina carried her full load of merrymakers! Then I heard the squeal of her brake blocks. Smoke, sharp and acrid, scented the frosty air. From inside the carriage I heard the cries of protest at the jerk when they were brought up sharply. That motion must surely must have thrown the hindmost passengers forward damned hard. But still the company sang on, their feet now stamping out the song's measure against the carriage floor. From the slur in the voice of the fellow who was bawling out a filthy version of the ballad 'My Lord Size'. Clearly the lad was already well on his way towards being swine drunk. Then I found myself sucking in breath. For suddenly there was an unforeseen mishap. As the carriage swung to a halt her near side door was flung open with a bang. I saw the man's body roll out sideways and heard its heavy thump as it hit the ground. Head first a passenger had tumbled and been spilled out. He came to rest, raised himself on one arm and looked around him. I've often heard it said that no harm comes to a drunken man. Perhaps! This fellow sat up with his tongue lolling. Then there was a gurgle. He put down his head down to the gravel and noisily spewed out his innards. He lay there, groaning with the side of his face resting in his own steaming vomit. At once from inside the carriage I heard another of the revellers call out. This fellow's would-be drawl broke suddenly and turned quickly into a querulous wail of outrage and disgust. Someone, still inside the carriage, it seemed, had also suffered an accident!

"Y'rrch! Y' filthy swine, y' have … haven't y'?" There was a little hiccup. Then:

"Ohhh…God! Eustace! You're a dirty dog, an' y' really have messed yourself! Jesu! It's enough to make a resurrectionist gag! Damn it all; man, can't you just smell yourself!"

Then I knew. These fellows could only be medical students, young lads apprenticed to physicians in the town. But then it seemed that another of these boys at least had kept a tight hold on some small corner on his wits.

"Now then, Algernon…" There was a forced slowness as the young man strove to fight his own befuddlement. "Never you mind poor Eustace… Whatever substance is to be found within the privities of this drunken young jackanape's linin's is now a private matter… something to be settled betwixt him and…" His solemnity turned to a silly giggle. " … and his washerwoman! But you, my young shaver, now just you play the sportsman… Jump down there and drag poor Harold's face out of his half-crown dinner…" He giggled again. "After all… it is the lad's birthday!"

I was more than a little puzzled. During my time most medical apprentices had seldom been able to afford half crown dinners. Seldom indeed too had any ever been able to get riotously drunk at their own expense! That for certain! Whatever Edinburgh's custom might be, down here in Newcastle most apprentice physicians I had known had been hard put to afford to keep their backsides decently covered,

Yet without doubt these fellows were indeed physician's apprentices and tonight they were out on a spree. My suspicion grew when I caught the whiff of their tipple. Without doubt it was brandy – good French brandy!

But then with a crunch as his boots hit gravel the driver jumped down from his box. This man at least was steady on is feet – indeed he sounded purposeful. Surely, I thought, these few drunken young lads could hardly be the discrete servants that Hetherington had boasted of? Then as the coachman passed by the carriage lamp its light fell on his profile. Even in the drifting mist there could be little chance I was mistaken. This fellow was our counterfeit gentleman farmer. This was that same blustering comedian who only yesterday morning had tried to represent himself to Dekker as the lawful owner of the collier-brig, *Countess of Raby*.

"Here! Garvie, bear a hand, man!" So I had guessed true. The link was made. Yes, this had to be that same Garvie – the would-be Redmond – he who had returned a yellow painted cart to Manley's stables. I smiled into the darkness. This was a chap who could likely tell me a deal about the kidnapping of Mrs. Brydon. But at that particular moment this same Mr Oliver Garvie sounded as though he had been badly nettled by the familiarity of his companion. Indeed his annoyance was only too plain.

"Here ya-sell, Kiddar! Haaad-up there, sailor!" Garvie's fury sounded to have been festering for a while. Now this proud cock-horse had the bit set hard in his teeth! "Mister Garvie t' you, m' man!"

"Aaa'm a ship's officer!" But the snarling anger in the man's protest was short lived. Indeed the mate got little further. Garvie's sarcasm cut him, as folks will say, clean off at his stocking tops!

"Aye, ma' bonny lad… well we've all heard the story about what sort o' ship's officer you were, Mr Caird!" Whatever it was that Garvie knew it clearly gave him clout enough to shear clean away any further argument. But then Garvie himself was reminded of what work he had yet to do. He pulled a roll of coarse sacking from his coat." Now, ma' jolly jack tar, you be civil and bear a hand – wi' this!" I guessed at that particular sack's purpose. This was the bag brought to carry away Doctor Mudie's corpse.

It was then too that I realised that I had also seen Garvie's companion before. But where? Memory served with a rush. Caird was that same seaman who had looted Eneas Knox's room. Well it takes all sorts to make a world! A ship's mate and a gentleman's manservant who had shown himself talented enough to act the part of an arrogant ship owner! Soon enough we would see what a handsome pair o' body snatchers these two made!

Amber light flickered and smoked as Caird took a flame from one of the carriage's side lamps. For a minute he hunkered down to light his lantern; he fiddled with a wick-trimmer until he had the flame cleared. Now the two men stood in a bright aura of light.

"We'll get him into the bag… no town watchman will want to stop this coach load o' young sprigs…that young bugger there a-rollin' in his own spew is Alderman Sorsbie's ssss…"

But Garvie did not finish. I heard his gulp. Almost it was as though the man reached out after his own breath as it fled. His own words seemed to choke themselves off dead inside his mouth. Audibly the hinge of his jawbone clicked. I realised then that at last the bold Oliver had caught sight of the bloodied handprint I had smeared against the wall's clean white stucco. The man's eyes grew wide as they followed the bold crimson streak along the wall. And I would really have had to agree that under the lantern's bright gleam the whole scene had a look that was pleasingly stark – even, as they say in the popular English novels, Gothic.

Then Caird saw it. He had followed Garvie's gaze. But this rogue had a seaman's ready eye. And it took him no more than the half of a quick glance to grasp at the many sharp edged implications held in this for his own near future. Yet even in these dire straits the fellow had still time to splutter out the filth that laced his rage.

"Oh, b' Jesus!" The ship's mate swept off his tricorn hat and slapped at his thigh with it. "Didn't aah tell ye? Y' daft buggers, this is what comes of givin' the job t' that friggin'… frog-guzzlin' landsman! "Caird's voice began to take on the keen edge of a whine." Didn't aah warn Mr. Hetherington; didn't aah speak up tae the gentleman, aal very civil like; didn't aa'h say outright what aah feared? So now aa'h asks y' plain an' honest… fuckin' fart guns? But, man, that French twat would still use his little elder stem popgun. That thing wouldn't ha' killed a bread-locker rat!" Caird's tight clenched fist rattled at the hilt of the cutlass that hung at his waist. "He should ha' give me leave t' use this! Aah told him that … no bugger ever gets up an' walks away after a good backhand slash wi' old Dame Sarah here!" Caird's right hand swung at the air. "Didn't aaa undertake fairly to lop that old sod's cauliflower clean off his bloody showlders – phwat? One slash! You heard me plain? Now the whole damnedboilin' o' us is all buried neck deep in the same midden o' fresh shite. And that's the fault o' that pox-bound French snot gobbler! Mudie 'll been up an away, long since. By now that old bastard will be raisin' the Watch! Why, man, them bastards o' the town's Watch 'll already be turned out and in full cry… now!"

Caird's spleen was quickly spent. And obviously he was not a man to tarry. The fall of the night's events had already made up his mind for him! Much as mine would have been!

"Well, shipmate," His grin at Garvie was mirthless. "Bully Caird can see the shadow o' the doomster's noose swingin' ag'inst yonder wall – that's as clear to me as it is to the next man…" He put the lantern down at Garvie's feet. Only then I think did the footman realise that he was being abandoned. Like sugar stirred into hot rum I watched the fellow's courage dissolve. He reached forward to pluck at Caird's shoulder.

"Wait, man! aah'll come wi' you. Aah've got money!" Already the footman was pleading. "Christ, Mr. Caird … Aah've never wanted no truck wi' murder… aah mean not to do it!"

"No fear o' that ma' bonny lad! Nor that not for this hat o' mine stuffed full o' spade guineas!" Caird had come all of a sudden into his own. Now it was his turn to sneer. "Nor yet for a slop-bucket filled up tae over flowin'!" He stooped suddenly to the prostrate drunk and caught up the lad's brandy bottle. He shook it. "Shipmate, aa'm just goin' t' stagger off singin' drunk into the fog - like the poor ignorant sailorman aah am. An' if aa' get stopped by the Watch…why then, Mister, I'll just start jabberin' at the daft buggers in Portugoose…" He cocked an eye at Garvie as he delivered his own final verdict on the venture. " Lad, this ship's pumps is aa'll smashed. She's a nail-sick old cow and aa'll her seams is wide sprung…'So you should …'leave her Johnny, leave her.' His black teeth showed up jagged in the lamplight. "Though mind you…" Caird's grin turned sly. "Not even some poor lickie-bum of a jumped-up footman like yourself should let his sel' swing for that pimp Hetherin'ton! Or maybe he should…Eh, Kidda?"

Playing the drunken sailor already Caird began to sway off away towards the gate. As he passed by the carriage I saw a pale face poke itself out of one of the windows. "Driver…" He got no further. Caird's fist hit him.

"Damn y's aa'll t' Hell!" His shout echoed out loud across the yard.

Now and even from where I stood I could see the pallor spread across Garvie's fleshy face. Though to be sure by then I was observing the man with all the dispassion I would have used had he been my own patient and suffering the last throes of the cholera. It was more than likely that this man Garvie had been a servant for most of his life though he obviously might have made an actor. And yet setting aside the slaps and curses that fall naturally upon one his class he may well have enjoyed a comfortable enough billet. Even, he might have revelled in some small status. Few folk in Newcastle, I fancied, would ever want to get on the wrong side of Arthur Hetherington's own body-servant. Now, and at a stroke, this night's work had changed all that. Or, to speak more true, what had wrought the change was my own little tuppenny-ha'penny theatrical ruse. For by doing nothing more than drag Doctor Severus Mudie's corpse away a few yards I had caused Caird to jump his ship. And Garvie too, I could see it in the fellow's expression, was already persuaded that unless he did the same thing he too was like to swing on the Town Moor's gallows. Ten minutes before this Oliver Garvie had been Cock o' the Walk. Now this same fellow- a fart-set-loose-in-a-bottle - had become a yellow canary bird fleeing the sparrow hawks! Already his wits were telling him plainly that he had been thrust out into a pitiless world – a place where a fellow like him might find it hard to scratch even a crust! I watched as the purple silk braiding on Garvie's livery coat swelled - he drew a deep breath. Yet, and to give the fellow his due, I could sense that he was a cunning dog. Already he was struggling to get his grasp around a new situation. And it would hardly suit my own purposes to have him recover his wits too quickly!

As Garvie picked up the lantern I shrank a step deeper into shadow. He began to walk towards the stable door. I was waiting for him inside. Forewarned by the light of his lantern I took a quick step forward and ground the cold muzzle of my pistol hard against his mastoid bone. It was effective. Though that much I had expected. For it was a sensation I had experienced myself! Garvie stiffened. Indeed for a few seconds I thought the wretch was about to be stricken by a seizure. But he was not. It was merely the ripple of stark terror through his mortal frame. Now this was a suckling pig ready to carve.

"Oliver Garvie..." Under the stable's high roof beams my tone sounded nicely sepulchral. "I have here a warrant issued by the King's Justices. It concerns the attempted murder of one Doctor Severus Mudie..."

By God I was good! All the powers of the State had seemed to be embodied in that poe-voiced declaration of mine. And as I uttered the words into Garvie's ear I could almost hear the last dregs of hope drain out of him. I was Justice; and there I was, standing all plain and present. "A charge of attempted murder has been laid against one Charles D'Oeuys... said to be a Frenchman. Also...and named as criminal accessory to that same felony... is your master, Mr., the Honourable, Arthur Hetherington..." I stopped. Sometimes it is perhaps better not to give too full a rein to an unfettered imagination.

"Dear God!" Were the only words that wheezed out of him.

"Now... Garvie..." I whispered softly. "Just you take me into the house. Show me where the gold Doctor Mudie spoke of in his sworn deposition is hidden!"

It was clear enough that simple fear of his situation was already tightening its grip on Garvie. Now the fellow was gasping on air, snatching at deeper and deeper breaths. Between each breath a shudder passed quickly through him. Soon, for I knew the full course of such fevers, his shaking could well become uncontrollable. Already in his own mind this Garvie was in chains and sitting in the condemned cell. Well, keeping him that way at least for the moment was, I supposed, the very essence of my trade.

To my surprise however we had only half a dozen steps to go. All Oliver Garvie had to do then was to stretch out his hand. He took hold of one of the wooden pegs set into the whitewashed wall and pushed it upward. Quite honestly I was amazed. A square of the most solid looking brickwork swung inward. Now, in my time, I had seen – and used – all manner of so-called secret passages. Though mind you they are mostly just clever cabinet-maker's work and easy enough to discover. Frequent use is what most betrays them. The rub of sweaty fingers on wood always puts a shine on the panelling. It shows up like a wart on a nose. But here this trap truly did display an English ingenuity worthy of Joseph Bramah. Everything about it was all so damnably cunning in its contrivance. The block of solid brickwork had been bolted into a stout strap iron frame. When Garvie had pushed at the stable wall a hair fine seam in that brickwork had widened. And as it moved it made scarce a sound.

We stood at the foot of a narrow stairway. Around us now there drifted the waft of quicklime mortar, pine shavings, and linseed putty. But then, and that almost at once, I caught not a smell but something almost as insistent. It was the barely perceptible tickle to your nostrils that comes when the dry fibres of hemp float on the air. And at once that was making me salivate!

"Lower the lantern…" Garvie said nothing, but he obeyed.

Under its light I could see where the edges of the stair treads bore a polish. That shine on new cut pitch pine was unmistakable. This I was sure had to be the marks where ship's fenders packed heavy with guinea pieces had been dragged. At the stair's head the marks changed. Here they turned into circular whorls. This betrayed the place where the heavy bags had been swung sharply to the right. And at that point their track was cut off clean by a sort of portcullis. Beyond that – about six feet beyond that – I could see riveted iron plates. It was a strong room door. On that door were four ornate escutcheon plates: each I guessed would cover a separate keyhole. Above them the lantern's light glimmering in through the bars showed a polished brass plaque in the form of a rising sun. Cast into the metal I read the legend: 'The Safeguard – Bartholemew's Patent No. 3424 – London, 1807'.

So Hetherington had placed his trust in an iron box! Fool!

I could hardly believe that the fellow would be daft enough! Had just this iron box been enough to make him think he was safe, safe enough to leave his treasure unattended and go to take a night's pleasure in a whorehouse? Obviously Arthur Hetherington had not had my experience! Once in

Strasbourg I had lowered a man down a chimney. It had taken Little Nellowski, the Pole, less than four hours to open the locks on the strong room of Gelderman's Bank! Though to be sure I doubted very much that even now there was a man in England with that kind of skill! Nonetheless I supposed that, even here, a local master locksmith, working with the right tools, might just break into that strong room. But even a skilled craftsman would take some days to do the work. Though before even Talaeus Dekker would be allowed to do that he would need to get an order from a court. Meanwhile Hetherington would have his own pack of lawyers all ready to show how unlawful it was for any honest merchant to be forced to reveal the extent of his own wealth.

One thought linked itself to another. What the very existence of this strong room meant was that, as he stood at that moment, Hetheringtion was already free - and damned near to being clear! For I knew then that, whatever else, every other merchant on Tyneside would be behind his defence! All the laws of England, of Property and Ownership, were on the man's – on the gentleman's - side. Nor of course would any court in the land even attempt to order him to open his strong room to inspection, not unless other strong evidence could first be offered as to why it should be done. It was remarkable that here in this Protestant England, men of Business are always able to hedge themselves close about with all the secrecy of the Catholic confessional. And here yet again I was reminded that what Robert Shafto would never be able to offer was his own testimony. Any oath of mine was already tainted pitch black. I would be arrested at once as a traitor! So if these arrogant bastards were not to confound us again I would have to find some tangible evidence for Talaeus Dekker to offer against Arthur Hetherington. And that before this night was done.

"Doctor Mudie was in here earlier?" I snapped my question sharply at Garvie. I would have to be careful. So far as he was concerned I was here to investigate only a charge of attempted murder. "So too then, all that gentleman's stolen gold will be here?" I gripped at Garvie's sleeve and raised up the lantern until I could look directly into the man's face. Under a growth of black stubble his hollow cheeks were still trembling. But the eyes themselves, I could see, were not quite dulled. There was no sign yet of the condemned prisoner's stumbling paralysis. This Garvie had a brain and he was still hard at work using it!

"Yessir..." The whisper faded on his lips. Then: " But all that gold isn't Doctor Mudie's alone... there's six more gentlemen in the syndicate... and they're all powerful men in Newcastle town!"

"I see..." I allowed a pause. Strictly speaking it was far too early on in the business to offer the rogue even the faintest glimmer of Salvation to come. But at this moment it couldn't be helped. I turned the lantern until Garvie was blinking in its light. "Give me the names..." I was quiet; I was reasonable. "Name them now my friend." I whispered. " Name them, name every one of them ...and I can promise you now that you will have a friend when you come before the court. Do this! Then make it your most earnest plea that - all along - you've been no more than a good, honest, manservant...acting entirely under his master's instructions. And I think I can promise you that I shall be able to see to it that the Bench... accepts your testimony." Probably it would. For long seconds Garvie hesitated. Then, very carefully and matching my low whisper, he began to give me both the names and the men's places of business.

"Thank you, Mr. Garvie. I think we can accept that as the act of an honest man...and I hope a prudent one!" That was all I said. A little sanctimony goes a long way!

So here at last I had six prime names. In one way too – in my own reckoning - I had now done all that Dekker had asked of me. What he had said to me was "Get me the bastards' names. Leave the hanging of them to me!" Well now the syndicate was named. Nor would these fine fellows be too difficult to lay hands on. Every one of them I was sure would be prominent in the pages of the Newcastle Directory. Mudie of course was already dead. And as I had expected Hodgson was already a named man. Moreover two of the other names I also recognised from the crabbed columns in Matthew Crowley's little book! Respectable men o' business it seemed could also be lads o' parts!

But what I needed myself at that moment was a little time to think. My discovery of the strong room had changed everything. Getting any court to order its opening would surely fill the pockets of any number of lawyers! But that was nothing I could be expected to help with. Now it was Dekker's turn! This game was now closing very near to a tight checkmate! Legally as well as materially this strong room in the house of the Honourable Arthur Hetherington was for all ordinary purposes impregnable. In my own mind that I fancied that all Dekker's efforts might yet be in vain was not my concern. All I could do now was take my prisoner and report back to Talaeus Dekker.

This was a time for decisions. Though it might not necessarily be a time for immediate action. I would have a strategy but not a plan. For a little while longer I would continue to do my job, but for a time I would put both snaffle and curb on my own intelligence. My report would be fulsome and true. But from this instant Bob Shafto was planning his own escape. After all, a few pounds in pay along with the fair chance of being hanged for your efforts at the end of it is hardly a reward to elicit any great espirit de corps!

But I had come that far. So it behove me to do nothing that would make Dekker suspect me. He was not a master likely to forgive. And he would certainly expect me to be able to reveal to him all the house's secrets. I shoved Garvie forward.

What was immediately clear to me was that this ingenious secret passageway had been built between what had been the wall of the old house and the new. Nowhere was it more than a yard wide. Smoke blackened sandstone blocks made up only the left hand wall. The other side was of new laid brick. Now before us the run of the passage turned sharp left. We passed through an ancient archway left in the thickness of the old wall. Nor did we have much further to go. In front of us there lay the machinery of another device.

What folk with money will spend it on! I put my hand on Garvie's shoulder and pointed to a handle. He nodded. It was obvious that the rogue knew how to work it. As he cranked the mechanism the whole inside of a wardrobe ready hung with garments was drawn backwards. I stepped forward. Now I was looking through glass, through the thinnest seams of light showing in through fine scratches incised on to the back of a mirror's silvering. Almost without having to think about it I found the handle. I turned it. There was tiniest metallic snicker; the door swung open. In a blaze of candlelight I stepped down from the open wardrobe on to the coloured intricacies of a Chinese silk floor carpet.

Rachel Brydon spun round at the sound and looked across the room. I think we were both equally taken aback. Though I fancied that I had by far the stronger cause for surprise. The girl who stood there in the firelight was wearing a garment that looked like the blue habit of a German nun. Indeed had Mrs. Brydon not already torn off her starched white wimple I don't think I would have recognised her at all.

"Mrs. Brydon... "My good manners were overwhelmed. "What the Hell are you doing here!"

But I didn't get so much as a word in answer. Already the woman was striding out towards me. She came at us like a harpie! As she moved, her beautiful face twisted itself up. This truly was the anger of a gentlewoman outraged.

"Filthy... scabrous... peeping Tom!" It was almost a scream.

I honestly do think that had Oliver Garvie not tripped on the carpet as he turned to flee I would have been ready to defend myself. But by then Rachel Brydon had thrust her way past me. She had the fellow! It was as though I was not there at all. Garvie lay prone. Rachel Brydon was upon the wretch! This was no boxing of a miscreant's ears! She tore at his sparse hair with both hands and hauled him face up. His teeth were bared with pain. Then I heard the crack of her fists against the fellow's cheek bones. At what polite lady's academy Mrs. Brydon had learned how to use her knuckles like that I could not begin to guess. But, by God, she had. And I could not help laughing when I saw how she even kept her thumbs tucked in like a regular pugilist. Soon enough too she had tapped Garvie's claret for him. The footman's blood spattered wide across the carpet as he tried to turn his head away from her blows.

"That's enough!" It was an order and I barked it at her. "Madame...get up! The both of you!" Garvie managed to fend off her next three blows with his forearms. I bent to catch at Rachel Brydon's raised fist. "I insist... that... will... do!"

It would have to be, for I could see now that the pain of Rachel Brydon's battering had begun to stir at the pride of the man who lived inside the servant. This much I knew: had any woman of his own class ever dared raise her hand to Oliver Garvie he would not have hesitated. By now she'd be wearing a mouse under both her eyes. What Charlie D'Oeuys had done to Ettie Bellis came to mind.

Somewhat to my surprise Mrs. Brydon did get to her feet. Though this particular Minerva was far from spent! When she stood upright over Garvie she lifted her nun's skirts and aimed a final vicious kick at the fellow's crotch! He flinched far backwards and she missed.

"You, my man, be assured of this... " Her eyes were narrowed as wagged a finger at him. "I am going see to it that you are sent to Botany Bay by the next transport. I'll teach you to spy upon a lady when she's..."

"Mr. Garvie already stands in a more present danger of being hanged, Mrs. Brydon...." I spoke softly.

Those words changed both their faces. " However if he is wise enough to stand witness to certain events...I think I can promise him that..." I allowed the rest of it to drift. "And now I will ask you again... how is it that I find you here. Joe Fletcher assured me that you had gone to the country to recover.

"They were waiting for me in the lane beside my aunt's house...that is twice..."

Rachel Brydon breathed in slowly, raising her chin and looking down her nose at Garvie. At once the rogue seemed to know what she was thinking.

"As the Lord is my witness, ma'am...that I did not!" It was that French fella', D'Oeuys... it was all his doin', so help me!"

Chapter Thirty

"**B**utton your gob, Garvie! Speak when you're spoken to, man – and not otherwise!" I heard the fleshy clap as the fellow's mouth snapped shut. Though, I also saw too that the footman had lifted his forearm ready to fend off any further blows from Rachel Brydon's tight little fists. My voice cut harshly at the fellow. "Your work this night, my man, must surely be to try to save your own neck. So that even if you possess only the parboiled wits of a born idiot you *will* see now that your one over-riding need is to grasp at this Heaven granted opportunity – and hold damned tight to it!"

The sharp edge I had ground on to my words silenced Garvie and, much to my surprise, silenced Mrs. Brydon too. Although I could see that the girl's eyes were still blazing angrily at the offending manservant. "What I want you to do now, my good Garvie, is to take a message to… to my superiors." Caution had made me pause. It still would not do to tell this rogue over much. "Downstairs in the yard is the carriage you arrived in… the berlina in which you were meant to cart away the murdered body of Doctor Mudie." I narrowed my eyes at Garvie. "Though, of course, I am already half persuaded to testify that when the cart arrived, you, yourself, were absolutely innocent of any knowledge of that foul crime… any knowledge what-so-ever!" I had guessed aright and saw at once that Garvie was already eager to reach out, to clutch at any thread of hope I might dangle before him.

"Make shift to throw out your drunken passengers. You may kick the backsides of those young sots out. Order the beggars off to their homes or lodgings directly! But then you will drive that little carriage, hard, back along the river road. Don't spare the horse! Get yourself along towards Wallsend. Somewhere along that road you will likely meet up with a gentleman who will answer to the name of Talaeus Dekker. You will know him by the company of armed men who come with him. And for that reason too you had best address the gentleman as *Colonel*! Or perhaps you could find him aboard the steamship *Perseverence*. Indeed you might well need to hale him from the riverbank. So don't you fear to shout your lungs out, Oliver Garvie! For – and be assured of this - your life will very much depend upon your getting that gentleman to hear you! Tell him everything you know about tonight's doings. But - and whatever else you may do - make certain sure that you get Colonel Dekker to come here as soon as may be. And, Garvie…"My last words had clawed at his shoulder as he turned away. "Wherever you go after that I do not greatly care. But what I have ordered you to do… without fail, my man, you *do* that thing. For, friend Oliver, if you should think to run off… Be assured o' this, Mr. Garvie, or if you prefer it Mr. Redman…Or indeed, as Sir Hugo Geddes?" My apparent omniscience as to his various identities gripped painfully at the rogue. "Be absolutely assured that the court's officers will not take long to run you down!"

"Filthy beast of a fellow!" Rachel Brydon hissed her words after Garvie as he darted off back into the panel behind the wardrobe.

"What exactly was Garvie's offence, ma'am. " Long since I had guessed that Oliver Garvie, along with his master and probably also that swaggering French turd, Charles D'Oeuys, had all amused their fancies by spying on the personal business of their lady prisoner. Rooms kept aside for such Peeping Toms are a common enough feature in most of the larger brothels. A few fine lines razor-scored into the silvering behind a mirror allows the discerning customer to sit there in the darkness behind the glass seeing, without his ever being seen. Though to be sure not many of the girls in our employ had ever cared one jot that their own fleshly antics being gaped at by some filthy old lecher. Just so long as they received their franc pieces for the service! Naturally though, I knew that certainly for our Mrs.Brydon even the suspicion that she was being spied upon must have been cruelly hard for her to bear.

"His offence, as you put it, Doctor Shafto…was to…to spy upon… to look at a lady while she…bathed… " For long seconds the girl searched for the words. Then her response came out with an angry rush: "You, Sir, are a man… so you must know precisely what that fellow is guilty of doing!"

"I see…" I allowed my own words to fall with a lowering tone. In most circles of Polite Society, of course, Mrs. Brydon's sense of outrage would be agreed with, to the fullest extent. Though, and I knew this only too well, if the girl had been spied upon, then the man Garvie had simply been snatching up a mere servant's portion, a scrap of the gentlemen's leavings. For surely Arthur Hetherington and his friends would have looked first and stared the longest, and no doubt have enjoyed the finer points of their spying. Under the brilliant light of the Carcel lamps that he had so thoughtfully provided very little could have been missed. Neither had the blue enamelled bath with its gilded lion's feet, nor indeed had the long elegant looking cheval glass, been placed in its precise position exactly for Mrs. Brydon's own convenience.

"Mary Dolan is safe, ma'am. We rescued her last night from Severus Mudie's house. Rachel Brydon's start told me at once that up to that moment she had not given the poor girl a thought.

"Now, m'dear, while we wait for Talaeus Dekker to come here with his men, We will need to look carefully around this building. It has many secrets: they must be found.

I led Rachel Brydon out of her luxurious room by way of the secret panel; not attempting in any way to hide the scored mirrors which had been used to spy on her. Madame, I saw at once, cast only the slightest glance over the mechanism. Under the light from the Carcel lamp I had brought with me the lass had obviously seen, seen and then deduced for herself quite enough! By that same brilliant light too I quickly found the second sliding panel which allowed us to get into the room beyond the barred door of her own little *chamber d' elegance.* Beyond that we found ourselves on a wide landing.

"There'll be a stairway here." I led the way forward, holding up the light. Rachel Brydon was following me closely, though still without saying so much as a word. As we stepped on to stairway I could feel the nipping chill of an uprising draught. Under my feet too now I could feel the grit of spilled sand grains. We were in the unfinished part of the house.

"Upward first, I think…" I raised my eyes and at once that same suggestion was sharply choked off by the catch in my own breath. But by then Rachel Brydon had seen it too. Her sharp little scream went echoing up and down the stairwell.

"Oh, dear God!" The rest of her words broke up in her mouth to come out as a little gurgle. "It is!"

There was no mistaking the long shadow. The body dangled over the gilded iron rails at the stair's head, hanging there like a child's doll. This time it looked as though Lady Donkin had got into a house but had not been able to escape from it – *no*, not this time she hadn't!

Her old fashioned chignon of white hair was scarce a hand's breadth from where the cord was tied to the banister rail. The old woman had been strung on a very short nip! Yet whoever had done the job had been damned apt to his business! Someone had thrown the noose about her neck and then lifted her bodily, tipping her over the bannister rail. Her heel marks were clear on the new paint. Her killer, her executioner, had to have held the noose in his hands while the old woman's legs had kicked out her life above the stairwell's space. It must surely have felt like playing a great fish at the end of a fine line.

Only when the woman was dead had he tied the cord to the rail – a round turn and two half hitches – neat!

There was no doubt that Lady Donkin was dead. If nothing else, the simple fact that her scrawny neck had stretched to such an obscene length alone told me that much. Indeed the stretch in her spinal vertebrae reminded me of nothing so much as a goose on poulterer's hook. But this was no time for any close examination of the body. Nor I fancied would any good be served by my cutting her down. Yet I did cast an eye over the corpse. Some things were obvious. No proper hangman's noose had been used. That much was certain. The noose itself was tied in a length of new window sash cord. Indeed the marvel of that was that the thin line had held at all. But it had. So Lady Letitia Donkin had not been allowed the mercy of the new English long drop. Her life had been strangled out of her at the end of that thin cord.

Yet this same lady's companion now looked so very tiny, so harmless, almost. And, at least as I reminded myself, now she was one piece of the game that had been knocked off the chessboard; and that for good and all. The mother of the man I knew only as Lieutenant Cable, was dead.

Of course I had been tempted to draw up the old woman's body and search it. After all it was a body - and that falls at once, as it were, into the purview of my trade. As Fouche had once said, "a good agent will seek intelligence even though it be written out on the foreskin of a dead cardinal!" And I had to suppose that the same cunning bastard would have known! Then I heard my own short cough of laughter. Gallows' humour is the means by which we make unspeakable horrors into a joke.

But I did retrieved Lady Letitia's bag. It contained what I might have expected of any other lady's companion: damned little! There were handkerchiefs and scent bottles; there was a little purse that held exactly nine pence in copper change.

The fan hung from the corpse's wrist by a black silk cord. I heard the clack of its slivers of finely tooled ivory even before the lamp's light fell on to it. Then under that same brightness I saw the blade. It was surely a thing of contrived devilry! Twelve leaves of thin ivory each pieced through with a pattern of elephants walking *en train*. But the last piece of carving carried its own surprise. Blade thirteen bore a honed steel edge to it. The thin ground steel was cunningly riveted into the ivory. I reached down and flicked open the fan. Then truly I knew.

This was the same blade that had slashed open Eneas Knox's windpipe so *exuberantly*. The same honed edge had sent Matthew Crowley into the Hellfire that he so richly deserved. Yet I recalled how Lady Letitia had done the work without disturbing the fat whore sleeping so peacefully at his side.

But who? Who had killed the old woman I had known as Lady Donkin?

Then the secret that I sought was delivered to me. In the lamplight's gleam my eye caught the glint of a faint redness. A single hair lay against the dark velvet of her dress. It was enough. Many men are red headed. Though few that I had ever had dealings with had quite the foxy redness of Monseiur Charles D'Oeuys.

I could not know fully the truth of the tale. But I could be sure that it was from beginning to end the woman I had known as Letitia Dobson who had been in the employment of the French.

Yes; it were better for all, or at least better for Bob Shafto particularly, that the old woman's body should disappear. In life the woman I had known as Lady Letitia Donkin had been my enemy. Well, now that she was dead the old bitch would serve as the ready slop bucket into which the guilt for many crimes would spill.

It was Rachel Brydon's sharp sniff at the air that decided me upon my next course of action. Some careless fool had been spilling turpentine about. But then at once I knew that this could be no mere carelessness. Earlier this night Hetherington's mansion had been set to burn. Why someone should set out to destroy a fine great house built in the new Palladian mode escaped me. For sure the honourable Arthur would be furious. But then the sweat of the two hundred miners hewing at the coal seams in his mines below us would soon enough make good the loss - within a year or two.

Then of a sudden I knew exactly why Lady Letitia herself had come to this place. Under the servants' stairway I found my nose wrinkling at the heavy reek of turpentine. That smell became especially rank when I stooped and opened a little cupboard. For the first time since the year '04, the neat chalk drawings done by a one legged, hook handed, military engineer danced before my eyes. Yes, it was then that I knew precisely what Lady Letitia had come to do. As I strode up the long flights of stairs towards the attics the white arrows of old Captain Le Monceaux's drawings clearly showed the flow of the draughts through a building. They zig-zagged their way across my mind. Even a little snatch of the veteran engineer's lecture echoed across the years to me.

"Gentlemen, wherever possible set your starting fire on the servants' back stairway – quite simply that is because painted pine will always blaze into life so much more quickly than the heavy oak or mahogany of any grand staircase." I saw again the powder seared blue of that old devil's face and found myself smiling into the darkness.

"Oh, Letitia!" But Rachel Brydon's call was wasted. For truly her companion was as dead as it was possible for any wicked old woman to be. Then I heard the soft choke in Mrs. Brydon's throat. Her fingers reached out and caught at the air. I knew that what she wanted was to have Letitia Dobson's body taken down.

Cutting down the corpse cost me very little effort. With the sharp blade of my jackie-legs I reached up to slash through the thin cord; that cut allowed the limp body to slump downwards, easily I drew the old woman's corpse in sideways. With scarce a grunt of effort I was able to drag the body inward over the banister rail.

From the battering the face had taken it was at once apparent that Lady Letitia had not gone down without a fight. The old woman had clearly been in a hand to hand struggle. And while manifestly she had lost the hard tussle it also looked to me very much as though the same old biddie had put up a damned brave cat-fight.

At once Rachel Brydon fell on her knees beside the body. I held the lamp close beside her while she fumbled in the cloth of the sleeved cloak to find the corpse's hand.

"I fear she's far beyond revival now, m' dear...far beyond that." Her patting of the dead woman's limp hand stopped; Rachel laid it aside.

Nonetheless I could be sure of nothing until I had lifted the fan's ribbon free. Then the weight of that plaything alone told me everything. With a slight flick of my thumb I riffled apart the twelve leaves of carved ivory. Then I heard the tiny click. Looked at as a piece of workmanship alone, the device was quite beautiful. The killing blade itself was attached to its leaf of ivory with little gold rivets. I flourished the open fan. How easily the weapon came to my hand. And in that same instant I knew precisely who it was had slashed Eneas Knox's gullet so deeply; just as I was as also certain now who had put paid to Matthew Crowley's game a few nights later. Doubtless too there had been and would be others. That was something I was sure of. So too, it occurred to me, I owed my own quayside reputation as a fearless man killer to this same little old lady. But exactly where did the late Lady Letitia Dobson fit into the guinea smuggling game?

It was not difficult to reconstruct a fair picture of what had happened on the stairwell that night. The old woman had not been in the building searching for her mistress. It was also clear too that, as I thought, she had again come disguised as an elderly serving woman – though this it seemed had been a ruse she had used just once too often. The white cotton mobcap, it was the same one she had been wearing on the night she had spilled the life out of Matthew Crawley. The thing was lying on the stairway at my feet. I remembered. This little old lady had been the same slight figure I had seen that night at Mrs. Gore's brothel, the same little old woman who had been bustled gently into the cupboard by one of Jesse Rea's shipmates.

Yet whoever it was had managed to get close enough to crack his loaded riding crop against Lady Dobson's jaw. That told me too that the old woman had very obviously not been taken by any kind of surprise. Nor, as things looked, had the female assassin's lightening fast stroke with her razor fan found any mark. Nowhere was there so much as one drop of blood on the stairway; not one anywhere that I could see. But what was also obvious now was that the same fellow had struck the old woman on the side of the face; and that blow had been savage. I had not to look too closely to see the fracture in the corpse's jaw. Though to be sure looking at a face that by then was the near the colour of a roof slate I had much to guess at. Even so, I knew for sure that just that one vicious blow had been the last thing that Letitia Dobson would have known in this world. The noose must have been a mere spiteful afterthought.

"We'll have to leave her, m' dear…at once…"

"I'm not a fool, Doctor, I have suspected for some little time now that Lady Letitia Dobson was the creature who murdered my husband." It was as though I was hearing the girl's voice for the very first time. The sheer, bleak, lonely coldness of that same sound was enough to send a chill around any man's heart! "And even more recently I came to realise that she herself knew – or at least had come to suspect - that I had learned too!" The girl looked up at me. The tears on her eyelids glinted brightly on the lamp's light. "But what pains me most of all is the memory of how tenderly this same old woman nursed me through all those bleak months after Martin's murder; truly, all through that time the woman was an angel to me."

"But at whose order did Lady Dobson kill your husband, Mrs. Brydon? Who was it who employed the woman in the first instance? What we must learn now is the name of the fellow who has all along been paying the assassin's bill. What is the real name of this worm; who is it who has been eating its way through our rosebud? Can you tell me how you yourself came to employ Letitia Dobson?"

It took a little while for Rachel Brydon to speak. Then when she did that her voice came haltingly, like that of a little girl unwilling to answer.

"When Martin died, was murdered... I was distraught for some time..."

"Yes, of course, you would be..." Those few comfortable words were costing me nothing. In the lamp's light Rachel's grey eyes were now sparkling bright with brimmed tears. Her betrayal was something hard for her to accept. The old woman who had been her angel for so long had just been revealed to her as a fiend. But as I looked at her I saw that the girl was struggling to summon up her courage. " Naturally, such a lady's companion does not present references: she is after all, herself, a lady."

That I myself knew that well enough. As a class, lady's companions would not be so much employed as appointed to their posts by word of mouth.

"But, in the end, my Dear, *who* did recommend Lady Dobson to you?"

"If it were anyone at all, it was Mrs. Lydia Doggart... Richard Grainger's married sister. "

My first thought was that the link could, of course, be entirely innocent. After all I had never found difficulty in insinuating myself into other men's households. Indeed I had to remind myself quickly of just how easily Rachel Brydon herself had contrived to get me my employment as the valet, Wilfie Nettles. This was all very much in the very nature of the game we played.

"Doctor Shafto... please understand this, Letitia Dobson was to me, in those early days, everything that could be wished in a trusted companion. For almost three months she kept the harsh world at bay. It was she who..."

"It was also *she*, Mrs Brydon, who murdered your husband…" The next thought sprang ready formed into my mind. "And you might also consider that it may well be that same Lady Donkin had not come here tonight to *rescue* you at all…" Our eyes met, gaze to gaze. I think that only then did she realise the enormity of what was being suggested to her.

The implications of her long betrayal were still twisting hard at Rachel Brydon's thoughts as she followed me about the new mansion. Together we walked through all five levels of the place. I found I was right about the building being readied to be set ablaze. Wooden casks of painter's turpentine had been broached and were laid out over floor. The great sandstone blocks of the house's outer walls were divided into levels by massive archways and pillars; but this solid framework had been floored over between with thick pine planks.

Soon enough, too it became apparent that Arthur Hetherington had to be a damned wealthy fellow in his own right. The black stencilled foreign lettering on the stacked boxes spoke of a very wide trade.

It was the smell of burning charcoal that set my nose twitching. On the ground we walked across an expanse of flag-stoned cellar floor. Down here on the first level what looked like a huge kitchen appeared to be almost empty. Then the broad shadow of a riveted sheet iron chimney stood across the lamp's light. My gaze followed it upward until it pierced its way up through the floor timbers above. In a few short paces I was over and looking at it closely. The heat coming from the firebrick furnace radiated out at me. Then when I swung about slowly with the lamp lifted high, I saw that all the necessary gear was laid out ready. I had found the workshop where imported silver ecus – the coinage that had been exchanged for English guineas - were melted down. Here any ill-fused silver coins would surely be a thing of the past. The explosion at Shield Field had taught the guinea smugglers a hard lesson. There was to be no more silver largesse blasted out for Newcastle's bairns to pick up from the street. Here in this tidy workshop everything was set up to ensure that the centuries old silver coins of the Bourbon kings could easily be melted and poured into cast iron moulds. My eyes swept across the work already done. From the little barrels that they had arrived in the blackened silver ecus would have easily been shovelled into big fire-clay crucibles. There was even a neat mechanical fan to force an air draught into the furnace. This surely had to be evidence enough. But even as that thought entered my head I knew that not even this show taken together would give Dekker all he would need to arrest the honourable Arthur Hetherington and his syndicate. I picked up one of the moulds. A sharp tap at the pin that held the hinged halves together allowed the device to flap open. A silver ingot fell out heavily into my hand. The bright metal brick bore on it the raised lettering it had taken from the mould: *Hetherington's Lead Works, Newcastle-upon-Tyne.*

But as always the Devil, as they say, hides himself away in the detail. This surely had to be quite the neatest dodge a man ever thought of. Silver is found naturally with lead. Indeed our local ores have always been noted for their richness in the precious metal. And a fellow who owns both lead mines and a refining works is surely free to extract all the silver he can from the metal he wins from his mines. But already I saw that already this could only be part of just an over stretched guess. For it would be near to impossible to distinguish betwixt silver refined from the lead his ponies brought down from Alston Moor and the same metal melted down from smuggled French ecus. It seemed that the Honourable Arthur and his partners had long been working at a damned rich seam for themselves!

Talaeus Dekker burst in on us as Mrs. Brydon was pouring glasses of Hetherington's best sherry for us. Like a wild bull the old man smashed his way in through the wardrobe's panelling. I saw at once that he was limping. Also that there was still the red blear of battle – or of powder smoke - in his eyes. Sight of Rachel Brydon stopped that sly old rogue dead in his tracks.

There was the double click of hammers as he un-cocked his pistols and hooked them into his belt. My own glass of sherry was plucked neatly from my hand. Dekker downed it in a single gulp; then he stood there before us, swaying unsteadily on his feet.

"Ma'am…"The rascal's bow to her would surely have passed muster at any soiree in Europe. Then he snapped out a terse few words at me: "Your report, Doctor!"

I gave it. For in the last hour I had been working over in my mind all I might say. And out it came: and damn me but Fouchet himself could not have faulted it.

"Aye, you would seem have done a sovereign piece of work this night. Then Dekker put his head on one side. "Did you happen to promise that man Garvie any sort of protection, Doctor?"

I cocked my head in an opposing slant: " In some manner…" It was as far as I wanted to commit myself. Doubtless Dekker already had plans of his own for using what information Oliver Garvie would know. That much was already clear enough.

"It seems the rogue has already heard o' King's Evidence. He started to bawl about wantin' to turn that way as soon as my lads had clapped the irons on his wrists."

The clatter of boots on the planks behind us distracted Dekker. We turned to see Mr. Partis, the Customs House jerquer stepping into the room crab-wise over the wardrobe's sill. The fellow was struggling two handed to lug in what looked like a large brown pineapple. I recognised it for what it was with a sharp little start. And within the same thought I fancied knew who had made the thing. At once the sight of it finally explained the calluses on the fingers of the supposed French nobleman presently lying secure in his coffin aboard the *Countess of Raby*. It was a ship's fender, a neat piece of seaman's handiwork, a bag of woven rope. This one however had never been hung over any ship's side to protect her timbers – it was brand new.

"Here y' are, Geordie, just you lay that fender down over there." At once I thought I saw that one sharp thrusting gesture of Dekker's thumb. It should have sent any other man scampering back the way he had come. But Partis was obviously ignoring the direct order. This was a prize that had been taken off a ship that was fully within his domain. Partis was clearly not a chap to let loose the Excise's share! Yet here was Dekker choosing to ignore the obvious slight.

"Now, my friends, here is proof positive… all the evidence I'll need to break up his pack o' treasonous dogs…This is one o' five new rope fenders we took from the hold of the *Countess of Raby*. They were neatly stowed in a space left for them under the coffin and all Flemish coiled around with the new ship ropes consigned to the Admiralty Dockyard on the Medway!" The rope bag had been closed with cunning knots. "I'll beg the loan o' y'r knife frim you, Doctor!" Dekker snapped his fingers sharply. Without a word I pulled open the blade of my jackie-legs and handed him the weapon. Dekker used my knife like a man taking the guts out of a new killed hare. Then I heard the old fellow's little grunt as he pulled open the neck of the leather bag inside.

I've heard it said often that gold in any great mass will always cast a magical spell all of its own. For my own part I will readily allow that I was at once aware of the sharp suck of my own spittle inward between my teeth. And I knew too that my eyes, like the other three pairs looking into the neck of that leather sack, were glinting back in the reflected golden glitter off those massed coins. Even Talaeus Dekker so far forgot himself as to allow a good Scots oath to escape softly from his lips.

"As jerquer to this port, Sir, and in the King's name, I have seized five bags o' this coin…but for certain sure there was a space under that coffin box to hold another hundred o' the same size." Partis's voice had a steadiness to it that was quite new.

It was then, as Talaeus Dekker turned his head to look directly at me, that he raised an eyebrow. It was perhaps as well that Nathaniel Partis saw nothing of it. But it was at that precise moment also that I realised that we had come suddenly to be at odds with His Majesty's Customs and Excise. I straightened my shoulders and looked away from the gold in the sack. I tried to think of all the cunning that lay in the trick of the hiding place itself. The lead coffin had never been intended as the container for the gold; instead it was a cover, a mere lid on a box! For I knew myself that even out on the North Sea the collier brig, *Countess of Raby* could still lawfully be ordered to heave-to. Like any ship under British colours her master would always have to submit to a sound rummaging, a full truck-to-keel search at the Excise's challenge. But then who would want to try move a leaden coffin? Fewer still too, I fancied, would wish to tamper with the cadaver within it... and to do that on a heaving deck in any sort of sea?

"Mr. Partis!" The order came with a crack like a whip. "I want you to turn this warehouse inside out." Talaeus Dekker flourished a sheet of thick paper and thrust it towards the jerquer. "This is my warrant... you'll find it gives you all the authority you'll need. So go to it, my man! Use your own lads upon these premises. You have my own leave to rip the very bowels out of it!" He swung sharply to turn to me. "One last small service, Doctor Shafto... lead me to the town's very best whorehouse..."

Chapter Thirty-one

Twelve men were packed into three hired hackney cabs, each carriage with its curtains drawn and its horses' hooves heavily muffled with sacking. They drew up silently before Mrs.Gomer's establishment on the Close. The jingle of harness betrayed the presence of the mounted men who were riding close behind those carriages. Few of the folk already hurrying along the street to their work stopped to gawp at our little caravan.

Talaeus Dekker was first man to jump out on to the pavement. But beyond that neither call nor signal was needed from him to send four of Mr. Partis's Excise men hurrying off – cutlasses ready drawn - directly into the narrow alleys that flanked either side of the building. Then from his coat's breast the old fellow drew out a sheet of paper. Under the pool of light from an opened lantern shutter I recognised the black imprint of the royal crest at the document's head. This surely, I fancied, had to be Talaeus Dekker's time of triumph. It was his warrant. He drew a long barrelled pistol from his belt. I heard the lock's sharp click as he cocked back the hammer.

"Right we are, m' lads. You are all herewith stood-to-arms…all lawful and in His Majesty's name…Remember also that this night we've still got three of our own lads to take revenge for!" Then it was as though the old man had of a sudden run out of the temper to sustain his words. Suddenly he bellowed out like an angered bull: "Chaaaa'rge!"

I stepped down from the hackney carriage. But before I too could give chase a hand reached out of the darkness and gripped tightly at my arm. "Stand well back, Doctor Shafto! Your duty here is already ended. The work you undertook to do in Newcastle town is now finished. Any plain measure o' discretion should warn you, now, that none of this business need – nor indeed should - be any concern of yours…" "It was only when I turned about that I recognised Squires Taylor. He was still wearing the scarlet coatee of a regimental officer; still wearing the disguise of one Captain Tolliver. "Shall we allow old Talaeus to gulp down his own last draught o' Glory! For I myself would have to allow that the old man surely does deserve it." It was at that moment that my own common sense returned. Taylor was right - of course he was!

Before us the heavy boots were thundering their way up broad wooden staircase. Above us they rumbled like distant cannon fire. Torches flared yellow as they were swung about over the heads of the charging men. Yet already at the top of those stairs Mrs Gomer was waiting. The fat little woman standing there in her quilted bed gown had raised her candlestick high. I could see then that the curly black wig that the old brothel keeper was wearing was tilted comically awry. Nonetheless, our Mrs Gomer had been in her business for many years. I fancied it would take more than any gang of armed hooligans to overawe this old woman. "Gentlemen…" The voice was steady. Indeed our Mrs. Gomer sounded almost confident. As indeed well she might. For her establishment was regularly patronised by many of the most important – powerful - gentlemen within the city of Newcastle, and indeed far beyond it. "What business have you here… sir?"

"King's business, my good woman…Treasury affairs!" Dekker's voice was oddly haughty; or, more like, proud - arrogant even. Indeed that emotion seemed to rise within him into an almost joyous shout. "What I have here is this signed warrant; it is an order to arrest a brace of felons… I am to arrest two fellows who came here earlier this night… after they had fired upon sworn officers of the Crown!"

Mrs Gomer, and this clearly, still possessed sufficient of her own wit to know that she was likely to get neither thanks nor profit from her other customers if she dared offer to delay a king's warrant. Her words were few. She spoke softly. But they were enough. "Rooms nine and ten, Gentlemen… at the corridor's end!"

That arrest was damned swift! Though, from the sound of it Charlie D'Oeuys's door had to be smashed in. Obscenities, screamed out loudly in the raucous French spoken in the port of Toulouse, were carried down to me. I found myself smiling. But the honourable Arthur Hethrington himself, it seemed, remained completely aloof. Which I knew must have been no easy thing for him to do. For by then both of the fellows were being frog-marched down steep stairs with either wrist manacled fast to those of one of Dekker's men. The first trio's progress was swift. And to be sure I saw that neither of the prisoner's feet looked to touch the pavement's cold flagstones at all before they were bundled up – bare arsed – into separate hackney carriages. Both men had the rosy, swollen faces of drunkards stirred all untimely out of a deep sleep. One of Dekker's hired runners followed the party on – smirking – carrying a great double armful of men's clothes.

But no common jail had been requisitioned to detain these two prisoners. Neither the decrepit dungeon under the Castle's Keep nor even any of the more secure cells beneath the Sheriff's Court, within the precincts of the Guildhall itself, had been requisitioned to satisfy Talaeus Dekker's warrant. I remembered then that the old fellow had lost prisoners before. Taylor's hackney followed the two carriages up the bank as they were driven up towards the house by the town's Meat Market, the place from where the carrier pigeons flew.

"Yes, this arrest must finish this business altogether…" Taylor's voice was still soft; yet there was a distinct rising note of certainty to it. "And thus you, my friend, would do best for yourself if you were to be well away from this town. You have done the task for which you were brought to Newcastle. So you, my good doctor, should be on your way – and that, my friend, is my own especial advice to you. Climb aboard any stagecoach you fancy – to any town you like! Sure enough, the honourable Arthur Hetherington may have been clapped into chains; but in this town you must know that even now that same fellow's softest whisper would be enough to get you murdered… Get yourself well away from Newcastle, Bob Shafto!"

I would have been a fool not to catch that little note of warning that lay within Taylor's words.

I looked him full in the face. "So this sudden fall of events means that our good Colonel Dekker will not be inclined to protect me further?"

"No; it is not that, not exactly. And while the *British Linen Bank*'s particular interest in you might not yet have fully faded…in the way that such bodies will. But what I do fear now is that friend Dekker might suddenly have quite another need for your services! And that might be more than you would honestly wish to offer… " It was clear from his face now that Squires Taylor had already told me over much. Yet when I turned again to look at him directly I saw that he was smiling. Suddenly he held up a forefinger.

"Within another hour I myself will be taking a fast coach for London." I saw his right eyebrow was lifted high. "I fear that I cannot ask you to share my hired coach with me, Doctor Shafto. But if you do follow me down to London…meet me there in three days time. Present yourself at the chambers of Messrs. Martinmass off the Strand. There I will offer to employ you. Moreover I will here offer to pay you a minted gold sovereign for every day you work for me. Such an appointment will also foot the cost of comfortable lodgings. Moreover, I'll see to it that you are handsomely mounted whenever the need arises…"

"And what precise service, Mr. Taylor…would you require me to do for you?" Of course I was asking a road I already knew. Yet my question was reasonable enough. But Squires Taylor only shrugged his shoulders a little. "Why, Doctor, pretty much what you have been doing in Newcastle these last days. I shall expect you to sit quiet, play at cards and smoke a pipe, to cock your lugs, to watch and listen carefully to all that is said…in French or Italian. Then every day I would have you write me a report, much as you did for Colonel Dekker…" His sudden laugh almost caught me unawares. "And of course I shall want you to tell lies, to cheat, to inveigle. Recently I have learned of a certain Mrs Helena Vardy who manages a popular gaming club, the Phoenix, at Proctor Lane in Westminster. That should launch you into a good start…"

I could sense then that there was already a plan in being, a scheme, forming in Taylor's brain. The man was obviously waiting for my answer. Then, of a sudden, Squires Taylor barked out another laugh. "As I say, I can give you three or four days…until the early morning's London stagecoach sets off south from the *Queen's Head*, Doctor Shafto. By then you will need to come to your decision. From that day on, Doctor Shafto, depending on the world's events, I can offer you, perhaps, three months of the work you do best, say a hundred days in all… After that I fancy you may then go wherever you please… without let or hinderance. Whatever new identity I give you in London Town will hold good for you wherever you choose to show it!"

So, it seemed I had half a week to do whatever business I needed to do in Newcastle. And in that time there were many things that I would have to do.

As though to emphasis the sudden change in my affairs, our carriage was sharply denied entrance to house by the Meat Market. The blue gate remained shut before us.

I stepped out on to the cobbles.

"Thank you for your kind offer Mr. Taylor…I will give it my honest consideration. Truly, I will!"

"There will be an inside ticket - paid for – waiting to be picked up at the coach office by a man who gives the name, Fry. It is my advice that you should collect it without fail…."

My first mission would have to be to collect the monies rightly owed me by Ralphie Hodgson. After all fifty guineas in gold had now become a damned important sum to me. For hadn't I fairly seen to it that every element of the services I had promised to Hodgson the Grocer had been carried out.

When I got up to the shop at the top of Pilgrim Street I was just in time to see the grocer being bundled into a closed carriage. Yet I boldly pushed my way between the crowding onlookers and stepped into the shop. The bell above the door chimed merrily behind me as I walked down the floor towards the brass scales at the end. That the lad in the yellow pantaloons had seen me come in there was no doubt - but the same fellow looked now to have other things on his mind.

"Sir?" Yes, clearly the day's events were having their effect on Hodgson's pup. The lad's breath was refusing to come. I stared hard at him:

"My name is Mr. Farrow…." I heard the sharp catch of his breath." Master Hodgson promised to leave a box here for me, a little box…" I framed the container with my thumbs and forefingers. Then I began to focus a hard glaring eye upon Rupert Hodgson through the rectangle. "It is very likely that you will find that the same box has my name upon it." His father would have been proud of him. The fat under lip curled slowly at me. "Ha! Not this time ma' bonny lad!" I mouthed at him, silently. Almost without thinking about it I reached out at the fellow. My fingers took a harsh grip on his neck cloth. I jerked him towards me. "Young man, if I were you I would not think to offer me so much as one instant of delay!"

Young Hodgson's surrender was absolute. Recent happenings had obviously borne down heavily upon our Master Rupert. He bent down under the counter and at once came up with a little parcel. From the weight of it alone I could feel that Hodgson had already met our bargain to the full. It was a little cigar box tight wrapped in brown paper and bound about with string. The knots were sealed with red wax. I plucked it from the lad's fat fingers and at once turned about. I was through the shop's door before I heard his plaintive bleat behind me. The younger Hodgson had summoned up enough of his damned impertinence to demand a written receipt of me. As I strode through the morning crowds on Pilgrim Street I hefted the box's weight in my side pocket. Two thick blue paper rolls, each holding twenty-five guineas apiece was what I knew the cigar box held. Busy folk walking up the Pilgrim Street shuffled to move aside from me as suddenly I chortled out something like a giggle!

Later I fancied that it had been my own boots that had galloped me down the bank towards Elsie Bell's cottage. I had only faltered a little when I had realised that I was taking the stone steps up to the door three at a time. I stood there paused for a long moment while I caught my breath. For a further couple of heartbeats I stood there shaking my head like a bullock dazed. There was almost no boldness at all to my knock. The door planks rattled a little. Then of a sudden I sensed it; I knew. I was a man whose natural volition was fleeing headlong from him.

I had not realised before how tiny that cundum maker's workshop room was. Though never had I seen it so full of folk. Jacob Storey was crouched down like an imp before the hearth's blaze. Before me a stranger sat at the table.

"Why Reverend...you've come..."

I caught Jacob's lie in its mid-air flight. Then before I had time to think further I looked directly at the fellow who was at the table.

At once there was no need for any other explanation. I suppose I would have been a fool entire not to gather that whole scene before me in one glance. But Eadie Bell's reckoning came even quicker.

"Reverend Shafto...I would like to have you meet Master Daniel Hutton..." The woman's eyebrows were semaphoring wildly at me. And at once I caught the message. Though the weight of that same news was already tugging hard at my heart strings - fit to pull them asunder it was. Nonetheless in that instant all the skills I had learned during my years in Europe came into play. Without hesitation I thrust out my hand in greeting. The fellow at the table freed a big hand from the bairn he was holding. Jesu! No man would have wanted that same lad to grip at him in anger!

"Master Hutton...it is my pleasure to take your hand, Sir..." There was, I supposed, damned little else I could find to say. For I think that even by then I already knew how things stood between Hettie Bellis and this fellow, this Daniel Hutton. I myself had come down ready to offer young Ettie Bellis a new life; though as I would also now have had to own it would have been a new life of very uncertain prospects. Danny Hutton's offer it seemed had already weighed heavier in Life' s scale pan.

His eyes were clear: plain Geordie blue. The fellow's smile was open and, damn him, honest. His handshake had in it all the power I might have expected. The man had shaved himself too, close, that very morning - which as I reminded myself I had not done. In the North the ordinary run of men are slow to change their fashion o' dress. Plainly enough this Danny Hutton had stepped out that morning as a Newcastle master craftsman dressed for his wedding day. And while among the class of tradesmen to which Danny Hutton obviously belonged new, Bedford cloth, knee breeches and knitted stockings might well be everyday wear. I could also see that the bright silver buttons on both his dark grey coat and the waistcoat beneath had been cut to make a matching set. At his neck he wore a kerchief of blue Shantung silk. So... and looked at anyway I liked, I knew then that this had to be a lad dressed as a bridegroom.

"Miss Bellis..." Ettie slipped out from behind the curtain. She was wearing a high- breasted dress of pale blue tulle silk. By some magic of her own the lass had contrived to cover most

of the bruises she had taken from Charles D' Oeuys's beating."
I turned my head away. "Ma'am…I would beg a private word
with you!

"Aye. Reverend…if you'd care to step outside, Sir." She
nodded shortly to her light o' love. "Danny, this is a last
private matter that must be settled…so, and by your leave,
the Reverend gentleman and I will go out on to the step…"

I heard the clash of the door behind us. We faced one
another.

"You'll surely have had the wit to see how things lie
between me and Danny Hutton?" Without a word and with
my lips pursed tight I found myself nodding!

I waited, allowing Ettie to gather her words.

"The lad came down as asked me last evening… It was the
third time o' asking." Her eyes wandered from mine. " And I've
promised him that I'll wed wi' him…this afternoon, at three
o'clock…up at St. Andrew's church…"

The girl's hand was laid upon my wrist. "Bob Shafto, you
and me both were stricken by the same daftness, lad. But we
both of us knew all along that there was never a chance for
either of us! Was there? This life has always been damned
cruel to the pair of us. But always I've had to do what I've
been forced to. And you must know that I have never spared
myself for that little laddie o' mine. I've kept him decent and
fed all along." The tears began to well up and fatten in Ettie's
eyes. I felt her hands take a tight hold of mine. "For the love
of God…leave me be! Danny Hutton is a good lad. He's a
widower with two little daughters who sorely need a Ma… He
has a canny little house of his own down by the North Shore.
Soon enough he'll come into his uncle's timber yard; already
he's a freeman o' the town…" For how long Ettie Bellis went
on retailing to me the virtues and prospects of Daniel Hutton
I lost count. Yet for every argument that Ettie put to me I
found my own defences falling back before it. She was right,
of course she was. And though neither of us mentioned the
fact, we both knew that Newcastle itself would never accept a

young woman of what would be called ' doubtful background as the lady wife of a physician. It was no good! And it was that which made my own arguments falter, before her own did. My own decision came with a sudden rush. I reached into my pocket and brought out one of the blue paper rolls. I reached forward and took Ettie's hand.

"Take this, Ettie, take it as an honest love gift... "I pushed the guineas firmly into her hand. "Always remember this, m' Love... When this new French war is over, this country will suffer hard times; and as always the North will take the worst of it. For me, I have still my own neck to save... and I know that I will be safest by far away over the seas!" I turned about and went off back down the stairs.

Chapter Thirty-two

For the rest of that morning I scuttled hither and yon about Newcastle's busy streets. Truth to tell, any man with even a half ration of his God given wits about him would already have made off by whatever means he could. And to be sure, too, I had already been making some plans in that direction. Though increasingly the none-conformist's black broadcloth I had bought from Mrs. Bone at Shields had become a suit of clothes I now *felt* myself wearing. It would have been foolish for me to go on walking the streets draped in that garb for much longer. Yet for sure my luck continued to hold. For before that day's noon I had found a tailor on Ridley Place who had a bespoke suit of what by courtesy could be called gentleman's clothing. It had been had lying by him, uncollected, for all of three months. The same tailor was as eager to be shot of the garments as I was to have them. While – as we had agreed - he shortened the sleeves of the dun-coloured coat for me, I walked two doors down the same street and stepped into a hatter's shop. There I paid out nineteen shillings for a brown beaver felt round hat. My confidence rose as I walked out among the street's good folk again as a town merchant in his workaday clothes.

It was in my new guise that I wandered across town towards Charlotte Square. As I had already half-expected I found Rachel Brydon's town house was closed, every window shuttered-up. So far as Newcastle was concerned – or even interested – that lady was no longer in residence. It had already been my own guess that she would certainly not be found to stand before any court and give her evidence against the guinea smugglers. Though I myself was strongly persuaded that the same lassie would sit in her closed carriage to watch any executions!

Everywhere I went about the town I heard the whispers about the arrest of Arthur Hetherington. Though like most gossip the fine detail of the same tale became more and more smudged as time drew on. Folk in every tavern seemed to know the simple broad facts of the case. An attempt had been made to smuggle golden guineas out of the port of Tyne – and, of course, the agents of the Emperor Napoleon were behind the business. I heard much wide-eyed speculation as to the sums of money involved: that ranged from a thousand coins to a fancied half a million. And of course, as all men knew, such an act was plainly a hanging matter!

I went down to Mrs Dilkes' house on the Butcher Bank. There was still gear I needed to pick up and, as I remembered, I would have to give the order to release the wounded Lieutenant Cable.

I found him in the kitchen. He was busy playing at *vingt-et-un* with Mrs. Dilkes nephew, Cuthbert, and it looked very much as though the officer was winning – and handsomely too! From the set of his shoulders I could see that his wound was at least comfortable.

"Mister Cable…"As his eyes lifted from his hand he folded his fingers to hide the faces of his cards.

"Doctor Shafto…" Plainly the fellow had not heard of Lady Dobson's death. I told him. There was no point in my sparing him. Though, while I gave him my news, I did not look directly into his face. "By all appearances it was the red-headed man, the Frenchman, who…who murdered Lady Dobson." I heard him draw a breath in slowly - through his nose. It sounded like a sigh. And while to be sure it is hard not to sympathise with a bereaved man, at that moment I could not help but picture the blue-white faces of the men with slit throats which came up at once into my mind: Eneas Knox... Mattie Crowlie. That same old woman had narrowly failed to sever the jugular vein of Geordie Humble – it had seemed only just! And I was certain that there would be others; lots of other men who had fallen to the sharp blade hidden in m' lady's slashing fan! So, and by any easy reckoning, Rachel Brydon's female companion had surely deserved everything she got. From my pocket I took out the carved ivory fan, twirled it round by its black silk cord. I allowed it to fall on to the table before Cable. "But have no doubt, sir, in this matter...I will lay before you the name of a Monsieur Charles D'Oeuys. Though the man is already under arrest, and that for more crimes than any simple murder..." Mr. Cable put his head down and went on examining his hand of cards. I could not see his face.

Mrs Dilkes brought me the note on a polished brass tray. Clearly she regarded the message as important. My thumbnail crackled off the seal wax as I opened the paper. I had to move across to the window to read it. The message was short.

> "Dr. Shafto,
> Pray oblige me by stepping up to Brunswick\
> Place at your, at your earliest convenience.
>
> Richard Grainger

For a long moment I hesitated. When I turned around I found Cable was looking directly at me. I smiled at him. "Tell me, Mr. Cable, have you any notion at all where I might find your Major Farquahar?" Twice during that morning I had reminded myself that the same dog was still ranging about in Newcastle...and likely as eager as ever to clamp his fat fingers on to the scruff of my neck!

I did not have long to wait for Cable's answer. "Given what time o' day it is, Sir, I would say that you would most likely find the Major playing at cards - with his friends from up at the barracks. You'll find him at the new *Turf Hotel* up on Mosely Street. He has of late been doing uncommon well at the pasteboards"

"Thankee…" I smiled at him. This was important. For a man would have to be a damned fool altogether to forget that George Ninian Farquahar was still possessed of a king's warrant sworn out against him. So it would be a damned bad business for me to be arrested this far along the road. By rights I should already have been on my way to Sunderland. Yet the attraction to talk with Richard Grainger was strong.

I made my way up to Brunswick Place. The city's streets were crowded with a market day crush of busy folk. I stepped in under the arch and into the yard behind the house. At once I heard a man's knuckles braying noisily at the glass panes above my head. I looked upward and saw Richard's own clerk, his shorthand writer, Martindale. It was obvious that the old fellow had been set there to wait for me. He lifted the window sash.

"Pray come in, Doctor. My instructions are that I am to offer you lunch; to give you a drink… and to beg you to stay." I followed the directions offered by Martindale's waving hand. A footman waiting in the doorway took my coat and hat. I followed him into the house.

By God, all things in Brunswick Place looked to be damned handsomely well managed. A tray with a black bottle and two glasses were already laid out for me. I had poured a small glass of Cognac brandy and lifted it to my lips when I heard the quick footsteps behind me. Richard Grainger pushed his way into the room.

"Thank God you could come, Doctor Shafto… "The voice was hushed. "I had feared that you would already have been away south on the morning's stagecoach." It was suddenly clear to me that this gentleman had been riding hard. I watched him pause. He hauled a long chamois leather bag out of his breeches pocket and began to spill out bright new coins on to the table. They were, I saw, new minted George III guinea pieces. "First things first, Doctor… Be so good as to accept from me the sum of twenty guineas in gold … these being the wages owed to you for your recent services to The *Linen Bank*. I would have been a fool to refuse the money. Most honest men must break their backs for half a year to get their hands on such a sum. Grainger stood there like a fellow who had just discharged a pressing debt. I watched as his eye fell upon the bottle of brandy; he grabbed at it and charged a glass for himself. I waited.

" Doctor Shafto…" Even then I had a curious premonition as to what was coming. "The offer I am about to make you, Sir, does not emanate from me…." I heard Grainger's mouthful of brandy gulped hard into his throat.

"To come directly to the point…" I heard him swallow the cognac. "I am requested to offer you what I will call a piece of work… it is short and it will be handsomely well paid." Clearly, Grainger was already uncomfortable with his commission. Then of a sudden his courage reasserted itself. "Damn it all, man, I represent certain gentlemen in whose interest it now lies to save that purblind fool Arthur Hetherington from his richly deserved place on the Town's Moor – on the gallows."

I felt my lips purse themselves together; then with a slow deliberation I allowed my breath to wheeze out softly. "Pray go on Mister Grainger…" Now I too was taking a gulp at my Cognac.

"Newcastle is an odd sort of place, Doctor. Mostly hereabouts men mind their own businesses. But every now and again a chap upsets the happy balance of the town's trade…" It was hard not to smile at Grainger. Clearly The Town did not want one of its wealthy citizens to hang!

"What you mean, Mr. Grainger, is that in this town any fellow with a sufficiency of ready money is able to break both every commandment in the Decalogue, and can moreover smash every statute of English Law…and to do that ten times over in any week - if he wishes." I tapped my nose with my forefinger. "And until the early hours of this morning your honourable Arthur Hetherington was just such a fellow. Now he is to learn that this is not so… However, now it seems that there are powerful men in Newcastle town who want this same wretch saved… want his backside lifted clear of the hot lick o' Hell's flames!" I knew my own town; as surely as I knew the men who ruled the place.

Richard Grainger looked even more uncomfortable. I went on. "But…sir, and as you yourself also know… Our friend Colonel Talaeus Dekker also desires, most particularly, to have the bold Arthur dance all at tippy-toe on the morning's air….." Now I smiled directly across at Grainger. "And as you warned me when I came to Newcastle, the Colonel is surely not a man to cross, to hinder, nor to thwart…"

What I had said had clearly struck Grainger hard. But I had not yet won the game. Grainger stepped over to an escritoire and let down the flap. I heard him grunt softly. Then I heard the chink from what he had let fall on to the table before me. My nostrils twitched at the smell of hemp. They were two woven rope fenders, pretty pieces of a sailor's handiwork. Grainger's slender fingers rove at the cords, pulling them open. It was the gleam of the gold coins inside those two coarse bags that set my heart to a wild thumping.

I was aware, almost at once, that Richard Grainger was allowing me plenty of time to look at that gold. He wanted me to be gripped by the money's own spell. And I was.

"What I want…what it is wanted of you, Doctor Shafto, is that you secure the escape of the two prisoners now held in the cellars beneath Maudant's Chambers. "

"*Two* men!" My voice was pitched upward, and that almost sharply. To be sure I had no love for the grocer Ralphie Hodgson – but leaving even that miserable little bastard to hang in place of a brace of rogues like Hetherington and D'Oeuys truly did stick fast in my gullet. The emotion must also have showed in my face. Grainger lifted the palm of his right hand before him.

"Aaah! But you could not know! There will be no need for your help to free Monsieur D'Oeuys. He was discharged from his arrest an hour ago."

"God damn him!" I think I heard my words catch in my throat! "But… how? How could that be so?

Grainger had obviously been as surprised as anyone else at this recent turn of events. "The simple answer to that question, Doctor, is fear! Monsieur was able to flourish a fat wedge of papers that were hidden in his shirtfront. Mere sight of those letters greatly disturbed this town's magnates. On their simple nods the Frenchman had his chains stricken from his wrists. As we speak that same gentleman is being offered fresh brewed coffee and slabs of new baked spice cake up at the house of a Mr. Farrington on High Friar Street. I have just seen him served with it!"

My own anger was still set plainly on my face. Grainger went on.

"The commands of kings…Doctor Shafto…the merest scribbled word of a king's minister. The Frenchman came to Newcastle bearing a written protection from the pen of Monsieur Fouche, himself. And as you will well know his own master, the Emperor Napoleon, is already nearing Paris. Oh, yes, there will soon be a battle, a great battle… but who is to say who will win it? And so the emperor's shadow looms uncommon large! Which means of course that many men in this country are already in something close to a muck sweat. This business has already set the dice rolling now. These same sensible fellows would sooner avoid taking any chances they don't have to. What they all most wanted was that the Emperor's servant be sent out of the town… and that at altogether the earliest moment!" For Newcastle, in common with most other of England's cities, is governed, as it has been for centuries by a coterie, if you like, by a cabal of men who can bargain with kings… Though no man will ever own to membership of such a body… yet it has its charter of ancient rights and its modern customs.

"So, tell me, Mr. Grainger..." I fixed him with my own gaze. "What precisely is it that your friends want me to do? And more importantly, to me much more importantly, what do you think Talaeus Dekker will do when he discovers who it is has freed his own prisoners? "

"When a decent interval of time has elapsed, Doctor, the Colonel will himself be paid off.... Though you might say that his venture is - has already become - entirely self-financing! Or say rather that all the end expenses of this game are being met by the Hetherington family themselves. They are damned rich. They can afford it! The good Dekker has, I believe, been on his way to Edinburgh this last hour. His own masters have summoned him North - at all speed!" I heard myself sigh. Grainger's answer to it was a little chuckle. "You know Dekker's own first error was to charter the steam-vessel, *Perseverence*. Bankers do not tell other men's secrets – but they will always discretely confide, one to another..."

It was soon clear enough that someone within Newcastle town had brought to bear a cabinet of the sharpest wits to bear upon this problem. The first sheet of a fistful of papers showed a drawing – a pretty piece of artist's work. It was simple enough; yet that sheet bore precise details and measurements of the respectable business chambers backing on to the town's meat market. There was also another sharply drawn pencil sketch showing, all clearly limned-in, dimensions for the cellars of Maudant Chambers.

Richard Grainger explained the plan to me very well. Nor did he cavil at any requests I made for whatever tools I might need. His faithful scrivener, Martindale, I noticed, was writing down whatever I asked for.

Over all, the plan was damned well conceived. Getting Hetherington and Hodgson out of the cells in Maudant's Chambers was likely on my own reckoning to take less than thirty minutes by any man's pocket watch.

But beyond the immediate escape it sounded to me as I listened to Grainger 's plans that Newcastle town entire had been marshalled to help in this business. The town's night watch was to be turned out early; sent to go off down river after a gang said to be looting moored barges. The troops of the Black Cuffs had already received special orders and had been marched off towards a field near Durham City to take part in a mock battle! Beyond that there were also such minor items as tallow slush spread on the cobblestones along certain streets; while here and there the torches that the town's bye-laws had long required householders to burn before their premises were left unlit!

Not a detail it seemed had been left unattended. In my own hands I even had the roster of the names of the men who would be on guard around Maudant's Chambers that night.

"These men, Mr. Grainger... they are town's own servants? I saw at once that Grainger had blinked. He was uncertain. That would not do! "Then we had best find out, hadn't we... By you leave, Sir, I would like to borrow the services of your Mr. Martindale, here." Grainger nodded eagerly. I wagged a finger at the old servant.

"Wrap up warmly, Mr. Martindale. For surely this is greatcoat weather!

We moved with the crowds around the meat market. The stench of animals, pigs and veal calves mostly I saw, was strong on the air. Then through the swirl of coal smoke from a brazier I saw the scarlet of a soldier's coat, then another and yet another.

"Christ! This is going to be a tough old chop to chew at Mr. Martindale...is it not?"

I had spoken to Martindale out of the corner of my mouth. The old fellow nodded: "Yet it is early on in the day, Doctor, damned early on in the day!"

But a close walk-by of Maudant's Chambers did nothing to lighten my spirits. The blue gate that let out on to the street was we saw guarded by two soldiers of the Black Cuffs. And as I noticed at once these were men chosen from the ranks of the regiment's leavening squad. It would have been only a small favour for Talaeus Dekker to have asked a brother officer for his help. Nonetheless on a quick glance I saw that both fellows were turned out in full marching order. Their boots and brasses gleamed; their cross belts were new whitened. I caught the oiled brown glint on the long blades of the bayonets fixed to the muzzles of their Brown Bess muskets. Yet, and clearly too, some inspecting officer had not cared to notice that the ball cartridges bulging out of the flaps of their cartridge boxes had quite spoiled the line of their dressing. Clearly these lads looked to have been warned to expect trouble.

All of six times we walked the circuit round and past Maudant's Chambers. Each time we learned a little more of how things stood there. We saw that the guard was under the command of a fat sergeant who sat across the road in the taproom of *The Three Featherss*. As ever the N.C.O. was sitting in the warm. I invited Martindale to take a glass of sherry with me.

We sat by the fireplace and waited. Once, a couple of clerks came into the taproom. One of them greeted Mr. Martindale warmly. That it seemed was our pass. We were no longer strangers; no longer a threat. Thus it was too that we were able to count the full complement of military guards. There were six men on duty; two before the gate and the other four elswhere within Maudant's Chambers. That guard was changed at the stroke of two o'clock.

The fresh redcoats had scarcely grounded their muskets before a little carriage drew up before the gate across the street. At once the sergeant stood up. He leant towards the window on the street. The old manservant who climbed down out of the carriage turned about and lifted out a large tray covered with fine linen. Together Martindale and I watched the little piece of commerce that passed between the two men. The guard lifted the covers from the silver dishes on tray. We watched the steam rise into the air. Then the manservant neatly palmed a coin to the soldier. All's well – pass friend!

Chapter Thirty Three

Martindale and I went back to Brunswick Place at the run. Within half an hour Richard Grainger had contrived to have the Hetherington's manservant taken off the carriage and standing before us in his kitchen. The old fellow shivered before the fire in his body shirt and drawers. "So, wor Razi-muss..." I thrust a pewter mug of fresh mulled wine into Erasmus Barnes' gnarled hands. "Mr. Hetherington's family solicitor, his lawyer, has demanded that the prisoner be fed from his own kitchens – that three times a day! And the magistrate did agree to this?"

"Aye...In England, Sir, a man is innocent until he's been proved guilty...they do say! Yet mind you, aa'am always well searched every time aa'h ga'an in wi' m' tray!"

"But will it work, Doctor, will it work? Richard Grainger was eager; but it was also increasingly plain to me that now his own anxiety was working upon him. Clearly this was a man whose loyalties had been drawn damned tight by two powerful parties.

"The nearer I can be made to look like our friend Erasmus, here...why then the more likely it is that we, *I*, can set the prisoners, both of them, free." The boldness of my own words had sent a shiver through me too. To be sure, though, Erasmus Barnes looked to be an almost easy figure to counterfeit. That was why we had stripped off his footman's livery almost as soon as Joe Skinner had frog-marched the poor fellow down into the kitchen at Brunswick Place. It had been Joe, too, who had overcome Erasmus' fears about the outcome of the imposture. "Do this for my master, brother Barnes...and you can depend upon it that you'll be secure in your service till your dyin' day!"

But I myself was not so easily pacified. It was Bob Shafto alone who was going to hazard his mortal frame within the next few hours. The disguise I was being eased into would have to be a deal more cunning, truer to life, than anything that might have deceived the audience in the front row at the Theatre Royal. It was my neck; so it would be my disguise. I worked at my face myself before a little mirror. Either I would be satisfied with myself...or.

"Mister Barnes' wig...if you please, Joe Skinner." Few footmen still wore wigs. The fashion for them was going out in all save the richest households. What the coachman fitted on to the top of my head was a mangy old thing of what had once been white horsehair; yet when he had tugged on the black ribbons it fitted my skull well enough. At least I would catch no lice from it – that for sure because the footman's skull was close shaved.

Rare for a Newcastle manservant, it looked very much as though the Hetheringtons had put up their footmen in a decent turn out of livery. The waistcoat front was worked in scarlet satin thread, on black serge. A wide shouldered dress coat was heavy with gilt. The white cotton gloves were dirty. Soup had splashed across the fingers of one of them. Without a word I handed them to Joe Skinner. They were back before I had climbed into the footman's knee breeks, washed clean and still hot to my hand from the flat iron

"Now for the tray!" It looked odd to see Richard Grainger walking forward with a big Sheffield Plate tray in his hands. That the more so because the fellow was, as they say, grinning like an arse! Then he made the tray turn over. This had to be the cleverest dodge I had ever clapped my eyes upon. The underside of the tray had been fitted with two thin rails of bright metal. Clipped into those rails by their belt-hooks were two brace of pocket pistols, each double barrelled, one pair were flintlocks, the other two had the new percussion locks fitted.

"Look after those, Doctor. One pair is mine, the other belongs to my father. Both come from the workshop of Durs Egg; and I may say that we're both uncommon fond o' those little beauties."

"Nonethless, Mr. Grainger, and by your kind leave, sir... I must insist upon re-loading those weapons with my own hands..."

I was ready; as ready as ever I was going to be. Even though my guts were tight and my teeth were beginning to clench themselves. The four of us waited while the hours between mealtimes passed.

The carriage wheels rumbled noisily over the cobblestones. Set before me the polished silver tray was loaded heavily with closed porcelain dishes. Over all a lace edged linen cloth was spread like a shroud.

"Dinnor f'r Mr. Hetherin'ton..." I rolled my r's heavily... Geordie is the accent of the county. Both sentries guarding the gate were Yorkshire Tykes.

"By, Lad...that smells good!" The soldier holding open the carriage door sniffed in the aromatic steam rising through the linen.

"Aye, but it's not for wor bellies, bonny lad ...is it?" I grinned up at the man.

As Barnes had warned me I was passed directly through the gate into the yard beyond. Only there was I called to a halt by an old fellow wearing a corporal's blue cloth tapes on his coat's arm.

"If you'd be so kind as to put your tray down on this table..." He laid his musket aside and began to search me. You know, I would have to own this fairly, that had I been attempting to smuggle in anything at all into Maudant's Chambers, then that old bastard would surely have discovered it. Yet the tray, the plated silver tray loaded with good things, suffered no more than a twitch at its linen cover.

"Aye, pass in! Take him down, Holdstock!"

With a young militiaman's boots ringing out behind me I walked down a narrow passageway. I think I heard the voice from a long way off. But at first it signified nothing to me. Then I saw him in the flicker of the firelight. A man was bending to the hearth. He had lit a taper at the fire and was transferring his flame to the candles in an iron candelabrum. The third candle's wick had flared into brightness when I recognised the man scanning me. He was in the fullest regimental fig that the regulations allowed. Above his tight neck stock the face was fat and the bulging eyes were bright.

"You are?" The question was sharp, cutting. And I responded to it as only a man like old Erasmus would.

"Barnes, sir...footman in the service of Mrs. Hetherington...Aa' have come down with the young master's dinner..." I allowed my answer to waver into a tremor. This was the hound who three weeks before had arrested me on a Paris street. Almost unconsciously I licked at my upper lip. I was remembering how on that night Major Farqahar had pushed at my nostrils with the muzzle of his pistol. Now though I was nothing more than a poor devil of a footman.

"So what's he got, then?" Without so much as a by-your-leave Farquahar swept the linen cover from the tray I was holding. The powerful reek of a Madras curry wafted on to the air. I laid the porcelain out on to the table, unrolled a napkin and laid out the table silver ready for my master.

"Fricassee of chicken in a rich Indian sauce that is, Sir. The mistress prepared it herself. She prides herself on doin' the foreign dishes, does Mrs. Hether' inton ... the master is very partial to such spicy messes." But by then Farquahar had turned away from me. I heard the jingle of keys.

The first of the pistols came away easily from the tray's underside. I stepped forward and at the sharp double snap-click of cocking the locks I whispered my command into the major's ear:

"Undo their manacles, man…and be damned quick about it!" Farquahar needed no second telling. First Arthur Hetherington then Ralphie Hodgson were loosed from their irons. At my finger's pointing both men lowered their chain links down quietly on to floor.

"Now, Major Farquhar…" It was at that instant that it came to me that my disguise was still holding up. Neither prisoners nor guard had recognised me, yet. Yet for sure no more than a whisk with a hare's foot drawn through powdered rust was standing between this counterfeit footman and Doctor Shafto, the traitor.

"So, Sir William sent you…" Arthur Hetherington was rubbing at his wrists. The fellow stood proud: a day sitting in the darkness of a cell had scarcely worn the shine off him at all. His neck linen was clean and spruce. I could smell the eau-de-toilette still wafting off him; but from the shadow under his chin he had not been allowed the services of a barber.

"I was sent, Sir, by the Glasgow Man…" At those words Ralphie Hodgson stiffened like a setter dog. My invented tale had truly impressed him! An agent from the Glasgow Man was a creature he could believe in. His face had sagged and his shirt collar looked to have been chewed at. But at my words the eyes brightened. He seemed to come alive. "Beyond that – and the fact that we've undertaken to get the pair of you down to the farther side of the Tyne Bridge – you'll not need to concern yourselves with us at all. " I smiled harshly at them both: "That is provided the principals concerned pay out the balance of the guineas owed to our league…"

Major Farquahar was looking hard at me in the candlelight. I watched his recognition slowly dawn; I saw his jaw fall. But my words got themselves out first:

"I have brought this dinner especially for you, Major Farquehar…allow me to serve you with a dish of India chicken. It comes highly recommended." Swiftly I spooned out a little white rice and then doused the entire mound of it with all the sauced chicken meat.

"Now, sir, sit…" I handed Farquahar a silver dinner fork. "…and eat!

How long it would take better than two hundred drops of surgeon's laudanum to work when it had been admixed with a rich chicken curry was something I had had to guess at. And to be sure at the third mouthful of the dish Farquahar's face began to twist. "Yes, Major, it is laudanum… sufficient, I fancy, for me to take off your leg at the thigh and for you not to scream even a little.

With the twin barrels of one of Durs Egg's little pistols levelled at his head Major Farquahar soon finished his curry. For long moments there was only the scrape of a silver fork on a porcelain plate. I had been right. Already those bulging brown eyes of his had an odd glaze to them.

"Gentlemen, if you would both be so kind as to assist the Major to his cell… No, Mr. Hodgson, there will be no need to manacle the prisoner." While the two men cursed at one another as they struggled to force Farquahar's fat body in behind the bars, I took the other pistols out from behind the tray and stowed them into my coat pocket. For a second or so I had toyed with the idea of giving side-arms to my rescued prisoners. The idea fled. I had reminded myself that this same Hetherington had also been - as the invalid, Briggs – the same mean-minded bastard who had caused Farquahar to stop both my food and my wine on the way from France. No; I must not allow such sentiments to sour my responses. This was a job done for money, it could be nothing else; it would be nothing else.

I fished out an iron key from out of the dish that held figs in custard. Licking the sweetness from my fingers stepped over to a door in the opposing wall. The key slipped round easily. The door pulled open with a little creak.

"Up! To the first floor…up three flights, then stop!" My orders were whispered; though there was a necessary harshness to them. I closed the door behind me and locked it. The two men had not wasted any time. They were scampering off up that stairwell like bairns at play. Then it happened!

King George's gunpowder gives a powerful loud bang. But even before that shook the house I think that I was aware of every last little sound. For sure, I heard Hodges give his little cry as he tripped over the cord. Then I heard the clash of the locks and saw the bright chips as red sparks flew off Brandon gunflints. The bright flash as the priming flared lit up the whole scene.

Talaeus Dekker was the name that screamed out in my head. So in the end the old devil had scored! Two Tower muskets – cocked - had been tied across a pair of carpenter's saw benches. Their triggers had been rigged with waxed threads. A man's ankles against those taut threads had loosed off the shots. Poor bastard! Both musket balls had taken Hodeson squarely in the chest. This was one grocer who had thumbed his last scale pan!

"One more flight to climb, Mr. Hetherington... Move!" I almost gagged on my words in the swirling powder smoke. Beneath us already the musket butts were crashing against the door.

The drawing I had studied had shown a large window on the first floor landing. As Grainger had promised, its lower sash had been left open far enough to receive my fingers. I threw, hurled almost, the thing upwards. Ordinarily any footman's shoulder knot o'ribbons is a mere fancy decoration. When I had pulled the top knot loose these ribbons unwound themselves to nigh on twenty feet of silk cord. I tied the end of it to the eye of the key and flung it out into the darkness.

"Pull away..." The voice came out of the moonlit gloom like a man caught in a yawn.

A rope was tied to the silk, and that rope allowed me to draw in the end of a workman's ladder.

"Not far to go, Mr. Hetherington... seven steps, no more."

I was right. Of course I was, even though the ladder itself looked thin and a little femmer. Behind and below us now I heard the timber splinter as the door was smashed in. Boots, heavy metal shod army boots began to thunder on the stairway. I grabbed at the fellow's shoulders and shook him as I would a wayward bairn.

"Get yourself on to that ladder man!" I was yelling at him now. "Come on… Eight steps and we're both free!" Then I saw Hetherington's expression in a glimmer of moonlight. It was plain, simple, bare-faced fear! From the cobbles in the lane beneath us up to the window where we stood could scarcely have been twenty feet. But Arthur Hetherington had seen it, had judged the height, and a fear, like as not some Duergar beastie from childhood tales, had gripped its claws deep into him.

"Doctor Shafto, man…are y' comin', or what?" There was alarm in Joe Skinner's voice. One flight of stairs beneath us I could hear the rush of men's feet. I discharged both barrels of one of my pistols down into blackness. Men fall back cursing and swearing.

"Mr Hetherington…!" I took my hands and turned his head round towards me. Then I hit him. The steel over and under barrels of my empty pistol cracked hard against the side of his jawbone. He collapsed and I caught him as his legs folded beneath him.

It is no light matter to walk rung by rung across a ladder, that at night, in near darkness, not to speak of standing and high above the cobblestones of a back lane.

Yet there are times in a man's life when the scourge of his own fear lends him wings. I could feel the rungs under my instep as I stepped out. I had gone all of five steps. The loud word of command seemed to hit me in the back of the neck like a blow.

"Stop! One step more and you'll get your bloody bowels blasted out. In the King's name, turn about…" I heard the lock of a musket being cocked back. I think I had actually paused, I was standing there on the ladder with Arthur Hetherington slung across my shoulders like a veal calf. Then a shadow passed over my head and I heard the crash and tinkle of windowpane glass being smashed.

"Come on, y' daft buggers..." Another pantile was lobbed through the air. Where it went I never knew. But for myself I was off that damned ladder ; aye, and booting Hetherington's backside to move him on his way crab fashion down the roof slope of an old house.

We dropped, rolling off a brick wall, into a lane and I found myself dodging the hooves of a shying coach horse. But then Joe Skinner was up on the box.

"For Christ's own sake, gentlemen... get yourselves inside."

From the instant we were thrown hard back against the cushions by that carriage's starting jolt, until we were charging down the steep bank of the Side. I fancied that I could never have sworn by which road we went.

But at the end of it I was sure that the carriage crossed the Tyne Bridge at an honest trot.

From that moment the plan that Richard Grainger had outlined for me looked to be coming into being; indeed it looked to have been brought about with all the drama and romance of Italian Grand Opera. Two riders, both men cloaked and booted, both men mounted on cavalry horses waited to relieve us of our rescued prisoner. Both men held the bridle of a spare charger. But it was Joe Fletcher who had received his orders. His voice whispered hoarsely down into the carriage through the coachman's roof trap: "These two gentlemen will take you down to Hartlepool... sir!" So that was where Arthur Hetherington was bound. And I fancied too that wherever overseas his journey took him the same mangy dog would nonetheless still spend a life that was a damned sight more comfortable than that of most other honest Tyneside fellows.

Chapter Thirty-four

Richard Grainger proved to be as good as his word. Two thousand guineas in gold coin was the sum I counted out myself on to the polished table top in his dining room table at Brunswick Place. With that money dropped into two leather saddlebags I rode my borrowed horse down to the Branch Bank of England by the Bailey Gate, on Clavering Place. There, bold as you might please, I had the money laid to my account, to the name of Robert Fenwick Shafto, Doctor of Medicine. And it was in that same name that later that morning I wrote a cheque in the sum of six hundred pounds. This slip of heavy paper I pushed across a table to sallow looking lawyer acting for a young fellow called Askew Bourne, Mudie. For my cheque I took possession of papers that made over to me, all lawful and entire, the house, the practice, all instruments, books, and apparatus belonging to the late surgeon of Newcastle, Doctor Severus Mudie.

It was later that same morning that I was scanning through a recent work by a Paris surgeon when I heard the knocker, my own door's knocker, rap briskly.

"A Colonel Dekker would like to consult you, Doctor..." Mrs Austin, the late Severus Mudie's housekeeper, pronounced her formula; I responded with my own, while at the same time I touched at the little pistol hooked under my coat behind me. "Beg the gentleman to come in, Mrs. Austin..."

"A good morning to you, Doctor Shafto... My, but Lad, but you do look uncommon well." Talaeus Dekker was smiling, nor was there any trace of the usual playful sarcasm on his face. This was a man found in an honest good humour. A trace of egg yolk at the side of his lower lip told me that he had breakfasted late, and a flake of dried blood under his ear told me that he was still shaving himself.

"What ails you, Colonel Dekker? I jumped to my feet and took a hold on the old man's pulse. I drew Mudie's silver pulse watch out from my waistcoat pocket and counted the beat. "Very fair it is, for a man of your years, Sir…very fair. Then I allowed my fingers to tighten. It was the merest shadow of a sign. My gaze met his; then he smiled.

"All that Grainger promised you will hold good, Doctor. Have no fear of arrest. The *British Linen Bank* always makes good on its promises, for good or ill! As Major George Ninian Farquahar will soon enough discover. "Yet I find myself surprised…" Indeed I myself was so surprised that I dropped Dekker's wrist.

"The Major was employed by me, from the beginning, to secure your person in France, then to bring you home, in a sufficiently subdued state." In spite of myself I smiled, though still a little sourly.

"That man is still the Devil's own bastard son!" Yes…I began to see. I began to remember the misery of my journey along the road from Paris - of lying in chains during a rough passage across the Channel in the hold of a merchant ship.

"Oh, aye, he's every bit of that. D'ye not know that he himself had made a firm deal to break Arthur Hetherington out of his prison in Maudant's Chambers. The bloody rogue was going to drag the wall out of the cellar with a team of brewer's horses…and those four beasts he tried to hire on credit!"

I poured two glasses of Doctor Mudie's good whisky and put one into Dekker's
hand. "Just so long as I don't have to meet with the fellow again…"

Talaeus Dekker's throat rattled with a laugh that was something to set a man's teeth on edge. "The major is already on his way to London by this morning's stage. He leaves Newcastle behind him…along with about a hundred pounds in undivided winnings from his recent lucky gambling. Two lieutenants of hussars would now greatly like to have words with our major on that matter. But no matter, with the battles that are undoubtedly coming in Europe, such matters are now trivial things. Napoleon is already close to Paris and no armies have taken the field against him, yet! The Bourbons, damn them, have already fled the city." Dekker laughed again, softly. "And the London Stock Exchange is already becoming more than a little nervous. " Dekker tapped at his left nostril with a finger.

"While I myself would always hesitate to offer any man advice on such matters, I will tell you that the country's markets will soon go stark daft… invest some o' your own new won guineas in something that needs a steam engine to power the work. That's advice I have myself from two canny Edinburgh bankers…"

"Thank you Colonel Dekker. It is something I will surely keep in mind" But the question that was in my mind that that moment now bubbled up into words. "Tell me, sir, if you will… The gold: how much was it we were chasing; and where is it now?"

Dekker's fingers sought the pockets in his waistcoat:

"Eighty-one thousand guinea pieces, which is to say eighty five thousand and fifty English pounds. It was indeed locked up in the strong room at the head of Mr. Hetherington's new stairway. Dekker looked up at the ceiling. He was enjoying the thought.

"Within an hour of us laying hands on the man, a cousin of the bold Arthur came along at the run. It was he who opened the locks on the strong room for us with the three brass keys he had ready in his hand. He also had two lawyers and of three of the town's prominent bankers close upon his heels.

At once he claimed that the gold was the lawful possession of the Hetherington family... and had his lawyers wave at us the documents to prove it."

"So, it looks as though you ran directly into a ram's horns!" I laughed; I could not help myself. But to my surprise Dekker was taking no offence.

"The money is held now in the strong rooms of three Newcastle banks. And there it will stay until I say otherwise... Your own freeing of the bold Arthur has already given me considerable leverage. A man sought by a king's warrant can hardly step up to claim his wealth...can he?"

There was a look on Dekker's face that expressed the rest of what was in his mind. And I could read it easily. The nub of this entire matter was he could not afford to call any testimony of mine into a court.

"Now, Doctor, as a personal request I will ask you to walk with me along to the yard o' the *Queen's Head*. I, myself, am under fresh orders for London. Nonetheless there is something I would have you see..."

We stood together while the *Union*, the stagecoach down from Edinburgh, turned into the yard. We watched the four steaming horses changed and heard the guard's hoarse cry for 'London passengers!' That trip the stagecoach was light: there looked to be only four folk who wanted to travel down to the capital. The first two were ladies. I saw they had a manservant with them. The fellow climbed up on to the carriage's roof and pulled a heavy rug around him. Then I saw the mincing step of another passenger as he crossed the yard. His gleaming boots had to be worth all of twelve pounds. Above those he was wearing a triple-caped great coat of pale blue woollen cloth, faced and lined throughout with grey lambskin. I think that, even by then, I knew him. When he doffed his hat as he stepped aside for the old lady had followed him slowly across the yard I saw the queue of red hair tied with a silk ribbon. Monsieur Charles D'oeuys was going back to his master. Only then and quite suddenly I saw something else. The Frenchman put his hand out to assist the old lady up into the carriage. He pushed at the elbow of her right arm, lifting it upward. It was then that I saw the flick of her left wrist as she twirled the black silken cord around her hand. I heard the laughter choke itself off in my throat. Somewhere along the muddy miles to London the young man I had known as Lieutenant Cable had a matter to settle. It was a family matter, one that had nothing at all to do with the Fate of Europe. And it would - I knew - be resolved.

Suddenly Talaeus Dekker knuckled at my shoulder. "Stay here, Doctor. Take up your new practice and work hard at it. Folk get sick in Newcastle town as readily as they do in London or Paris. Find yourself a bonny young lassie, a virgin o' seventeen, a girl wi' a rich father. For be sure with the all battles that are coming about soon there's like to be a rare shortage o' lads in the North. Marry her. Bob Shafto... Sit this dance out. Truly, that's my own plain advice to you..."

Printed in the United Kingdom
by Lightning Source UK Ltd.
121575UK00001BA/1-9/A